BOOKS BY J. D. EVANS

MAGES OF THE WHEEL SERIES

Reign & Ruin
Storm & Shield
Siren & Scion
Ice & Ivy (2022)
Mountain & Memory (2022)
Fire & Fate (2023)

THE PRELUDE TO MAGES OF THE WHEEL

Wind & Wildfire

J. D. EVANS

Published by Whippoorwill Press LLC 2020
North Carolina, United States

Cover Art—Tatiana Anor
www.artstation.com/tanyaanor

Cover Design, Interior formatting & Design—Terry Roy
www.teryvisions.com

Editing—Michelle Morgan
www.fictionedit.com

ISBN: 978-1-951607-07-4

AUTHOR'S NOTE

This book takes place before the events in the *Mages of the Wheel* Series. You can read it at any point in the series as it is a standalone, but you will probably enjoy it most AFTER you have read *Reign & Ruin*.

To those with strength enough to see a better world for everyone, and who sacrifice to make it so.

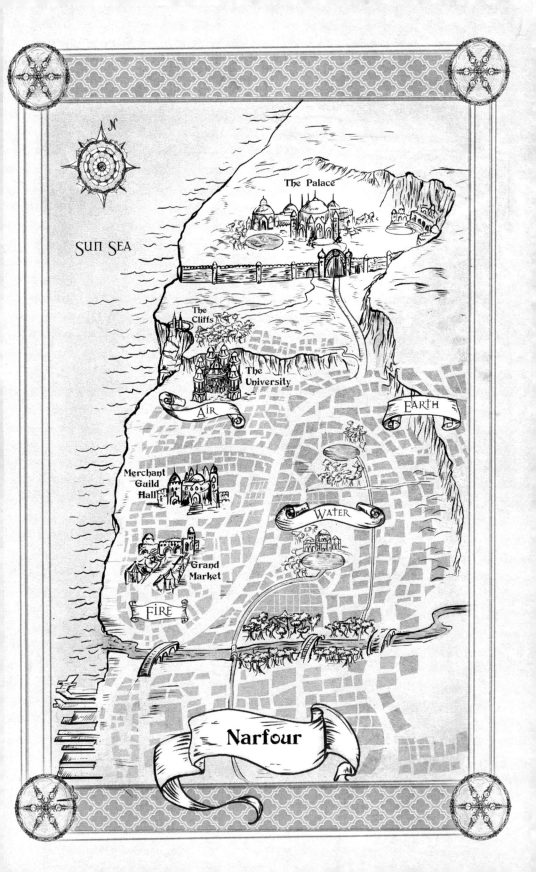

ONE

Wheel's Turn: A.S. 215

ILAY MOVED SEVERAL STONES FROM one divot in the earth to the next, grinning triumph at the ground, instead of at her friend, Seda. Seda groaned her irritation. They sat side by side on the edge of the stone tiles that marked the entrance to the Merchant Guild Hall, where their parents were.

"This is boring," Seda sighed, dragging her feet through their makeshift gameboard and drawing her dirty, perpetually skinned knees to her chest. She rested her folded arms and chin on them.

"It's only boring because you're losing," Dilay retorted. Seda bolted to her feet.

"No, it's boring because it's boring. I'm going inside," she announced. Dilay sniffed as Seda flounced inside the guild hall, then turned back to the scuffed-up dirt. She began to trace the board anew with a stick, squinting around at the early morning scene. The Grand Market was coming to life. In another candlemark the crowds would be so loud she'd be able to hear them all the way to the pier road. A steady hum of humanity that was the background noise for life in this particular area of the city. Maybe the honey candy vendor was open.

She still had the single coin she'd won from her father two days ago, playing the same game, but on a real board. Dilay swept the stones she had won from the step into the street and stood.

She slapped her hands against her thighs to clear the dust and headed toward the market. Old Ali, who ran the smallest honey candy stand in the market, was also the easiest to charm. Especially if one was a girl of only ten Turns. He had three daughters, all older than Dilay now, and so he was susceptible to nostalgia. At least, that's what Dilay's mother said every time Dilay simpered her way to a handout. She didn't want to spend her coin. She wanted to save it for something special. Her father had promised the next time the book vendor came up from Menei he would pay half for any book she wanted. Within reason.

Dilay took the route behind the southern edge of the market. Dodging vendor carts and early morning shoppers on the main path this time of day was a recipe for a cuff on the head. Ali wasn't far, and he was just setting up his little stand when she arrived. Dilay helped him spread a clean linen over the rough-hewn table he used as display. He raised an eyebrow as he smoothed the cloth with hands beginning to curl with arthritis.

"Good morning, Little Moon. Have you come to work in Old Ali's shop this morning?"

Dilay clasped her hands behind her back and twisted from side to side. "If you need me, Bey," she replied, dutifully. Her mother would sell her as a cart goat if she refused to help an elder. The scruffy brow rose higher, and a smile twitched at the corners of his thin mouth, making his grizzled mustache quiver.

"Not today, my Little Moon. My own daughter is coming to help me. But, I do have one problem you may be able to solve. I seem to have made too much today. Do you know anyone who might be able to take one of these off my hands?" He gave the jar of candies he held a little shake. Dilay did her best not to appear greedy and thrilled, and gave her most solemn nod.

Ali chuckled and held the jar down to her. It was filled with amber-hued disks of honey candy affixed to little sticks. Dilay carefully selected one and smiled. "Thank you, Ali Bey."

"Tell your anne I said hello, yes?"

She nodded as she started to turn away, then remembered her manners and turned back to offer a quick bow. His chuckle followed her as she dodged between two stalls and toward an alley. As she took her first taste of the candy she contemplated whether to return to the guild hall or simply go home. Home was a long walk through parts of the city her mother would not be pleased she had traveled alone.

Dilay turned toward the Merchant Guild Hall.

Ahead and between two closed shops, an apothecary and a bakery, a scuffle and a pained shout drew Dilay's attention. She crept forward. She'd seen many a fistfight, though her mother liked to pretend she'd been sheltered from such things. But they lived too close to the pier and the crime-plagued sections of the city for Dilay to be sheltered from anything. She didn't like to see it, and usually went in the opposite direction whenever she sensed something brewing. But the shout had a higher pitch to it. A woman's. Or a child's.

She peeped around the corner of the apothecary, into the narrow alley. Three boys stood nearly at the back, where a retaining wall for the hill above barred further progress. She could only see their backs, but their height suggested they were a few Turns older than her, at least.

"Ha! Look—he's going to cry," one crowed. Dilay fumed. Bullies. She despised bullies. One of the other boys bent and picked up a discarded board from a broken pallet and brandished it like a sword.

"We haven't given you a reason to cry yet, fancy boy."

Dilay could see between them to a fourth boy, on his backside on the ground. Blood had trickled from one nostril. He glared up at the others, lips pressed together and angry, even if his skin was washed of warmth.

"Let's see that fire, little mage. Got any? I heard you can't summon a flame at all. Better get to it before I whack you so hard with this board you forget your House." The biggest one laughed, and the hurt boy's lip quivered as his fingers clawed at the dirt. No flames came.

Dilay took a step closer. Maybe he didn't have magic yet. Hers hadn't come yet either. "Well, if you can't do magic, then pay us coins. Spread all that wealth around."

The boy on the ground spit at them, splattering red-tinged droplets on the speaker's caftan. "Slug!" The bigger boy swung the board up.

Dilay darted into the alley and sprinted to their backs just as he cut the board down as if it were an axe. She slammed into his back, sending him stumbling in a heap into the retaining wall. He landed on top of the boy on the ground and his friends wheeled to face Dilay. She recognized one. Her heart pounded, and the heat of fear and anger filled her face.

"Zeki," she said his name in scorn. His father and hers were acquaintances. His face scrunched in a confusing mix of outrage and shame. The other hauled their leader to his feet and all three rounded on her. "Zeki, you better go home or when I see Baba again I'll tell him about this." She wasn't so valiant she was going to take on three boys nearly twice her size alone. Zeki's brows snugged together, while the lead boy snorted.

"Going to tattle, snitch?" He made the title a filthy word, punctuating it with a sneer.

"Happily," Dilay sneered back.

"Her father's a judge." Zeki tugged the other boy's caftan as he spoke under his breath. A judge who had put Zeki's father in prison on two occasions.

Dilay folded her arms, hoping she looked big and unintimidated. All her insides were shivering. She didn't want a bloody nose like the other boy. And she wasn't big at all.

"Bah, forget it. Who cares about a sniveling noble and a little snitch anyway." The leader looked at the boy on the ground, snapped his fingers and pointed, and small flames erupted on the hem of the boy's entari.

"That's how it's done, you little disgrace." He stalked away. The second boy followed. Zeki hesitated, then followed, his head ducked and his cheeks bright. Dilay ran past them to stomp out the flames on the boy's clothes. He sliced a hand beneath his nose and cut his gaze away from hers.

"I didn't need your help," he snarled as she took a step back.

"You need somebody's help. Are you a Fifth House mage?" she asked. "Couldn't you burn them?" He looked older than her, he should have his magic, even if he was late, like her.

He glowered, turning his face down. He looked like he might cry, and his fists flexed closed as he whispered a bad word. But he didn't look at her again. "It's none of your business."

Dilay squatted in front of him. "My magic hasn't come yet either," she said. His eyes narrowed as his gaze turned to hers, though his head was still angled away.

"I have my magic," he growled. "Why are you still here?"

She stood and turned, ready to stomp away. She should have let them beat him up, with a temper like that.

"Where are you going?" he said to her back. Dilay spun.

"I helped you and you didn't even say thank you. I'm leaving." Obviously.

"Oh." He pulled his knees to his chest and wiped the trickle of blood from his nose against the red cloth of his salvar. Dilay returned to him, then slid down to sit next to him. He radiated heat. Like a cook stove. He had to be her age at least, if his magic was awake. Ten Great Turns or so, she thought one or two older.

She smiled. Anne always said a smile was worth a thousand words. "Here." She held the honey candy out to him. He looked at it side-long, as if it were going to transform into a snake. Dilay held it closer. His gaze flicked to hers. It made her sad, how sad he looked. "They're really good, and I can get more whenever I want."

"What is it?" he asked. The heat faded. Maybe he just couldn't make flames. His magic certainly felt awake.

Dilay blinked. "Candy."

He looked surprised for a moment, then unfolded from his huddle and took it gingerly from her. Dilay crossed her legs in front of her and tucked her hands into her lap. He examined the candy for a moment before trying it, then more surprise lit his face when he discovered the taste.

Dilay smiled again. They sat in silence for a moment, him with the candy, her wondering if she should get back before her father finished at the guild hall.

"What's your name?" he asked, looking at the candy instead of at her.

"Dilay." She beamed. It felt like she'd won a game of chess. "What's yours?"

"Behram," he said. He looked at her with the tiniest of shy smiles. "Behram Kadir."

Two

Wheel's Turn: A.S. 229

THE SMALL COURT WHERE Dilay's father headed the four-judge tribunal sat on the border between the poorest district of the city, and the richest. All her life her father had walked that line, a lower noble among the highest, and a highborn among the starving. Dilay was learning to walk it too, just. She attended as many of her father's courts as her schedule allowed. The law fascinated and repelled her, and she had vowed to master it, in knowledge at least. It had been struggle enough to earn her place among the University instructors; becoming a woman judge was certainly a bridge too far for this bygones-worshiping city.

The building was circular, as so many public offices were, to represent the Wheel that turned and the balance of law. She blinked to repress a snort, shifting the bag of books she hugged on her lap. The laws of the Tamar Sultanate took their cue from the histories of the Old Sultanate, but they were hardly balanced. They far over favored the upper classes. She glanced up at the domed roof, then through the doorway and three arches beyond it into the afternoon sun. It

7

was getting late. She might have to leave before the tribunal was concluded. She couldn't keep her students waiting.

The judges had already heard all the arguments, and stood behind the lattice screens at the back to deliberate. The low hum of their voices blended into the greater noise of those attending. This was a larger turnout than usual. But it was also a different kind of case. Usually her father dealt in territory disputes among merchants, tax law, and theft.

This case was proof that the rumblings Dilay had been hearing about unrest within the governing families of the Merchant Guild were true. The man on trial was a longtime trade-level member of the guild, standing accused of underselling his competitors. Those kinds of petty disputes had always, as long as Dilay could remember, been handled internally in the guild. Never brought before a public tribunal. The implications were troubling. Her father had called it the first strike in a looming faction war.

The voices of the attending, a random scattering of guild members and onlookers trying to fill an empty afternoon, turned chaotic as a tangle of shadows darkened the arches outside the entrance. They filed inside and Dilay blinked the sting of the sun from her eyes as she watched them stride up the central aisle toward the round room and the man on trial. He stood on a small platform in the circular box designed to make him appear contained. As though he were accused of murder instead of pricing his imports a fraction below his competitors in the guild.

Dilay's hands tightened and her gaze automatically dropped to her shoes when she recognized the new arrivals. Six palace guards bracketed two nobles. They wore brown and tan caftans and entari, yataghan belted low, and expressions as sharp as their weapons. Dilay could not help but shrink back, hugging the bundle in her lap harder, but she glanced up, unable to constrain her curiosity. She was the only one who dared lift her gaze to watch; she sat among the lowest born of those attending, and most were nearly bent over in their deference.

Behind the first three guards strode the Grand Vizier, Eymen Demir, obvious for his gold-embroidered finery and the staff of office he carried, a bejeweled, gold monstrosity that glinted in shafts of light from the windows above. He smiled amiably to those who dared not look at him, nodding miniscule greetings as he walked.

A younger man in white, silver, and blue walked at his side. His hands were clasped behind his back, his shoulders rolled forward and his gaze turned down. His clothing, and the bright white, silver-adorned turban that crowned his head, identified him as one of the two Sabri princes.

Dilay's fingers curled against her books. This was a guild dispute hearing. There was no reason for royalty to be present. Or rather, only one reason, and only one of the royal family who could execute it. Her stomach twisted as she tried to get a better look, but the prince was past, and the three guards bringing up the rear of the procession blocked her view of his face. Not that she could tell the difference between the Vali Ahad and his younger brother, the Sehzade, to confirm her nauseating suspicion.

The chatter in the hall stuttered into expectant silence. The four judges, including her father, stepped from behind the screen to meet the new arrivals, bowing and muttering the necessary niceties.

Her father's face, stern and held in an expression of tense deference, did not fool Dilay. His gaze stayed on the prince, his hands unsteady as he bowed and spread them in recognition of the prince's more powerful magic.

Fast steps and hissed voices snapped her attention back to the entrance, where two more men had appeared, walking quickly to catch up. She recognized both, father and son, and the younger's darting gaze caught hers. His black brows drew down, then he ripped his gaze from hers to commit himself to the same bows and greetings as everyone else.

What were Behram and his father doing here? As the judges spoke with the newly arrived palace officials, the guards spread out around the circle of seats. Dilay was sitting next to the aisle that led out of the circular main room and to the doors. She had a good enough view of the proceedings to see the sweat beading and trickling down the accused man's temple as he stared at the Grand Vizier and the prince.

Behram cast a quick look back at her, then returned to his whispered conversation with his father. They were showing uncharacteristic composure, but Dilay could tell by the tense lines in Behram's face that they were arguing. He gestured at the prince. Dilay followed the movement.

"This is a minor matter, Efendim. Surely not something to waste your time and magic on?" Dilay's father spoke purposefully loud enough that the entirety of the hall could hear him. His gaze slipped between the Grand Vizier and Kadir Pasha, Behram's father. He was still half bent forward in a bow, to add respect to his words, as the prince was looking right at him.

"This is by order of the Sultan," Kadir Pasha said, and though his back was to her, Dilay could perfectly picture his smile. A smile she had learned to hate over her decade-long friendship with his son. Kadir Pasha was the head of one of the factions involved in the growing dispute within the guild. The man on trial was one of his own merchants. This was strategic, if this was his doing. Summoning the Vali Ahad to prove the innocence of his man, without a doubt. It showcased his personal relationship with the palace, and cast his opposing faction—that run by the head of the Merchant Guild, Altimur Pasha—in a very poor light indeed.

The man in the trial box stared at the Vali Ahad as though he were a creature of fangs and talons. Dilay had never seen the magic of a Veritor. A mage who could open the minds of others and mine them for truth like diamonds ripped from the earth. It was a rare manifestation of First House power, the House that held dominion over air, and the mind. A trait the Sabris had encouraged in their own lines and discouraged elsewhere. The Vali Ahad was the only living Veritor that Dilay knew of.

"Truly, an unnecessary inconvenience for the Vali Ahad, our tribunal has all but announced the verdict," Dilay's father began, but the Vali Ahad turned his back on him to face the accused. Dilay thought she saw the prince's gaze catch on Behram's for a moment, but it was so fleeting she couldn't be certain. Behram, who had been gripping his father's arm, spun on his heel and stalked to Dilay.

"Come on," he ordered. Dilay stared up. He loomed over her seat, his jaw set in anger, fire snapping in his irises.

"But—"

"You do not want to see this."

"I'm not leaving," Dilay argued, in a savage whisper. Behram reached down and hauled the bag of books out of her lap. The people around her turned their shoulders and shifted away in an effort to avoid involvement. Dilay fumed, clutching the strap of the bag as Behram tried to pull it from her hands. The accused stammered as the Vali Ahad stepped to the front of the box and reached for him.

"Please, Efendim, I already told everything I know, I told the truth. Master Kadir, you know I am innocent, please—"

"We've already determined his innocence, Efendim," Dilay's father said, more firmly.

"By order of the Sultan," the Grand Vizier replied, amicably, though his smile wavered, "you are to be verified."

The room shuddered with shocked rumbles. Behram tugged Dilay to her feet. The Vali Ahad, whose face might have been carved of marble, reached forward. Dilay tried to slip out of Behram's grasp, slapping at his hands as she tried to watch, despite the sick misgiving swimming circles in her belly.

"Please, Dilay," Behram said. "It will only upset you." But she could not take her gaze away from the scene, no matter how he tugged her. The prince put his hands on the man's face and head, and magic thumped the air. White light poured from the prince's eyes, obliterating the irises and pupil, fluxing across his face and hands. Both he and the accused rocked as if struck by a force.

"Please!" the accused screeched, his back bowing, and the back of Dilay's throat burned with angry tears. Vile, invasive magic. The crowd recoiled, the man's pain louder for the horrified silence. Someone invoked the Wheel's favor.

Behram pulled Dilay into the aisle and toward the door, wrapping an arm around her shoulders, but she craned to watch. The accused's mouth gaped, and a low-pitched whine cut through the air. A trickle of blood slid out of his nose and over his lip. Dilay's throat tightened, her eyes stinging, and anger brewing in the place of her nausea. The prince released him, dropping his hands to his sides. The magic sizzled away.

The accused slumped to his knees, then fell backward out of the trial box, unconscious.

Dilay's chest vibrated with the thunderous beat of her heart, and her teeth clenched together so hard that her head ached. Behram held harder, forcing her forward steps.

"Innocent," the Vali Ahad announced.

The accused man woke with a scream, clutching his head and pitching forward, as several onlookers helped him to sit up.

Behram forced Dilay out the door, and the last thing she had a good glimpse of was the Vali Ahad's face, undisturbed and unfeeling. He'd broken into that man's mind like it was nothing. *Monster.*

The sunlight stung her eyes, hastening the tears she had been holding back at the man's cries.

"I do not understand," she said, as she swiped her tears off her cheeks and looked away from Behram. He had never been one with patience for weakness. Even hers. But then, how could he? He had never been allowed any.

"It is politics that does not concern you," he said. "There is nothing to understand."

Dilay whirled to face him and shoved his hand away from her shoulder. "What are you doing here? How could you let that happen to a man who works for you?"

"Let it happen?" He gave a bitter smirk. "Do you think I can deny the Sultan?"

"What interest does the Sultan have in a low-rank trade merchant? What is your father up to?" Behram might not have strings in the palace, yet, but his father had many. And an inverse number of scruples. This was dirty dealing, Dilay was certain of it, but she could not understand why.

Fiery sparks in Behram's eyes flickered out. "I am needed inside. Unless you need an escort back to your home?"

"Of course not," Dilay snapped. "When have I ever needed your protection?"

He started to smile but repressed it. "Never."

Dilay inhaled slowly to calm herself, then dipped her head to him for show, as they had gathered a few onlookers. He did outrank her. Technically.

"Be good," he said under his breath, as he turned toward the doorway. Dilay watched his back as he walked into the darkness of the hall. An involuntary shudder made her hug her arms around herself.

As infuriating as Behram was, as arrogant and entitled as any noble, at least he wasn't *that*. That man, the Vali Ahad, dead eyed as he filleted open a man's mind to obtain answers that had already been given.

It was as good a reminder as any of why Dilay risked what she did. Why she did the things she did, in the dark of night—breaking laws. Defying edicts and class. Because the Sabris did not care a wit for the city, the Sultanate that they ruled.

They were tyrants, every one.

Three

OMAR STRODE DOWN THE aisle of his father's receiving hall. The Sultan sat on his bench on a dais, the Queen Sultana seated beside him on a smaller, silver-inlaid stool, her hands folded in her lap. Eymen, the Grand Vizier, reached the Sultan first. He bowed, then ascended the dais to bend in and whisper to Omar's father.

Omar stopped three paces from the bottom of the dais and bowed. The Sultan waved Eymen away with a twitch of his fingers as he examined Omar.

"It is done?"

Omar ducked his chin, his right hand tightening around his left wrist as he held them at his back. He only needed suffer through a few moments more, then he could wallow in his misery in private.

"You seem none the worse for wear this time," the Sultan said, as though Omar had finally forfeited in some contention between them. He had, to an extent. His father believed that Omar's magic should not be causing him pain, and if it was, it was Omar's fault. And in a manner of speaking, Omar had conceded. He had decided to conceal its aftereffects better, in the vain hope his father would cease trying to

14

prove to Omar that he was, in essence, doing it wrong. Not that Omar or the Sultan would know. Omar's only example of another Veritor had been his uncle, ten Turns deceased.

"The Council will be pleased to see you using your powers for the betterment of Narfour society. You are dismissed until the evening meal."

"Yes, Efendim." Omar bowed again, spinning as he straightened. He couldn't look his mother in the eye at that moment; she would see through his charade no matter how he tried. He made his way out of the hall, waving away the personal guards that made as if to follow him.

By the time he reached the tower that felt like his only sanctuary, his nose was bleeding again and his head was pounding. He collapsed onto the bench that stretched beneath the arched windows. His hands were shaking as he pressed his face into them and dug his fingers against his throbbing temples. The blurriness in his vision faded in shrinking circles with each slow inhale and exhale, until there were only twin points of light that obscured his sight. When he looked up at the scuff of feet on carpet, annoyed, Master Bugra, his tutor, stood obscured by the pale glow in Omar's vision. His annoyance fizzled.

"Is he all right?" Omar asked about the man whose memories were still popping open in his thoughts like grains on a hot pan. He'd tried so hard to be careful. But…

The tutor did not speak, which was more than enough answer. Omar closed his eyes.

"Are you all right, Vali Ahad?"

No, he was not all right, would never be all right.

"Efendim—"

"Please don't," Omar ordered. He was tired of the apologies. Of the assurances that they would try something else. Find a new way. Tired of the headaches and the voices and the fear in everyone's eyes. Tired of his father's disdain of his failure. Of his weakness. That he was always measured against an uncle he had barely known, against an imaginary ideal of magic while his own sense of self was eaten away by the rats of shame and anger. He was nothing beyond this…curse.

Master Bugra moved to the bench and swept his gold and brown entari and caftan out of the way as he lowered himself beside Omar. At a respectable, and necessary, distance.

"You need help," Master Bugra said, in a tone that held both deference and insistence. But there was no help. He'd been through every tutor at the palace. Every physician. Every book he could find on the magic of Veritors. No one knew what to do with a mage who could not master his own power. Children could do it, for Wheel's sake. If Master Bugra—the most gifted instructor of control and intention the University had ever known—could not teach Omar, there was no hope.

"Maybe this is my destiny…" Omar began. To be punished. He tried to think of the tribunal, but he couldn't. He could not think of the man. Of the terror. It would call it up into his own mind, and take him over, erase him. And it was only going to happen more frequently. More minds invading his. Retaliation for his magical brutality and his lack of control.

"Vali Ahad," Master Bugra said, "my prince. You must not allow yourself to become a pawn. To allow others to dictate who and what you become, what you are. If I have taught you nothing else, please tell me I have taught you this."

"Of course I am a pawn," Omar said with a bitter laugh. "I am my father's puppet, just as he was his father's before. That is the Sultanate."

"But you are not the Sultanate. Not yet. I have"—he stared unseeing at the arch that led to the spiral staircase down—"one other thing we might try."

"I am done trying, Master." Omar swiped at the ooze of blood under his nose. Master Bugra produced a square of cloth from the pocket of his entari and handed it gingerly to Omar. Omar wiped his fingers clean.

"Do you know that your friend, Behram, could not summon his fire for many, many Turns?"

Omar swallowed a sound of surprise. Behram was the most gifted fire mage in Narfour, as far as Omar knew. But he did not speak of childhood much, beyond what they shared in domineering fathers.

"It was erratic. Dangerous, even."

They shared a brief moment of silence. It was still dangerous. Behram was known for his temper. For his fire was always so near the surface. All the more reason for Omar's surprise at discovering his volatile friend once could not summon it at all.

"Did you teach him?" Omar asked. Master Bugra had salvaged many an erratic, powerless, or overpowered mage.

"No. I could do nothing for him. His father brought me in privately when Behram was just into his second Cycle. Twelve Turns, perhaps thirteen. So withdrawn."

Omar almost laughed. He could not imagine Behram as withdrawn. But he did have an inkling of what Behram's younger Turns had been like, violent, oppressive. Only from oblique hints that Behram occasionally let slip.

"I could do nothing for him. His fire was always tied to his anger, and he could control neither."

"Why are you telling me this?" It seemed a private thing, and Omar did not know how to navigate his friendship now, knowing something Behram perhaps would not want him to.

"You may have noticed he controls it well enough now." Master Bugra adjusted the collar of his entari and pursed his lips, something he'd always done when he was thinking how to phrase a distasteful subject.

Well enough. Omar squinted. Behram got away with allowing it to surface far more than any other mage. People did not trust him. Because of his father. Omar had never found Behram to be anything but loyal. He had made it through University with nothing but praise from his instructors. He had obviously learned control somewhere.

Though being unable to summon one's magic was a very different problem than that which plagued Omar.

"I am not certain, but I have long held a hunch about who helped him, and I believe that person is now an instructor at the University. Quite a gifted one, a prodigy of mine, if you will." He smiled. Omar did not care for the sly look in the old man's eyes.

"Summon him here then," Omar said. The Master's smile faltered.

"Ah. No. That will not be possible. Instead, I thought it a fine opportunity for you to tour the University, attend a class or two. The University is the lifeblood of your city, my prince. It would not be time wasted."

"Oh? Are you going to tell my father that? You know how he feels about the University." Omar touched his fingers to his upper lip and felt crusted blood in his mustache. Had his father noticed? There was no way the Sultan would approve of Omar *wasting* time at the University, for any reason. He had always felt it beneath the royal family to attend, and had procured private tutors for them instead. Even though many of his and his brother's friends and peers had attended.

Omar had only barely gotten over the bitterness of it. He did enjoy learning, studying. And while the palace had the most extensive library in Tamar, the University had books the palace did not. Though he doubted any on Veritors, or Master Bugra would have brought them to his attention during his many-Turn tenure there.

"At some point, my prince, you are going to have to defy the Sultan in one way or another. This is a fine, innocuous place to start." The Master slapped his hands to his knees and stood, accompanied by the crackling sound of his aging joints. He cringed. "If you do decide to seek out Behram's teacher, you are looking for Instructor Akar."

Why did that name sound familiar?

"And you are personally vouching for him? That he has the discretion necessary to assist me?"

Master Bugra laughed. "I cannot promise that. You'll have to ascertain trustworthiness yourself. But since no one seems to know who taught young Master Kadir his control, it is plausible that whoever it was is quite capable of keeping a secret. Good day, Vali Ahad." The Master bowed and left, ducking beneath the arch that served as doorway and disappearing down a twist of stone staircase.

Omar turned to look out the windows, which gave him a sweeping view of the city skyline and the sea beyond. Prominent in the view were the domed towers of the University. They shone copper and white in the early summer sunlight. He had always loved the view, a small way to escape, to imagine what it would have been like to attend, as every noble mage did. If he did what Master Bugra asked, he might have a little taste of that. Greed filled his thoughts with visions of long talks into the night with young instructors full of new ideas. Debating the dynamics of the Wheel, the interaction of magic. Whether theories about magic's effect on the user's personality were assumptions or fact.

Familiar, quick steps announced his brother's arrival before Omar turned to greet him. "Mazhar."

The Sehzade proffered a smirk and slung himself on the bench beside Omar, twisting to follow his gaze out the windows.

"Eymen tells me Father was uncharacteristically sweet with you. Playing a good lapdog are we?"

"I bled less than usual, and arrived under my own power."

"Bravo," Mazhar said, growing thoughtful. "You have things so easy. I do that every day and he hardly notices me." The brothers locked gazes for an instant, then both returned to staring out the arched windows. "I saw Master Bugra in the hall. What new schemes does he have for you today?"

Omar huffed a chuckle. "He wants me to attend the University. He is under the belief that one of his former students, now instructor, might be able to help me." But how was a novice instructor going to teach him something every else had failed to?

"Brilliant. When do we go?" Mazhar crowed, jumping to his feet. He had always been the animated one, energetic and unbridled to Omar's subdued, careful demeanor. But then, he was second born, both a blessing and a curse in the case of their father's attention.

Omar could not help but smile. "As soon as we convince the Sultan that we are absolutely not going to expose the biggest family secret to the general public."

Mazhar winked. "You leave that to me, brother. I'll have us in those doors before you can throw your voice down the hall." He paused, contemplating. "The women there must be absolutely starved for someone with a personality."

Omar snorted, turning his attention back to the University's profile in the sun. He did not belong there. Or here. Or anywhere.

FOUR

ILAY SLID A BOOK BACK onto the library shelf then glanced down at the stack she held propped against her hip. Ten more to go before she could go prepare for class. She tilted backwards just enough to scan beyond the library shelf to the entrance, where Master Fahri was in his usual place, ensconced on a horseshoe-shaped couch with whichever ancient tome had caught his interest, ready to pounce on anyone who was too loud, inappropriately dressed, or just generally offensive to his sensibilities.

She returned to her task when she was certain he did not appear fixated on her progress. She took a book from the stack she was supposed to be replacing and slid it into the bag she wore slung over her shoulder and against her hip.

It was against University policy to remove any books from the premises. Even instructors needed to put a request in through the Headmaster and Master Fahri and such requests were rarely approved. But Dilay felt her need warranted such treachery, and she always returned the books each day, in perfect, undamaged condition.

After replacing another book, the sound of hurried steps scuffing against the worn rugs warned her of impending company, and she forced a smile. Seda was late to take over the library shift, and Dilay was in far too much of a hurry to listen to her rambling apology.

No doubt it involved at least three overturned carts and one or two distressed animals that needed saving. Or perhaps a young man who had warranted extra attention. Dilay loved her friend, but she could be so…distractible. Fire, jumping from fuel to fuel.

"Dilay," Seda gasped, practically tripping into her and knocking her against the library shelf in an effort to spin her around.

"You're late." Dilay wrenched out of Seda's grasp and gave her a glare that lacked any heat.

"I know, I'm so sorry, but you have to see this." Seda confiscated the remainder of Dilay's stack of books and shoved them haphazardly onto the nearest clear shelf. As Dilay fussed in protest, Seda grasped her hand and tugged her into the main aisle, then toward the door and atrium beyond.

Master Fahri looked up at the spectacle of them, frowned, and snapped his current page over as his narrowed gaze followed them.

"Seda!" Dilay protested.

"Look," Seda said after she had pulled Dilay into one of the alcoves that circled the main atrium. Ostensibly they were for students who needed a place to study between their classes. But there was no possible way to concentrate in the atrium, the heart of the University. Everyone had to traverse it while they traveled between the House Wings, from class to class. At this exact moment it was filled to the brim with students loitering until the very last moment before their first class. Their talk, laughter, and movement were deafening in the perfect acoustics provided by the soaring atrium dome.

"You will have to be more specific," Dilay said dryly. Seda pointed toward the spiral staircase that led directly to the entrance to the First House Wing. There was another, broader staircase on the far side of the atrium from the University entrance, easier to navigate in a crowd. But right now the narrow spiral of the auxiliary staircase was not crowded, except for the throngs gathered at the top and bottom to witness the climb of the small group halfway up.

Dilay shifted her bag, confused. She recognized the Head Proctor, leading a group of seven men. He and his subordinates oversaw all testing, which students went to which classes, and the occasional tour of the University. It appeared to be a tour, though the Head Proctor seemed discomfited, turning every other stair to say something to the man ascending behind him.

"Seda, what—"

"Oh would you open your eyes!" Seda snapped in an impatient whisper-shout. "Is that who I think it is?"

Dilay examined her friend's excited, and perhaps panicked expression, took a moment to focus herself, and looked again. Seven men. Five in brown and tan…her hands closed hard on the strap of the bag she had slung across her chest, heat draining out of her. Those were palace guards, though they were without the swords they had worn two days ago at the tribunal. Tan caftans and salvar, brown waist wraps and leather belts and armguards. The two men in front of them wore finer clothes, though not in the traditional colors of silver and white, or blue. But she did not need the visual clue of their clothing. One of them had hair shorn to the same scalp-hugging length all over. He would not grow it longer until he was named in his father's place.

The Vali Ahad. What was that monster doing in the University? She thought the Sultan turned his nose up at public education.

"What are they saying?" Seda whispered when the Proctor turned around once more, gesturing more urgently with his hands as he spoke to the Vali Ahad. The man next to the Vali Ahad must be his younger brother, unless it was some other noble. She did not know many of the highest-ranking nobles on sight, she simply wasn't exposed to them enough.

"How should I know?"

"Well, listen!" Seda said urgently. "Don't you want to know why they're here…and headed toward your wing?"

"You want me to spellcast on the Vali Ahad, have you lost your mind?" Dilay hissed.

"Oh? You don't think you can do it without him realizing?" Seda raised an eyebrow in challenge. "I thought you had better control than even Master Bugra."

Dilay exhaled forcibly through her nose, whipped her gaze back to the men on the staircase, and whispered a listening spell. She directed it on the Head Proctor, Burak Akdari. He was a water mage, and so would be less likely to detect the touch of the spell. The spell, woven together like the finest of gossamer threads, fell over Proctor Akdari like a net. Dilay held her breath, waiting for any of them to realize. But no one reacted. They continued climbing the stairs, Proctor Akdari practically walking backwards up them, his voice carried to her by the threads of her spell as if she were standing among them.

"Are you certain you would not rather observe Master Gur's control class? He has been teaching much longer," Proctor Akdari wheedled. Dilay's eyes narrowed. "It is just—"

"I thought I had made my wishes clear, Proctor." The Vali Ahad sounded impatient. But in that she could hardly blame him. Proctor Akdari could strip even an old, tired ox of its tolerance if given half a chance.

"I am just not certain you understand the…" Proctor Akdari fidgeted and nearly fell backwards over a stair. "Well the, uniqueness of Instructor Akar's class."

Dilay cursed. What was happening? Seda watched her, eyes wide, hands gripped together in front of her mouth, likely to explode with excitement with her very next breath.

"Uniqueness is exactly what I want, Proctor."

Dilay severed the spell. The Vali Ahad, who was framed perfectly in her line of sight, lifted his head, and started to turn it, as if he might look her way. He knew. Flashes of watching him pry open that merchant's mind only days ago flickered in her memory. But the Vali Ahad did not turn, only continued to the top of the stairs. Then down the hall to the First House Wing. To her classroom, it seemed.

"I feel sick." She swallowed, slumping against the arch of the alcove.

"What happened?" Seda gripped her arms.

"They're going to my class. He wants to see my class." But why?

"It's about time the palace took notice of the first woman instructor at the University," Seda said triumphantly, as if this were good news.

"Are you mad? I cannot go up there."

"*You* are going to skip your class." Seda folded her arms. Dilay winced, tipping her head back against the column. She could not skip it. There were plenty of her esteemed colleagues who were carefully tallying every wrong step she took. An unannounced absence during the Vali Ahad's visit would be just the giant hook they needed to hang their case against her teaching.

"Seda. I told you about the tribunal. I can't be in the same room as that…" She glanced around to make certain no one was watching her. Seda looked up, to the second-floor walkway that circled the atrium and overlooked the floor below.

"It is one class."

"What if they know about my *hobby*?" Dilay dropped her voice to the barest whisper.

Seda made a face. "Yes, they found out about one low noble doing things she should not and have now sent both royal princes to deal with her." Seda flicked her on the forehead. "Don't be daft. Go to your class. Don't look at him, be done with it. Then come tell me all about it." She grinned and turned, practically skipping back to the library. She would be the queen of her district for a day with gossip like this.

Dilay kept her gaze fixed on her friend's back until she disappeared into the library. Then she turned, slowly, toward the stairs.

The atrium crowd was beginning to thin; it was getting too close to class time to linger anymore. Dilay forced herself to walk to the staircase and to move quickly up them. She was never late to class. She could not let this be the first time.

The balcony that circled the upper level of the atrium opened onto six hallways that led to the six House Wings. Dilay followed a few stragglers toward her small classroom. She wished this session were in the big room at the end of the hall. With its many tall windows and archways open to the sky, she would not feel trapped.

With each step that brought her closer to the room, from which she heard uncharacteristic silence, her pulse grew faster and heavier. Was she afraid of him? Of course she was. Any rational person who had seen him at work would be afraid of him. He was only one step away from ruling all of Tamar. He could crush her. End everything she had worked so hard for, and all she had to do was take one misstep. Or, he could simply rip all her secrets from her with a spell.

Dilay peeked around the arch of the doorway, clutching her bag against her belly. She could only see the front half of the classroom from that vantage. Proctor Akdari leaned arrogantly against the podium, one elbow propped on it, fingers drumming against the wood as he surveyed the class with clear distaste. Her lip curled and she swallowed a groan. It was possible, slightly possible, he was even more detestable than the Vali Ahad, whom she could not see.

"Looking for someone?" an unfamiliar male voice said from behind her, quietly. Dilay straightened and spun, choking on a half-formed denial. Her first view was his chest and arm, which sported a tiraz just below his shoulder of white and silver embroidered with three air sigils. A Sival of the First House, the highest order of mage. Dilay flicked her gaze to his face. He straightened, hands clasped behind his back, head cocked like an owl and dark eyes trained unblinking on her. She opened her mouth, then closed it. She had never seen his face, not really. Not until this moment. It was the short hair, no longer than the first joint of her thumb, that made her realize who stood before her and blurred the rest of his features as panic seized her thoughts.

"Efendim." She pitched forward in a bow, nearly smacking her face into his chest, which was only narrowly avoided by them both taking a fast step away from each other.

"I did not mean to startle you." He had an unusually resonant voice for an air mage. Something more suited to an earth mage. But he was tempering it now, to keep their conversation quiet. It was not…she had thought he would sound more…violent? If she ever had occasion to speak to him at all.

A shiver slipped down her arms and she hugged them around herself as she straightened, then forced herself to drop them to her sides and roll her shoulders back.

"I was not startled, I was…" She bit the inside of her cheek. She was looking for him. A guard stood several paces behind him, silent and severe, staring at her as if she were an unsheathed sword. The braids on his shoulders indicated he was of some high rank, though she had never spent time learning such details of palace life.

"You are Instructor Akar." The words fell somewhere between a statement and a question, as he studied her instructor's caftan and entari of grey over blue.

"Uhm. Yes." Her hand crept instinctively toward the strap of her bag and she curled her fingers around it, her comfort. His gaze caught and followed the movement, which resulted in his staring square at her chest. A heartbeat of awkward silence followed before his gaze wrenched up and away, and red crept up his neck as heat flushed her own face.

"You appear young to be an instructor," he said, then cleared his throat. She and he were exactly the same age. Four Cycles, or twenty-four Great Turns of the Wheel. It was not odd that she knew his age, though she did not know him. Everyone in the city of Narfour knew how old the Vali Ahad was. Knew what he had eaten for breakfast. What he had worn on any given occasion. But she did not think many would recognize his face were he taken from the palace, and his entourage.

"I am," she said. It should not be charming that he was still blushing and flustered. She had encountered much worse, and far less accidental, leering, on her daily market trips. "Are you lost, Vali Ahad?"

"Yes," he said, then, "no. I would like to observe your class." He finally turned his head to look at her again. "If that is all right with you."

Dilay blinked. "I do not understand," she said. He could do whatever he wanted.

"I do not want to be a distraction."

A small, sharp laugh burst free, and Dilay clapped a hand over her mouth, eyes wide as she stared up at him. His eyes, which were a warm shade of cinnamon, widened, then crinkled at the edges. There was no smile. Dilay lowered her hand. He was toying with her. Surely. Like a cat with a doomed mouse.

"If I said no, would you leave?"

The guard took a threatening step forward, beginning what was surely to be a correction of some unfriendly nature. The Vali Ahad raised his hand and the guard froze in place.

"Yes," he said, then clasped his hands behind his back again. Relief had barely had time to be replaced with suspicion when he added, somber-faced, "but I would return tomorrow."

"Ah," Dilay said. Best get it over with, as Seda had said. She stepped to the side and gestured toward the room. "It would be my honor to have you in my class, Vali Ahad Efendim."

There were more guards inside the room, lined up along the back wall like statues. In their midst stood the man she assumed to be the Sehzade, dressed almost identically to his brother. He stood with arms folded over his chest and one foot propped up on the wall, appearing bored. They looked alike, the two men, both swarthy and, she admitted reluctantly, handsome. But swarthy was an adjective for nearly every person at the University.

"Instructor Akar, you are late," Proctor Akdari said.

"I detained her," the Vali Ahad said in a voice that more closely matched what Dilay would have first expected. Something hard, with an edge that suggested his father, sitting high on his gold dais and meting out harsh punishments for the smallest of offenses. Perhaps his real voice and tone, not the one he used to put young instructors at ease. Proctor Akdari executed a quick bow and scurried away from the podium. Dilay rarely used the thing for more than a place to put her bag or prop up a book she was reading.

"The Vali Ahad would like to observe our class today," she began. "You should thank him, I had planned on a test of our lessons so far. But that would be uninteresting for him to watch." She chanced a look at him. "Would you care to pick our exercise today, Efendim? Feathers or countering."

"I did not come to be disruptive," he said, his declaration made lie by the many, many gazes fixed, unwavering, on him, "as I said. Continue with your planned test."

His statement was met with groans and shuffling as everyone selected a cushion on the floor and situated their small desks in front of them. Dilay turned away, confused. Perhaps he was here because of her. Because his traditionalist father had caught wind of the very non-traditional instructor. What did they want from her? Why seek her out especially? There were much more seasoned instructors at the University if he wanted to observe teaching methods.

She picked up a piece of chalk and began writing out questions. Control and containment were fascinating to her, and had been since she was a child, and especially since she had known Behram. He had made her begin to realize how inextricably tied to emotion magic was. And she had wanted to know more. To understand why a mage who was not in control of themselves, or whose lives were particularly harmful or chaotic, could not effectively control or target their magic. That was also why she had begun to wonder about those left behind. The poor and lower classes who were not allowed to study at the University. Who were given only the barest of education concerning their magic or that of others.

Chalk ticked against slate as students wrote out their answers. Dilay circled the room, checking answers as they worked, and noting only those that were grossly wrong. Only a few, and she gave them the benefit of the doubt. She could hardly think straight with five palace guards, the Head Proctor, and two princes staring at her. She doubted even she would have performed well on an unexpected quiz with that kind of distraction.

Her gaze strayed only once, or perhaps twice…to the Vali Ahad. Was it that he did not wear a turban today? Was it because he was standing at the back of the class like a student being punished, appearing just as uncomfortable? Or was it the pained furrow that seemed permanently etched in his brow that made it hard for her to reconcile this man with the one she had seen perform that brutal confession at her father's tribunal?

Why was he here? This was too much pretense if the palace was displeased that the University had appointed a woman as instructor. The Sultan was not a man who tiptoed around things. If he did not like it, he abolished it, with no arguing permitted. She wondered if the prince would tell her the reasons for his presence. Or if Proctor Akdari would.

Dilay's mouth quirked down. No. The man would delight in keeping it from her, whether he knew the answer to her question or not.

She finished writing her last question and faced the class again.

"That is an interesting question, Instructor Akar," the Sehzade, who had not spoken once so far, said. "How would you answer it?"

What is more important, intention or control?

She waited until everyone had put down their chalk and their boards before she erased the question. "Master Bugra argued that intention was the greater of the two."

"Someone has since changed his mind," the Sehzade said. "Because that is not what he espouses now."

Dilay smiled in memory of their many long discussions on the topic.

"In truth, it depends upon the mage," Dilay said. "No one mage can master all the theories of magic. What one might lack in control can be made up for in sharply defined intention. What another lacks in spell force they could make up for in pinpoint control. Master Bugra did not discuss this with you?"

The Sehzade did not answer, instead looked briefly at his brother, who did not move or respond.

"That is all for today. Tomorrow, exercises in the sky room." Dilay took a wet rag from a bucket near the board and wrung it out so she could wipe the board clean. She forced her gaze to stay trained on her task, which she did more slowly than necessary. If she did not look at them, perhaps they would simply leave, and not require anything else of her. The tension of waiting seemed to beat drums beneath her skin. When the classroom was quiet, she relaxed, slinging the rag into the bucket. She turned.

The Vali Ahad stood in the center of the room, hands clasped behind his back, waiting. Dilay's lips twitched to frown, but she controlled it.

"Do you believe that?" he asked, either politely ignoring her tangled and unfriendly expression, or oblivious to it.

"Believe what, Efendim?" In the corner of her vision, just outside the room, Proctor Akdari paced, and the Sehzade watched her from his position across the hall. She shivered, and rubbed her arms, leaving them hugged around her for comfort.

"That mages who lack in one tenant of theory can make up for it in others."

"Oh." She released her grip on herself. "Yes, I do. I have seen many examples of it."

"Like Behram Kadir?"

Her heart thumped in her chest, heat followed by cold wisping over her skin. Behram's lack of control in his younger Turns was widely known, but that he was assisted by a lowborn judge's daughter was not an acceptable rumor to be spread. They never spoke of it. Partly for his safety and hers, because his father would retaliate for his loss of face in the only way he knew how. With violence. Dilay managed to clear her face of anything except for a wan smile.

"I never had the privilege of teaching Master Kadir, so I cannot answer that. But I am a good enough example. I lack spell force, despite being a Sival. But I have spent countless candlemarks fine-tuning my control."

"I was told you were the very best at control." He took a few careful steps closer, and Dilay resisted the urge to back away. She did not want him within arm's reach. "And you apparently have enough confidence in that control to dare to place a listening spell on the heir to the Tamar Sultanate."

For one blinded, dizzy moment, Dilay thought she would faint. Words were birthed and died in the moment it took her to meet his gaze. He did not appear angry, and perhaps that was enough for her fool self.

"I did not place a listening spell on you," she said. "I placed it on Proctor Akdari." Oh Wheel, her heart was racing. She could barely breathe. What was he going to do to her? Why did she ever do anything Seda told her to?

"It was well crafted. I would not have sensed it at all if you had not cut it so abruptly."

"You cannot prove it was my spell." There was almost no way to trace a spell back to its caster unless they were seen. Although he was uniquely suited to force the truth from her. Dilay's boldness died an icy death. Her eyes widened. His face went taut, his gaze skating away from hers.

"I would like to see you demonstrate your control," he said.

"Like a trained monkey?" Dilay said. His brows rose in surprise. She bit her lower lip.

"I would rather you did it from a sense of duty—"

"That is exactly why a monkey performs," she said.

"I thought they did it for rewards."

Her cheeks flamed and her temper mirrored the heat in her face. She snatched up her bag from the podium. "Since you haven't offered any sort of compensation, then no, Vali Ahad Efendim, this monkey will not be performing any tricks. Good day."

She marched from the room, casting Proctor Akdari a scathing look that matched his, and hurried down the stairs. She could hide in the library. Wheel and stars. He was going to have her arrested. What was wrong with her? Baiting, not only the crown prince, but a man who could easily, and with no other reason than his wounded pride, have her sentenced to prison. Or worse.

FIVE

"HOW HAVE YOU MADE IT so far with so little sense?" Seda asked.

Dilay could only agree. Normally their walk home from the University was full of their chatter. Today it had been silent but for Dilay relaying the disaster of her interactions with the Vali Ahad.

They reached the intersection where she and Seda usually parted.

"Are you all right?" Seda asked.

Dilay adjusted her bag along her side. "I think so."

"Are you going to tell your father?"

"I don't know." Dilay glanced up the street, toward her house. He would be as distraught as she was. Perhaps it would be better to wait and see what happened, before worrying him. "Go home. I'm fine."

Seda squinted at her, then gave her a quick hug. "I'll see you soon." She waved as she turned toward her own home. Dilay watched her for a moment as she strode between the twin rows of low, narrow houses with arched roofs. These were built of stone. In the poorest parts of the city they were mud brick. Dilay only turned away when Seda disappeared inside her house.

She turned onto her street and nearly ran into the wall of the shop that shadowed her home because of her distraction. With a soft curse, she swerved at the last instant and tried to shake the tension from her shoulders to clear her head. She was being absurd. But the entire encounter had been so strange. The Sabris were not known for their leniency. It would be completely reasonable of her to be terrified of the consequences of her loose speech. Especially considering what she had witnessed at the tribunal.

He could have threatened her. With a variety of punishments. He had not. Even when he knew she had listened to his conversation with the Head Proctor, he had done nothing. That did not inspire terror so much as curiosity. What did he want? And why had he brought up Behram?

If Behram had known anything about this he would have told her beforehand.

She pulled open the door and went inside. It was not like Seda's, like a cylinder cut longways down the middle and plunked on the ground. Their house was a square, single story, a halfway point between the houses of the lowest classes, like Seda's, and those richer ones just up the hill. Those usually featured two stories instead of one, a common area and kitchen downstairs for entertaining guests, and a living area upstairs. All that was combined into one room in Dilay's house, a room which her mother kept immaculately clean and her father replastered every few Turns. The interior was white, with cushions of blue and white. Both Dilay's parents were First House mages, and preferred a breezy feel to their living area. They kept an urn of earth next to the entrance, to balance their magic with its opposition. Dilay dipped her hand into it and let the sand run through her fingers as she stepped out of her shoes.

There was less innate magic in the world than there once had been. If the books she read were to be believed, which she did, the world had once sung as strongly as the void with magic. But the Sundering War had broken the Wheel, and the subsequent imbalance had resulted in a recession of magic. She could still feel the slightest hum of magic in the earth she touched, because she was in opposition, because it stirred hollow breezes in her thoughts. Her own magic being antagonized. And a Fourth House mage would have felt it too, more strongly than she, for their affinity to their House's element. They would feel the earth the way she felt the air around her—as if it were a living thing. To her the sand between her fingers felt like cat's tongue on her skin, sent a skittering feeling up her arms like the shock of friction from fabric rubbed briskly together.

Dilay withdrew her hand and wiped it on her caftan. The central room was furnished simply, with a rug woven by her mother's grandmother before they moved to Narfour from the valley. There were large, plush sitting cushions and a few low-set, round tables. A cushioned bench ran the length of one wall. Once a small turn her father's fellow tribunal judges gathered on that bench to smoke and discuss matters of *import*.

"Baba?" she called, sensing his presence even if she did not see him. It was magical and habitual. She could feel his power, his agitation. A little breeze that scooted over her temple. And he had scuffed the carpet out of place on his way through the room.

A crash came from the kitchen and he poked his head and one shoulder out, with a guilty look on his face.

She gave a scandalized gasp. "You are not eating the rice pudding Anne made for tonight, are you?"

He took a moment before answering, a moment punctuated by a hard swallow. "No." He popped back into the kitchen.

"You live dangerously, Baba." She smoothed the carpet down with her feet as she crossed the room then sank onto the couch. It ended just outside the door to the kitchen, so she could speak to him while he conducted his illicit sampling.

"I have earned this," he groused, and something else crashed as dishes toppled. He cursed, then reappeared from inside, taking a seat beside her. He handed her a small dish of the pudding.

Dilay kissed his whiskered cheek before taking a spoonful of the creamy, sweetened rice. He did not fancy it up the way her mother did, with a sprinkling of pistachios and a dash of rosewater. Or it might be that they were out of pistachios. The price had gone up recently.

She dipped the tip of the spoon into the rice and swirled it, then took another bite, gripping the spoon in her teeth as her thoughts wandered again.

"Your mother would take your food away for that," her father said. He circled his own spoon around his empty dish, scraping up every last morsel. Dilay set her spoon in her bowl. Her mother hated when she bit the utensils.

"Did you not have a tribunal today?"

"It was rescheduled to the morning," he said.

Dilay glanced at him in surprise. His black brows were drawn down over his eyes and his mouth curved down beneath his bushy mustache as he stared at his empty bowl. Or rather, stared through it.

"What is it?"

"He is using it too much," he said in a voice uncharacteristically quiet.

"He?" Dilay asked.

"The Sultan. Uses that foul magic instead of evidence, a court, judges. The tribunal was rescheduled to the morning, because that is when the Vali Ahad has time."

The rice in Dilay's stomach soured. He had been busy at the University this morning.

Never in recorded history had a Sultan relied so heavily on magic in the justice system. The Sabri line had always contained Veritors, but they had reserved that magic for the most egregious of crimes, when no one would confess and there was simply not enough evidence. But Sultan Murat Sabri, born without Veritor magic, had utilized his brother's until his death ten Turns prior. And now…his son had taken the uncle's place.

"If he goes on like this, the Merchant Guild will not be his biggest problem. Rebellion will." He forced a cheerful smile. "How are your students?"

"Which ones?" She tried to smile back.

"The important ones." He winked.

Dilay hummed in thought. "I will find out tonight. If only they would take their assignments more seriously."

"They are not afforded the time to take them seriously, you must remember that," he said, a gentle reminder. No, her night students, her "hobby" as her mother called them, were not afforded time to study. They were not welcome to study. The children of the poor. And voids. They were expected to work, not like their wealthier peers, who were considered the important future of Tamar and their schooling paramount above all else. Primary school taught a mage their powers, gave them opportunities into the University, into skilled work. Without that...well. It was impossible to climb upward without a ladder.

Dilay wanted to be a rung on that ladder for them.

It was illegal for her to use her University education and apprentice appointment to teach the poor and magically devoid. Imprisonment was the least she would pay if anyone found out. And Wheel knew what sort of punishment the children and their families might endure. But so many were eager for it, she had to turn some away. Seda was helping her, in the hopes that she would one day be able to man a second classroom. She had wanted to do the same thing Dilay had done, become an instructor.

Even if the University headmasters would have allowed another woman into their ranks, Seda's parents had been vehemently against it. Not a woman's place, they argued.

"The Vali Ahad came to the University today." Dilay picked up her bowl of pudding and handed it to her father. His sweet tooth was the bane of her mother's existence.

He looked at her sternly. Perhaps it had been a mistake to tell him. His political leanings were not toward the Sabri Sultanate. In fact, if there ever was a revolution, her father would be on the side opposing the Sultan, and the wealthy. He bemoaned the widening gap between the wealthy and the poor whenever he was afforded even the narrowest of opportunities.

"Dilay Akar, you are not to go anywhere near that man," he said. Her father was not a man of anger. She had never seen him lose his temper, though he could give an impassioned speech. Her mother joked that he was the most Fourth House air mage she had ever met, with a temper like polished stone. But he was angry now.

"Baba, if he attends the University, then I am obligated—"

"He is vile. Just like his uncle. Taking what he has no right to. Ripping people open without a care. What is the point of having a system of justice if you simply intend to break anyone who defies you? And make no mistake, daughter. That is what is happening in the courts today. Innocent people are being broken to obtain proof of their own innocence. I will not have you anywhere near a monster like that." He stroked his hand over her hair, his face lined with concern.

Dilay laced her fingers together, staring at her father, her thoughts tumbling.

"Promise me."

She gave a single, mute nod. He seemed satisfied, and retrieved their dishes, which he returned to the kitchen before he left again. Dilay sat where she was for a time, trying to stop her thoughts from circling. But dark was approaching, and she did not wish to be late.

Her bedroom was the smallest room in the house, hardly the size of a wardrobe. Her bed took up all the space, and the three caftans and two entari she owned were hung on a line secured across one corner of the room. She removed her University uniform and changed into the pale-grey salvar and caftan she wore outside of work. The entari she chose to put over that was dark blue. It blended better at night, when she felt the need to fade away from eyes that she did not wish to see her. Like those of the City Watch.

After unloading her *borrowed* library books from her bag and replacing them with chalk and the precious paper she had stolen, one sheet at a time, from the University, she slung it across her shoulders. It looked like a messenger's bag and made her travel at night appear less out of place. When her mother was home early enough, Dilay used her laundry basket and apron as disguise. She tidied her father's mess in the kitchen before she left, smoothing over the places in the pudding where he had scooped out spoonfuls. She ate the two remaining bites of hers, after realizing she had not eaten since her break at the University that afternoon.

Dilay clutched the bag's strap and hurried out. Her father's words circled in her thoughts, interrupted by her memory of the Vali Ahad.

There was a face to go with the monster she had seen at the tribunal. And wasn't it funny how monsters with faces were so much harder to despise.

But was he the monster she had seen before…or just a man? A man who expected people to do exactly as he wished. Her irritation returned.

She turned down an alley which let out on the road that would take her to the neighborhood that bridged the Earth District and the Merchant Pier. The poorest and most dangerous neighborhood in the city.

The sun had set far enough that in the shadow of the buildings it was dark. When she neared the warehouse that was her destination—a long, earthen building with a thatched roof—two shapes broke away from the larger shadow of the building. Her muscles jolted, but then she managed a smile.

"Evening, Dilay," one of the burly men growled, and bent to tap his cheek against hers. The other offered a small bow.

"Zeki, Turgay. How are you tonight?"

"Well enough," Zeki, the more serious of the two, said. "The Watch was by earlier, but I think it was one of those using it as an excuse to go to the Lily. He hasn't been back."

"I see," Dilay said. The Lily was a brothel, the most squalid of its brethren in the city. It was also the largest, as it served the merchants and sailors that quartered in the Merchant Pier. And occasionally nobles with…particular tastes.

"Your patrons are eager." Turgay grinned. Dilay raised an eyebrow and stepped past the men, though Turgay jumped ahead to pull open the patched-together door. Dilay ducked into the space. It was lit by a slew of poorly controlled mage orbs, bubbles of light popping into life and extinguishing just as quickly, those that maintained flickering. Her *patrons* remained oblivious to her entrance, chasing each other about the room, doing a poor job of keeping quiet to avoid drawing attention. A girl shrieked from the far end of the warehouse. A group of boys laughed.

Dilay clapped her hands sharply as she strode down the aisle between the threadbare cushions people had managed to gather together for her makeshift school. Her students ranged in age from ten Turns to sixteen, though she had taught several adults as well. They often preferred private instruction, embarrassed to tower over their classmates. It was also difficult to study the fundamentals of magic when one was the target of spitballs and stares.

There were thirty students total. Teaching outside the University was illegal, except for sanctioned primary schools that none of these children could afford to go to. Or, in the case of the five who were voids, were unwelcome at. And while it was very rare for children of the poorest families in the city to have magic strong enough to be a danger to them, Dilay resented that their education was not considered important. Her father called these children, the future labor and workforce that would keep the city running, the foundation of the Sultanate. Dilay agreed.

"Sit." Dilay used her magic to cast her voice to the ears of each student as she strode to the back of the room, where Zeki had cobbled together a stand for whatever materials she planned to use for class. It was not a lectern, by any means, but it was sturdy.

"Tonight," she said, then paused. They fidgeted as she looked from face to face. Some were eager, some not outwardly so. But they listened to her. Often better than the privileged adults she taught at the University. These children worked. All of them. With their parents. They worked all day at whatever labor their family was slotted into, whether because of their magic or their lot, then they came here. Many of them would, at one point or another in their life, turn to crime out of desperation or necessity.

Wide-eyed faces stared back. What could she teach them to ensure there would never be a day in the future when a mind she had taught, had helped to shape, had been broken open by magic?

"Tonight we will speak about crime, and punishment. How the laws work. What it is legal to use magic for, and what it is not."

Six

"I WAS NOT AWARE THEY were allowing women to instruct," Omar said to no one in particular. This nightly gathering was a habit of the few he considered true friends. A habit they had begun when they were young, hiding away in the tower at a time of night when most of their fathers were smoking the nargile or busy on other tasks. He was not in the mood for company now, but it felt selfish to turn them away because of that. It was usually his brother Mazhar, Behram Kadir, brothers Kudret and Sirhan Yavuz, and Osman Altimur. But tonight Osman was off on business for the Merchant Guild and his father, who currently controlled the guild.

"That is because you do not know anything at all," Mazhar lamented. "Poor, cloistered little prince."

Omar shot him a glower. His brother laughed, stretching out in a chair between Kudret and Sirhan. Omar was cloistered. He had always wanted to go to the University because all his friends were there, having experiences he did not get to share. Having fun he did not get to have. No, he spent his free time in Council meetings with his father, in visits to the central valley to meet with regional governors. In sleep-inducing discussions with the guilds.

Omar turned his attention out the windows of the tower toward the University's domed halls. They glinted in the setting sun. The mosaics in all the colors of the Wheel that circled the towers dazzled even from a distance.

"Do not fret too terribly about your ignorance. They are not allowing women to instruct. They are allowing Dilay Akar to instruct," Behram added, from where he sat near a bookstand. "She is the only female instructor. I was surprised to hear the Headmaster had allowed you access to her class. He is not thrilled to have his legacy be defined by allowing a woman to teach. If Master Bugra had not personally vouched for her I doubt she would have the position." He drummed fingers against the bench he occupied. She had deftly avoided answering Omar's question about helping Behram. He did not know her well enough to know if she had lied by omission. But he would know if Behram did.

"That was enough to get her the position?" Omar doubted that.

"She graduated early just to be able to apply for the single open position," Kudret interjected. "She had some of the highest test scores in Turns. Several of her instructors spoke on her behalf, though I think that had a great deal more to do with them wanting her around to look at, than wanting her around to instruct the eager young minds of Narfour."

That was not the impression Omar had gotten from Master Bugra. He had heard genuine respect in his tutor's voice. And while he could not deny she was lovely, he thought her magical prowess was too impressive to be overshadowed by such a trivial thing.

Omar stared at the floor. Why had Master Bugra not mentioned Instructor Akar was a woman? What else was being kept from him? Or were they trying to keep things from his father? Or perhaps it was his father's doing, hiding him from the world.

More likely the world was hiding from his father and his tenacious insistence on tradition. The world, the city—his city—moving on without him while he stayed stuck in the past, where his father wanted him to be. Some of those students had not even recognized him until they had seen his guards. Though Instructor Akar had been immediately aware. Why did she look familiar? Even her name sounded familiar.

"Watch your words," Behram snarled at Kudret.

"Behram"—Kudret tugged at the end of his short goatee, a taunting smile on his mouth—"it is unusual for you to be so interested in the affairs of a woman. Or her accomplishments."

Behram's face turned crimson, made only more so by the fire that flared beneath his skin. That piqued Omar's interest. It was unlike his friend to speak about any woman in more than passing. "The Vali Ahad asked about her specifically," he sneered.

"But are you not friends with her? Or perhaps…more than friends?" Kudret said. Sirhan cleared his throat and caught Omar's eye to wince in apology. Kudret had always been the more impolite of the two.

Mazhar, seated on the bench near Omar, chuckled into his glass of arak. Kudret and Behram were always at odds, something Mazhar found ceaselessly amusing but only gave Omar a headache.

Behram cast a disdainful look at Kudret. "Do not be absurd. What possible interest could I have in her?" Omar knew that tone of manipulation in Behram's voice. There was more there than friendship, it seemed.

"She is smarter than you," Kudret said. "She received higher marks than you in all our classes. She received higher marks than almost everyone."

Omar could not imagine Behram being attracted to anyone smarter than him, mainly because he doubted Behram believed there was anyone smarter than him. And for the most part, he would be correct. But Master Bugra seemed to think Instructor Akar had helped Behram, and gratitude could turn to attraction, he supposed.

Behram flicked his gaze up to Omar, flipping a page in a book he was not actually reading before he collapsed back against the couch. "She also has exceptional control," he said. "As noted, ad nauseum, by every instructor who has ever taught her." Behram stretched an arm across the back of the couch. "Why are you so interested in her?" His dark eyes were sharp, and Omar raised an eyebrow in mockery of the question.

Behram knew exactly why someone like that would be of interest to him. Perhaps he was attempting, in his way, to protect Instructor Akar. Omar did not care for the notion that anyone needed protecting from him, but it was not untrue.

"I do not like being so uninformed about strides made by one of the largest establishments in Narfour," Omar said. Kudret and Sirhan did not know of Omar's secret. Behram only knew because Omar had once confided to him in a fit of desperation. No one else could know.

"I am disappointed I missed witnessing all the instructors preen and monkey about for your favor." Behram rose, his crimson and orange caftan and entari swishing as he did. "Please excuse me, my father has summoned me for yet another guild meeting about this feud."

Well, one instructor had been uninterested in monkeying for his favor. Omar pressed his lips together so he did not smile. "Stay a moment, Behram. I have a matter to discuss with you." He caught Mazhar's gaze and his brother rolled his eyes.

"Come then, gentlemen, it seems we are dismissed." Mazhar stood, and Sirhan and Kudret followed him through the arched doorway, their steps echoing as they made their way down the twisting stone stairs.

Behram watched him for a moment, then crossed the room to the chessboard that had a game halfway in session. He put a finger on a pawn and said, carefully, "What were you doing at the University today?"

"It was Master Bugra's suggestion."

Behram cast his gaze toward the ceiling with a huff.

"Did Instructor Akar teach you control, Behram?"

Behram flicked the chess piece over. "I could not summon my magic. It is an entirely different problem than yours, is it not?" His irritation raged in his eyes, tiny fires flickering like dancers over and between his fingers. Behram's pride was a fragile thing.

Omar forced back his curiosity. "And that is why you never mentioned her to me, though you knew how desperate I was to find a solution?" He tried to keep the accusation out of his voice.

"She is a lowborn noble, my friend. I could not imagine someone like her would be of interest to you." He smiled. Omar considered him. Protecting her, indeed.

"Did she help you?"

"You saw her today, I assume. Did you ask her?"

"I did."

Another smile, this one directed at the floor, clearly pleased. "She might be able to help you, but you understand how having a woman come to the palace as your private tutor might be…misconstrued." Behram righted the pawn.

"She did not seem particularly inclined to speak to me, and I am unsure if she is even trustworthy enough to task with assisting me."

"She is trustworthy. I trust her more than I trust even you," Behram said, softly.

"Then help me. Will you speak to her?"

"Do you know she was at the last tribunal you attended?" Behram caught Omar's gaze with a weighted look.

Akar. Of course. "Her father is a tribunal judge for the guild," he said in defeat.

Behram tipped his head. If she had been present at the last tribunal, she would have seen his hack job of a confession, torturing that innocent man for his father's agenda. No wonder she'd looked at him as though he disgusted her. He also knew enough about the tribunal judges to know which supported his father and which did not. She would never help him. Behram watched him as he tore his own thoughts apart, and some of the hauteur smoothed away.

"She is enamored of books. And since you have an entire library at your disposal that she would never be allowed access to, I should think you have all you need to bribe her." Behram gave a strained smile.

"What kinds of books?"

"She is the daughter of a judge and an instructor of magical theory. I am certain you can puzzle it out. Now, if that is all, I am late to meet my father."

Omar waved him away. Behram reached the top of the stairs just as Mazhar appeared, and the two passed each other with twin looks of dislike.

"Wheel and spokes, I do not know how you bear him," Mazhar blurted.

"He is a good friend to me." Omar turned back to the windows. Behram would happily take Omar's place, roosting in the palace, his every whim tended to, safely away from the people he considered so below him. He was not so unusual among the noble families in his sentiments about the lower classes. He thought Omar's problem was a great boon, a way to get a leg up on almost any person he encountered. But that was Behram, always aware of how any situation or person could benefit him.

Omar did his best to at least appear to feel as Behram did. But he simply could not. His mother said he and Mazhar were not fashioned that way. The First House did not share the Fifth's arrogance. Usually. Perhaps his father was the backspin that proved the Wheel's true direction.

"You needn't go with me to the University tomorrow if you do not wish to," Omar said.

"So you are going back?" Mazhar laughed. "She seemed…prickly."

"She did."

"Of course I will go." Mazhar crossed the sitting room to stand beside Omar at the window. He folded his arms. The two of them looked alike, though Mazhar favored their mother, with finer features and hair a lighter shade of brown than Omar's. Omar looked like their father. Had his build, his mouth, and his jaw. It was well he did, he supposed. The old guard of the Council would take comfort in that when he replaced his father on the Sultan's seat. "Perhaps she was just dazzled by her first encounter with you."

"She did not appear dazzled," Omar said wryly. She had seemed to oscillate between annoyance and disgust.

Mazhar laughed again. Always laughing, his brother. Amused by everything.

Omar pondered the University. It sat south of the palace, encircled by the cliffs the palace had been built atop. He could see it from any part of the palace with a southern exposure, and had looked at it often. Wondering what it was like to be a student there. Instead of locked away in his rooms with his tutors, most of whom were too old to teach at the University anymore, or come up with an interesting lesson plan. Wheel, they could make even the most interesting of subjects into a mind-numbing mental trial.

"Father requested you," Mazhar said, and turned away when Omar nodded. Mazhar led down the stairs, one hand trailing along the stone of the tower wall. At the bottom, through the doorway at the bottom of the stairs, Omar's steward stood waiting. He was only two Turns younger than Omar, not quite to his full fourth Cycle. He had an entourage of apprentice stewards and servant girls with him. All bowed when Omar and his brother appeared.

Omar wiped a hand over his face, averting his gaze from all of them. He and his steward, Ruslan, were friendly enough in private. The others came and went too often for him to become attached.

Ruslan stepped forward and adjusted the collar of Omar's entari, careful not to touch anything but fabric, then straightened the hooks that buttoned it closed. "You do not wish to change before you see the Sultan?" he asked, eyeing the hem of Omar's garments with a displeased frown. Omar looked down. They were a bit dustier than they should have been to see his father.

"We haven't time." Omar twitched his entari, fruitlessly. The eternal curse of wearing silver and white for even the most mundane activities.

Ruslan turned a fraction toward the people gathered behind him and gestured. One of the young apprentices stepped forward and dropped to his knees in front of Omar, producing a brush from Wheel knew where. He applied it to the hem of Omar's caftan, also careful to touch nothing but cloth. The servants did not know why, though doubtless there were a variety of rumors, they knew only that the Vali Ahad was not to be touched. By anyone.

Mazhar snickered behind him, until the boy moved on to him, then his smirk soured and he rolled his eyes.

"Thank you, Ruslan," Omar said when the boy had finished and retreated to the gaggle of his comrades.

When Ruslan ducked his head, Omar moved past him, with Mazhar at his side, toward his father's receiving hall. It was late in the day for him to request they come see him; he usually met with them in the morning, to tell them about their expectations for the day, or had his Grand Vizier do so. Their relationship with their father was neither strained, nor loving. It simply was. He managed them the way a business owner might arrange his assets to his benefit. Deploying them here and there as was needed.

Ruslan sped his pace when they reached the hall, to open the doors and announce them, then stepped to the side as they entered. The shifting sea of other attendants moved like a bird flock through the sky, or a school of fish. Individual, but as one large swarm, to huddle against the outer wall.

Omar expected to see only his father, as usual, seated at the back of the room. But their mother was beside him, which was most unusual, and Omar resisted the urge to look to Mazhar for a hint that he knew the reason.

He could not relax his stiff posture as he approached the dais where his parents sat. He bowed. Mazhar moved in time with him, and as Omar straightened from his bow, he chanced a look at his brother. His face reflected Omar's same wariness.

Omar's next glance was to his mother. The Queen Sultana wore a tremulous smile, her hands gripped together in her lap.

"Sultanim," Omar began, but his father raised a hand for silence. His Grand Vizier, Eymen Demir Pasha, bowed when Omar cast a questioning look his way. Eymen took a step forward and bowed.

"Vali Ahad, the Sultan has fortunate news about your future."

Omar's heart plummeted into his stomach, and beside him, Mazhar's quick inhale hissed. There was only one thing left unsettled about Omar's future. A decision he could neither avoid nor control, and which he dreaded. It would explain that apologetic look on his mother's face.

"The High Council and I have decided it is time for you to choose a bride," the Sultan said gravely. Omar was not certain he had ever seen his father be anything but grave. He motioned with his hand once more, this time to indicate Eymen. The Grand Vizier bowed. "The High Council has scheduled to convene in two small turns to present the Sultan with their suggestions."

Before Omar could take so much as a breath, the Sultan spoke again. "The engagement will be held at the quarter."

Omar stared at his father, words rising and dying. That was only a few more small turns away. But it was futile to argue with him. He had never once won an argument with his father. He cut his gaze to his mother. Her warm skin was pale, her lips pressed so hard together they had almost disappeared.

"Thank you." He ejected the words too sharply and bowed to hide his face. "Efendim," he added before straightening. The Sultan dismissed him and Mazhar with a nod of his head.

Mazhar strode silently by his side as they left the hall. Omar signaled Ruslan to leave him alone with a wave of his hand, and the steward dismissed the others with a similar gesture. Only Mazhar walked with him as he returned to the study.

"Brother," Mazhar began when they reached the little foyer and the base of the stairs.

"Go," Omar said. Mazhar ducked his head, waited a moment more, then turned and left.

Omar climbed the stairs and returned to the window to look out over the city. He stared once more at the University, a place that was about moving forward. Not like the palace. Backward and stuck. But it did nothing for him now. For his pulse that raced in anger, despite the calm expression he managed. It was the only expression he was allowed. Composure was expected of him. Always. At least by his father. Omar's hands, gripped together behind his back, tightened so hard the fingers of his left went numb.

He turned, releasing his hands and snatching a vase from the little table beside the tall, arched windows, and smashed it on the floor. Regret flooded him immediately. Omar crouched, righting the base of the broken piece, and began filling it with the smaller bits.

Steps echoed on the stairs, then Behram entered through the arch. He paused to consider Omar. After a moment of silence he moved to Omar's side and knelt, helping him pick up the pieces.

"I thought you had guild meetings," Omar mumbled. Behram made a dismissive sound.

"They were postponed." He dropped a few pieces of ceramic into the broken vase as silence stretched between them. "I am sorry," he murmured after a moment.

"For what?" Omar turned his face away. Behram did not answer. He did not need to. The very few people close to Omar at all knew he had dreaded this day with every fiber of his being. His own parents' marriage was a miserable affair, his earliest memories full of their fights and his more recent ones their icy distance. He did not want to inflict that on anyone, or be afflicted by it. And besides, how was he to be a husband? To father an heir? Those things required touch.

His skin prickled. If he even wanted to touch whatever woman they chose for him. Or her touch him. He had never been under the delusion that anyone would ever love him, not for more than the comfort and titles he could provide. There was certainly no love in him to give to anyone or anything but Tamar. He had realized that long ago. His duty, and care, should be for Tamar and its people. There could be no room in that for anything else. His father had proved that to him over Turns.

Behram and Mazhar were the only two people Omar had ever admitted the last bits too, about love.

"If it is any consolation at all, my father told me the same only a few days ago." Behram stood. "Come with me to the meet. It will be a good distraction, and the guild leaders will behave better with you there."

"Not tonight." Omar stood and placed the broken vase on the table he had knocked it off of. The last thing he wanted was to be surrounded by people who could not see him as a person. As a man. Just as his father could not. He was nothing but a crown to those in the palace. And a monster to everyone else. It was all they saw when anyone looked at him. Except Behram. Behram understood, because he was his father's pawn, too.

"Then I will skip it. We can take a bottle of arak to the roof."

"You hate the roof," Omar said.

"If it will cheer you up, Vali Ahad, then I will endure." Behram gave an elaborate bow, and smiled as he straightened. "We can toast an end to our bachelorhood."

Omar returned his smile with less enthusiasm. "All right." He stood. Behram took the bottle of arak that Mazhar had been sipping from. The tower had a door to a narrow walk that led to the broader roof over the Sultan's wing. He and Behram occasionally sat out there, to escape the bustle of the palace, and everyone else. They rarely talked. Sometimes they drank.

The night was cold, despite that the day had spring's enthusiastic warmth to it, and dampness threatened in the air. The sky was clear though, so Omar lounged back on his elbows and looked up.

"Do you know who your father wants you to marry?" Omar asked after taking his first sip of arak. Behram shrugged. He sat stiffly, feet braced against the ceiling as if he were always afraid the roof would spontaneously reject him.

"It doesn't really matter, does it?" Behram said. "I have had plenty. Enough to know they are essentially the same. Trade one fault for another."

"It must be impossibly difficult, being faultless," Omar snarked. Behram looked at him sidelong with a raised eyebrow and snagged the bottle from him.

Omar rubbed his eyes. His head ached, painful, shooting throbs streaking up his temples that made him want to curl into a ball on the floor of his room in the dark. If he could control his magic completely, would the plague of pain cease? It was certainly worth demeaning himself by trying to bribe someone into assisting him.

He wanted to ask Behram more, but it was clear he was not in a talking mood. Behram took a long swig from the arak bottle and glared into the night. Somewhere an owl called, then another nightbird.

"What will you do?" Behram passed him the bottle. Omar shook his head.

"The same thing we always do. Accept it."

"Not this time. I have my own plans. Someone I could bear."

"Hmm." Omar held the bottle by the neck, swinging it in a slow circle. How did Behram plan to broach that with his father? Semih was even less reasonable than the Sultan. Still. Someone he could bear. That was a luxury he dared not hope for. It hardly seemed fair to ask that of someone when he was not certain he would be able to return the favor.

What was the Wheel turning him toward? He was blind to it. It felt like swimming against a rip current—no matter how he tried to change his course, it drove him further and further away from himself.

Silence was their third companion for a long while, as it usually was. Then Behram shifted and looked at him. "How are you feeling?"

"Generally like a great pile of steaming horse dung, thank you for asking." Omar looped his arms around his knees, swinging the nearly empty bottle back and forth as he stared down at the Sultan's garden.

Behram chuckled, in the fire-tinged way he had of making the worst things seem funny. A dark laugh and bitter smile. But he was the only one who understood what enduring pain for the sake of a father felt like, the only one who could make Omar feel the humor of it.

"What did you do to forget when it was bad, when all you wanted to do was run or fight back?" There was no fighting back. His father was Sultan. Omar's opinions only mattered when his father did not have one.

A wall went down between them, something Omar only rarely sensed between him and Behram. Behram opened his hand in front of him and a tiny flame sparked in his palm, and danced across his fingers as he turned it one way then the other, staring as if he were under its thrall.

"All it takes to banish the darkest night is a tiny flame," Behram said, in a rare flush of wisdom. "You just need to find that thing which lights you up."

"Just do not set me on fire in a misguided attempt to help," Omar said, uncomfortable with the mood of the conversation. Behram laughed and closed his fist over the flame, extinguishing it.

"I should go," Behram said, "and you should rest."

"Yes, Anne," Omar said. Behram snorted disdain, then made his awkward, stutter-stepped way back to the walk and the tower door beyond. Omar waited a few more moments before he did the same.

Ruslan was waiting for him in the tower. He eyed the bottle in Omar's hands, which Omar set carefully on the table where he had gotten it. Ruslan had clearly tidied up the rest of the mess Omar had made of the vase. Guilt nipped at him.

They had never been friends, though he was not certain if that was Ruslan's doing or his own. There were so few people who knew his secrets, it would make sense to be friends with the man who spent more time around him than anyone else. But more than anything, Omar felt like a burden to his steward. How could he also ask him for friendship? He was hardly worthy of anyone's friendship.

"Are you familiar at all with Judge Akar?" Omar asked.

Ruslan maintained his bland mien and spoke as if reciting. "He is well known for his better-than-passing knowledge of the Old Sultanate laws and for ruling fairly. He is also deeply embroiled in the Merchant Guild disputes."

Omar's exhalation whistled. That was an entanglement he did not need. He was already far too involved in something the palace should not be interfering with. He could not be seen to be showing favor like that.

Although his father was clearly choosing sides. Semih Kadir's side.

He went downstairs, and headed for the library, Ruslan trailing behind. Omar rubbed his temples and grumbled his own indecision. He had not read every book in the palace library, it was too expansive for that. But he was familiar with all the law books contained therein. He had a set in mind that might pique the interest of someone who enjoyed law.

If he gave her books, as Behram had suggested, was that really showing favor? He could not control how they affected the outcome. The real question was whether his own peace of mind was worth this betrayal of his father.

Voices whispered in the back of his mind, quiet, but separate.

SEVEN

ILAY GLANCED OVER HER SHOULDER. It was quiet in the library before classes began, only the most studious of attendees spent time here instead of sleeping or time with their friends or family. The courtyard in front of the University was filled to the brim with students mingling and chatting. Master Fahri was dozing in the front, though he had roused enough to welcome her. Dilay circled her arm around her bag and slid it forward on her hip, digging out the books she had borrowed for her class the previous night. Her young students tried very hard to be respectful of the materials she *borrowed* for them to reference. She had not used these last night, inspired by her talk with her father to branch out to a discussion of the laws.

She pushed one book into place then moved down the aisle and ducked her head as she dug through the bag for the next.

"Good morning."

Dilay gasped, her instinct to turn away in order to hide what she was doing causing her to lurch forward and drive her face into the bookshelf.

"Oh," she groaned, pressing her palm against her head where she had smacked it on the shelf. She turned to look at whoever had addressed her. Cinnamon eyes in a stern, though amused face. Dilay immediately bowed, nearly dumping her bag of smuggled materials on the floor. She slapped her hands together against the flap to hold it closed.

His shoes were filthy. Had he walked from the palace? Was he out of his mind? She was surprised he had not been mobbed on his way.

"I seem to always manage to startle you. Please." He wiggled his fingers in her line of sight so she would straighten. Dilay obeyed and swept stray hair from her face as she did with one hand, clutching the bag's strap with the other. Afforded an opportunity to look at him again, she was surprised to see his skin washed of color, dark circles beneath his eyes and the lids red-rimmed. A man she had not seen the day before lurked behind him, dressed in palace finery. At the entrance to the row, three guards stood in a wedge.

"Perhaps if you did not always approach from behind me, I would not be startled."

"I shall keep that in mind," he said. His distinctive voice was hoarse, and he appeared a bit unsteady, his feet set wide to keep him from swaying. Was he ill? Her first instinct was to cover her mouth with her sleeve, but she did not. Consumption ravaged the poor areas of the city, but she doubted the Vali Ahad had been anywhere near the affected areas.

Or…her father had said he was to attend another tribunal today. Dilay took an involuntary step back, smashing her back against the shelves. His demeanor tensed. He turned to the man behind him, who stepped to his side and held out a small, leatherbound book.

"I have brought you a"—he paused, blinked—"a book."

Dilay looked at it, then the man, who must be a steward, and finally, at the Vali Ahad. "You came to bring me a book and made someone else carry it for you?" she asked, and before she could stop herself, blurted, "was it quite heavy?"

His expression relaxed in disbelief, and her own scrunched in regret. The steward's mouth twisted, though whether it was amusement or outrage, she could not determine.

Seda was right. She truly could not keep her mouth shut when she needed to. Well, at least if she was caned for speaking back to the crown prince, rumors about her being his lover because they had been sighted speaking together would die before they ever started. She was not entirely certain which would be more painful.

"Quite." He appeared amused, although it was hard to tell if that was humor glinting through his stern countenance or just irritation, or perhaps pain. There was definitely pain, amidst the other flitterings of emotion. The man did not look well at all. Was that perhaps an aftereffect of using his magic? If so, then she could not help the brief thought that he deserved it. He took the book from the steward and held it out to her.

Dilay took it gingerly, casting her gaze at the floor. The more she looked at him the more he resembled his father, and the more uncomfortable she became in his presence. She had only ever seen the Sultan from a distance. But they shared the same broad shoulders and height, hair that was neither black nor brown but both. She wondered if his father also shared that particular shade of warm, red brown in his eyes. She could not imagine she would ever be close enough to the Sultan to determine that answer.

"Thank you for the book," she said, confused by the gift, "but please do not let me keep you."

"You are not keeping me," he said with a soft noise like a laugh. As though the idea that she could keep him anywhere was absurd. Which it absolutely was. This conversation was equivalent to a lion having discourse with an ant. Still, it raised her ire to be dismissed, even if he were perfectly within his rights to do so.

"Well, you are keeping me, so if you would not mind." She bowed again and pointed between him and his steward to indicate she wished to leave. He blinked again, then a broad smile broke over his face, unmooring Dilay's good sense for a moment.

"If I might have a single moment more?" He turned his head to give his steward a tiny nod. The man drew a sigil against his palm, which glowed briefly then disappeared, and the sounds around them were snuffed out as his dampening spell buffered them from the rest of the library.

"Spellcasting on University grounds, outside the classrooms, is strictly forbidden," Dilay said, brow creased. Being locked into a dampening circle with a Sabri seemed like the first step toward something she did not wish to be involved in, something that ended in prison. That broad smile returned, and he winked, which completely flustered her.

"I believe they will make an exception, this once," he said. She flushed. Of course. He was a prince. He could do anything he wished. What must that be like?

"That"—he pointed to the book he had given her—"is Judge Hanim's book of laws."

Dilay took a moment to understand, glanced in surprise at the nondescript book she held in her hands. Her fingers tightened possessively.

"Have you read this?" She took an unconscious step closer in her excitement. He stepped back, as if afraid she would touch him, and fumbled to grab a shelf when it seemed to upset his balance. Dilay tried not to let her offense show on her face. Did he think her unclean? Or too lowly to touch him? Not that she had even intended to.

"I have studied Old Sultanate Law," he said. "To include this one. I was told you are interested in law." It took a moment to think of a reply that did not reveal how far outside the normal role of *woman* she chose to step. A reply that did not tell him she studied law looking for bits to help mediate the guild dispute, through her father, of course. Or old laws that might be leveraged to help with her extracurricular endeavors. What would he think of that? His father would assume her intention was to undermine him.

"It is the best measure of a civilization, is it not? How their laws are written, who they punish, who they include, who they exclude. Much can be gleaned about the past and present by studying the laws and how they were and are enforced."

He dropped his gaze on hers, and it held her. "Then you will be interested to know this book has three brethren. That are only available in the palace library."

"Oh," she said bleakly. One book was better than no books, she supposed. Perhaps when she was a full instructor, and not just an apprentice, she might be afforded a chance to browse the palace library.

"The others go into the more interesting aspects. Such as how the Circle of Chara'a integrated themselves with the tribunal and the Sultan's Council." He had a pleasant voice, she decided. Voices had always been her particular talent. She could remember them, even when she could not remember faces. It was not an unusual talent for an air mage, for whom hearing was such an integral part of their House. His had a restrained resonance that she liked. As if he was always holding it back, trying to shrink it to a volume it was not made for.

But why was he talking about books? With her? Surely that did not require a dampening spell. She glanced at his face and found him studying hers. She twitched her gaze away.

"Why did you bring me this?"

"Would you like to see the others?" he asked. Dilay's gaze zipped back to his, and he smiled triumph. "Behram tells me you are known for your magical control," he said, clasping his hands behind his back.

"It is not a concept that caused me challenge," she said warily. Bragging to a man about her magical prowess always ended in her annoyance at best when he tried to prove her wrong; at worst, she knew women who were beaten for embarrassing their male counterparts, though that was far less prevalent now than it had been when her mother was young. Who knew what measures the Vali Ahad might take to elevate himself?

Muscles twitched across his face, then he cast his gaze up and to the left.

"Then you would be well suited to assist me in finding the answer to a problem," he said. Dilay glanced to his steward, then drew a look above them as if she might be able to see the spell that cocooned them. He cleared his throat. "I would like to engage your help. And in return, I will see to it that you are granted access to the palace library as often as you wish."

Her thoughts swirled into a tumult of nonsense. Her father's disapproval, the fact that only the highest-ranked of instructors were ever allowed into the palace library and only with approval. The idea of being beholden in any way to the man before her. A man who could, in a fit of pique if she did not prove capable of whatever it was he wanted, put her in prison. Or simply cast about in her mind with his magic looking for interesting bits.

"What would helping you entail, exactly?"

His eyes narrowed, as if pained, and he moved his head from one side to the other, quickly, as if trying to expunge something that nagged him. "We can discuss it in more detail later, but it would require meeting with me on regular occasions that fit both our schedules."

Meeting with the Vali Ahad on regular occasions? Her father's face flashed in her mind, as did the scene at the tribunal. But the book was warm and heavy in her hand, full of new knowledge.

"May I"—she hugged the book against her—"may I think about it?"

"Of course." He released his hands from behind his back and turned to say something to his steward. The movement made him sway, and he clutched a hand over his face, digging against his temples. His steward's eyebrows shot up in alarm. The Vali Ahad grunted, and a drop of blood trickled from his nose.

"Efendim." Dilay took a step closer. "Forgive me, you do not appear well. Can I…shall I have someone summon a carriage to take you back to the palace? My father has headaches and rest is the very best medicine." Though this seemed like something far worse than a headache, if it was causing him to bleed. She flipped open the flap on her bag, realizing too late it revealed her illicit borrows, but dug between them for her single, rumpled handkerchief. She held it out to him, fumbling the flap closed as the steward eyed the books within it with a raised eyebrow.

"If I return to the palace like this, I will never leave it again," the Vali Ahad mumbled as he lowered his hand. He noticed her outstretched hand, glanced at her eyes, then took the bit of cloth reluctantly to wipe the blood from his face.

"Is there somewhere the Vali Ahad might rest, in private?" the steward emphasized *private*, as though she might suggest he rest in the middle of the atrium.

"I could find an empty classroom?" she offered. The steward glanced behind him, toward the main aisle of the library and beyond. "If we could not parade him in such a state in front of every noble's son—"

"I am not in a state." The Vali Ahad tried to prove his point by straightening his posture, but his skin went a shade greyer. This was more than a headache, to be causing such weakness. Perhaps she had the wrong idea of the cost of his magic.

"There is Master Fahri's office, at the back of the library. He allows me to study there sometimes when he is in a benevolent mood. I can show you." Dilay turned and strode through the aisle, glancing back once to see if they followed. The Vali Ahad followed at the front of his small entourage, doing a very good job of pretending he had not almost gone to his knees a moment before. Her fingers tingled, and a little catch lodged in her throat. What was she doing? She should just ignore whatever was wrong with him and go about her business. Any help she gave him was tantamount to condoning his disturbing magic.

She opened the door to Master Fahri's office, and the assault of must and the unidentifiable smells that had always permeated the space made her scrunch her nose. No lamp was lit, but the light from the library was enough for her to see her way around. The square table in the center of the room served as a workspace, and Dilay quickly tidied it, making neat stacks of books and papers to create room. She kicked the sitting cushion into place just as the Vali Ahad entered.

His guards stayed just outside, but Dilay did not see the steward.

"Your steward?" She shuffled out of the way; the small room was not meant for more than one person. He sat on the cushion.

"He went to inform Master Fahri that I have commandeered his office."

"Oh, but I am certain it is fine. You are the Vali Ahad after all," she said. One of the guards ducked his head in, murmured a few words, and a mage orb bubbled to life and floated to the ceiling, casting the dusty, disheveled space in pale light.

"Am I?" the Vali Ahad said, as dry as packing salt, as he propped his elbows on the table and pressed his palms to his eyes.

"I did not mean offense," Dilay said softly. She fidgeted with the flap of her bag and yearned for escape.

"I know." He folded his arms on the table in front of him. Dilay traced the edge of the fabric flap, then knelt across the table from him with her back to the door. She set Judge Hanim's book in front of her, arranging it exactly parallel with the edge of the table.

"You said if you returned to the palace you would never leave it." Could it be that he was at the University seeking help against his father's wishes? That intrigued her.

Cinnamon eyes met hers, and a little jolt went down the back of her throat. It was perfectly normal to find him handsome. There was not a woman she knew who would disagree with her. Though she was not entirely sure it was because of those warm brown eyes and broad jaw, or because of the promise of wealth and power that so many lauded his looks. Besides, there were plenty of handsome men in the world who were also terrible people.

"I have a specific set of duties. Being here is not one of them," he said. There was no mistaking the sharp tone. Bitter. "If the Sultan believes that time at the University will hamper my usefulness to him, he will not allow me to return here."

Dilay sat back on her heels, watching him. Was he speaking about the tribunals? She had not considered that he was not a willing participant in them. But she could only assume this violent, bleeding headache had something to do with his magic. She had seen students give themselves bloody noses when they were trying to transition from controlling a spell with words to mental spell craft. An affliction of Sival—Aval and Deval did not have enough power to overload their own bodies in such a way. But the tribunal would have been a few candlemarks ago. Any aftereffects of his magic should have cleared by now. Though she knew almost nothing about a Veritor's particular power. If she helped him, would he tell her more about it?

"Is this headache"—she paused when his bearing hardened—"is this the problem you want my help with?" If she enmeshed herself with something involving the palace, her father would never forgive her.

"This is part of it, yes."

"I am not a physician, Vali Ahad."

"I am aware." He touched the cloth she had given him to his nose again, and it came away with a fresh mark of blood. "I have seen a dozen physicians. I have studied under countless tutors. And still, still I am…" He dropped the blood-spotted cloth between them as though it were evidence.

I am pathetic. A fire mage that cannot burn.

Dilay realized why she cared at all that the Vali Ahad was bleeding in front of her, despite what she had seen him do. Despite what she thought of his father's policies. Despite her own father's vehement opinions. Despite that he was a man grown and not a sad, lonely little boy. He was just like Behram. His magic and his self completely separate, dictated by someone else.

She rubbed the spot between her brows. Wheel, why couldn't she just take in stray animals, like Seda did?

"I will try, Efendim, but you must promise not to throw me in prison if I fail." Or rip her mind open. Dilay gripped the table edge instead of recoil from him.

His shoulders slumped and he lowered his forehead to his arms. "No one can know about this," he said into his arms. Of course not. Tensions were too high in the city, in all of Tamar, in fact, for anyone to know and likely exploit the fact that the Vali Ahad did not have his considerable power under control.

"When do you wish to meet? And how will we do so without starting rumors?"

"At night." He stirred, shifting his head so his eyes appeared above his forearms. His gaze fixed on the book then rose. She was sitting across from the Vali Ahad. And he wanted her help. She could never have imagined such a turn.

Dilay glanced down to hide her consternation. Surely he understood that private meetings between them would cause both of them issue? Not only was that when she taught the children, meeting the Vali Ahad at night was a sure way to ruin her reputation and give those who opposed her appointment as instructor exactly what they wanted.

Always there had been rumors. It did not matter that she had worked tirelessly to graduate a Turn early. Master Bugra had chosen to retire from the University, and the subsequent shuffling of instructors after his departure had opened a vacancy. So Dilay had worked through sleepless nights and endless days to finish early and apply. Master Bugra had spoken for her. As had two of the younger, more liberally minded instructors. Enough to get her the job. On probation, of course.

The slightest slipup and she would be gone. And they watched her for it. They claimed it had not been work that got her the position, but that she was pretty.

Beauty, her mother had told her, was both weapon and liability. But for Dilay, her even average beauty had been nothing but a problem. Used both to elevate and demean her. *She was only chosen because she is beautiful.* And, *Why waste your time with all this work when you can have anything you want by simply seducing the right man? How can our male students be expected to concentrate if she is teaching them?*

Perhaps none of that would occur to a man who was used to the entire world bending to his schedule, who was accustomed to people doing exactly what he wanted without him having to consider the consequences to their lives.

"I cannot," she said.

He blinked. "Classes are over then. Your work is finished. Why?"

"Work does not stop at the end of the day for most of us, Vali Ahad." She tried to keep her tone subdued, and maybe managed a bit of respect, but she thought some of the edge of resentment remained. "Your steward, for example, and your guards do not stop when you are at ease."

"Brother," the Sehzade said from the doorway. Dilay twisted to look up at him. He glanced at her, then apparently dismissed her completely, as he stepped around the table to stand at his brother's side.

"Ah good. My nursemaid has arrived," the Vali Ahad sighed. The Sehzade raised an eyebrow.

"What are you doing back here?"

"I think that is obvious." The Vali Ahad straightened, and held a hand up to indicate Dilay. "Recruiting Instructor Akar to my cause."

Her temper bristled at the wording, and it must have shown on her face, because when the Sehzade looked at her, his mouth stretched in a taunting smirk.

"I am not so certain about that."

"You seem to be in good hands, Efendim." Dilay rose. "I have classes to attend."

"I would like to meet today, Instructor Akar," the Vali Ahad replied. She looked down at him and raised an eyebrow.

"I do not think that is a good idea."

"Today."

Dilay put her hands on her hips. "No."

The two men stared at her in silence.

"Did you"—the Sehzade made a sound like a tiny laugh—"did you just tell the Vali Ahad no?"

"First, I have no idea where to even start. I need time to assess and prepare. And second, you can hardly walk and will be useless in any kind of class," Dilay said, borrowing her mother's stern tone, the one she used when there was absolutely no arguing. The one that could make complete strangers stop and recoil in preparation for her rebuke. "Come to my class tomorrow, Efendim, if you are able. Under the pretense of observation. I can assess you then."

"Very well, Instructor Akar," the Vali Ahad said, doing a poor job of suppressing a smile. He thought she was funny. Novel. Not so different than any of her other students. Well, he would learn, just as they did, that she was no less willing to make his learning life a misery. "Everything you have seen, and everything we have discussed, is not to leave this room," he said. "You understand."

"Of course." She bowed and snatched up the book at the very last moment before she turned and left.

EIGHT

DILAY MUNCHED ON A FEW slices of carrot, and a cold wedge of kibbeh, with more buckwheat than meat in it. They had been trying to stretch the lamb they had, since it would be some time before they could afford anything more than a chicken. It was cyclical, when her father was paid for his tribunal duties, and crime was lowest in winter and spring. Spring was in its full glory now, unfortunately. Her mother set a bowl of greens down in front of her, and Dilay looked up in surprise.

"You are too skinny."

"These take too long. I need to get to—"

"Eat," her mother said, gently, and pushed the bowl closer. They grew what they could in pots along the front of the house, the only south-facing exposure not shaded out by neighbors and the taller houses of the more wealthy. Much of it was pilfered by passersby, but what they could glean helped a bit. Her mother had dribbled oil and vinegar and a healthy dusting of za'atar on the greens. Dilay dutifully ate them, watching as her mother tied her apron about her waist and tucked her hair beneath a wrap of white cloth. "I have picked up two more houses in the Air District. So I will be home late tonight."

"I will be in the warehouse after my classes at the University. I will not see you until tomorrow," Dilay said around a mouthful of bitter greens. Her mother nodded, the corners of her mouth pinched in the manner Dilay had named her "not frown."

"Be careful, Deedee. I heard someone speaking of your hobby the other day, though they spoke as if it were just a rumor. You do not wish for that rumor to become talk of sedition."

Dilay nodded. She needed to talk to someone, anyone, about the Vali Ahad. It was frightening, and confusing. Her mother would at least listen. But she was also certain to tell Dilay's father, eventually, and he would not listen.

Her mother hoisted her basket, with its empty bags for laundry, up to her hip before bending to kiss Dilay's temple. The door that led from the kitchen to the tiny patio in the back, where their oven was, creaked closed behind her mother.

In her absence the house settled in silence. Dilay pushed the bowl of greens away. She wiped her fingers on her salvar, making certain none of the oil from the greens lingered. Then she reached beneath the cushion that kept her off the cold stone of the kitchen floor and withdrew the book the Vali Ahad had given her.

She set it on the table and opened it carefully. None of the books available in the University dealt so specifically with the laws of the Old Sultanate. Tamar was all that was left of that empire, which once stretched to touch most of the known world. From the Odokan plains in the east, to the easternmost reaches of Menei and its neighbors in the south, beyond the Sun Sea, nearly to the north, where barbarians who still cavorted in furs and hefted spears were rumored to live. And where the Old Sultanate had reached, so had magic. In everything. Every life, every plant, every grain of sand had been touched with it.

Six Houses spun the Wheel, balanced in harmony and opposition. The mages of the Circle helped write the laws of the Old Sultanate, known for its justice and fair dealings. At least until the Sundering War, when the seeds of prejudice sprouted into mighty vines that broke the world and reduced Tamar to a fraction of its former size.

Dilay wanted to know why. Desperately. She wanted to understand how a world had gone from harmony and balance, six Houses, to four. First House, air and intellect. Second House, water and emotion.

Fourth House, earth and duty. Fifth, fire, and passion. And once, now lost, the Third and Sixth. Creation and Destruction. Life, and death. Joy, and sorrow. She wanted to know if it could ever be brought back to balance, and restore that which was lost.

She opened the book, and marveled at the fading inscription once again. This had been written by someone just like her father, who lived before the Sundering War, at the height of the Old Sultanate's glory. She knew of Judge Hanim. He was renowned as the father, alongside Omar Sabri the First, of Tamar law. Dilay had not known any of his writings still existed. So much knowledge had been lost during the Sundering War, books burned and destroyed.

There had once been a branch of the University entirely dedicated to training tribunal judges, but that was now accomplished by apprenticeship. Some of Hanim's outlines of law had survived into the modern age, were still informing and serving as the structure for the system of laws the current Sultan relied upon.

Unfortunately, there was no time to dive deeply this morning, she was already running late to get to the Grand Market before it was overrun. But she flipped carefully through some of the pages. Laws governing marriage, the sale of goats—an important commodity then, and to some degree still—and trade disputes. That was the section she needed most, and had yet to find time to devote to it.

The Merchant Guild was headed by the Altimur family. In fact, some believed it had been controlled by the Altimur name dating back to before the Sundering War, though those kinds of records had been lost in the violence of the war. In the last decade, Semih Kadir, father of Behram and governor of three quarters of the territory that made up Narfour, had been painstakingly gathering supporters. Now, he was making a bid to take control of the guild. The Merchant Guild was the most powerful guild in the city. Its umbrella encompassed all of the trade guilds, which meant its reach stretched even into the valley, where agriculture ruled more than commerce. Whoever controlled the Merchant Guild was eclipsed only by the Sultan in power.

There were many, particularly in the less-powerful trade guilds, and the poorer parts of the Water and Earth Districts, who were frightened by the prospect of Semih Kadir taking over the Merchant Guild. He was not a man known for fairness, the way Altimur Pasha was. Osman and Behram, who would one day take over in their fathers' places, were also entirely different people. Osman was mild-tempered, smart, but simple. He saw things in black and white, and had a strong head for business and fairness. Behram, at least as a friend, was loyal, protective, and confident. But he could also be, in contrast to Osman, the truest manifestation of the Fifth House's darker side that Dilay had ever seen in one person. Arrogant, abrasive, and selfish. She did not know what kind of leader Behram would be, as he had yet to hold a position of any kind. But she had seen Osman, and trusted he could lead a guild into the modern age.

The laws under the Tamar Sultanate stated that guild leadership could only change hands under two circumstances—death with no heir or a three-quarters majority vote of a panel of tribunal judges. She hoped her research into the old laws would yield guidance on any similar circumstances that she could use to help her father, and the other judges, in mediating. She wondered what the Vali Ahad would think of that. Behram would be livid; though he already knew which way her father leaned, he would feel betrayed that she was doing anything to move against him.

Just as she began reading, someone knocked on the back door then flung it open.

"Great, spinning. Wheel," Seda exclaimed, dropping into a heap at the little table in the kitchen. She scooted a cushion about to her specifications, then planted her elbows on the table. "We are going to be late." She plucked several lettuce leaves out of Dilay's bowl. Dilay pushed both the greens and her plate of kibbeh toward her friend. She knew Seda's father, an ironworker in the Blacksmiths' Guild, was struggling to get enough work. The tides were shifting already in the trade guilds, and nothing had yet been decided about the Merchant Guild.

Seda paused in her chewing to eye the plates and then Dilay, preparing to argue. She had her own fire mage pride, though it was not so immolative as Behram's. But she relented, eating enthusiastically. It broke Dilay's heart, because she knew Seda and her family were not the only ones suffering the consequences of the Merchant Guild's instability.

"I heard…" Seda said around a mouthful of kibbeh. Dilay took a carrot slice and ate it as she looked at her friend. "…that the Vali Ahad has taken a special interest in one of the instructors."

Dilay's mouth went dry, the carrot's flavor withering. Seda met her gaze, accusatory. Heat threatened to spread up Dilay's neck, and she banished it with a whisper of cool magic. It had begun already.

"What does he want?"

"He wants my help," she purged. A weight felt lifted, then settled back with emphasis when Seda gasped.

"Your help with what?" Her eyes widened, and she stabbed her spoon into the kibbeh without taking a bite. Dilay's fingers tightened against the book. Seda was an incurable gossip. But she also had a solid, no-nonsense approach to problems that Dilay found herself keenly in need of at the moment. Dilay was not a fool, she understood the dire consequences if the greater public realized that the Vali Ahad lacked magical control. Any mage who lacked control could be dangerous, but one who lacked control who could also bore into a mind? She blanched. But he wanted control. Was that not a good thing? No, she could not speak to Seda now. The secret would definitely get out if her friend knew.

Perhaps, if she earned his trust while helping him, she could get influence enough to speak with him about ending trial by confession. And the access to the library in the palace was invaluable. A privilege only the Headmaster himself had, and only on special occasions or on research subjects assigned by the Sultan himself. But the Vali Ahad had said whenever she wished. It would be exactly the advantage she needed, the kind of advantage she had never had, had never even dreamed of having.

So, Seda had helped her make a decision, in a way.

"He wants my help with preparing a study of theory for Master Bugra," Dilay said. "The Master recommended me." Fire mages were gifted by the Wheel with an affinity for lies. They could tell them, but were notoriously bad at scenting them out. That was water's realm.

Dilay said silent thanks to the Wheel that her friend was not a water mage. Because Dilay was a very poor liar.

"That seems like cheating." Seda sniffed, then took a bite of the kibbeh. "I should not be surprised. I suppose you can't exactly refuse a prince. What are you going to do?"

"Oh…" Dilay lowered her eyes to the book so she would not have to look at Seda while she lied, "recommend books and read his work."

Seda made an exasperated sound and pushed the food away as she stood up. "Let's get out of here. At least it is only one paper."

Dilay stood, tucking the law book into her pocket, then followed Seda out the back door. Dilay snagged an empty basket from the front of the house as they passed. They wound their way around the house and into the street, heading for the Grand Market.

"Does your father know?"

"No. Please do not tell him, it will only make his headaches worse," Dilay said. "Which reminds me, help me remember to buy more herbs for him." Her father held all his tension and stress in his shoulders. Which led to occasionally debilitating headaches.

Seda nodded, threading her arm through Dilay's. They spoke about the forge, about her father's work, and Seda's. For now, she apprenticed one day a small turn in the University library, but she also helped her mother run a market stall selling the small goods her father made, the everyday things people needed, nails, wire, bucket rings. She and her mother braided rope as well, for smaller applications. They were typical of this section of the city, handy at a variety of smaller jobs and crafts, to make ends meet and feed themselves. Just enough to get by on, never enough to move up.

Seda also helped Dilay teach at night, which Dilay could not pay her for, since she did not get paid.

Dilay hoped that someday she would clear a path so that Seda could join her at the University. She was just as bright a student as Dilay, and Dilay had no delusions. It was that her father was a judge, with some pull, which had allowed her to attend and be noticed at the University. Were Seda's parents different people, it might be her teaching at the University, instead of Dilay.

"Broken spokes," Seda whispered and veered, tugging Dilay to the other side of the street. Dilay followed her friend's line of sight to see Behram Kadir seated on the patio of a tea shop. A tea boy was just setting a tray with pot and cups out on the table. Osman Altimur sat on a cushion across from him, and he appeared angry.

"What do you think they're discussing?" Seda asked, looking curious. It was odd to see Behram and Osman together. They did share the same group of friends, according to Seda's gossip, but Dilay could not think of a time she had seen just the two of them. Behram had a look on his face like a cat with a mouse.

"You tell your father to call off his thugs," Osman said, loudly enough that Dilay could hear him, with a little help from her magic. "I will prove he is bribing those price-fixers."

"Will you?" Behram smiled. "That will be difficult, considering he is not."

She briefly considered crossing the street to interject herself. She hated it when Behram used his considerable intelligence to trap people. Just when Dilay started to turn away again, Behram looked up. Their gazes snagged, and his demeanor changed. His smile softened, and he said something to Osman before waving to Dilay and Seda to come.

"Don't you dare," Seda moaned under her breath, her dark eyes wide.

"You will be fine," Dilay asserted. Seda and Behram were fire and pitch together. All Seda knew of Behram was what he was now, not the bullied little boy Dilay had grown up with. The one who had shared his books with her and taught her to play chess. "We shouldn't be rude."

Seda protested again as they crossed the street, only going silent when they bowed to the men.

"Join us." He indicated two cushions. Seda and Dilay glanced at each other. Teahouses were men's places.

"You know we cannot," Dilay chided Behram, and he gave her a taunting smile in return.

"I thought you enjoyed inserting yourself into places women do not go," he said. Dilay folded her arms and raised an eyebrow, then sat on one of the cushions. Seda made a sound of annoyance, sinking beside

Dilay, so close their sides were pressed together. But her mood quickly warmed, as she had been nursing a starry-eyed crush on Osman for as long as Dilay could remember. Osman had the good sense to look embarrassed at their presence, glancing around at the other patrons, who all wore appropriately scandalized visages.

"You are my informant when it comes to matters of the tribunal judges and their talks about the guild dispute. I thought to ply you with tea." Behram pressed a cup toward her and poured. Osman's attention riveted on her, a disapproval showing in the curve of his mouth despite his thick mustache. Dilay offered him a weak smile. She liked Osman. She did not know what Behram was scheming, bringing her over to them like this and mentioning the feud. As a boy Behram had been shy and sweet. As a man…he was something else. Like a dog beaten too many times to ever be anything but feral. But there was still hope, still some of the boy left that had so much potential.

"I have overheard nothing of use to either of you." She used her father's most neutral tone, one she had practiced in preparation for teaching at the University. Osman's shoulders relaxed, his gaze flashing to the edge of the market, just up the road. Dilay could not help her curiosity. She followed his line of sight. A group of women stood chatting before entering the main square of vendors. She recognized Zehra Demir, the Grand Vizier's daughter. His only child, in fact.

"A pity," Behram said, with a tone like he did not believe her at all.

Dilay glanced back to Osman. He dropped his gaze to his hands and his cup of tea, then took a sip, trying to appear as if he were absolutely fascinated with the process. Dilay looked sidelong at Seda to see if she had noticed, and Seda did not return the look, but one corner of her mouth did turn up. Osman's pale eyes narrowed at both of them, his ruddy cheeks darkening.

"The entire student body of the University has been swept up in having the Vali Ahad and Sehzade visiting," he said, in a poor attempt to turn the conversation. "Are the instructors in a similar state?"

"We have been given several instructional lectures on how to treat the princes."

Behram laughed. "They would have made the worst students. What would the instructors have been able to do if they turned in unsatisfactory work? I will chance a wager. Nothing."

Dilay dipped her chin in agreement. No instructor would dare give a prince a failing mark.

"I cannot imagine the Vali Ahad turning in unsatisfactory work," Osman said. "The Sehzade though." He shrugged. Behram sniffed disdain.

"A man known for pranks around the palace surely would not have taken his education seriously. What about the goats?" His eyes took on a sharp glint, and Osman flinched, his gaze flicking between Behram and Dilay.

Dilay looked at Seda, then at Behram. Behram set his teacup down. "The Sehzade released a herd of goats into the High Council a few Turns ago. During a very important deliberation. If you want more details than that, you shall have to ask dear Osman."

"You didn't help him?" Seda blurted. Osman glowered at Behram, who bore a tiny, pleased smile.

"I helped," Osman said. "My mother still falls into melancholy anytime someone mentions the animals even in passing."

Dilay burst into laughter, and quickly put a hand over her mouth. All the teahouse patrons recoiled as if her laughter were the most grievous of affronts. She glanced at Behram, but he only stared back, neutral faced. Fire burned around his irises. Most mages leashed their magic unless they were actively casting a spell. Behram let his show as augment whenever it suited him. Like someone playing with a dagger in front of a rival at a dinner table. When she looked at him he looked down, snatching up the teapot and pouring another cup.

"We should go," Dilay said to Seda, when her laughter subsided. Seda nodded enthusiastically, all but leaping to her feet.

"You owe me a chess match, soon, Instructor Akar," Behram said as she rose and bowed again. Dilay offered him a smile.

"I will attempt to fit you into my schedule," she teased. Fire remained in his irises, not the flames of a moment before, but light, like a lamp shining inside, its glow leaking through the brown of Behram's eyes.

Seda grabbed her arm and dragged her across the street and up the hill. "You need to be more careful, Dilay."

"What?" Dilay adjusted her basket so it hung from the crook of her arm, and straightened her clothes.

"You will be the death of me," Seda groaned. "How can you know everything in the world it's possible to know, except what is going on around you?"

"Stop talking in circles," Dilay said. They passed the group of women Osman had been watching. Zehra waved a hand in greeting and smiled, and Dilay returned it. She could not blame Osman for staring at her, she was lovely. A Fourth House mage, earth showed in her gentle face and eyes, sweetness in her smile. She was one of the kinder nobles Dilay had ever met.

"You told me things between you two were over, but that man is *still* in love with you. Or whatever passes for love in Behram Kadir's mind."

Dilay's stomach launched into her throat. Turns ago, just before his father's meteoric rise in standing, before they were old enough to begin in the University, Behram had admitted feelings for her. Had kissed her. And she had kissed him back. He was handsome, and at the time, there had still been gentleness in him. But not now. He knew she did not want him as he was now. She had told him that, only a few days after that kiss. When she had seen him strike one of his father's servants. They had never mentioned any of it again, and their friendship continued, if a bit more formal and distanced than before.

Surely all that was gone? Behram lived by the divisions between nobles and the lower classes now, and while Dilay was technically a noble, she was only barely so. He had no use for women like her as more than they were.

"We are friends," Dilay said.

"That was not what I saw in his eyes when he looked at you. Be careful." Seda looked at her earnestly. "A fire mage's care can easily be warped."

Dilay closed her eyes and exhaled harshly. "I will be careful. Please do not worry. Despite what you think, he can be reasoned with. Now can we talk about something else?"

They made their way through the market, selecting a few bits and bobs of spring produce. Dilay made her stops along the section dedicated to remedies and herbs. It had taken a great deal of studying nearly incomprehensible notes in ancient texts, but she had finally come up with a particular concoction of herbs that seemed to work for her father's headaches. She paid for extra, mixing those together in their own little burlap bag.

She could not put Seda's words, and warning, out of her mind. Her friend had to be mistaken. Dilay had known Behram for Turns. Wouldn't she know if he was infatuated with her? Yes. Of course she would. Behram would never be able to stand someone like Dilay. He wanted a wife shackled to a splendid house, whelping highborn heirs. Dilay was not suited for any of that, and Behram knew that better than anyone. She had helped him to tame his temper, to find his control. He had helped her study, helped her practice her magic until they were both exhausted.

He knew what she wanted most: the path she was clearing for herself, one miserable brick at a time. A life in the University, a chance to teach others who were bright, and curious, and could make a difference in Tamar for everyone, not just the nobles. That was not the kind of woman who would present well in the high circles.

Behram could not love her. She did not think he could love anyone. He did not even like himself.

NINE

THE SKY ROOM AT THE top of the Hall of Air took Omar's breath and held it hostage. Nowhere in the palace was there such an unobstructed view of the city, of the ocean to the west and the Kalspire and its ridge of mountains to the east. He was entranced by it, and walked to the windows as if physically drawn, unaware and uncaring about the way all conversation ceased when he and Mazhar entered. Birds circled and dove through a crisp blue sky just beyond the windows, and the spring sun glinted and sparkled off gilded domes and wicked spires. For a moment, while the other students stared in silence at his back and the world shone outside, he felt like he could breathe. Like he was free.

He resisted the urge to put his hands and face against the glass, instead clasping his hands behind his back as he stared. There, nearest, and below, the Air District was like a skirt around the University. The homes there were built taller, and slimmer. The Fire District lay just beyond that, which also encompassed the whole of the Grand Market, a riot of color and movement even at this early time of day. Beyond that, the shoreline and the bay, the Merchant Pier and its inns and wayhouses and storerooms, the darker veins of the city. The Earth District…his mood sank. The Water District. They were too far away to make out details, only differences. Squat, windowless houses, narrow streets. Dinginess that did not plague the loftier districts. Tension pinched between his shoulder blades.

"Vali Ahad Efendim," a stern female voice said. "Do you intend to disrupt my class by standing at the window all morning?" He raised an eyebrow and chanced a look over his shoulder as the other students either chuckled in amusement or whispered in disbelief. Those were his same feelings. Both humor, and disbelief. No one dared to speak to him like that, save his brother. Even Behram treaded carefully in his phrasing on most days. He should reprimand her. But he found himself more intrigued than angry.

"Forgive me, Instructor Akar. I was taken with the view of my city." He attempted a smile, but his father's demeaning tone found its way into his voice anyway. Her eyes, hazelnut, he decided, narrowed, and her full mouth thinned before she swept a hand to indicate the classroom.

"Perhaps you might ponder the beauty of your city from a seat."

He recognized his brother's muted snicker, followed swiftly by a symphony of whispers. All the students were seated on the scattered cushions that peppered the rugs.

"I am only here to observe, as I was yesterday."

"Very well," she said to him before addressing the class. "Today we will circle. Please do so now."

The students shifted, scooting their cushions around to form an open space in the center of the floor. Omar joined Mazhar near the doorway, their backs pressed to the plaster wall. She carried a lidded basket into the center of the floor and upended it in on the carpet, dumping a pile of feathers. She set the basket outside the circle of her students. Ah yes. Every First House instructor's favorite teaching tool.

Mazhar physically recoiled from the cascade of white as they pooled on the carpet. "Poor bastards," he whispered. It almost elicited a laugh from Omar.

"Everyone select a feather," she said.

"I thought the University was known for using new techniques, not ancient torture schemes," one of the young men whispered as he selected a feather.

"If you find the exercise too familiar, then you should be able to accomplish it with little effort," Instructor Akar said. The man, perhaps only a few Turns younger than Omar, scowled, and the others glanced at each other. Of course every air mage knew about exercises using feathers. There was no better way, and none more frustrating, to learn finite control. But these were children's exercises, used to teach newly awoken power. Direct a feather from the ground to the ceiling. If these mages could not do so already, they had no business at the University. Omar folded his arms.

Once everyone had selected their feather from the pile, Instructor Akar stopped her pacing and stood in a gap between students. She reached up to tuck errant strands of hair behind her ears. Her fingers were ink-stained and there was a streak of chalk along her jaw. These were things he associated with men in education. A universal kind of never-quite-existing-where-they-were, but perpetually worrying some problem in their mind. He had never seen a woman in such a state. He could not take his gaze off her. It was...disconcerting.

She dropped her hands to her sides, and her fingers flexed open as she stepped into the center of the circle of students and faced the one who had spoken against the exercise. Magic woke on her skin. Sparkling, tumbling points of light, as pale and whimsical as the drifting feathers. Wind swept around her, and she held a hand open over the pile of feathers. They swirled up in a small cyclone before twining around her, tracing a spiral through the air she commanded around her. Mazhar made an interested sound, and raised an eyebrow when Omar glanced at him.

"Now"—she held her palm open in front of her, within the cyclone of wind that whipped the feathers around her—"put your feather in my hand."

"Fiendish," Mazhar whispered. Omar nodded. But ingenious. Completely possible, but only with extreme focus. Or...there was always cheating.

He watched as each student tried, twenty of them in total. Three students succeeded outright, and three more got very close. The dissenter was not successful, and Omar found smug pleasure in that. Omar marveled that she was able to hold her working for so long without appearing fatigued. It did reaffirm that Master Bugra was right, a mage with precise control tired less easily than one who simply charged their way through a spell.

"Would you care to try, Efendim?" That voice…cold like a crisp winter day, bright like the sparkle on the water below. It took him a moment to realize the question was directed at him. She had said she meant to assess him today.

"Brilliant," Mazhar said, straightening immediately from the wall and stepping forward eagerly. The other students leaned forward, probably equally split in their desire for him to succeed spectacularly or fail miserably.

Omar tried to concentrate on his brother's efforts, but his attention kept straying to her eyes, glowing with sparks of light, like twinkling stars against the dark of her irises. High-order magic was always beautiful, and manifested differently for each mage. It only manifested for those mages of the third order, Sival. Those who could cast spells with intention and focus alone. First and second order mages, Aval and Deval, needed words and symbols to cast their spells, tired more easily, and could cast fewer spells.

"Damn me," Mazhar conceded with a chuckle when he failed to get his feather past the wind that whipped around the instructor. She turned to Omar. Between the storm of feathers that swirled around her, Omar was certain she had a taunting smile on her face. He should not use any magic at all, not with his head pounding as it was, with fatigue weighing down every limb. But it was impossible to resist that look in her eyes, the challenge. *Impress me.*

The wind from her spell stirred his clothes as he moved into the circle and selected a feather. The power of the wind funnel threatened to whip his feather away before he even had a chance to try. Everyone else had taken her instruction, and the setup, literally. To pierce the cyclone of wind and place their feather in her hand. An exercise of precision.

Spellworking was a game of balance, between power, precision, duration, and energy. To focus on one aspect one had to pay with the other three. He released his mental hold on his own magic, which the others had not done. Instead of trying to drill his way into her spell with concentrated magic, Omar chose a route without finesse. He raised his other hand palm toward her, and blasted her own wind away from her. The feathers exploded across the room and students behind her, and her hair tore loose of its twist at the nape of her neck.

As she gasped in surprise, Omar reached between them and dropped his feather into her palm.

For a moment it seemed like her shock might turn to anger, but instead, her mouth twisted to prevent her smile. She lifted her palm and blew the feather at him, keeping its course true with a thread of magic that set it unerringly on his face.

"An unintended lesson on problem solving outside of the parameters you are given." She ducked her head to him as she placed the basket in the middle of the circle. She swirled her hand near her cheek, and a breeze swept in a circle around the room, collecting up the feathers and depositing them in the center of the rug. It looked simple. She made it look simple. But feathers were the bane of every air mage's existence, because they were so difficult to control, so unpredictable. The thoughtless way she did it, as if it were mundane, was enough to assure Omar that she was at least capable of the kind of control he needed.

When hope brightened his mood, he squashed it down, reminding himself that many gifted instructors had tried to help him. She was half the age of all of them. Just because she had control did not mean she could teach it. After all, only a handful of students had succeeded at her exercise.

"Remember"—she knelt and began scooping the feathers into the basket—"that each aspect of a spell is a choice you make. That your feelings and your magic are inexorably tied together. If you are distracted, frightened, anxious, this will affect how you perform a spell. Someone who is preoccupied may have no trouble casting a powerful, undirected spell"—she cut her gaze sideways to him in a distinctly accusing look—"such as an air blast. But will be unable to focus enough to cast their voice across the courtyard."

His temper prickled, and he clasped his hands behind his back to silence his retort that he had absolutely no trouble casting his voice, anywhere.

Mazhar chuckled at her callout, and Omar fumed. She hoisted the basket and removed it from the circle.

"That is all the time we have for this class. But we will repeat the exercise next turn. If you wish to practice, I am happy to assist you during one of my free periods." She folded her hands behind her back and bowed. The students chattered as they collected their things and exited. Mazhar got to his feet beside Omar and thrust his chin toward the exit, indicating he would wait outside.

Omar followed Instructor Akar to the far side of the room, where she was placing the basket, picking up a few feathers that had wiggled their way free. She pretended not to notice him.

"You do not care for me much, do you, Instructor Akar?"

She straightened and measured him with an up-and-down sweep of her gaze, punctuating it with a raised eyebrow.

"I do not feel anything for you at all, Efendim. Forgive me if that is offensive."

He was neither crown nor monster to her, if she was telling the truth. A fraction of his ever-present tension eased, and he tried his very best to use a friendly tone. "It is not offensive." Her vigilance relaxed and he added, "I find it refreshing."

Her eyebrows ticked upward.

"Are you satisfied with your assessment?" He put a thread of magic in his voice to lower it even softer than a normal whisper, as there were several students lingering to watch him.

"I cannot assess someone who cheats," she replied in a similarly spelled whisper. She deftly gathered the cascade of her dark hair that his magic had blasted loose and worked quickly to put it into a careless braid that she left to drape over her shoulder. Omar tried to look away and was unable to. He had never watched a woman style her hair before.

"Is it cheating if it achieved the desired result?" he finally said. She made a face of exasperation and dropped her hands to her sides.

"I have a free period after my next class. Meet me in the Hall of Destruction, and we will try again." Her demeanor, censored and wary, reminded him that she was likely not a supporter of his father and so, not of him. Not as unfeeling toward him as she professed, if her father and his politics were anything to judge by.

"Why did you agree to help me?" he asked.

"Teaching people to use their magic is what I love most," she said. "Everyone deserves to have proper instruction."

The weighted tone of her words was not lost on him. He suspected she was not simply talking about him. Would the lessons with her afford him a chance to know her better?

"Or perhaps because I bribed you." He could not help that she intrigued him. A woman whom Behram spoke of with so much respect, who had achieved a place where no woman had been before. But why would she talk about any of that with him?

"Bribing me with books and a library was not unhelpful in your scheme." Her gaze lifted to his, and it shone with mixed shyness and greed. It was the most charming thing he had ever seen. She offered a smile that felt like truce.

Omar returned it. She brushed her hand against her cheek again to move a bit of hair that she had missed with the new braid. Wheel, she was lovely. There was something settled about her. It radiated invisibly, so that when he stood close to her like this, it grounded him. Someone who knew exactly who they were, and what they wanted, and were moving toward it like an arrow loosed from a bow. What would that be like?

"Are you feeling well enough to do this today?" She flicked a look past him, toward the door, then back.

"I am fine," he said, all his tension returning. "I will see you in the Hall of Destruction." He turned away and strode for the hall. It should not have irritated him, she was only asking. She did not mean to imply he was not strong enough, good enough, to imply he was weak or sickly. That was what his father thought. That did not mean anyone else did.

Mazhar stood in the circle of the three guards, the commander at their front.

"Are you certain about her for this?" he murmured, with a spark in his eyes Omar did not like. "I trust you not to be influenced by things that do not matter to the issue at hand."

"I am certainly more capable of making rational decisions than you are, in that respect," Omar snapped. Mazhar's slight smile vanished, his brows knitting together. Omar turned from his brother.

This was a bad idea, meeting with a woman. If word of it reached his father, he would be more of a prisoner in the palace than he already was. Not to mention the rumors.

TEN

DILAY GRIPPED THE STRAP OF her bag in one hand and held the book the Vali Ahad had given her in the other as she stared up into the gloomy dome of the Destruction Wing central foyer. A cluster of large, human-sized urns and pots sat in the very center of the light-starved space. Presumably, once, they held plants, living things to balance the magic of destruction. Now they were dust-covered and some cracked, abused over the Turns.

It had been, and still was as far as she knew, a right of initiation to run into the abandoned wing at some point during a student's first Turn and retrieve a tile from the interior mosaics that circled this central space. Dilay had not been able to bring herself to destroy something so old, and had been mercilessly jeered for it.

Each wing of the University was built similarly, the building itself circular, with classrooms along the perimeter. They were tailored to their House, for example, the Fourth House Wing had more class-rooms on the ground floor, with pits of earth for the mages to practice within. The First House Wing had more rooms in the upper level, some were even open air like the sky room, to practice higher-order spells without concern about damaging anything.

The Sixth House Wing of the University was stripped to the walls and floors. There were far fewer ornaments, vases, statues, tables and benches than there were in other wings. The mosaics around the central room were pillaged nearly to the plaster, with only small bits here and there, fractured remnants of a magic House wiped from the face of the world. Sadness settled like a mantle as she surveyed the expansive room. Dust swirled, and silence seemed heavier.

There was not a destruction mage alive in Tamar, so there was no need to teach the forbidden magic and the hall had languished, abandoned. She was still curious why they had not, in their xenophobia, destroyed the Sixth House Wing of the University when they had chased out or killed every Sixth House mage in Tamar during the Sundering War. She was also grateful, because despite the haunted feeling that permeated every nook and cranny, that the wing still existed in somewhat whole condition gave her hope.

Hope that one day things could be set right. That there could be balance again.

After a few more moments she returned her attention to the book. She had hoped to read the law book while she waited for the Vali Ahad to arrive, but it was too dark in the hall to do so. Cloth, now threadbare and dust-covered, had been tacked over all the windows that circled the top of the soaring dome, blocking out most of the sunlight. Some weak shafts did make it through holes in the moldering cloth or places where it had torn away from the tacks.

There had only been a few stolen moments during the day to glance at the book's pages, enough to see there was much greater detail than anything she had ever found at the University, each tenant described through use of case studies. Her father would be thrilled. But could she show him? How could she possibly explain how she came by the book?

"Oh you do look upset."

Dilay glanced up, surprised to hear Behram's voice. He emerged from the unlit hallway that led out to the main atrium and halted beside her. He was dressed in caftan and entari of subdued reds and browns, hair and beard perfectly trimmed, and an arrogant smile on his handsome face. Leagues from the drably dressed, uncomfortable and unsure boy she had known and cared for. She still cared for him, but sometimes, like now, she wanted to shrink away from him. The fire was too much for her, especially here, in a place that felt more like a mausoleum than a place of learning. That emberous anger in him. Not fury, no longer the rage that had erupted from him as a boy, pent-up frustration that had no other outlet. But a coal that had been carefully banked, and that he nurtured, anger that was now fuel.

"What are you doing here?"

His attention went immediately to the book and he reached to take it, but she instinctively tugged it away.

"What do you think I'm going to do?" He laughed, making a second, successful grab for it.

"Hold it over my head and make me jump for it?" A favorite pastime of his when they were younger.

"Tsk, how childish." He opened the leather binding to find Judge Hanim's inscription. "He did better than I thought he would," he said. He snapped the book closed and handed it back.

"He? Did you tell the Vali Ahad to give me this? Behram, what is going on? He asked me about you. If I helped you."

"I know." His eyes narrowed. "And are you going to help him?"

She hesitated, wondering if she was allowed to tell Behram. The Vali Ahad seemed to have shared a great deal with him. Were they friends? Behram did not talk to her much about others he spent time with. They walked in much different social circles. His was so much higher than hers she would break her neck trying to look up at them.

"You did not tell me why you are here."

"I came to see you, why else would I be here?" He raised an eyebrow as he said it, but did not look at her.

"And how did you know I was *here*?"

"I am well informed." He turned his head, taking in the decrepit hall with distaste.

"You have never come to see me before." Dilay glowered up at him. He smiled, canting his head sideways so he could meet her gaze.

"You sound so distraught. I did not realize my absence had upset you."

"That is not what I said," Dilay corrected, closing her eyes. Should she try to convince him to leave? What would he think when the Vali Ahad showed up, to meet her in a dark, empty wing of the University?

A bell rang up from the atrium, echoing strangely in the empty wing where they stood, the signal to change classes. The noise of people pouring into the atrium carried down the long hall of the wing to them. Dilay hugged her arms around herself. She should not be nervous. Behram's presence was the Vali Ahad's problem, not hers.

The Vali Ahad emerged a few moments later from the hallway to the atrium, his bright clothing seeming to wink into existence out of the shadow of the hall. Three guards and his steward walked closely behind.

Nervous, she glanced at Behram, who had also caught sight of him. She was surprised to see a broad smile on Behram's face. She had never seen him smile at anyone but her that way. Behram bowed, and Dilay was so distracted by him that she almost forgot to, and hers ended up being choppy and awkward.

"Thank you for coming," the Vali Ahad said to Behram, but his gaze strayed to Dilay, catching against her own before zipping away again. Had he asked Behram to come?

"You said you came to see me," Dilay hissed.

"Also true." Behram grinned at her. "Consider me your chaperon."

Dilay drew back, glancing between him and the Vali Ahad, who had a look on his face that reflected her same offense. But Behram continued on, oblivious or uncaring.

"Who would have thought you had an affinity for the macabre?" He bent to pick a broken piece of mosaic tile off the floor. Dilay stole it from him and set it back down, even though it was clearly just detritus. It felt wrong to disturb anything here. As it felt wrong to disturb the ground where ashes were laid after someone died. This was a tomb, for a long-gone House of magic.

There were no books on destruction magic in the library. No one spoke of the mages. The hundreds upon thousands who had been murdered. Persecuted. Driven away.

"I needed a place free of distractions." Dilay picked a drifting bit of cobweb out of the air. "This seemed the best place to go unnoticed."

"If the Headmaster discovers you are teaching outside your classes, you will be banned." Behram smiled helpfully, then gave the Vali Ahad a look that Dilay could not interpret in the dim light. She blew the cobweb away.

"I am aware. I hoped, since it was at his behest, that the Vali Ahad might be willing to put in a good word for me, were the occasion to arise that my integrity was questioned." She looked at him sidelong, and the Vali Ahad tipped his head to one side in acquiescence.

"Shall we begin then?" He dismissed his men with a little flick of his fingers. The guards retreated back to the hall. Not exactly out of sight, but certainly out of the way. His steward found an ancient stone bench along the wall, gave it a fastidious dusting with his hand, then looked disdainfully at the dirt before he sat down.

Dilay flipped her bag open and pulled out three feathers she had stolen from the classroom. She was going to have to stop thinking of it as stealing, but it would never really feel like borrowing. Pushing boundaries and roles was fine, but blatantly breaking rules would always feel wrong.

"Where is the Sehzade?" Dilay asked. She had been thinking to use him in her assessment exercise. If she was going to help the Vali Ahad gain more control, she had to see how much he did, or did not, possess already.

"Entertaining a pack of young women with his comic genius," Behram said, dryly. That earned him a chuckle from the Vali Ahad. "I saw him in the atrium when I came up."

"Then you could assist?" she asked Behram.

Behram made a face of disdain. "I am not a teaching assistant."

"Then at least make yourself somewhat useful and give us some light," the prince grumbled. Behram ducked his head and snapped his fingers. Three mage orbs blinked into life and floated up and away from each other, casting pale, steady light as they rose.

Mage orbs were the first spell a fire mage learned, even the least gifted of the Fifth House could conjure them, though their strength and duration varied greatly from mage to mage. Conjuring and controlling multiples was a difficult task, but Behram had been able to do it from the moment his magic manifested. A prodigy, many of the instructors called him, despite the fact it had taken him much, much longer to summon his actual fire.

Dilay's talent was control, giving her the ability to cast spells that far outstripped her power level because she did not waste a modicum of energy. But Behram, he was a master of intention. Another tenant of theory. Intention was the beating heart of a spell. Dilay often thought even more important than control.

If one could not narrow the focus of their intention, then power was wasted in a spell. It had unintended consequences, or veered off course. Dilay had never met another mage that had such an innate grasp of intention.

"Arrogant prick," the Vali Ahad muttered. The walls echoed the utterance.

"I only thought to inspire your growth with my prowess, Efendim." Behram gave a little bow.

"Inspiring is not a word I would use for you, my friend," said the Vali Ahad.

"Perhaps I should leave you two to this…chest puffing?" Dilay suggested. "If I am not needed." She did not have time to waste, but it did make her happy, and confused, to see Behram and the Vali Ahad exchanging friendly heckling. It pleased her to see Behram had that kind of relationship with anyone. There had been a time she had been his only friend. But this man? Who was known only for his ability to pry into the minds of others? What could they possibly have in common? Unless it was just their positions in society. Perhaps that was connection enough.

"No, please, Instructor Akar, I apologize." The Vali Ahad faced her, clasping his hands behind his back. Dilay shot Behram a warning glance and he held his hands up, backing away to sit beside the steward. He could learn something from the Vali Ahad's easy apology.

"I had meant to have you do this with the Sehzade, but as he is not here, I will have to do." Dilay held the feathers out between them and looked up, into the soaring dome above. This was an exercise she often gave to her young air students in the Earth District. It allowed them to use some of their boundless energy and work on their magic simultaneously. She only had Aval in that class, for whom the act of controlling a feather and running about was the very upper limit of their capability. It would be interesting to see what the Vali Ahad, arguably one of the most powerful air mages in Tamar, could do.

She searched for a suitable place to serve as goal, and found one in an alcove on the balcony that circled the upper reaches of the dome. It was used to frame a mosaic, and had a little stone basin jutting from the wall, which might once have been a fountain.

Dilay pointed to it. "The first one to get two feathers into that wins the game."

"A game?" The Vali Ahad scowled up at the alcove, then turned it on her. "I do not have time for games," he said.

"I need to assess where we are starting, Efendim." She shrugged, then held the feathers up in front of her face. "Besides, we learn best when we do not realize we are learning. And when we cannot cheat." She blew on the feathers as she gave him a pointed look, casting magic into the air expelled from her lungs. They spiraled toward the roof. Had he never been given a game as a learning device? His displeasure continued as he watched them, then looked at her, clearly at a loss.

"You should stop scowling and start playing, my prince, or you will be bested in one breath," Behram jeered. Dilay slipped a tendril of air around one feather and scooped it away from the others. This game was not for winning; she wanted to see how the Vali Ahad handled the task. The trick with feathers, she had discovered over endless marks of practice, was not to engage them directly. But to deny them a direction, thereby forcing them where one wanted them.

She had the first feather in the fountain before the Vali Ahad had even reached with his power for the other two. Dilay stole one away from him with a quick push of air, sacrificing the third as he directed it into the fountain. He used his hands, a habit of even the most practiced of Sival. It was not necessary, but a trick to emphasize their intention and focus.

Theoretically, a Sival needed only to focus mentally on the outcome they wanted, and the magic would do the rest; the most powerful and accomplished of mages did not even need to be looking at an object to apply their power to it. But most needed the direction of motion, of sight, and hearing or their other senses. Even those who did not need movement utilized it, to save energy and time.

Dilay played with the second feather, keeping it just out of his attempts to steal it from her, watching his face and body as he walked a circle around her. His head was tipped back so he could watch the feather, his brow knitted, jaw set. Energy wasted, but not an egregious amount. Dilay stood in the center of the room, only moving to keep him in sight.

She shifted her stream of air, sending the feather dipping toward the floor. The Vali Ahad lunged forward, toward her, commanding the feather back up with a palm angled toward the ceiling. He ended up in front of her, close enough to touch. The air he shifted had force, cutting through hers like it was gauze. And his control was good enough to direct with surety the feather when she was not fighting him for it.

As he made a bid to guide it into the fountain, Dilay stepped forward, closing the distance between them and spearing her own shaft of air through the middle of his. The feather spiraled wildly, and he spun to follow it with his gaze, trying to direct it out of her magic. Dilay followed him around, reaching across his chest to interrupt his magic again.

This time she got too close. He bent back to avoid the sweep of her arm, then stepped hurriedly away and dropped his arms to his sides. Red flashed in the peripheral of her vision as Behram surged to his feet.

"Don't," the Vali Ahad barked and Dilay stood rooted in her shock at the tone. He paused and swept a hand over his shorn hair. "Please do not touch me," he said in a more reasonable tone. The feather drifted toward the floor, free of the guidance of their magic.

She glanced to Behram, who avoided her look as he sank back to the bench.

"Are we finished?" the prince said. Dilay lowered her hand, trying to maintain a neutral air despite her surprise and irritation. The Vali Ahad avoided her gaze.

Behram laughed, and the feather burst into flame, and was ash before Dilay blinked. She looked over at him. Behram had his arms folded over his chest, his head propped back against the wall, his eyes closed. She huffed in annoyance.

"I do not think the Vali Ahad understood your little test, Dilay."

She strode to the bag she had left on the floor and picked it up, her pride still stinging. Behram's dismissive laughter only made her feel sillier. As she slung the bag's strap over her head, the Vali Ahad approached her.

"Forgive me, Instructor Akar, I—"

"You asked for my help, Efendim." She tugged her braid loose from beneath the strap before she rounded on him. With a cold smile she patched together her pride and ignored her confusion. "Do not worry. I have no need to touch you to conduct these lessons. Nor can I ever imagine having the desire." She turned on her heel. Behram popped to his feet and fell in stride beside her.

"Instructor Akar." The Vali Ahad's resonant voice was not held back now, though she could not tell if that was anger or simply disbelief at her abruptness.

Dilay stopped, turned, and bowed as a peace offering. "Tomorrow, here, the same time." Dilay glanced to Behram as she turned and walked away, wishing she could outpace him as well. She was embarrassed, and that always felt like a weakness when she was around him. Something he could attribute to her trying so hard to be something she was not. Their few, short interactions had not suggested that the Vali Ahad was a man like Behram. That he was not so caught up on station as to be offended by the touch of someone lower born than him.

So, what was he afraid of, exactly? Perhaps the rumors. Though that seemed a stretch considering he had chosen her to help and met her in secret. Her irritation settled into curiosity. A puzzle to be solved.

Behram's uncharacteristic silence drew her attention out of her thoughts and to him. For a moment she considered asking why he wore such a brooding look but decided against it. She did not have patience to deal with his mood as well as her own.

Wheel help her, men were exhausting.

ELEVEN

"**F**ATHER," MAZHAR SAID, THOUGH HIS gaze was locked with Omar's, "please consider his health. You push him too far." Mazhar had their mother's soft heart, her concern for Omar's welfare. Omar had always been, by necessity, more pragmatic. He was the heir, and more tool than person.

He was not pleased to be spoken around as if he were not in the room, but this fight between his brother and his father was not a new one, neither was it productive. The Sultan was not a Veritor, and though he was a Sival, the highest order of mage alive, he possessed only the First House's more mundane powers. Sound and the manipulation of air in the space around him. Omar, like his father's now-dead brother, could dig mental fingers into the mind of another and pry it open for its secrets. The price he paid for that power was pain.

He would be lucky if headaches continued to be the only effects of his youth being used as judge and jury. The occasional whispers in the back of his mind suggested otherwise. But his father would not be swayed. Omar's uncle had not suffered ill effects from using his Veritor magic. The fact that he had died young of the consumption did not seem especially relevant to their father. Nor had he been as sensitive to the power as Omar had proved to be, at least by his father's account. The Sultan was rooted into his belief that Omar was affecting

95

any ill effects in order to weasel his way out of conducting any more "confessions." He considered it an affliction of laziness. Perhaps it was. Omar could not say for certain that his hatred of the task, of the magic, did not manifest as the pain that plagued him. Repulsion so deeply rooted it could masquerade as real aftereffects.

Their father believed using Omar's Veritor magic was the best way to dig evil out of the city at its root. That knowing there was no way to lie one's way out of court would stop crime before it started. There was no turning him from the notion. No matter how many alternatives Omar studied, in between the headaches that denied him the ability to read or concentrate, or the voices that whispered in the back of his mind sometimes. His father did not believe in looking anywhere but tradition for answers, and he had a great deal of support in his High Council for that notion.

Omar could understand, to an extent. The traditions of the Old Sultanate had made it a power in the world. But Tamar's past was also bloody, filled with atrocities some thought better forgotten than examined.

"Mazhar," Omar chided. Mazhar turned his back on both Omar and their father with a noise of irritation. Their mother sat quietly in her chair, staring out into the garden. She had fought, countless times. Omar knew it because he could hear it all the way down the hall in his own rooms. But she never did so in front of anyone else. Embarrassing the Sultan publicly was the surest way to make certain he dug into his opinions, never to be swayed at all. Mazhar liked to address these fights head-on, bluntly. But their mother, she fought a war of attrition. Omar did not know if she would win it before it did not matter to him anymore. Before the headaches split his skull open, or he performed a confession when he was too tired and killed himself and the other person.

"I have answered these doubts before," the Sultan said. "He will condition himself to the level that is demanded. As with any magic. You must work on your stamina. And if your interest in the University is affecting you—"

"It is not, Efendim," Omar said. "I can continue my duties at the palace as you see fit."

His father rose from his chair, and the servants in the room scurried to open the door to the hall. "Very well."

"I am grateful for your indulgence, Sultanim." Omar bowed. Mazhar did the same, and they remained so as their father bent over the back of their mother's chair and kissed her cheek, then left the suite of rooms.

As the doors shut, their mother glanced at her lady in waiting, Beste. The woman bowed at the silent command then made a quick gesture with her hands. Silence blanketed the room, muffling everything for a moment before Omar's ears adjusted to the dampening. The Queen Sultana took up a more relaxed pose in her chair. She smiled a secret smile at Mazhar and Omar.

Omar dropped onto one of the couches as if he were a puppet with its strings cut.

"Tell me about the University."

"I enjoy it. Though I do not know how he can," Mazhar said. He sat on the couch beside Omar. "With headaches that prevent him concentrating."

Omar shot him a look that commanded silence but it was too late.

"And have you found someone who seems suitable to assist you?" Her tone indicated she already knew the answer. Omar pressed his fingers against the bridge of his nose, nodding. It felt like defeat. His mother wanted him to pretend his magic did not exist. They had never outright fought over it, but her disapproval and his desperation often clashed in silent stares between them, as it did now.

"An apprentice instructor. A woman," Mazhar said. And while Omar was certain that his mother would be very intrigued by the idea of a female instructor at the University, he had the strangest, anxious desire to keep anything and everything to do with Dilay to himself. He did not wish to bring it out and speak about it with anyone, examine it too closely, look at it directly. He was very afraid of what he would see. When he had offered her the palace library as payment for her help, her eyes had burned like dark suns. And he had realized how desperately he wanted people like that, who wanted knowledge, who wanted change…people like her, around him. How isolated and repressed he felt. Conforming, bending to his father's will, contorting himself into the man his father thought he should be. But she…she was exactly who she wanted to be and it did not matter that it did not fit into a mold others had made for her. And he wanted that same thing so badly that he could taste it, like too much salt blistering the inside of his mouth. Looking at her was like looking at his own, true self standing outside his body.

"A woman? How extraordinary." His mother gave him a sly smile that did not normally make him sick to his stomach. But today it did. "She must be most sympathetic to you, then."

"I have not had the impression that she is a particularly sympathetic person," Omar said. He had been kicking himself all night and morning for overreacting to her movements. She had been so insulted. That was the last thing he needed. Today he would not allow anyone in with them except Ruslan. So he could apologize.

His mother's sharp black eyebrow rose. "Oh? A woman of intelligence and backbone. How delightful. And is she pretty?"

"What does that have to do with her qualifications—"

"Pretty enough to put Behram Kadir upside down. He is *nice* to her," Mazhar said as if it were the greatest of scandals. The feeling that Omar did not want to feel scratched harder, and he was suddenly irritable. "And smart enough to help Omar with his problem." His mother's smile lost its joy at Mazhar's latter statement.

"I see," she said, carefully, her dark gaze fixed on Omar's. He did not like what her expression told him she saw on his own face.

"We should go." He stood. "Because Instructor Akar is, in fact, not sympathetic at all, and if I am late to meet her I have no doubt she will terminate our agreement."

That brightened his mother's face, her smile making her radiant. That radiant smile had appeared much more often before he had come into his powers, whenever she chased and caught him as a boy to sweep him into her embrace and cover his scrunched face in kisses. But he had not embraced his mother since he was ten.

"Bring her to me," she murmured. Omar straightened, staring down at her. He frowned, but her face was earnest, and lacked the wily glint in her eyes that was there when she was scheming.

"If Father finds out that I am being taught by a woman," he began.

"He will not. Bring her to me. I wish to meet her."

Dissect her, she meant.

OMAR SAT ON THE BENCH where Behram and Ruslan had watched the day before. He had left his guards halfway down the hall, and Ruslan with them. Perhaps it was inappropriate to have them so far away. But the entire exercise was inappropriate. He had no intention of doing anything untoward to her, he simply wanted a moment to apologize without everyone's eyes on him.

His head pounded. This one was not the aftereffects of a tribunal, but one caused by the tension in his neck and shoulders. Part of the joy of going to the University had been the freedom to walk outside the palace. But that joy was quickly diminishing. Each day since the first the trail of people had grown more, as word spread. He'd had to bring five guards today instead of three, and even Mazhar was growing annoyed. Soon they would have to take a carriage to the University. Or not go at all. He had the person he needed. Besides the pleasure of simply learning for learning's sake, he needn't attend the University any longer.

He heard her footsteps before he saw her, and she rushed into the central room. Perhaps she thought she was late. He supposed she was. Omar did not move, or speak. It was frustrating, how much he had thought of it…of her. Of her help. Of having opportunity, or rather an excuse, to speak with her more. He should not feel that way.

She turned a slow circle, her brow knotted in confusion until she saw him.

Her gaze swept up from his feet to his face, and a slow trail of heat followed in its wake. Her hazelnut gaze met his, and he could see wariness lingered from his unintentional slight the day before. The tension at the base of his neck twisted tighter, zinging into his skull. He stood as she approached. Without Behram's mage orbs, the hall was dimly lit by the light that managed its way through the dark fabric hung above, over the windows.

She stopped in front of him, clearly torn between curiosity and uncertainty. After a moment, she exhaled impatiently and bowed, quickly. When she straightened, she opened the bag at her hip and withdrew a small packet.

"Forgive me if this is presumptuous." She started to hand it to him, then stopped herself. She pulled her hand back and moved around him, to set the object on the bench behind him. Omar retrieved it as she withdrew. A sachet of herbs.

She smiled, reserved. "For your head." She brushed her fingers against her temple, tucking one loose strand of hair behind her ear.

When Omar looked at her she held his gaze this time, the smile teasing the line of her mouth, bright like threatening daybreak. His body relaxed a fraction. Simply looking at her was calming. Freeing. A few wisps of dark, silken hair had slipped loose from the braid that circled her head, touching her face, so much more real and true than the perfect hairstyles at the palace. No one ever had a hair out of place, there. They never looked sweaty and disheveled, as if they had run from somewhere. Run to meet him.

His heart thumped, like he had been the one running. His fingers tingled. The tension in his neck spread through his entire body.

"They are not poison, but I can brew them where you can see, if you are concerned. My father uses this blend." She reached to take it back.

"What must you think of me, that you assume I think you are trying to poison me?" Omar slipped the little packet into the pocket of his entari. His heart still hammered, and his fingers remained gripped too hard around the gift. "I wanted to apologize for yesterday. I…" The words died. Felt worthless, because they were lies. He could not tell her the truth, and so what was the point of an apology?

"People want to touch you because they believe you are Wheel blessed. I had not thought how awful that might be, how often you must deal with it. I will not touch you, Efendim." She ducked her head in lieu of a bow, and Omar did not know if he had ever hated words more than he hated those. "You do not look well today. Would you like to postpone?" Her cool voice, calm and even, was perfect.

"What lesson did you have in mind today?" He did not want to leave. He did not want her to leave. It did not matter that hammers were beating against his skull.

"Vali Ahad"—she seemed reticent, searching his face then looking away—"yesterday in class and here, you did not lack control." She shrugged out of her bag and laid it on the floor. "Though you do tend to use power instead of finesse."

"No, I am not known for my finesse," he agreed.

"You are not telling me everything I need to know to help you," she said, folding her arms over her chest. Being intelligent enough to help him meant, of course, that she was intelligent enough to be curious. Omar stifled a wince.

"You know what you need to," he said. "Behram has faith in you." Mentioning his friend's name made him more tense. He flexed his hands open against his legs to banish it. She rolled her eyes and turned her back on him as she paced away.

"I have known Behram since we were children," she said, absently, pacing a path through the dust. "I do not know you at all. How do you two know each other?"

"My father maintains relationships with the most powerful families in Narfour," Omar said. He did not wish to talk about Behram. About the palace. About anything having to do with his day-to-day life. "Behram and I found we had things in common, when we met a decade ago." They had fathers in common. Fathers who utilized them like pieces on a chessboard.

"Oh?" She wheeled to face him. "Keeping all his wealthy friends close?"

"The wealthier and more powerful your friends, Instructor Akar, the more likely they are to become your enemies. A sultan does not have friends."

She recoiled, gave him a searching look that flashed to pity. Before he could say anything she turned her back on him again. "You may call me Dilay. If it pleases you."

"Mistress Dilay," he said, around a mouth that was oddly dry. She gave a little laugh and turned on him, farther away now than she had been.

"No. Just Dilay."

"Yes," he said, like all his wits had fallen out of his head. Her brows knit together, her smile shrinking.

"Yes what?"

"Yes, it pleases me," he forced out. Then felt even more foolish for the way it sounded. The room was not dim enough to hide the way she softened and transformed, from teasing to embarrassed. He cursed himself.

"Good. Then, we can begin." She took an abrupt step forward and swept a hand up in an arc from her hip in his direction. The dust from the floor billowed up and toward him. The gust of wind hit him, then the assault of the dust, into his eyes, mouth, and nose and all over his clothes. "Oh, dear." She laughed, and his irritation was erased. "I thought you would be quicker than that."

"You might have warned me," he coughed. The grit coated the inside of his mouth, and he wiped a hand down his face, picking cobweb off his face. "What was the point of that?"

"If you refuse to tell me how to help you, I will have to determine it myself. You do not lack control of expressing your power, though your reaction time does leave something to be desired."

He clapped the dust free of his hands. "Is this a lesson, or an excuse for you to take your personal grievances out on me while I am defenseless?"

"Yes," she said, flatly.

"I am going to add a law into the books about dusting a prince," Omar said. Her mien brightened and broke into another teasing smile.

"Dusting is the act of removing dust, not the act of applying it," she said. "But of course you would not know that."

"I know impertinence when I hear it. What makes you think you can talk to me like this? Or, apply dust?" He slapped at his clothes, because he needed to move, otherwise he was going to cross the floor to be closer to her. He hoped she never stopped taunting him. Only

Mazhar and Behram ever dared, and that caused an entirely different emotion. Not this…fizzing pleasure. Addiction. As though he could happily spend candlemarks trading barbs with her.

"Because I am your instructor and you are my student." She crossed the space back to him. And with each step nearer his body wound tighter, protective instinct demanding he move back. He could not bring himself to, even when she stopped only a step away. Something floral hung in the air around her. It pierced straight through the headache fog. "Control"—she had to angle her head slightly to meet his eyes—"is intricately tied to a mage's emotions. What we feel, what we think, what we want, and love, and hate. This tension"—she pointed a finger at him and angled it up and down to indicate the length of him from head to toe—"is energy wasted. Worry, problems you are trying to solve"—she tapped her temples—"these distract. Even when we do not realize they are."

"Ah," he said. He could not take his gaze from her cheekbone, where a strand of hair danced as she moved and spoke. That was a simple thing, was it not? To be able to reach out to touch someone, to slip a bit of hair behind a small, delicate ear? Was that…something other people could do? How could he tell her that? That he wanted to be able to do that. Without violating someone, without being subjected to the parts of another's mind no one else was meant to see. "I am afraid I may never be able to clear my mind of those things."

"No, I imagine not," she said. "You will have to learn instead to compartmentalize." The way she looked up at him, wide-eyed and more subdued, suddenly, he wondered if she understood what he was thinking. Was his face so telling? Her hand lifted, fingers stretching toward his face, and for the first time in a long time, he contemplated staying. Letting her finish the movement. But she aborted it herself, before he could be the better person and move away. "I apologize. You have"—she brushed her fingers over her own chin—"more spiderwebs."

He dusted them away from his chin and looked to her for confirmation. She nodded, a little smile tugging at the corners of her mouth.

"I amuse you?" he grumbled.

"It is nice to see that the man who will rule us is a real person, who sometimes gets cobwebs stuck in his beard. I cannot say that I believe the same of your father."

"Me either," he said. "In fact, I think my father would likely frighten cobwebs away."

She giggled. He thought if this was all it ever was, talking instead of fixing his problem, if he could make her laugh, it would be enough. To be a real person, as she said, not a prince. Just, who he was. With someone who treated him, not with kid gloves and pageantry, but with humor and realism. He could survive like that.

A bell rang in the hallway, the signal for the classes to change. Surprise registered on her face, and in his thoughts.

"Forgive me, Vali Ahad, I am afraid I was late and now I have wasted our time in banter." She gave a small, apologetic bow.

"Omar, please," he said it before he could think it through. "When we do this. Just Omar."

Her face smoothed in surprise, then a conspiratorial smile drifted across her mouth. A mouth which made him think of things he should not. Made him want things…his magic coiled, gusting up into a storm inside him, as want burned just beneath his skin. He would have to remember not to stand so close to her, so the urge to reach out was not so unbearable.

"Omar," she said, her smile turning friendly and pleased as she gave a little nod. This was the worst idea he had ever had, and he could not look at her a moment longer and prevent himself from saying or doing something foolish. He managed something like a smile before he turned abruptly and left.

Only when he had passed Ruslan and his guards had fallen in around him did he realize he had forgotten to tell her that his mother wished to see her. Damn him to the void. He could not go back now. She had a final class to teach, and he had just left her standing there with no explanation about his abrupt and awkward departure.

He would find her, later. After he had his sense back.

TWELVE

"I BROUGHT THESE." SEDA HELD out a fistful of cotton rope, cut into finger-length spans. Dilay nodded.

"That will do well. Can you work with the Fifth House? And the voids tonight as well. I will take the others," Dilay said.

Seda nodded, and Dilay clapped her hands loudly, to be heard over the children as they settled in on their cushions.

"Fifth House and voids with Mistress Seda, everyone else with me," she called. The children obediently stood up and shuffled around the small warehouse. At the door, Turgay took a head count before ducking back outside, into the alley to keep watch. Seda sat on a cushion and her charges formed a circle around her as she handed each budding fire mage a length of rope.

Tonight's lesson was, ironically, on control. Starting a fire and keeping it burning at a steady pace. Containing a breeze into a cyclone, moving water from one end of a trough to another without splashing, and for earth, directing a small quake.

"Second here." She pointed to the trough, which Turgay and Zeki had filled with buckets from a nearby well. "First with me, and Fourth"—she pointed to the back of the warehouse, where, the winter before, she had spent days tearing up floorboards to reveal the earth beneath—"you remember this exercise. We will pick up where we left off last turn."

A boy in the huddle of earth mages tugged a younger girl's braids when they turned to their work.

"Mert!" Dilay stood from where she had knelt by the trough and crossed the warehouse. He immediately snapped his hands down to his sides, contrite, and the little girl, Belma, stomped her foot. Earth shot up, spraying all three of them with sand and small stones. One sharp bit of gravel scratched Dilay's temple.

"Ow!" Mert screeched, and immediately began to cry. Dilay cast Seda a martyred look, and Seda stifled laughter.

"Mert, the Wheel turns in whichever direction you push it. If you push it with rudeness, then that is what you will receive in turn." Dilay turned to Belma. "That was a very good improvement of controlling your temper, Belma." Last small turn, the young girl had sunk a classmate a handspan into the earth. "But?"

"We do not use our magic against people," Belma intoned. Her chin quivered. It was not entirely her fault she lacked control. So did her mother.

Dilay gave each child a hug, wiped the dirt and tears from Mert's face, and rebraided Belma's hair. "I would like you two to work together to see what you can do. I imagine it will be wonderful." She smiled, and they traded glowers, but obeyed. Belma had potential, a Sival. But she would never have the advanced training she needed to use her power for the good of others. If she was anything like so many others who were low class but had power, she would learn to use her unmanaged talent in criminal ways to survive.

Dilay checked on the three air mages, all of them Aval, juggling a few feathers back and forth. Because they were of the lowest order, they had to use spoken spells to control their magic, which limited what they could manage. This type of exercise was the upper limit of their control over air. Listening and controlling their voices came easier to lower-level First House mages than control of their element.

"Very good," Dilay said, and moved back to the water mages. She had five of them. Three were Deval, the second order of mage, who could control their spells with spoken words or drawn sigils.

"Try this sigil," Dilay said to the eldest and most powerful of her water mages, Bilal. She pulled a bit of chalk out of her pocket and drew a sigil for movement on the side of the wooden trough so he could practice it. Each line of a sigil was an instruction, a direction for the spell. Much like a corral with a chute to direct livestock in a certain manner, a sigil was how a Deval told their magic what to do and how to do it. Sigils gave power and duration to spoken spells. But not as much power as a Sival could leverage. Instead of the power of words, or gestures, Sival could utilize their own energy and focus to cast a spell, giving them capability to cast spells of fantastic complexity, as long as they could manage their concentration.

Bilal, who had just taken his sixteenth Turn around the Wheel, nodded in subdued excitement. Every mage enjoyed learning a new sigil, but Bilal was particularly sharp. If Dilay was in position to do so when he reached adulthood in a few more Turns, she planned to petition the University to allow him to go. If he were a Sival, it would be easier. Or, she smiled, if she had someone with enough influence to speak on his behalf, and who might owe her a favor. And if she could talk Omar into speaking for one, perhaps he would speak for two.

She looked at Belma again. Of course, Omar owed her nothing. She was duty bound to do whatever he wished of her.

Dilay cursed herself when her thoughts turned, for the millionth time that day, to him. She had analyzed and re-analyzed every moment she had spent with him and still could not understand what had happened. Why he had left without a single word or explanation. What had she done? And then, in the same circle they had been turning all day, her worry turned to irritation. How arrogant and self-absorbed could someone be, to just leave another person standing there like a fool? And without saying a Wheel-damned word.

Perhaps he had been upset that she had wasted their time. She still felt a bit guilty for that. Not guilty enough to forgive his sense of entitlement. The entire event felt much more like something Behram would do than Omar. But then, what did she really know about the Vali Ahad? Nothing. Any friendliness she had imagined between them…any of that gut-pinching magnetism she had felt. Well, she had clearly imagined it. And even if she hadn't, what did she think would happen?

Dilay corrected a girl's pronunciation of the spell words she was using to guide a feather in the air stream of the girl across from her. The smell of smoke from the burning bits of rope Seda had brought made Dilay sneeze when she spoke. Tendrils of the acrid stuff were filling the warehouse with haze.

"Sorry!" Seda said when Dilay made a sour face. "Next time I'll find something better. I thought this would burn more slowly." Seda stood and moved to Dilay's side.

"It's fine, we make do. Let's open the doors and get some fresh air in here." Fresh air in this part of the city was debatable. It would smell like refuse and stagnant water, but at least it would clear the tear-inducing smoke from the place. Dilay went to the door. It was sagging on its hinges, and she had to press her shoulder against it and lunge to get it open. It moved, then smacked into something. Something that let out a curse.

"Oh no," Dilay gasped. She must have hit Turgay or Zeki on their way in. "I am so…" The darkness outside had blinded her, and the man she had hit straightened up, his hand lowering from where he clutched his nose. Blood covered his face and hand. Dilay did not know whether to be more horrified by that, or by the fact that it was Omar standing in front of her, in the poorest, most crime-ridden part of the city, in clothes that stood out like polished silver in a pile of coal.

She lunged backward and yanked the door shut.

"Get up," she ordered to the children, "get up, out the back, now." Seda stared at her in confusion, and Dilay pointed to the back. "Everyone out, get out, go home." If he did not see them, see their faces, she was the only one he could punish. "Hurry up," she pleaded with Seda with a look, and her friend began herding the children toward the far door.

They ran, confused, and Dilay threw her body against the back door to jar it open, just as the front was wrenched open. Dilay grabbed Seda by the wrist and slung her out the door, then put herself between the children still trying to flee and Omar as he strode toward her. Two of his guards came after him, and two others prevented Turgay and Zeki from entering. Dilay threw her arms out to the side like she could stop Omar from moving past her.

"What is this?" he said. With the blood on his face, and the wrathful look in his eyes, he was frightening. Bilal ducked under her arm and dove for the water trough.

"No!" Dilay gasped. But he slapped his hand against the rune she had just taught him, traced his finger over the chalked outline, and slung a troughful of water at Omar's back with an upward arc of his arm. It drenched him from head to toe. A more powerful Second House mage could make water feel like a whip, do real, physical damage. All Bilal accomplished was to soak the crown prince from head to toe.

She could barely speak, her heart was pounding so hard. Omar wheeled, and Dilay darted around him, grabbing Bilal by the hand and tucking his head against her chest to hide his face, then ran for the back door.

"Stop," Omar barked. Dilay shoved Bilal out the door and put her back to it. Omar's two guards moved as if they would follow.

"No." Dilay held her arms in front of her, offering her wrists. "You have me, and you will never catch them."

"What are you doing?" Omar growled, swiping water and blood off his face and slinging it away.

"Teaching them to play chess." Dilay glared. Omar returned it, a narrow-eyed look of fury. The evidence of what she was teaching them was strewn about the room. Still smoldering bits of rope, earth piled in unnatural formations, water sloshed everywhere around a trough that had no business inside an old warehouse.

"You foolish, stone-headed—" Omar started. His guards moved around him, reaching for Dilay's outstretched hands. "Do not touch her," he snarled. Dilay lowered her arms as his bewildered guards took a step back. Zeki, built like a pile of stones, broke through the two guards at the front door and made a head-down rush for Omar.

"Zeki, don't!" Dilay cried, too late. His arms cinched around Omar's waist from behind, driving the prince forward and nearly into Dilay, so what happened next was unmistakable. Omar's face contorted and magic like pale fire burned beneath his skin. His eyes bleached, going completely white, like marble, and behind him, Zeki's did the same. Zeki's head snapped back and his back bowed as Omar wrenched at his arms around his waist. Zeki let out a sound like a whimper as the guards ripped him away.

"Do not touch me," Omar said in a shredded voice. The white faded from his eyes and he took a step, then dropped to a knee, catching himself with one hand to prevent himself toppling completely. The guards left Zeki on the ground to circle around Omar. Dilay put shaking hands up to her mouth, her breath coming in short, sharp intakes and exhales. Omar's head hung for a moment, and she thought he might collapse completely.

"I'll touch you!" Turgay threatened from the front door as Zeki managed to clamber to his feet. "I'll put my fist through your ribs. You son of a—"

"Stop!" Dilay said. "Go." She managed to force calm she did not feel into her voice. "There will be City Watch here any moment. Please. Go now, I will deal with this."

She would have to check with them later, if she had a chance. They were smart enough to know it would do the school no good to go telling the entire district that the Vali Ahad had shown up. Everyone would pull their children and then there would be no school. Or in acts of self-preservation families would out each other, hoping sending some to prison would protect them from the same.

Turgay grabbed Zeki by the arm when he reached the door and they disappeared into the dark.

Dilay crouched as Omar collapsed to his haunches.

"How am I going to explain this?" he said to himself, wiping blood against the hip of his shining white entari. What had the fool been thinking, wearing something like that down to the Earth District? She was surprised he was not bleeding out in an alley with a knife wound to his belly.

"Vali Ahad Efendim," Dilay began. What could she say?

His gaze, warm cinnamon turned dark and angry in the fading light of one of her student's mage lights, locked on hers.

"Go," he said, in a broken voice that held only anger.

"Please," she murmured. How had she not realized?

He didn't need help using his magic, he needed help stopping it.

"My father will hang you for this," he said like an accusation. Blood dripped through his beard and off his chin, onto the entari, marring the pure white and silver with more garish red. "Go. And tomorrow, you will bring yourself to the palace, or Wheel help me, I will have you brought."

THIRTEEN

THE WALK FROM HER HOUSE to the University was usually her favorite part of the day. The city was just waking, the sunlight beginning to pour down and illuminate the riotous colors in a way mage orbs could not do justice to. And the streets themselves transitioned from the depressed parts of the city to those with more hope, sections that had once been poor becoming more built up, happier faces to see and greet. But today she did not see it. Only the questions and fears spinning like leaves in a breeze. And she only got a brief stop at the University, to drop a note for the Headmaster that she would not be teaching her classes that day, by order of the palace.

It was further ruined by the presence of her father, dressed in his most ominous of dark brown caftan and entari, bordered with gold and fastened with the sigil-laden belt of a tribunal judge. For the most part they walked in silence, punctuated by his occasional sharp sigh, which then led into another rant about her foolishness.

"How could you keep something like this from me?" he railed. "How could you even agree to such a thing? You were already putting yourself at risk with that damned school, and then you decide to play personal attendant to the son of the man who would have you hanged for it!"

"What did you wish me to do, Baba? Tell the Vali Ahad no? Should I also tell the Sultan himself?" Dilay snipped. She did not need his lectures at the moment, wound as tightly as she was.

He returned to his stormy brooding, marching up the merciless incline of the palace road with a vigor Dilay could not match. By the time they reached the gate to the palace courtyard she was sweating, despite the cool spring morning, and her hair was falling out of its braid.

The Morning Gate, named because it was built to highlight the morning sun when it appeared from behind the peak of the Kalspire and its mountainous companions, was colossal. Large enough to drive ten carriages through side by side. People were already coming and going in droves, even at this early time of morning. Her father led the way, plowing ahead with intensity. Dilay followed more nervously, half convinced the guards would be looking for her—to whisk her away to a dank, lightless cell in the Cliffs.

As she passed between the arch and the grouping of guards to either side, and above, on the spired towers, her heart took up residence in her throat, drumming so it was all she could hear and feel. Each laugh or exclamation from the conversations around her startled her, making her tense and step away. By the time she was through the gate and crowds, she felt like a ball that had been paddled this way and that between a gaggle of children. Dilay pressed a hand to her heart, feeling its staccato rhythm.

Her father gave her a once-over when they were past the crowds and his iron visage of outrage softened. He took her arm and patted her hand.

"It will be all right, it will. No daughter of mine is going to prison or…" he said the last more softly, as if steeling himself instead of comforting her.

They crossed toward the palace's broad steps. There were guards there as well, two to each side of the monstrous double oak doors. The doors were thrown open to reveal the shining marble hall beyond. Her father released his grip on her at the top of the stairs and addressed the nearest of the two guards on the left.

"My daughter has been summoned." He drew himself up with shoulders back and head high, and Dilay did the same. Three people shoved by Dilay, distracting the guard. Someone laughed as they passed into the hall. "Summoned by the Vali Ahad," her father said more loudly, to bring the guard's attention back.

The guard's brows shot toward his receding hairline, his gaze darting down and back up as he looked at Dilay. She was a mess, dusty from the walk, and her hair mussed and sticking about her face. Disbelief, horror, and confusion passed over his face.

"You are Dilay Akar," his comrade said, or asked. Dilay ducked her chin, every muscle seizing as he came around the guard nearest her and her father. Was he going to grab her? She took an involuntary step back. "This way," he said. His face did not show as much emotion as the other's, which was comforting, and frightening. Dilay glanced to her father and he nodded, and they fell in behind the guard.

No matter that the entrance foyer was filled to the brim with people, chatting, waiting, moving from one wing to another, all Dilay could hear were her own shoes, tapping against cold, pale marble tiles. Her slow march to punishment. Prison, or…if there was no mercy in Omar, hanging, the word her father would not say. Teaching forbidden subjects to forbidden students. Sedition. They could accuse her of anything they wished. Truth was what the powerful made it.

"I might suggest," the guard said, "that you take a moment to put yourself in order before you appear before the Queen Sultana." He stopped, indicating a small room to the right. Panic overwhelmed the shivering nerves that had predominated, and she looked at her father.

"Queen Sultana?" Her heart departed her throat to plummet to her stomach, which in turn twisted and cramped. There might have been hope to plead her case to Omar. She was certain she had not imagined that they enjoyed each other's company. But the Queen Sultana might as well be the Wheel itself for all she knew of the woman.

"I do not understand," her father said. The guard blinked, in a manner devoid of interest. "She was summoned by the Vali Ahad."

"To meet with the Queen Sultana. Do you wish to tidy yourself, or take your chances as you are?" The guard looked at Dilay and pointed again, suggesting the latter was not truly an option at all.

Dilay turned from him and opened the door, which was just a simple panel of wood carved in the pattern of the Wheel, lattice to let the light from the hall windows in. Beyond it was a small, narrow room, the walls and floor sandstone. She pulled the panel shut behind her and the guard and her father turned their backs.

A narrow wooden bench lined one wall, and there was a pedestal with a basin and pitcher, with a stack of rolled linen clothes to one side. An earthenware bowl held a wooden comb, a stiff brush for cleaning shoes and hems, and bits of ribbon. Dilay did the best she could, washing her face and hands and tidying her hair into a fresh braid, which she wound and coiled with some of the ribbon. She used the brush on her shoes and the worst of the dust on her caftan. She had chosen her University caftan and entari, shades of grey and blue. Not because they were flattering, but she hoped it would elevate her in their esteem. Though what could the Queen Sultana care about a woman teaching? No one outside the palace had seen the woman in Turns; Dilay wondered if she had any concept of what went on outside the palace walls.

When she emerged, her father took her arm again and the guard led them onward, down a marble hall with carpets woven in patterns of the First House. The Sabris had always been First House, as far as the histories were concerned. The palace reflected that, bedecked in cool colors and a dizzying array of windows and open spaces. She had expected to be taken to the receiving hall, the only place in the palace she had ever been. Her father had brought her once, Turns ago, when all the tribunal judges met with the Sultan about territories and division of labor. But this was an entirely different section of the palace.

He stopped before a set of gilt double doors and gave three quick knocks.

"Her chambers?" Dilay's father parroted, his face twisting with confusion. After a moment that was also a lifetime in which Dilay's heart pounded faster and her hands grew cold and clammy, the doors opened. A woman stood in between them. The guard bowed. She was older, dressed in fine clothes, but not the finest Dilay had ever seen. The tiraz on her arms marked her a mage of the Fourth House, so it was not the Sultana, who was a First House mage, but likely one of her servants.

"I was told to deliver Instructor Akar," the guard announced. The woman's gaze cut to Dilay and her father, assessed, judged wanting, then she dismissed the guard with a nod. Dilay stood rooted to the carpet, her hands coiled in her entari. Her father's arm tightened possessively around hers.

"Welcome, Instructor Akar." The woman smiled. She was in her seventh Cycle or so, with grey deadening the brown hair that was pulled into elaborately coiled braids. Dilay tried to smile back, but it must have been more of a grimace. "I am afraid you will have to wait, Judge Akar. You may do so here, or in the main hall."

"I will wait here." Her father folded his arms and set his feet. Dilay squeezed his arm before she unwound her arm from his. Then she bowed to the woman before them, because the servant of a Queen Sultana was still a highborn noble. Higher ranked than Dilay would ever be.

"The Queen Sultana has been looking forward to meeting you." She stepped aside as Dilay straightened, revealing the room beyond. It appeared to be a sitting room, with couches and a table set with food and coffee. Dilay forced herself to move forward, her mind unable to quite process that she must be entering the Sultana's personal rooms. She glanced behind at her father, who gave her an encouraging, if unconvincing smile.

"A bit farther, if you please," the earth mage murmured, and Dilay took a large step so the doors could be closed behind her. She gripped handfuls of her entari, over her belly, as the door blocked her view of her father. She faced the room, taking a moment to steady herself.

This was no different than facing the Headmaster to plead her suitability to teach at the University. She told herself.

The Sultana sat in a chair by an entire wall of windows that overlooked a garden beyond. She was lithe and elegant, dressed in silver embroidered upon silver, her near-black hair cascading over her shoulders but for a single braid that wound her head to hold her diadem in place. A teardrop sapphire hung against her brow, so large it could pay Dilay's entire pittance of a salary for a Turn. The woman's hands were in her lap, one finger tapping against her leg in patient rhythm. Dilay did not think she had ever seen anyone sit so straight-backed, as though their spine were a rod of iron extending from head to hip. Warm, cinnamon eyes assessed her.

"You may come in, my dear," she said. "I have enough ornaments in my entry already, I do not need another one. Especially one that does not quite fit." Her delivery was dry, so Dilay could not tell if the woman was having fun at her expense or delivering an underhanded insult. Dilay did not understand what she was doing in the Queen Sultana's sitting room. The single room was larger than Seda's entire home, and doors to either side were likely bedrooms, or even a bathroom. Dilay could not imagine having a room to bathe in one's home. She had to hike through the city to the public bathhouses to have a proper wash.

Dilay stepped forward, and when she had entered the circle of seating, bowed low.

"Sit," the Sultana said. Her servant came forward as Dilay sat on the very edge of one of the couches, and poured them both coffee. Dilay had not drunk much coffee in her life. It was a drink for the wealthiest, saved for moments with friends and guests. She found it bitter and overwhelming, but when a Sultana gave you coffee, you drank it.

Dilay took a sip, her hands shaking so the cup rattled against the table as she set it back. "Forgive me, Efendim," she said. "I do not understand why I am here."

"Because you are instructing my son, and I took an interest in you," she replied. So, this was not punishment for what Omar had seen? Dilay could not ask, or risk revealing a secret the Sultana did not know. But her confusion was only slightly alleviated. "Why else would I have sent for you?" The Sultana cocked her head, like a falcon, and Dilay felt laid bare, as if the Sultana could see straight through to every lie and failing.

"I am not very interesting," Dilay said. The Sultana smiled, genuine enough that Dilay relaxed a fraction.

"No?" the Queen said, something flashing in the depth of her eyes. "You are a woman who has invaded the University, not as a student destined to be a wife, but as an instructor. I find that very interesting. I think we have a great deal in common."

Dilay nearly choked. "What might that be, Efendim?" She did not mean to gesture to her University clothes, drab in comparison to the Sultana's glorious brocade and shining sitting room. To the circle of sweat that had dampened the neck of her caftan, or the unrepentant dirt on her shoes. But she did, and the Sultana saw and gave an amused smile.

"The outside of a person does not always represent what is inside them, do you not agree? Gemstones"—she touched the sapphire on her brow—"come from the poorest of rock and earth, and are made all the more beautiful for their beginnings and surroundings they are found in."

Dilay forced herself to breathe, and the Sultana continued to smile.

"Or perhaps you are nothing more than you appear to be. Though I doubt that. To have done what you have done, you must be tenacious indeed. Being a young woman in the province of men…we both know the struggles of that, I think." The Sultana's servant came forward, offered to pour more coffee. "No, thank you, Beste."

Dilay also declined, and Beste retreated again.

"I know Judge Akar has a reputation as fair yet unrelenting in his administration of justice. That he favors those of poorer birth in his rulings."

When Dilay made a surprised sound, the Sultana raised an eyebrow and turned her gaze out the windows. "People believe because I am the Sultana, and not the Sultan, that I know nothing of the politics and machinations of my husband's court. Because those are the province of men." Her gaze met Dilay's. "Assumptions made at a distance are rarely based on knowledge or fact. Which is why I wish to hear from you—why have you done this thing? Defied tradition and laws? Defied the Sultan himself?"

Though cold swept through Dilay like a tide, stiffening her posture and making her mind momentarily slow, the Sultana's face bore no malice, or accusation. Only curiosity. Dilay glanced to the servant by the door, then back to the Sultana.

"Beste, might I trouble you for a dampening, so our guest knows she is safe to express herself?"

"Of course." Beste traced a sigil against her palm, casting a dampening over the room. Dilay rubbed her ears to stop the temporary ache.

"I did not bring you here to extract secrets and reasons to punish you, my dear," the Sultana said. "Please."

"I believe things must change, or Tamar will crumble on rotten foundation," Dilay purged. The Queen made a soft sound of amusement and gestured with an open hand for Dilay to elaborate. Apprehension crawled like insects in her skin.

But when would she ever have a chance to say this again, to an audience that actually mattered?

"I grew up on the cusp of noble and poor. I have seen the disparity between the two. How gifted mages go untaught, simply for accident of birth. And how nobles with far less to offer to their country sit fat and happy and provide nothing in return." The words poured forth, uncensored, dangerous, traitorous words. As though the Sultana had lanced a festering wound.

There was nothing that could be done to take the words back, and something about saying them out loud also purged Dilay's nervousness. She forced herself to meet the Sultana's eyes.

"A revolutionary." The Queen aimed the tart comment at Beste, who made a thoughtful noise. "The corrosive kind. Slow, but ultimately, the most effective. Society has always changed in such ways. Either by war, the sudden, violent upheavals that pepper history. Or by this. By people like you. Termites eating away at the way things are, forging trails through the old by which the new infiltrates."

Dilay forced forced the mask of calm her father had taught her, the one he wore at the tribunals. No one should know anything of your mind that you do not tell them in words, he said. She did not want the Queen to see her fear, or know nausea made her lightheaded. The Queen's tone was even, cool, just as impossible to interpret as Dilay hoped her expression was. But she was not certain being compared to a termite was not an insult.

"Change is not always for ill," Dilay said, trying her best to match the Queen's cool tone. The older woman rose, turning to face the windows to the garden. The thought struck Dilay that it appeared lonely, the Sultana standing there, staring out at a garden devoid of anything particularly beautiful to look at.

"Change is inevitable, my dear, whether for ill or good. The Wheel turns. The seasons change, we grow old, and die. Anyone who tries to stop change is a fool. And there are so very, very many fools." She turned toward Dilay with a smile like she held back floods of secrets, and Dilay saw Omar in that smile, and relaxed incrementally. Perhaps he was not his father's son at all, but his mother's. He had not sent her to the hangman, after all. He had sent her here. "Yet, some change requires force, as you are aware, and have experienced."

Dilay sensed the Queen's push toward something, but there was no way to avoid it. She could only offer a reluctant nod.

"I know what my eldest has asked you to do. Do you?" The Queen turned her back to the windows, her clothes cast in gilt by the morning light.

"A mage uncontrolled is a dangerous thing, Queen Sultana. Some may argue a Sultan uncontrolled is an unforgiveable thing," Dilay said, quietly.

"You know there is always a price for magic. Many believe the worst price for magic is mage sleep, when a mage has exhausted their power and themselves." The Queen lowered her gaze to the table, over the coffee set before she turned halfway around to look at the garden again. "But there is something worse. A higher price."

There was death. Dilay curled her fingers against her knees. When a mage had exhausted their energy, their well of magic, they could draw, purposely or accidentally, on their lifeforce. Until the magic killed them. Everyone knew that.

"Do you know how the Elder Sehzade died? My husband's brother?"

"Consumption," Dilay said. The Queen's mouth curved in a tiny, bitter smile.

"My husband will be pleased to know you think so." Her gazed traced an arc, following the invisible bubble of her servant's dampening, then landed on Dilay. "He went mad. His head filled with the memories and minds of all he had used his powers on. They filled his dreams until they overflowed into his waking moments. Until he was erased by them. Until he became a liability to my husband."

Dilay went numb from head to toe. Her fingers tingled and her throat itched as she swallowed.

"Are there any books in the University library about Veritor magic?" the Queen asked so casually that it left Dilay's thoughts whirling for a moment. When she shook her head, the Sultana made a noise of affirmation. "No, I thought not. It is the very best-kept Sabri secret." Her brows drew together sharply, sorrow overtaking her face. "A secret kept even from those who wield the power."

The numbness buzzed in Dilay's body, filling her ears and pinching at her eyes. Omar did not know?

"I have asked you to come here so that I might request something of you, in the interest of change." The Sultana sat again, leaning forward. "Do not help my son. If he controls that cursed power with any precision, his father will only force him to use it more. Doom him more quickly. No Veritor has ever lived past forty Turns."

The pinching in Dilay's eyes made her nose itch and tears perch at the corners. She swiped the heels of her hands against them.

"Whatever he has offered you, I will give it to you now, to make you stop." The Queen's gaze followed the motion of Dilay's hands.

"He…" It felt too silly and childish to say now, knowing what the consequences were. "He offered to grant me access to the palace library. At my whim."

The Queen looked shocked, then she laughed, looking at Beste, who also giggled. "Of course he did. My scholar. I see why he chose you, if you are so easily bribed with knowledge. It is yours. By my edict, if you obey me. And I was distressed to find out I had not heard of you until now. I would like to change that. I would like all of Narfour to know about your accomplishments. About the inroads you are making for others to follow."

Elation lasted only as long as it took cynicism to root into place. Obey her, and leave Omar helpless to his power. Dilay murmured, "He cannot touch anyone, can he?"

The Queen raised an eyebrow and looked away.

Dilay asked, more forcefully, "When was the last time you embraced your son, Efendim?"

The Queen's face blanched, and her gaze dropped as she reached again for her coffee. A mage's power manifested as their awareness began to stretch outside themselves. The age of ten Turns was common, but could take less time or more. That was a very long time for a person to go without touch.

"You wish that for him? Isolated from everyone for the rest of his days?" she tried to ask gently. If what the Queen said was true, there was no right answer to the problem. Dilay swallowed back her dismay. She could not afford emotion where Omar was concerned. The fate of the city, of all of Tamar, was tied up with his. "What about heirs? What about Tamar beyond his reign?"

"Those are my concerns, not yours. If I cannot convince you with kindness, then I will do so by force. You will desist with assisting the Vali Ahad, or you will find your time at the University has come abruptly to an end." The Sultana caught her gaze and held it, the warmth in her eyes gone.

"I can help him," Dilay said, desperately. "I know I can. Control is all about what takes up space in a mage's mind." She could not mention helping Behram, and even if she did, it proved nothing. He had suffered from exactly the opposite problem of Omar's.

"Every mind he touches leaves a crack in his own. You think you can save him from that? Or will you be plugging a leak with a stopper made of sand?"

Dilay did not have an answer. The Wheel demanded balance. It did not give great power without cost. But this cost…

"Continue as you are, Instructor Akar. I will give you some time to decide before I summon you again." The Sultana stood. She was tall, and willowy. Perhaps that was where the princes got their height, because their father was not known for his.

Dilay stood as well, then bowed.

"Beste, see to it she is unmolested." The Sultana turned her back on Dilay, staring out the windows into the garden. Dilay wanted more words, more information, but she was already mired with all of it and could bear no more.

"This way, Instructor Akar." Beste indicated the doors after she pulled them open.

FOURTEEN

"WHERE ARE YOU TAKING US?" Dilay's father asked as Beste turned right down another hall, this one wide and open on both sides to a garden on one side and a series of fountains on the other. People were scattered about the gallery and the open spaces, chatting and enjoying an unusually warm day for the season.

Beste did not answer, only touched a finger to her lips when the question drew attention to them. When they turned again, into an interior hall, Dilay realized she would not be able to find her way back out without assistance.

One more turn brought them to a circular area situated in the middle of a round room with five archways surrounding. Four led into deep alcoves with cushioned benches and tables for socializing. The fifth opened to a stone staircase that wound out of sight.

"Where are we?" Dilay's father demanded.

Beste glanced behind her before she said, quietly, "The Vali Ahad requested you be brought to him before you leave the palace."

Dilay stifled the urge to ask if the Sultan himself would also like to see her as well. Perhaps the Grand Vizier? She exchanged a look with her father.

"To what end?" he asked Beste, his gaze flitting from the stairs to her and back again.

"I am not privy to the Vali Ahad's wishes, Judge Akar. I was only told he wished to speak to your daughter." She held a hand toward the stairs. "Only your daughter."

"That is hardly appropriate. Can he not see her in the receiving hall?"

"He can see her wherever he wishes," Beste said. Her father's face flushed and his jaw set.

"It is all right. I will return in a moment." Dilay touched his arm, then followed Beste's indication to the stairs. She gathered up her caftan and entari and marched up the narrow stone stairwell, pausing only once to look out a bolt hole, hoping to catch an awe-inspiring view of the city. Something to shore her against whatever Omar had in store for her. Instead she was treated to the sight of the palace rooftops, all gilt domes and spiked spires. A flock of sparrows exploded past the hole and nearly frightened Dilay into a tumble down the stairs.

At the top, the stairs ended abruptly at an arch without a door. Dilay stopped in the frame of the arch to survey the room beyond. It was hot in the tower, and she was already sweating. Being hot and sweaty fueled her temper enough to inoculate her against any more nervousness she might feel. The room was a study, with a bench along the wall beneath a series of triplet arched windows. Omar sat in the middle of it, with a bookstand in front of him. The stand was the typical type, two wooden panels fit together to form an X into which the book was cradled. This one was far more detailed than any she had utilized in the library at the University, intricate filigree carved into the panels.

He turned a page, head bent down. Was he ignoring her? Surely he had heard her huffing and stomping up the stairs like a winded bull. Dilay could not see if her accidental slamming of the warehouse door into his face the previous night had done lasting damage. She could see that a pair of spectacles perched on his nose, and the sight pierced straight through her irritability so that she started to smile despite herself. It was unbearably charming to see one more human crack in the armor of a prince.

"I do not believe your mother likes me, Vali Ahad," Dilay announced as she stepped through the archway and onto the carpet with an audacious weaving of the Sabri crest.

"My mother"—he turned another page without looking at her—"has a severe predilection for all creatures of the female persuasion. The surlier the better, and so I can only imagine she adored you."

"If I am surly it is your fault."

Now he looked up, and Dilay realized she had been mistaken. Omar Sabri in spectacles was not unbearably charming, he was heart-stopping. And for a brief, stunned moment, it did not matter that spectacles were a luxury of the wealthy. One that many of her children who needed them to read at all would never be able to obtain.

She glanced away from him. Fire flared in her cheeks and she snuffed it with magic, forcing cool into every limb and thought, so she could look at him and not be forced to feel affection growing like choking vines. He was, she reminded herself, likely about to dispense punishment for her crimes.

"My fault?" He pulled the spectacles off so he could massage the bridge of his nose. He winced and dropped his hand. "That you were illegally teaching?"

"You lied to me," she said.

"I lied to you because I barely know you." He stood. "Do you think I can just go around announcing to anyone that I cannot contain my magic?" He was not wearing an entari over his caftan and salvar, and in the heat of the tower the thin linen clung to his broad chest and strong shoulders so graphically that Dilay had to look away.

"You asked me for help and did not tell me what I needed to know to help you." She curled her hands into fists, trying to keep her voice level. "You put me in danger."

Omar edged around the bookstand and crossed to her, his brows drawing a sharp V on his forehead. "No I did not. I had no intention of letting you touch me. And you lied as well. You did not inform me that I was consorting with a criminal," he said. "You are putting yourself at risk of imprisonment at best, and I cannot even think of the other outcomes." He grit his teeth and rubbed his fingers against his temples.

"That is entirely up to you, is it not, Vali Ahad? What were you doing in the Earth District?" She wanted to remind him he could have been killed, with only a few guards and that foolish choice of clothing that practically begged someone to rob and beat him. But she did not. He was a grown man and could make his own stupid choices.

"I was supposed to tell you yesterday that my mother had requested to speak with you. I…forgot." He blinked hard and his gaze cut away. "So I searched for you."

"How did you find me?" Narfour was enormous. He could not simply have happened upon her. Even her parents did not know where the school was.

He bared his teeth. "Earth mages are invaluable, do you not agree?"

Dilay closed her eyes to hide her frustration. Deval and Sival of the Fourth House could use their magic to track individuals they were familiar with. His steward was apparently familiar enough with her to track her through the city. The magic of her students was distracting enough that she had not sensed the spell as she should have.

"There are laws against tracking citizens who have not committed gross crimes." Dilay pressed her lips together. It was difficult to keep her indignation stoked when he was so close. He smelled good, like soap and clean male sweat. His honey-brown skin glowed with it, especially in the hollow of his throat, which Dilay had an irrational desire to touch. Especially irrational considering her newfound under-standing of his power.

"You were committing a crime," he said, a smile starting on his mouth, "as it happens." She mocked a sneer.

"It must be very nice to have high-order mages of every House at your disposal. Those of us with more mundane means would simply have sent a message. Or just told me." He was certainly powerful enough to have cast his voice, even if she was not in sight.

Color bloomed around his neck, drawing her attention to the hollow of his throat once again. She did not understand her fascination with it. With the way the caftan cut in a small V to frame it, how just enough of his chest showed below the intersection of fabric to make her want to see more.

"Were you not the one who expressed some doubt that I could cast my voice with any precision? Besides, I did not think you would enjoy having a stranger's voice suddenly whispering in your ear," Omar said, a bit unevenly. He swallowed.

"Your voice is not so unbearable," she said before thinking. He exhaled sharply.

"No?" His voice, made to fill halls and Council rooms, growled when he lowered it to speak to her this way, and it made shivers echo over her skin in supplication. She shook her head. "I had thought you might be more penitent for being discovered at your crimes."

"Did you?" She raised an eyebrow. He conceded with a tilt of his head and a shrug. "No. I am not penitent," Dilay managed. She could not concentrate. His smell, and his nearness, and the look in his eyes were turning her simple. "I am the only chance those children have of ever being anything more than what they are now. To deny them schooling, basic instruction on their magic, or the mages they are surrounded by, is cruel. And dangerous. Do you know—"

Was he laughing? His eyes were crinkled at the edges, his smile broadening slowly. Dilay glowered at him.

"That is amusing to you? Those families are afraid, Vali Ahad. They are afraid you are going to take their children from them, or punish them. Families that hold your city up. What are you going to do to me, and them?"

"Are you finished?" The humor disappeared.

"For now." She forced her gaze up. Traitor thing that it was, it landed first on his mouth before flashing higher.

His brow furrowed, and he made a jerky movement to clasp his hands at his back. "I have no intention of punishing anyone for last night, except the miscreant who slammed that door in my face."

Relief flowed cool and bright through her limbs. "I am sorry."

"I do not think you are." He scowled at her, but in mockery, his eyes full of teasing. "You will pay me recompense for the humiliation of having to come back to this palace and lie my way through every question asked of me. Such as why I was covered in blood. My own blood. I could not even claim I won the fight against the brute that assaulted me, because that was obviously untrue."

"Brute?" She laughed a little. "Is that what you think of me?"

"No." He straightened, his mouth tightening and his gaze lowering. "No, I think you are brilliant. And brave. And kind. All the things I wish to be and am not. You help people. I…" He released his breath. "I hurt them."

Oh. That explained so much. Magic was intricately tied with a mage's emotions. When their emotions were high, their magic fluxed. If they were powerful enough, a Sival, it would show on their skin, react with the world around them, reflect in their eyes. But it did not attack without a mage's direction.

For his magic to do such a thing, to lash out at everything that touched him, he would, deep down, have to want it to.

When she had first met Behram, his magic was erratic. So powerful, and so dangerous. He could not summon it on command, but things would explode around him when he was angry, bursting into flames. Still that anger lived in him, always too near the surface, though he had learned to control it as they had become friends.

But Omar's was not anger. It was shame. He was punishing himself.

"I will keep your school a secret for you," he said, interrupting her thoughts, "if you will keep my secret for me."

"Your mother asked me not to help you," she said. His eyes rolled up and he made a frustrated sound.

"I thought she might. I will not force you," he said. "What did she threaten you with?"

"She said I had to decide whether I wanted to continue teaching at the University, and implied that if I agreed with her wishes, she would also give me access to the library, and make certain my accomplishments were known throughout Narfour."

He smiled in defeat. "I cannot offer you the same, I am afraid." No. He could not publicly acknowledge her in any way without making the whole of Tamar believe they were lovers. Ironic, considering any lover he had would be one in name only.

"She made some arguments that trouble me," Dilay said. The Sultana had made it clear that Omar was unaware of the long-term price of his power. Was it her place to tell him? Keeping such a thing from someone…it was needles in her skin, prods to speak and to remain silent, restlessness that made her thoughts twirl. These schemes and lies were unbearable. How could anyone live their life embroiled in them? Like a sucking morass that prevented any real change, trapping those who might accomplish something in endless rounds of intrigue instead.

"I see," Omar said, warily. "Are they arguments you will give me a chance to defend against?"

"I do want to help you," she said. Because she did. A mage was not meant to be controlled by their magic, and his control of his was vital to Tamar. Besides, against her good sense, she could not help that she was enamored of him. Of the parts of him that had revealed themselves to her in moments like these, when he was freed from outward expectations. She had helped Behram. Surely she could do the same for Omar?

His face relaxed and he graced her with a smile that made her understand why she had overheard so many noblewomen talking about him in the halls of the University. He somehow managed to be beautiful and handsome at once. So one moment she was drawn to the masculine, to the breadth of his shoulders or the hard line of his jaw, and the next he was beautiful and untouchable. Like the frescoes that graced the interior of the palace domes. Something to be admired but never reached for.

"Your friend from last night, the man who grabbed me, is he all right?" His shoulders flexed, as if he was fighting to keep his own hands behind his back. Dilay forced her gaze from him to the window, because her thoughts were beginning to wander in an embarrassing direction.

"I am told he is fine, surprisingly. And somehow oblivious? He says you hit him."

"If the contact is brief enough, my magic only touches the surface. I simply see whatever they were most recently thinking of." He did not like talking about it; his posture stiffened, his face tensing, his gaze darting. "Whatever they see and feel. And they often do not feel me at all mentally, only the physical. I did not hit him, but his mind may have interpreted it that way."

That was control. If his magic was unleashing, but not fully, he did not lack complete control.

"We should speak about your penance," he said. "For my wounds." He finally released his hands from behind him, indicating his bruised nose with a tap of his finger. Dilay folded her arms over her chest and cocked a hip and an eyebrow. Omar looked out the window. "I would like to observe one of your classes, the night classes. And afterwards… I thought you could show me my city, the parts that my father and the others pretend do not exist." He stood stiff, his gaze trained hard on the windows, as if afraid to look at her.

She scoffed. "You wish me to escort a crown prince and his entourage of guards and royal foot-washers through the parts of the city that hate him most. No thank you. I choose prison."

"We can leave the royal foot-washers behind," he said with a laugh. "In fact I meant for it to be just me."

Dilay stared wide-eyed. "Just you? You are mad."

"Is it mad for me to want to see my city? The people who feel forgotten?"

Did he mean that? "Behram is better suited to this task, for innumerable reasons, not the least of which is that the last thing either of us needs is rumors of us spending time alone together."

"They would not be rumors, would they?" he said. Her gaze clashed with his. An impending feeling of doom enveloped her, making her both giddy and melancholy. She was not going to be able to suppress this growing fondness. Not when he looked like that, shy, and unsure while also exuding the carefree arrogance only someone accustomed to having things their way could manage.

"Rumors may not be of consequence to you, Vali Ahad, but they matter a great deal to me. I cannot afford them. I worked incredibly hard to attain my position at the University, and they will not have to work hard at all to take it from me."

He relaxed and gripped the back of his neck with one hand while rubbing the other over his eyes. "Forgive me. I…"

"You are not accustomed to having to think of such things. That is why you must be surrounded by people that do. For your own good." She tried to keep her voice tinged with levity and earned a reluctant smile.

"I thought I told you to call me Omar," he said, lowering his hands to his side.

"Omar." Dilay liked calling him by name far too much. Liked pretending he was a man who could be a friend…that he was a man she could be attracted to as she was.

That attraction was probably more treasonous than her secret school. A lowborn noble looking doe-eyed at the future Sultan of Tamar. It sounded like something from a cautionary tale for children. The kind that ended with a painful lesson.

"If you are finished doling out my punishment? I have left my father sweating at the bottom of the stairs."

"I can escort you back." He moved for the door. Dilay put a hand out to stop him, but remembered herself at the last moment, yanking it back even as he dodged out of the way.

"Perhaps you could dress first?" She clutched her hand against her chest. His face flushed and he crossed back to the bench to grab up his entari. He shrugged into it and buttoned it closed.

"I keep having to ask your forgiveness. I did not remember I had removed it."

"No? I thought you might be trying to distract me on purpose."

His fingers fumbled a button, and his gaze shifted to hers. "Was it distracting?"

The heat came into her cheeks again, but she felt bold, bolstered by that shy look in his eyes. She gave a quick nod.

"I apologize," he said, but looked pleased.

"You needn't." She clasped her hands together and let them fall against her legs. His fingers resumed their work on the remaining clasps. When he finished he returned to her, standing far too close, and not close enough. "It was not an unpleasant distraction."

"Now you are distracting me," he murmured. She dared not look at his face, or the expression that accompanied the alluring hitch in his voice.

"And I did not even need to remove my clothes," she said, regretting it even as the words poured forth. Then she did look at his face. His warm, burnished gaze drifted over her hair and her face, so slowly he might as well have touched her, the weight of it pressed and burned against her skin.

"I think"—he cleared his throat when his voice broke—"that it would be best if I did not escort you this time."

Dilay could only manage a jerky nod. Even a simpleton would notice her blushing and fumbling because she had opened her foolish mouth and spoken about undressing in front of the Vali Ahad. Her father would be incensed if he pieced together she felt any warmth at all for a Sabri.

"Will your father be at the guild mediation tomorrow?" he asked. Dilay nodded again. Omar echoed the movement, and a moment of silence passed before he added, "Will you?"

"Yes," she said, her discomfiture obvious in the scratch of her voice. Annoyed, she dug deep, past her shyness, and forced a smile and a straight back. "Good bye, Vali Ahad."

"Omar," he demanded.

"Omar," she repeated.

"Good bye, Dilay."

He drifted after her when she turned to cross the room to the stairs, and he lingered in the archway as she descended. Before she made the first turn that would put him out of sight, she looked back. He had his hands braced on either side of the arch, flexing forward so that he appeared to be holding himself back from coming after her. Dilay could not help her giddy smile, or the bolt of pleasure that went through her when he echoed it.

FIFTEEN

THE MERCHANT GUILD HALL STOOD in the heart of the Fire District, just on the outskirts of the Grand Market. Dilay did not know how old the building was, but it certainly predated the Sundering War. There were blackened, man-sized chunks blasted out of the outside of the northern wall. Evidence of a battle within the city during the war, the damage the most powerful of fire mages could cause. But the building, with its high walls and gloriously tall, arched windows, remained.

The walls were lined with benches carved from wood imported from the north, before the fall of the Old Sultanate and the closing of the routes on the Spice Road that went north into the Republic and beyond. Rugs from Menei covered the stone floors, some with so many colors they dizzied her, others that were stark black and white. All beautifully and intricately woven. Dilay loved it, all the history contained within it, though today some of the wonder was gone because of the proceedings she watched.

Mediation by a panel of tribunal judges was the final step before an all-out guild war, replete with bogus accusations and trials based on spite that would tear the guild to pieces. Mediation was a three-step process, and the meeting Dilay attended today was the first of those steps. It was also the least useful, in her opinion. Two tables of people shouting at each other while four judges looked on, most likely considering other, more useful things they could be doing. The idea was that the groups could air their problems and talk through them with assistance. That was, in the few times Dilay had been present at such a thing, never what happened. By the time mediation was called for, the groups were well past polite discourse.

The largest room in the building had been transformed from general meeting hall to mediation room, with long, low tables placed in the center, parallel, so the two opposing sides could sit across from each other. There was just enough space between the rows to encourage the two sides to shout every time they wished to make a point. It very much reminded Dilay of fighting dogs she had once seen in cages on the pier. They paced the bars, barking and snarling at each other, trying to assert dominance with posturing and volume. But here, the men sat on cushions, sometimes rising to their knees to lob accusations and rebuttals across the table.

She positioned herself in the far back corner of the room, nearest to the doors that led out into the hall and offices. There were cushions around the perimeter, and people had begun the mediation seated, but all were standing now, often jeering or cheering as they thought the situation warranted. Dilay listened when she could, but there wasn't much being said that would be useful.

"It is time to bring the guild into the modern age, Altimur Pasha, and you are not interested in that, because it will not line your pockets," Kadir Pasha said, smoothly and calmly. Dilay had to give him credit despite her personal dislike; he was not acting the volatile fire mage at all. Instead he maintained a convincing mien of reasonable calm. He made no effort to stop the others at his table from shouting and arguing though.

Meanwhile, Altimur Pasha sweated and stammered in rebuttal. To rouse an earth mage's temper to such ineffectual blubbering was a momentous feat. They were the steadiest on the Wheel. It did not help his cause that Altimur Pasha was ten Turns Kadir Pasha's senior, and looked considerably less fit and sharp than Semih Kadir.

Appearances, Dilay knew well, could be everything. Even if Altimur Pasha was not the only one concerned about lining his pockets.

"My pockets"—Altimur Pasha swept a hand over his greased-back, silver hair—"are just fine."

Dilay sucked a breath between her teeth, switching her gaze from the pages of Judge Hanim's book to Osman, Altimur Pasha's son. His jaw was set, his hands balled into fists on the table.

Laughter speckled the room, and Kadir Pasha smiled indulgently. "We are aware, my friend."

At the head of the tables, the four judges sat, quiet. Dilay's father sat in the middle of them, his face impassive. Though, even at this distance she saw his eyebrow had ticked up.

He had to carefully consider the consequence of the judges choosing to continue on with mediation. Both Kadir Pasha and Altimur Pasha had passionate followers. Men and women perfectly willing to be brutal in their search to secure what they believed to be theirs. There had already been one attempt at mediation, and it had failed when one judge's home had been set aflame with him and his family inside. They had survived, thanks to quick-thinking water mages from the nearby market. No one had been punished or accused, and neither Altimur Pasha nor Kadir Pasha admitted to having anything to do with the attack.

Dilay and her father agreed that Altimur Pasha was no match for Kadir Pasha when it came to verbal combat. Osman might have a better chance, but it would be by a small margin. She liked Osman, liked his deliberate way of speaking. There was intelligence in there she was not certain his father possessed, not anymore. She had gone through the University with Osman, Behram, and the Yavuz brothers. Behram had been leagues smarter than all of them, but Osman had been quietly only a step or two behind. However, Semih Kadir could speak circles around some of the smartest people Dilay had ever met, had made his way quickly up the ranks thanks to his gift for twisting people around their own thoughts. If it came down to this, winning a popular vote, the Kadir family would take over the guild. That was why she hoped Judge Hanim's books might contain laws she did not already know. Something, anything she could leverage to keep Osman Altimur in line to take over the guild.

Behram leaned in to whisper something to his father.

Dilay turned her attention back to her book as Altimur Pasha stumbled through a clarification of his statement. But her gaze, as it had been doing all evening, slipped away from the page and to the very back of the hall, where Omar sat, flanked by six guards and three attendants. More of the palace's guard contingent surrounded the building outside.

The Sultan's seat was set back from the rest, and raised upon a hastily constructed platform above everyone else. Omar, despite looking every inch the Vali Ahad, did not seem to sit comfortably in the seat. It did not fit, him perched above and behind everyone, more ornament than participant or ruler. It did not fit the troubled, kind, smiling man she was coming to know.

But, there was this side of him too. The one she had seen at the tribunal, dressed as the Sultan he would be. Silver caftan and entari embroidered with blue and white, the colors of both the First House and the Sabri Sultanate. He wore a turban, though not one as audacious as his father's usual white and blue cloth with an unwieldy bejeweled pin in the front that bore the Sabri crest. His was only white, smaller, with a pinned sapphire in the front. And his face was cast of marble. Not the soft-spoken, shy man she had left grinning in the tower. Which was the more truthful? How many faces did he wear?

She had since convinced herself she had imagined all of the charge of that interaction. Her mind had been muddled by the heat of the tower and the drugging effect of her relief that she would neither be imprisoned nor hanged. She had gone on a flight of fancy. And said the most ludicrous things.

She closed the book, hugging it to her, pushing away the thoughts, again. None of that mattered. He had conscripted her to help him, not to wonder what kind of person he truly was. But how could she help him? Magic did not act without intention. That was an inarguable fact. So, she had to identify whatever deeply buried intention he had that was causing his power to attack like a snake every time someone touched him. If there was one.

Her greatest hurdle was that she did not know Veritor magic. It might be an exception to the rules that governed all other magic. That was difficult to believe. He had promised her access to the library. There might be books there. Or if they were hidden from him…would the Queen Sultana allow her to see them? Doubtful, considering her threats.

Maybe she could just talk to him. Dilay's fingers tightened on the book. That seemed more difficult than it would have a few days ago. Before he had begun to fluster her. But she could stay calm and reasonable in the face of men who would deny her accomplishments and abilities. She could do it for someone who was mildly attractive. Dilay sniffed and looked away from him and back to the tables.

Behram sat next to his father, one hand extended to fiddle with a coin against the table's surface. His gaze was fixed on her, his mouth set in something between irritation and determination. Dilay offered a little smile, which made him relax, and his gaze shifted from hers.

How much did he know about Omar's problems? And could he be objective enough about it to be useful to her? Objectivity had never been Behram's strength. Fire *felt*. They rarely worshiped at the altar of logic.

"There could be a balance between moving forward and honoring the things that have brought us this far," Osman said, not loudly, but with the quiet authority Dilay had always associated with him. There was potential in him to be a fair and honest guild leader, which was only partially true for his father. As for Behram…Dilay was unsure. Or was too tangled in their history to be able to make an accurate assessment. Her instinct warned her that he would not. But she did not want to do to him what so many had in his life, underestimate him. He had proved them all wrong. Perhaps he would settle her doubts during the mediation.

"I think," Behram said, calmly and with a congenial smile leveled at Osman, "if that were true you would not be fighting so hard to keep things exactly as they are."

A very brief shimmer of hope had opened in Dilay when Behram started to speak, but it shriveled.

"To keep those in the poorest positions of the guild exactly where they are. To ensure the same families stay fat and happy generation after generation, with no rewards for innovation or effort." Behram punctuated it with a disappointed twist of his mouth.

Those crowded at the edges of the hall clapped. A disturbing majority. Dilay closed her eyes against the sound. He spoke beautiful words. He had learned early to say what people wanted to hear, to say what his father wanted to hear, to avoid his father's anger. But he was viciously intelligent, and had honed that into a gift for manipulation. If there were not so much anger in him, so much fear, there was such potential there to be a great man. Could she talk to him? Convince him it was finally time to step out from beneath his father's looming shadow?

"*You do not hide very well,*" Omar's voice ghosted near her ear, as if he were standing next to her. Dilay opened her eyes, her gaze darting to the back of the room and the dais where he sat. His posture and position had not changed. Neither was he looking at her. He had said he had not voice cast at her before because he thought she would not appreciate a perfect stranger whispering in her ear. Which was, essentially, what a voice cast was. But he was no longer a stranger. And the sound of his voice made her skin prickle.

She ducked her head to hide the movement of her lips and spoke in the softest whisper she could manage, little more than shaping the words with her lips.

"Am I hiding?"

"Your thoughts. I can see each one on your face."

Dilay watched him, but from her position at the far end of the room, he did not appear to even move his lips. And did not, like most lesser air mages, cover his mouth as he spoke. Well.

"*I did not give you enough credit for finesse, that day in the sky room.*" Dilay cast a look around her to see if anyone had noticed her illicit spellcasting.

"*You were lucky I was in a benevolent mood that day.*" Even in the spelled whisper, she heard humor, teasing in his tone. And when she looked at him, she could see the smile threatening to crack his stone facade.

The tables erupted into chatter, and the onlookers began arguing amongst themselves, surging forward and blocking Dilay's view of Omar and the tables. She pressed her back harder to the wall to avoid being jostled.

A loud, sharp crack broke through the raised voices, then three more times. One of the judges, likely her father, rapping the floor with a staff. The arguments died down, and as the onlookers slunk back to the walls, Dilay's view was cleared so she could see all four judges on their feet.

"This is clearly going nowhere," Dilay's father announced. "Mediation will continue by tribunal. At the end of next small turn, bring forward all your grievances. All must be verifiable by witness outside the families involved." Her father paused, stiffening, then turned and bowed to Omar. "If that decision pleases you, Efendim."

Omar merely dipped his head in affirmation.

Osman let his head fall back to stare at the ceiling, frustration cutting a line down his brow. Behram appeared pleased, and he glanced to Dilay once, with a smile that disappeared quickly. Everyone at the table stood and bowed to each other. The onlookers shifted more toward the doors, only a few steps from where Dilay stood wedged in the corner.

Her father would be in a mood, ranting. She suspected their house would be full to the brim with tribunal judges by sunset. She had hoped to read at home, but now the library at the University might be a safer bet. Dilay slid her bag around to her front and tucked Judge Hanim's book into the front. Or perhaps…would Omar let her into the palace library? She hadn't exactly made any progress on helping him.

Red and brown filled her vision as she raised her head.

"Take a walk with me," Behram said. Dilay brushed her hair away from her face, and Behram tsked, reaching to swipe at her cheek with his fingers. "Always so disheveled."

Dilay narrowed her eyes at him and caught her sleeve in her fingers to wipe against her cheek. Chalk or ink. She was constantly smudging the stuff everywhere. "I was going to read."

"I have seen you read and walk. I will make certain you do not collide with anyone." He slung his arm through hers and tugged her through the doors into the main hall that passed by all the offices and smaller meeting rooms. They walked out into deepening light of late afternoon. Dilay had to make an effort not to turn and look for Omar. It felt wrong to leave without even waving goodbye. But it also felt wrong to think that a prince would care at all about whether she said farewell.

"Where are we going?" Dilay asked.

"Anywhere but here." Behram glanced over his shoulder as they passed through the twin walls of palace guards and onto the street. A group of five men, Behram's father in their midst, exited the hall. Behram turned abruptly, dragging her sideways and in between two other buildings as Semih Kadir looked around. Searching for Behram, she suspected. Dilay tried to manage herself so her dismay did not show. When was he going to stop running from the man?

He watched the progress of his father from around the corner of the building, ducking back when the group passed. Dilay pulled her arm free of his and gripped his arm.

"Behram—"

"No lectures, I haven't the patience today," he said without looking at her, his gaze trained unblinking on his father's back. "You have no idea what he has been like, this past quarter. All he speaks about is the guild this and the guild that."

Guilt chewed a hole in her chest. She had not been a very good friend. Too busy with her own path forward to do more than think of Behram in passing. This was good. She could spend some time with him and, if his mood was high, she could see if he had any ideas about Omar.

"Would you like to walk the Fire District gardens?" Dilay asked. Behram made a disdainful sound of dismissal. He found no peace in beauty. Dilay still was not certain what made Behram calm. Chaos, she thought. Or the organization of it. As children, he had found calm in their play. Chess. Hide and seek. Stones and trenches. As they had gotten older they'd examined whatever they were studying together. But now...

"*Where are you?*" Omar's voice shocked her into a little jump, and Behram glanced at her, giving her a once-over before turning his attention back to his father. She peeked around Behram's shoulder to look at the entrance to the guild hall. Omar had exited, and the judges had caught up to him. He turned, and she could tell they were speaking, but she could not see well because of Behram and the guards that surrounded Omar and the judges. She did not want to distract him from the conversation, nor did she want Behram to catch her spellcasting. She wasn't certain she wanted Behram to know that Omar was whispering to her.

"Why did the Sultan send him instead of attending?" Behram seethed. "Likely so it did not have to be him sitting up there like a statue and trying not to fall asleep."

Dilay stifled a giggle, and Behram looked at her sidelong, a smile crooking one corner of his mouth. "We can go to the market," he said. Dilay shrugged. If she let him decide what he wanted to do he might be more open to be questioned about Omar. He looked back to the guild hall, and his father turned and headed up the hill toward, presumably, his home. Behram took her hand in his and stepped out of the alley.

They were not far from the guild hall, and their emergence caught Omar's attention. He looked at them, and when her eyes met his, he started to smile, then schooled it. "I should greet him," Behram declared as he turned up the little hill to bow to Omar.

Dilay hesitated a heartbeat, enough time for Omar's gaze to drop to her hand, clutched in Behram's. He cut it away.

"Efendim," Behram said as Dilay pitched forward into a bow and twisted her hand free of his grip. Her cheeks were hot, and she flushed the feeling away with a slice of magic. She wished frantically she had hurried out of the hall ahead of everyone else. She could be safely tucked into the library by now instead of awkwardly stuck between Omar and Behram.

When Dilay straightened, she looked at her father. He wore an expression of annoyance and exhaustion, both of which he directed unequivocally at Behram.

"Ah, Judge Akar," Behram said, with antagonism in his voice. They had never liked each other. Semih Kadir was everything her father thought was wrong with the higher nobility, and he assumed all the same attributes in Behram. Despite Dilay explaining Behram's situation, her father had never held anything but dislike for him. Her mother tolerated him, in a worried sort of way. "What a pleasure to know you will be overseeing the mediation."

Her father's mustache twitched as he glowered harder. His fellow judges managed to at least appear much more neutral. Dilay cut her gaze sideways and up, to Omar. There were questions in his eyes, as he met her gaze. But she could not discern what they were about. Her and Behram? Behram and everyone else? The weather? She raised her brows at him.

"Your father was looking for you, young master," one of her father's companions said, pointing up the hill toward the Fire District.

"Yes," Behram said. "But I promised Instructor Akar a trip to the market."

Dilay managed a smile. Behram could make anything sound domineering. Omar's brows knitted then relaxed.

"Dilay," her father began, and she could see him mentally reaching for any excuse to deny her. It did not matter that she was twenty-four Turns old. When it came to Behram, he would treat her like she was five. But she wanted to be stuck at home with pontificating judges even less than she wanted to be strolling about with a fuming Behram.

"Vali Ahad Efendim," the words tumbled out, and she could not swallow them back once she had begun, "had you not expressed a desire to explore your city?" She couldn't move. As if she had been turned to stone, her muscles locked, her mouth went dry, and her palms turned clammy. Behram would be incensed.

Omar's marble mien faltered, then returned, and his gaze darted around the group of people, every one of them staring. Dilay chanced a look at her father, who appeared as if his eyes might boggle from his head.

Behram shifted. "Surely the Vali Ahad has more important—"

Omar laughed. A real, loud laugh, and the sound put everyone else on edge, but calmed Dilay immediately. She had not offended him, at least.

"I am needed at the palace, I'm afraid." He looked at her as he said it, and words like a breathy whisper caressed her ear. "*I will find you.*" Dilay's lips parted. How could he do that without her seeing his lips move? There were barely four steps between them.

She took an involuntary step, excitement bolting through her, then remembered all the eyes on her. Omar's mouth threatened a smile, but he looked away from her.

"Good day, gentlemen." He started to turn, then glanced at Dilay. "And you, Instructor Akar."

He left, his entourage of guards and attendants swarming around him, toward a carriage parked near the north side of the guild hall. Dilay cleared her throat and smiled wanly at her father, whose eyes had narrowed. No, she did not want to be anywhere near her home for several candlemarks at least.

Dilay turned abruptly and marched down the hill that led from the guild hall to the Grand Market, praying she did not trip on the cobbles and splay herself in the street in front of everyone.

Behram jogged to catch up. When they were out of sight of the guild hall he caught her upper arm and pulled her to a halt, spinning her to face him.

"Are you mad?"

"It just seemed polite," she said. "I doubt he likes being trapped in conversation with my father any more than I do."

Behram searched her face, transforming from angry to worried. "Just…be careful of him, Dilay." He flicked his gaze away and dropped his hand from her arm. "I know you have to help him but do not get too close. The way you do, with every poor lost soul. Promise me. Don't let him touch you."

"I know," she said, and touched his arm, squeezing. When he looked at her in surprise, she hesitated. She could not tell him exactly how she found out. Behram would not be sympathetic to her night-time teaching. "I know."

He nodded, then affected a smile. "Good. I have a sudden craving for honey candy. Be a good girl and buy me one."

Dilay rolled her eyes.

Sixteen

"**E**FFENDIM," Ruslan protested once more. Omar ignored the slight whine his steward's voice had taken on. Mazhar gave a martyred sigh from Omar's other side. Omar poked his head around the edge of the carriage to see the Morning Gate, watching the movement of people in and out. What he wouldn't give for another way out of the damn place. It was likely harder to leave the palace unnoticed than it was the Cliffs, and those were prisons.

Omar shoved his change of clothes into the carriage and Ruslan clambered onto the driver's seat with a pointed snort of indignation.

"I would just like to point out, again," Ruslan said, "that I am doing this under duress."

Mazhar ducked into the covered carriage and Omar followed, and immediately proceeded to change into the servant's clothes he had borrowed from Ruslan. Or commandeered.

"I was fine with this until it included me having to see your naked ass," Mazhar grumbled, tilting his head back against the wooden wall as the carriage lurched forward.

"You do not have to look," Omar snarled, sitting abruptly when the carriage turned and he lost his balance. He pulled on tan salvar and caftan and wrestled into the entari as they moved. They were stopped at the gate, as he had expected, and he quickly wound a worker's cloth wrap around his head to hide his shortened hair. Mazhar shifted forward and adjusted it with a click of his tongue as the curtain on the side of the carriage was yanked open.

The guard took a cursory look, which settled briefly on Mazhar, then he whipped the curtain back into place. They were accustomed to Mazhar leaving the palace.

"Who knew your frequent city visits would ever be anything but embarrassing," Omar said to Mazhar as Ruslan urged the pair of horses forward again and the carriage bounced over the cobbles. Mazhar shrugged. They had been aided by the tricky light of early evening, when the sun was gone, but its glow remained, muddying faces and colors. Omar touched the tiraz around his upper arms. They bore earth sigils, since they were Ruslan's. That was good. One more step removed from himself. His heart was beating too fast, but he felt like laughing.

"I really do not care for the idea of you alone in the city with some…" Mazhar pressed his lips together when Omar shot him a warning look. "…one not trained as a bodyguard."

"I will not be going anywhere dangerous."

"You are the Vali Ahad. You think there aren't people who would not love to get their hands on you to punish Father for some perceived wrong?" He knew. He knew everything about his plan was foolhardy and childish. He had never done anything remotely close to this. Mazhar caused enough trouble for the both of them.

"I am not helpless, Mazhar. You go all the time with only a few guards."

"But I have not spent the better part of my life with my face buried in books. Shut off from…" His words faded and he looked away from Omar, reaching to pull the curtain open to watch the scenery. "Just try not to come back covered in blood this time. All right?"

"I did not plan to." He certainly had no plans to visit that part of the city tonight. The first time he had gone he had three armed guards, not to mention his own magic. That Dilay spent every night there made his skin crawl. Though the two bruisers she employed as door guards had seemed…moderately capable. She said the man he had touched was all right.

Sometimes his magic struck and the victim was none the wiser. It was just him who felt it, who saw things no one else was meant to. That man…it was always painful, but Omar had already been angry and his magic lashed out like a cobra. He had seen a mother, a child, laughter, anger, sex and drunkenness, greed, violence, the children in the room from a stranger's perspective. It was only the space of a breath. Anything longer than the most fleeting of touches and he could see an entire lifetime. Omar forced his thoughts away.

"Are you sure?" Mazhar asked, more gently. He could always tell when Omar was lost to thinking about his power, about the things he saw.

He had been absolutely sure that morning, when he saw her, tucked into the corner of the guild hall, the book he'd given her held up like a shield between her and everything else. Her quick, unthinking words to him in the tower. About his voice and distracting her, the look in her eyes and flush on her cheeks. That had kept him awake nearly the entire night. He'd be willing to climb the cursed palace wall to get out and spend even a few moments with her, away from the palace. Away from the University, just her. And him, and maybe he could be a real person, and not a puppet, for a few marks.

It had been a miracle no one had noticed him staring at her like he had been spelled to. That she had not noticed. Or that he had managed to retain enough of the proceedings to appease his father's questions that afternoon.

But then there had been Behram. He was also staring at her. Omar had been troubled by it, and he was still unable to decide if that was because he was jealous, or because something in the way Behram stared at her made him uneasy. She had seemed unbothered. Unbothered enough to hold his hand in full view of the Wheel and every living person in the vicinity. What was between them?

Omar rubbed his hands over his face. His neck was beginning to ache and his temples throbbed. He could feel the rhythmic pulse of Ruslan's spell as he cast it at intervals to find Dilay and the antagonism of his steward's magic only made his head ache more. He would have to apologize to Dilay for the intrusion.

"Omar." Mazhar propped his arms on his knees. "Are you certain you want to do this?"

"Certain," he said. Mazhar raised an eyebrow.

"I did not realize you'd spent enough time with her to have it this bad already."

"I don't have anything. We have an agreement."

"Speaking of which, I haven't noticed that she's done much of anything except turn you addled." Mazhar slumped back against the bench.

"I am not addled," Omar snapped. "And she has hardly had time." Mazhar raised both eyebrows and cast his gaze sideways.

The carriage turned suddenly and halted. It rocked as Ruslan climbed down. Mazhar batted the curtain aside and Omar climbed out, into the very last bit of waning evening light. Ruslan had maneuvered the carriage onto an empty side street and angled the door toward the wall of a shop with no windows.

"Please let me come with you," Ruslan said, glancing down the street. They were near the Grand Market. The street where he had parked ran parallel and was occupied in the majority by tea shops and small businesses with houses above. The lamps along the street, each designed to tether a single mage orb, were being lit by a trio of Lightbringers, the nickname for Aval of the Fifth House, working their way down the street.

"Not one day in my life have I ever not been the Vali Ahad," Omar said. "Let me have a single evening. I will be cautious, and then I will be the Vali Ahad again."

Ruslan's expression crumpled and he nodded. "Down the street, perhaps three hundred paces. On the left. If you need anything…"

Omar smiled, waved at Mazhar, and strode away from them. For the first few steps he was disoriented, waiting to be surrounded by guards and attendants, crushed in, if not physically, mentally. But no one came. Then he feared he would be recognized immediately, but no one even looked at him. His lungs filled. His pace slowed. He did not have to rush, he was not running from one shelter to the other to avoid too many questions, too many eyes, too many requests and needs and expectations.

When he saw Dilay, he wanted to cast to her again. He had taken too much enjoyment from the intimacy of it. From her voice in his ear. He could almost imagine what it would be like for her to actually, physically whisper to him. The closeness of her, so her hair brushed his skin.

She was sitting on a cushion in front of a small, low table with her knees hugged up to her chest, a chessboard in front of her, her chin resting on her knees as she waited. Behram sat across from her, his back to Omar, clearly contemplating his next move. That it was so easy for them to be together, in any capacity, irritated Omar, but he shoved the feeling away.

Dilay's dark hair was braided and pulled up, spun around her head and pinned tidily in place. What would it be like to be able to touch her hair? To pull it loose with his hands like he had accidentally done with his magic in the classroom? His fingers twitched against his legs, making him realize he had halted in the middle of the street. He had to stop thinking about these things. Her gaze suddenly shifted, touching him then slipping away as she surveyed the street, as if looking for something. Omar wanted it to be him. But she did not even see him. Because all people saw of him were his shining clothes and his shorn hair and his guards and attendants… her gaze skated back and locked with his.

His heart thumped as a teasing smile appeared and disappeared on her mouth, then came back, and she ducked her chin behind her knees to hide it. He couldn't tell if she was pleased to see him or laughing at him, and he did not care. He settled into his skin in a way he rarely did, relaxing from head to toe as some invisible, unidentifiable tension loosed within him.

Dilay said something to Behram as he reached for a chess piece, and his hand stilled as he looked over his shoulder. She rose and walked up the street toward Omar. He glanced from her to Behram, who winked at him and turned back to the board, quickly moving several pieces to more advantageous positions.

"He's cheating," Omar said, when Dilay reached him. She smiled patiently.

"He always cheats. I can usually still beat him." Dilay folded her hands in front of her. "You have to take his soldiers before he sacrifices them all."

"I shall keep that in mind. I have never beat him at chess."

"Are you hungry? Behram has been whining for a candlemark about starving to death, but I…" She glanced to Behram, then up to Omar, her gaze darting over his face then away. He wanted her to say it, to say that she had been waiting for him. He wanted her to say it so badly that his chest ached with it. "I thought you might be hungry too, but I suppose that's silly. Surely they would not allow the pr—" She clenched her teeth together.

"I am hungry," he said. He would have told her the same even if he were stuffed to illness.

She smiled sheepishly and turned away from him to lead him to Behram. Behram hooked an elbow over one raised knee and regarded Omar from head to toe, a taunting smile twitching on his mouth.

"You look ridiculous." He smiled fully. Omar laughed. He felt ridiculous. He dropped to his backside beside their table.

"No, no," Dilay admonished. "We are going to the market. I am starving."

"You said—" Behram started, but she stared at him icily. He cast Omar a feigned look of suffering and stood, and Omar followed. Dilay led them down the street, and around a corner that opened into the sprawling chaos of the Grand Market. At this time of evening most of the vendors who remained open sold food or drink. Dilay walked with purpose, not even stopping to gawk at all the little food stands, with their cookfires and mouthwatering smells. Omar lingered at a few, watching people as they ordered. Everything from modest mezze plates with hummus and pita to huge, boat-shaped pide with ground meat and vegetables.

Dilay stopped at one of the smallest stands, just a man with a little flag held in place with sandbags and a small metal brazier with bright coals. Sticks were propped in a pyramid over the coals, each skewering three to four kofta.

"You should not be the one paying," Behram said as Dilay reached into a pocket. He looked sideways at Omar, who cringed. Behram laughed. "Of course you would not think of something practical, like money."

Dilay paid, and the man, short and squat and balding, retrieved three sticks from the fire. Dilay distributed them between the three of them. "Next time," she murmured as she handed Omar his. Her gaze flicked too briefly to his then away and he stifled a smile. The kofta, ground lamb mixed with herbs and spices and shaped into logs that would stay on the skewers, was singed on the outside so it had a crust when he bit into it.

He had only ever had it simmered in tomato sauce, never cooked over coals and eaten too hot while watching a bright parade of people and activities before him. This was a much better way to enjoy it.

Dilay stood between him and Behram, shorter than them both but somehow taking up all the space around him, his thoughts and every sensation. He breathed around a burning bite of what he thought might be the best thing he had ever eaten, as she glanced up at him and smiled playfully.

"Perhaps we should have bought you a silk napkin," she teased. Behram peered around her to see as Omar hastily wiped dripped grease off his fingers on Ruslan's borrowed clothes. There was another apology he owed.

"I did not think he was so base as to ever need anything like a napkin," Behram added. Omar ignored their teasing as he finished the kofta, and glanced longingly behind him toward the stand as more people crowded to buy their own.

"They do not make them like this..." He jerked his head toward the palace, where it perched on the cliffs overlooking Narfour.

"Good?" Dilay asked as she picked lingering bits from her skewer. Omar nodded, trying not to stare as her fingers pressed the scavenged bits to her mouth. "I thought we could walk the pier, and come back up through the lower Air District. Do you have a time limit?" She looked up at him, and he was certain every intimate thing that had gone through his head in the preceding moment showed like lamps on his face. He nodded mutely.

"I hate the pier," Behram groused.

It was too close to the water for him. But it was not a fire mage's natural dislike of its opposing element that fueled Behram's discontent. Omar was not privy to the entire story, but he did know that Behram had, at some point in his childhood, had a harrowing experience with water. They joked about it, because that seemed more agreeable to Behram than actually speaking of it. Perhaps Dilay knew.

"Was that enough?" Dilay looked up at Omar again. "Do you want to try something else?"

"All of it?" he suggested.

Dilay laughed. "If Behram is feeling generous, we could share some pide."

"Only if you get it without eggs." Behram fished inside his entari and withdrew a small pouch.

"Absolutely not." Dilay snatched the bag and stomped away. Behram smiled to himself.

"It's better with eggs," he said. Omar looked at him and Behram shrugged. "She is more fun when she's irritated."

"Why does she like you?" Omar said caustically. Behram's smile shrank and he looked away, into the darkening market.

"You know me well, my friend, but she knows me better. Has known me at my worst, and my best, and that is a rare thing, is it not?" he said. "That is Dilay's special magic. She can see the potential in anything. Even the most broken and crumbling of objects. And people." He cast Omar a weighted look before turning it to search for Dilay.

Omar's mood sank. He was broken, wasn't he? Behram knew it. Dilay did too, now. Perhaps that was what he saw in her face when she looked at him. A tinkerer's interest. Something she could fix. The weighty silence that took up residence where Dilay had been was almost too much. Omar fought a sudden, overwhelming desire to run straight back to the palace.

"Here we are," Dilay said as she appeared between them, the oval pide balanced on her hands. Behram grumbled at what was clearly extra eggs, baked onto the surface, one for each of them. He helped her tear the bread, bubbling with cheese and herbs, into thirds, their hands brushing and tangling as he did. It was so easy for everyone else. Touch wasn't something they had to think about. It could be absolutely meaningless to them. But Omar was unable to do even that. Help. Behram carefully deposited a portion into Omar's hand.

"This way," Dilay said, her cheerful voice counterpoint to Omar's steadily blackening mood. The bread was delicious, but he could not taste it the way he had the kofta. Not with the same ease and delight. This had been a foolish idea. More excited child than logical man making the decision.

The pier was darker than the market, fewer lamps and orbs. The market had felt bright and happy. Busy. The pier was different. A definite sense of caution permeated the place. The lack of orbs and lamps made each dark alley feel sinister, and Omar couldn't see faces until people were too close. Dilay led them on a side street that put a row of buildings between them and the water. Omar could still see the soaring masts and furrowed sails of many of the merchant ships, paused in unloading their cargo for the night. The docks were busy, shouts and laughter and the general cacophony of work loud enough to stymy any conversation between them.

Dilay made a point of identifying the rows of squat, ramshackle houses that served as homes for most of the workers. Many were little more than slapped-together structures, though some were obviously older, built of bricks and stone. Families ate their dinners seated in front of their homes, looking up with vague interest as the three of them passed. Many of those families greeted Dilay with warmth.

The food in his stomach felt heavy when he saw how thin some of the children were. How threadbare their clothes were. He wiped his still grease-stained fingers against his clothes again, disgust at himself coiling around his simmering discontent.

It was so easy to sit up in the palace and do the things his father told him and feel like he was reaching for something, achieving something. Becoming someone worthy of anything. But what good was he actually doing?

Their path curved through the district and began climbing the hill that led from the pier, through the Earth District and lower Air District. He thought Dilay would lead them straight up the hill, but she cut left suddenly, as if she meant to head toward the water.

Instead she led them to the back of a tall, narrow building and began climbing the stairs that zigzagged up the back of it. Behram voiced protests the entire way, with Dilay hushing him twice before they reached the roof. It was tiled, as opposed to most Omar had seen in the area, which were either the curved kind of the long houses, or thatched. Dilay climbed the peak and over the other side, then sat abruptly.

"I can never get Behram to go to the roof with me," Omar said as he settled beside Dilay.

"The palace is higher than this," she suggested.

"I am *right* here." Behram slipped a little and fell more than sat on Dilay's other side, which made both Omar and Dilay snicker.

"Well, Vali Ahad"—Dilay reclined back, staring out over a beautiful view of the ocean and the night sky—"what do you think of your city?"

"That is complicated, isn't it?" he answered. She tipped her head to look at him and offered an apologetic smile.

"It should be."

"For Wheel's sake, Dilay, don't drown the man in your political nonsense." Behram tugged at his entari, straightening his clothes beneath him. She bent sideways to bump into Behram in admonishment. That jealous ache started in Omar's belly again. Just casual touch. It didn't mean anything. It shouldn't have to be a threat, frightening.

"I thought we could try something, for your magic," Dilay announced. She scooted back a bit and turned to face Omar, folding her legs in front of her. Behram moved, haltingly, casting irritated glances down the slope of the roof, to sit below and between the two of them. "I think you have to retrain your magic." She wiggled her fingers in his direction. Omar grit his teeth. "When you take someone's confession, do you cast your magic, or simply let it happen?"

"I cast it. Otherwise…" Otherwise it would kill someone, and him, to open the floodgates of his magic unhindered.

She nodded. "If you can turn it on, you can turn it off. You just don't want to."

He recoiled. "Of course I want to," he said, too sharply. She pressed her lips together.

"No"—she pointed a finger at him—"you don't."

Omar looked away from the ferocity in her eyes and met Behram's stare. Behram dropped his gaze. Omar did not wish to speak about any of this in front of him. It was too much. Too hard.

"All right," Dilay soothed. "Just try this." She touched her eyelids. "Close your eyes and breathe."

He complied. After ten breaths, when the urge to open his eyes had become consuming, she said, "Now, cast your Veritor magic."

His shoulders tensed. He opened his eyes, and Dilay nodded once, as encouragement and order. Omar exhaled and allowed his magic free of his tenuous grip on it. His fingers clenched against his folded legs, clawing against his knees. His eyes closed again.

"Just hold it," she said, using the same tone he'd heard teachers use on the youngest of new mages who were both terrified of and excited about their newfound power. "Hold it to my count." Dilay counted, breathing audibly between each number, until Omar found his pace by her. "When you disconnect, do you silence your magic, or stop touching the person?"

"I take my hands away," he mumbled, "and the magic ebbs." That was not how it was supposed to be. But his uncle had died before he had a chance to teach Omar anything at all.

"Turn it off," she ordered, "and pay attention to the way it feels. Everywhere. In your skin, your breath. In your bones. We will repeat this until you can identify the switch."

Behram and Dilay's silence while he struggled was distracting and infuriating, and he finally silenced all his magic with all the force of closing a portcullis. But it was not what she had meant, and he knew it. When he opened his eyes to look at her, she had a frustratingly pleased smile on her face. But there was also pity.

Omar looked at Behram instead. His friend had turned his attention to the sky and begun to fidget with one of his rings.

"It is going to rain," he said in an uncharacteristically quiet voice. "We should go." The temperature had dropped, cooling the sweat on Omar's skin.

"I want to try one more time. Meet us below, all right?" She smiled at Behram in a way she had never smiled at Omar. Like there were hundreds of stories between them that tied to this moment and situation. That jealous gnawing, wishing he shared as much history as they did, trailed through his body. Behram raised an eyebrow as he looked to Omar and back to Dilay.

"Do not touch her," Behram said. He had never said anything like that to Omar—alluded nearly directly to Omar's failings.

"Behram," Dilay scolded.

"Of course not," Omar said, his voice lacking any authority at all. Behram scaled the roof, almost on hands and knees, and disappeared down the other side toward the stairs. Dilay turned her attention back to Omar.

"He doesn't mean anything…"

Omar laughed grimly. "Oh, he does. But I know it is because he cares about you. That is a rare thing. I don't think I can name anything else Behram cares about."

"You." Dilay smiled as she tucked a bit of loose hair behind her ear. "He laughs with you." Wheel, why did that small, innocuous gesture make his thoughts veer madly in useless directions? She lowered her hands to her knees once more. "Again, please," she said.

"I might be too tired for this," he said.

"Of course you are," Dilay said, gently. "And that is exactly when you most need control. Again, Vali Ahad."

He made a face of disapproval. "Omar."

"After you do it again." She smiled. Or grinned. Whatever name he would put to it, it was teasing. Alluring. There were words in that smile he did not believe she would ever say out loud, but his body heard them, and that new distraction made forcing his eyes closed and trying to concentrate all the more impossible.

"It is like any other spell," Dilay said, just above a whisper. "Yours to command."

The light of his magic, awake and dancing on his skin and behind his eyelids, flickered and pulsed like a dying mage orb as he tried to wrestle it under control. He muttered a curse.

"You can, Omar. I know you can." Conviction. She did believe it, he could hear it in her voice. There was no admonition there, no disappointment, or disgust. No boredom like the ones who had given up on him. She simply knew he could.

And so he did.

He huffed, his eyes squeezed harder shut, and his magic swirled away under his mental control. Dilay exclaimed in triumph. Omar relaxed, but did not open his eyes, panting as if he had sprinted up the murderous hill of the palace road.

It was too hard. But he'd managed it. He opened his eyes.

"I like it when you call me by name," he said, his voice rough in his own ears. "You are the only person outside my family who does so."

Her ease vanished, replaced with tension he did not care for. He hadn't meant to make her uncomfortable or overstep.

"Do you want to try again?" She lowered her gaze. He wanted to kiss her. That was what that fire sizzling through every limb was. He wanted to kiss her in thanks and in triumph, or at the very least hug her, and he could do nothing but sit there like a fool.

"The rain scared off our fire mage"—he smiled a little—"so it must be close."

The smell in the air had taken on the wet, verdant scent that warned of a storm. He had wanted her alone, all day. Now he had her and he had to give it up. But Behram was waiting, and he couldn't very well ask her to sit in the rain with him. He looked up at the sky, the stars slowly disappearing behind a curtain of clouds.

"Why does Behram hate the water so much?" He dropped his gaze back to hers. Dilay scrunched her face and looked down. Had she been looking at him?

"His father." She scratched at one of the clay tiles with her fingernail. "He thought he could force Behram's fire to come."

It was enough explanation to paint the beginnings of the story. Sometimes an element's opposition on the Wheel could frenzy magic. As could imminent death.

"He…" Dilay's voice quavered and Omar regretted asking as her eyes glazed with tears. "…he held him under the water"—she took a breath—"over and over again. Until he passed out." She swiped at her eyes. "Forgive me."

She tried to smile and Omar ached. He wanted to hold her, to wipe the tear that had escaped down her cheek. And he wanted to hug his friend. To tell him he was worth so much more than his usefulness to his father.

And he wanted to hold Semih Kadir under the water until his breath didn't come either.

"I didn't see him for turns after that. And he was…different. It took me an entire Great Turn to get anything close to the truth out of him, and only in little pieces."

Omar pressed his palms to his eyes. It burned behind his lids, a vicious stinging, and his head began to ache. What use was he? All these people around him suffering, and him, pampered and sheltered and useless. Mad because his father was not what he wanted him to be.

"Oh." Dilay scooted closer. He heard the rustle of her clothes and sensed the heat of her. He dropped his hands away from his face in panic, but she was leaning in to peer up at him with excitement in her eyes. "You must tell me how you voice cast without moving your lips."

She was offering him a path away from the emotions that overwhelmed him, and he was grateful and sad for it. Who else could he talk to about any of it? But she was so close. Unbearable, in the best of ways. She was so beautiful, lit by starlight and curiosity.

"Practice," he croaked.

Dilay flicked an imaginary bit of dirt at him in annoyance and leaned away again. "I would hit you if I could, you deserve it," she declared. He'd take it. Anything.

"Everyone is always looking at me…I just learned. You do it down here." He touched two fingers where his jaw met his throat. He and Mazhar could both do it. Had learned so they could make commentary during the endless meetings and dinners and numbing court celebrations.

"You can teach me? And also how you knew I had cast a listening spell on Master Akdari at the University."

He squinted. "That is part of my Veritor power, I think. It works best with First House magic, there is a resonance. It sounds the same as the mage it comes from." Her magic was…light and calm. Less piercing than other air mages he knew.

"I…resonate?"

He smiled. "It is difficult to explain. Do you know how often one can look at someone's handwriting and recognize it, or the work of a craftsman, but not necessarily say why you know it belongs to them? It is the same. I just knew when I stood near you that it had been your spell." It had sent shivers down his arms.

"Oh," she said, disappointed. A sharp, bright point hit Omar's cheek. The rain. They both looked up. "How are you getting back to the palace?"

"I'll summon Ruslan when I am ready." Could he tell her he wasn't ready? He would stay up all night, just walking, sitting, anything just to continue talking to her.

Dilay raised an eyebrow as she looked at him. "Is that poor man just sitting somewhere, waiting on you?"

Omar winced at the assault of guilt. "I imagine he has been escorting Mazhar to every teahouse in Narfour." He laid his arms in his lap and looked out over the sea, which was growing hazy as the mist and storm rolled in. "Would you ever let me watch you teach the children?" he asked quietly.

"Oh," Dilay said. She sounded reluctant. He couldn't blame her. How could he possibly do that without disrupting everything? Omar started to rescind the request, but she nodded. "I would like that," she said. "I teach every day of the turn except Sixth day."

Destruction's day. In the Old Sultanate a day of rest, the end of the small turn and beginning of the next. Most of Tamar did not honor it now. Today was Sixth day.

More drops splattered his clothes.

"Tomorrow," he said. Dilay nodded, staring at him with wide eyes.

"We should go," she said, and he hoped he did not imagine the reluctance in her voice.

"Yes, or Behram will burn this building down beneath us."

She laughed as she turned to ascend the peak of the roof and down the other side. Omar followed, and when he hopped off the last step, Behram had a fiery glower waiting for them.

"Well?"

"Things take time, Behram. You know that." Whatever look she gave him Omar could not see because her back was to him. But Behram's demeanor changed and his mood lightened.

"Come along, little prince. Best to deliver you back to the palace before you turn into a fig tree."

Omar rolled his eyes at the reference to an old children's tale. "Thank you, Instructor Akar."

She turned, looking up at him with a smile. "Practice," she said. "I will test you when I see you again."

SEVENTEEN

"ALL I'M SAYING IS"—SEDA dropped her bundle of sticks on the floor of the warehouse—"I would suffer through those mediations just to stare at Osman." She tsked. "Those eyes."

"What about his eyes?" Dilay asked. She was glad that Seda was buzzing with gossip from the guild mediation. It helped keep Dilay's bubbling nervousness from turning her into a wreck. What was she going to do with Omar? How was she going to keep the children from touching him? At least she had convinced Zeki and Turgay to take the evening off. Her First day classes were far less attended than any other day, due to the rhythms of the city.

Seda glowered at her. "You are so oblivious. They're *gold*."

"They are *not* gold." Dilay laughed. Pale, washed-out brown, like jasper. But Seda was prone to exaggerating everything about attractive men, and she had a particular soft spot for Osman. He was sweet. And his pale eyes were striking with his dark hair and beard, Dilay could give him that. Unusual. But unusual eyes were not enough to hold her interest.

In truth, outside of Behram and their complicated friendship, she had only had one romantic relationship, and it had been brief and frivolous. She had too much in her heart that she wanted to accomplish.

Those accomplishments were too important, took up too much space, to allow room for much romantic emotion. Besides, Fifth House was much better known for its devotion to love and passion. First House was the realm of logic and plans.

"Perhaps you're too preoccupied with someone else's eyes?" Seda wheedled. Dilay did not look at her friend, who made a sound of discovery that made Dilay wince. Was she that obvious?

A stuttered knock issued from the front door of the warehouse. Seda paused in arranging her sticks into piles, and turned to the door, bewildered. Dilay had no time to move before it opened.

First Ruslan, dressed very plainly, then Omar, entered.

"Fire and water," Seda gasped, dropping the sticks she was holding and scrambling to her feet.

"No," Dilay said, "it's all right. I…" She winced. "I invited him."

"You what?" Seda squeaked, then looked at the two men with wide eyes. She started to bow, stopped mid-movement to shoot Dilay a vulpine grin, then ducked her head. Dilay also bowed, refusing to meet Seda's pointed stare.

"You invited him to your illegal school?" Seda whisper-hissed. "Did you crack your skull on a bookcase?"

Dilay scrunched her face at Seda.

"Please," Omar said. When Dilay rose and looked at him his hands were clasped behind his back, his demeanor tense and uncomfortable. "I admire Instructor Akar's teaching, and I asked to see more of it."

"Her teaching, is it?" Seda purred. Dilay elbowed her, banishing the embarrassed heat in her skin with a thread of magic.

"He already knew about the school," Dilay said, cutting a quick look at Omar to see if he had heard Seda's remark. If he had it did not show on his face. When Seda glanced at her in surprise, then understanding, Dilay smiled sheepishly. Seda made a thoughtful sound as she went back to her task. Ruslan watched her with newly narrowed focus, wary.

Omar crossed toward Dilay, the rotted floorboards creaking and cracking as he came. Even in his drab attire he stood out. Did not belong.

"I thought you might observe from over there, if you wish," Dilay spoke quickly as he approached, pointing toward the back door. "You'll be well out of the way."

His face was too serious, like the stranger she had seen that first time at the tribunal. How could someone be so different from place to place? He wore similar clothes to those he had worn on their excursion the day before, brown and tan, but without any tiraz at all to mark his magic. His head was wrapped like a worker's, with more brown and tan cloth. Dilay could just catch sight of Seda, kneeling on the floor absently dropping sticks into piles, unabashedly watching Omar and her. There was no hiding attraction from Seda. The woman could sniff it out at eighty paces.

"Aren't you going to ask me if I practiced?" He smiled then, slowly, a smile that acknowledged all the secrets held between them. Seda had been teasing, but also correct. It was not that Dilay didn't get swoony over striking eyes, she decided, but that warm red-brown like cinnamon in a stern, shy face, appealed to her leagues more than pale gold and all the charm in the world.

"Did you practice, Vali Ahad?" she asked. His hands remained clasped behind his back, his posture stiff. He tilted his head to one side in answer. "I am afraid you'll have to wait until I am through with this class to assess your progress."

"Yes, Instructor Akar," he said.

The door opened at the front of the warehouse, and a gaggle of children poured through, laughing and chatting, which stopped abruptly when they saw Omar and Ruslan. She could not tell if they recognized him. They had never had anyone watch their class before, except a curious parent or two. But strangers in this part of the city were always met with suspicion.

Dilay stepped away from Omar and gestured the children in. "Is that how you treat elders? You gawk?" she asked. They all bowed, eyes still round, bodies tense. Dilay urged Omar to the back corner with a shooing motion, then herded the children to their customary places on the floor. "It's all right. We simply have guests observing today. I want everyone on their best behavior, and we'll do practical exercises so they can see how well you're doing."

They divided into their groups obediently, though gazes roved repeatedly to both men, and whispers filled the warehouse. It was an odd change from the usual rowdy conversation and horseplay that heralded the start of class. Dilay could sympathize with their inattentiveness. She was distracted too, constantly having to remind herself not to look at him.

Ruslan seemed intent on keeping Seda under watch, until Dilay set about putting the young Fourth House students to their tasks. She saw his head turn several times to look, craning to see over the group of children around Seda. Finally he stepped around them and wandered over, hesitantly. Dilay waved him closer. She had never had an earth mage to use as example for them.

"This is Master Ruslan. He is a Deval," she said. Belma sat up straighter, gripping her twin braids in her hands.

"How many sigils do you know?" Her eyes narrowed.

"Hundreds," he replied. Her eyes went round and she scooted closer.

"Please," Dilay said in invitation when he looked at her askance. He sat on the edge of the floorboards she had broken away and leaned forward to begin scratching in the dirt. The students gathered around him, rapt, if only because he was novel. But more likely because a mage was always in better hands with their own House than with any other. She turned her head to smile at Omar. He was crouched down, speaking with one of her youngest students, a void. Dilay sprang to her feet. The motion attracted his attention, but he gave his head a little shake. She did not know how Omar felt about voids, but many looked upon the magicless with superstition and prejudice.

Dilay could not hear them, because he was speaking quietly to her. He sat abruptly, folding his legs in front of him and drawing something in the dirt near the door. The little girl, Toulin, sat too. She repeated his gestures, and he nodded, saying something that made her smile at him.

"I see why you did not wish to tell your father," Seda said in her ear.

Dilay turned to her friend, who wiggled her brows. "I don't know what you think is happening here—"

"Yes you do," Seda tsked, but Dilay continued.

"He saw the school that day I made you leave. He knew what I was doing, but he did not turn me in to his father. Then, he asked if he could observe. I thought seeing the children might increase his sympathy."

"I recognize one of your strays when I see one, Dilay, you aren't fooling anyone. And this one keeps making eyes at you."

"He does not, and he is not a stray. We have an agreement," Dilay protested. It did not sound like much of an argument, when she said it out loud. Seda raised both her brows, still looking at Omar instead of Dilay.

"I see," Seda said. "Helping him with a paper, was it?"

Dilay closed her eyes briefly before she glanced at him. He had his back to them, drawing the Wheel in the dirt for Toulin, and the sigils for each House, oblivious to their conversation.

"He is the future Sultan of Tamar. A Sabri. A tyrant, your father would say. Is this a good idea?"

"Yes, just look at him," Dilay said, "terrible."

Toulin had swept away his drawing of the Wheel and replaced it with a game of jumping stones. He carefully picked up bits of rock and debris to use as pieces.

"I didn't say he was," Seda said. "I am worried about you though. There is not a single person in Tamar who would be pleased to see you two…working together."

Dilay could not argue. The Sabri Sultanate had done very little besides widen the gap between the poor and the rich, though there were some notable exceptions. They had abolished slavery. Created a guild system that allowed advancement to even its poorest members. But it had also encouraged arranged marriages among nobles to maintain stronger magic within the bloodlines of the rich. Encouraged divides in the classes that had not been so broad during the Old Sultanate. Anyone who knew Dilay would think she was pandering, and any noble would think Omar was slumming.

"We are just friends," Dilay whispered, before she turned from her friend and attended the water mages.

"That's what you said about Behram too," Seda chided as she stepped back to her fire mage charges.

When Dilay announced the class over, and the children said their goodbyes, their bows to Ruslan and Omar were more enthusiastic this time. Ruslan walked Belma to the door, and she chatted excitedly the entire way. Omar came to Dilay's side.

"I did not realize you taught voids as well."

"I teach anyone who wishes to learn," she replied warily.

"But what can they learn in a class about magic?"

"Have you ever considered what it might be like for them? Not only born into a society where almost everyone else is capable of something you are not, but to be assumed too inferior for even the basest of educations?" Dilay clucked her tongue.

He was silent for the remainder of the time it took the students to file out. Toulin stopped in the doorway to wave an enthusiastic goodbye, which he returned. His smile disappeared when Seda gathered up her things and came to stand in front of them, staring at Omar.

"If you harm any of these children or their families, I will crisp you like fish skin," she said. Dilay made a sound of protest.

Omar clasped his hands behind his back. "That is unlikely," he said in a friendly tone, "but I appreciate your concern. No one here is in danger from me."

Seda gave Dilay a loaded glance, then marched away and out the door.

"You dare to cast spells on a prince, and she dares to threaten one. What a pair you make," Omar said.

"She didn't mean it." Dilay attempted to sound believable. He chuckled, looking at her from the corners of his eyes.

"No? She was very convincing."

Dilay clicked her tongue as she retrieved her bag from where she had propped it near her makeshift podium.

"May I escort you home?"

Dilay straightened, slinging the bag over her shoulder. The offer made her fluttery. "Escort me? You are more in danger in this part of the city than I am," she said, trying to hide her nervousness with a taunting smile.

"Perhaps you could indulge my ego," he replied.

"I think you have plenty of people to indulge your ego," Dilay teased. "Any woman in Narfour would be happy to let you escort her, Vali Ahad." But she did not care for that idea. It rankled more than it should have, made her mood take a sudden dip. At least he asked her. Behram never asked, he just invited himself along.

"For reasons that should be obvious to you, I have never asked any woman if I could escort her."

"Because you never have to ask?" Dilay said over her shoulder as she headed for the back door. Omar followed, Ruslan a few paces behind.

"Guess again." Omar fell in beside her, hands clasped at his back. The darkness of the back alley hid details from her, but she could hear play in his tone.

"Hmm. Because none of them dress in a manner that will not clash with the eye-searing silver of the Sabri palace?"

He snort-laughed. "Silver and white are conveniently easy to coordinate with," he said sternly.

"Then I can only imagine you are as bored by nobles as I am." Dilay didn't need to say the reason. They both knew escorting someone you could not touch was difficult. Especially if you also could not tell them the reason you wouldn't touch them.

"You are a noble," he said. They turned up the hill away from the warehouse area of the Earth District and toward the homes.

"Barely," Dilay said.

"You think very little of the nobility," he said.

"Mmm," Dilay agreed, quietly. She glanced at him sidelong, concerned she might have overstepped, but also to keep her focus on the uneven, broken cobbles.

"Except Behram." Omar's voice held too much neutrality. Dilay made a face.

"We have been friends since childhood."

"Only friends?" He cleared his throat, and when she glanced at him again he was staring resolutely at the street.

"Friends," Dilay said firmly. "Did he say something different?"

"No. You just seemed particularly close."

"We are. Close friends." Close, complicated friends. Omar stopped abruptly and turned. Dilay nearly tripped trying to manage the same.

"I will meet you at the carriage," he said, into the darkness behind them. Ruslan stepped into the pale light of the mage orb that hung listlessly in its holder above them.

"I'm certain you won't listen to my protests," Ruslan said, tiredly.

"No," Omar said. Ruslan pressed his lips together, cast Dilay a look that said *he's your problem now*, and strode past them. Dilay turned to watch him go, afraid he might be lost in the unfamiliar area, but he took an appropriate left turn ahead of them.

"No need to worry about him," Omar said. "Ruslan is incapable of getting lost. I tried constantly when I was younger."

"We should hurry, another storm is coming," Dilay said. "Do princes melt if they get wet?"

"Probably," Omar said. "I wouldn't know."

"What? You've never been wet?" She laughed in surprise. He'd bathed, surely.

"I have never stood in the rain. Unseemly, you know." He looked up into the sky, the stars blotted by billowing grey clouds on an inky sky.

"I do not wish to pity you, but you make it very difficult." Dilay was feigning annoyance. He gave a wry smile, dropping his chin and meeting her gaze.

"I suppose I'll take what I can get. Though I would prefer awe or adoration."

Dilay made a sound of disdain, though her heart beat a bit faster. Did he know? Was he mocking her? Omar did not strike her as someone who took pleasure in mocking others.

"From a lowborn noble? Whatever would you need that for?"

His shoulders hunched a fraction toward his ears then relaxed and he looked at the ground as they walked. "I thought it was obvious."

"What?"

His eyes crinkled at the edges, something between a grimace and a smile. "Because I like you, Dilay Akar."

"Oh." She looked down as well. Somewhere, Seda's ears had certainly pricked up. Numbness spread from her chest outward. An odd reaction to the thrill the words had sent through her. Behind her, a sound like rushing wind caught her attention. Dilay looked at the wall of rain washing up behind them. "Run!" She laughed and broke into a sprint. That was probably punishable, letting the Vali Ahad get caught in a spring rainstorm.

She glanced twice to make sure he was following, leading him out of the Earth District and to the north end of the Air. The rain caught them as she reached her street, and she bolted for her house. They went around the back and burst into the kitchen, which was dark but for a nearly extinguished mage orb floating in the common room. Dilay lit an oil lamp in the kitchen. A neighbor would replenish the orb in the morning, they did not need much light anyway.

"Your family?" Omar asked, trying to look into the main living area from where he stood, not soaking but not exactly dry either.

"A baby was born this turn, one of my father's colleagues," Dilay said. Half the neighborhood would be at their house until the lamps burned down, cooking, cleaning, helping. And of course, celebrating. He pulled off the cloth that wrapped his head and looked curiously around, obviously more relaxed. Dilay turned her back on him and stood on tiptoe to reach the shelf where her mother stored towels and rags and pulled down the biggest she could find. "Here."

He smiled thanks and used the towel to dry his neck and face. They had only been caught by the very edge of the rain, so were only damp.

A familiar laugh, muffled, but dangerously close, sounded outside.

"They're back," Dilay said, dropping her voice. "My parents. Quickly." She snatched up the cloth he had dropped on the table then darted out of the kitchen and across the common room toward her own room. When she shoved her door open she turned to make certain he was behind her, and he almost trampled her. He turned sideways at the last moment, slipping in past her. Dilay swung the door shut, leaving it open just a crack so she could watch the front. It opened, revealing that she was correct, it was her parents. Her mother shook her hands, spraying water from her wet sleeves, and patted at her soaked hair with another laugh.

Dilay eased her door closed the rest of the way and pressed her ear against the wood to listen.

She didn't dare light her lamp. If her parents thought she was sleeping they would leave her be, but a light in her room was license for them to check on her. She could cast a listening spell to hear their conversation more clearly. But she knew the rhythms of their speech by heart, and they sounded happy, undisturbed, for now. Casting a spell was unnecessary, and they might sense it anyway. Then she would have to explain why she was casting spells on them. And they would discover that she was not only hiding a man in her bedroom, she was hiding the next Sultan. Her throat was dry, and her body wound too tightly.

Omar felt too big, and loud, and obvious. She could hear him breathing, feel the heat of him at her back, or imagined she could. At least she had a bedroom to hide him in. Seda slept on a mat on the floor with her siblings.

Dilay turned, carefully, afraid she might bump him, but he was against the far wall, where the single, small window was. Just enough light filtered under her door for her to make out his form, three paces away. Her fingers dug into the balled fabric of cloth for his head, which she still clutched. The silence between her and him, with the quiet murmur of her parents' voices in the other room, was necessary, but felt oppressive.

He seemed to agree, because after a moment, he came forward. "I am a prince," he whispered, with magic dropping it even lower than was normally possible, "why am I hiding in this closet? I am allowed to be anywhere I want."

She almost laughed, but his nearness stifled her humor, as did the thought of having him burst out of her room while her parents were sitting just on the other side of the door.

"This is not a closet, it's my bedroom. And"—she paused when his breath hitched and her own did something similar. Dear spinning Wheel, he was in her bedroom. Heat stormed up her body. She could not remember being more embarrassed in all her life. "I apologize, I didn't know what else to do. If my father found you here..." she stammered, "...you know not everyone agrees with your father and his tactics."

He shifted, raising his arms to press them against the door above her head. Dilay forgot how to breathe. Her heart bolted like a loosed horse, thundering in her ribs and her ears, and she was stone and heat and nothing else. His body was so close that the balled fabric felt like the only thing separating them, and every tiny movement he made pressed it against her belly. He dipped his chin, and whispered, so his exhalation danced over her skin. "Do you?"

Dilay's eyes slid closed in agreement with the shiver that coursed her skin. She had to think, hard, to understand what he was asking.

"You know the answer to that. You found my school."

What a stupid, silly thing to feel. She was a mouse longing for a soaring eagle.

"I did," he murmured. "I wanted to find someone who could help me. And instead I found a criminal, and someone who makes everything so much worse."

"Worse?" She turned her head to say it, so her cheek was parallel to his and the question sent her breath over his skin. She wished it was light enough to see if she affected him the way he affected her. She could hear the rush of his exhale, and sense the way he shifted his feet, the pressure change of the ball of fabric. It would be crumpled beyond explanation by this. But she didn't dare move, and did not want him to.

He tipped his head against the door near hers. She wondered if she could hold his magic, hold it enough to touch him without being attacked by his power. It was possible to hold another's magic, to

contain it. But there were limitations. One had to be in magical oppo-
sition, so an earth mage might be able to resist an attack of Omar's
Veritor magic. Or be of higher rank, or have incredible force of will.
She and Omar were both Sival, though he was the more powerful.

"I am in your bedroom," he said. "You could light me on fire and
it would be less torturous."

"There is a window. It might be loud—"

"I don't want to leave," he said.

"What…" She paused to steady her whisper and her thoughts.
"What do you want to do?"

A shimmer illuminated him, ghosting beneath his skin, outlining
him more clearly. Magic. A mage could not control everything of
themselves at once. Strong emotion could overwhelm a mage's hold
on their power. Anger. Joy. And most famously, lust. Lust stole focus
and control more reliably than any other feeling. The shimmer of his
magic waking in his skin revealed his to her. Knowing her feelings
were mutual did not comfort her. In fact it made her more reticent.
What could he possibly want in her, beyond physical attraction?

"But—"

"You are safe. I have no intention of touching you." His voice was
too rough at such a low volume, and she adored it. She wanted. She
wanted to touch him so badly that holding onto the rumpled cloth
in her hands was the only thing keeping her from doing so. Not her
good sense. Not her fear of his power. She couldn't say that—say she
didn't want to be safe.

"No? You are standing terribly close to someone you have no
intention of touching." The last was boldness she had not realized
she had in her. Bravery in intimacy. Admitting, a little bit, that she
wanted to touch him, to be touched. It was almost as treasonous as
maintaining a secret school to teach the poor. Wanting to touch the
son of the Sultan.

"I did not say I did not want to," his whisper groaned. Glowing
heat lit in her core. A steady, thrumming rhythm that lied to her about
what she could say and do. Made her feel languorous and uninhibited,

made her magic uncoil and rise to meet his, though she held hers back better than he had.

Then he spoke again, and erased those feelings. "But I do not deserve it. This magic is…my magic is nothing but horror. I deserve what it does to me. What it keeps from me. That is the balance for what I take from others."

There they were, the words he would not speak in front of Behram. That not containing his magic was the whip he used to flail himself.

"You should not punish yourself for something the Wheel gifted you."

"Gifted?" he said in scorn. "Do not speak to me about the Wheel's gifts. It spins at random, and for cruelty, if I am any indication. Look at Narfour. So many suffer, suffer so harshly that they have grown to hate the people who should be taking care of them. Me. I should be helping. But all I do is hurt people. I do not want to be the Sultan my father is. I do not want to be the man he wants me to be. But I do not know how to be anything else, cannot be anything else with this vicious thing in my skin."

"Oh," she said softly, sorrowful. "Omar." She wanted to reach out to him. To connect. To plant comfort with the pressure of her hands. To feel his heart beat and his heat, and offer him something for his confession, because she could not imagine he had said it to many people. "No one deserves this. Isn't it lonely?"

"I do not know." He had shifted his head up, so his breath stirred her hair. "I almost can't remember anymore. What it feels like…if I have ever felt any different than I do now. Numb. Do you know…the first time I accidentally took a mind, it was my mother's?"

She stilled.

"It was just a hug. The same hug she gave me every day. And the last one she ever gave me. I think I broke something between us that day. We are not meant to see the mind of another like that. To know the secrets they keep even from themselves. I don't even know how she feels about me now, if she is afraid of me or hates me for what I took."

"She loves you. She worries for you," Dilay said. "She told me."

He lifted his head in front of hers so she could just barely make out his features in the darkness. Pale, pale light danced in his irises. Swirls and eddies of magic that blotted out the dark of his irises.

"Help me," he said. "What must I do?"

"Your problem is not control, it is intention. You have to find something you want more than you want to punish yourself." But was that helping him? Or was she being selfish? His fate…there was no happy fate for him. Whether he controlled his magic or not. How many people had he already confessed? How many people had he idly touched? How many minds lurked in his own, ready to devour him?

She had to tell him. She could not keep it from him, the way his parents seemed willing to do. But first, she would help him master it. She would. Even if it broke her heart.

He made a sound that might have been a laugh or a groan. "You think I have not wanted things? That I don't…don't want things right now?"

"Of course," Dilay said, though it was hard to whisper with her pulse pounding in her ears and her body burning from head to toe. "But until what you want becomes more important to you than what you hate about yourself, you will never silence your magic." She did not know how to respond to his hesitant admittal that he wanted what she wanted. More. What could possibly be between them that would not be more painful than joyful? "You have to accept what you are, and that wishing and punishing yourself will never change it."

"It is easy to accept yourself when you do nothing but good in the world. When you are free to choose what you want to be. I am less than powerless." He straightened a bit, giving her room.

"You are freer than anyone to choose what you want to be," she said. "If I can free you from this"—she paused before forcing the rest out—"promise me you will be the man you want to be. The Sultan you want to be. Not what anyone else tells you to be." This was the chance she had wanted. To beg him to be something else. But when she had that idea they had been complete strangers. Now…could she call him a friend? "Choose to do something good in the world."

"That is a promise I could easily lie my way through. Would you trust me to keep it?"

"I will trust that if you do not, you will know, every day of your pampered life, that a poor judge's daughter was braver, and more determined than a prince. And did far more, with far less."

The pale swirls of his magic grew brighter and brighter, a rising sun in his eyes, illuminating his face and hers, the space between them, swirls of white light spinning down his neck and beneath his caftan, and she could see their light trails even beneath the fabric.

Magic manifested differently for each mage, and fluxed only for the strongest, Sival. His magic was beautiful. Light from the dark, the Sabris had once been called. Because it had been the Sabris that had risen up to drive destruction mages out of Tamar. Dilay had never cared for the term, because she did not believe in the breaking of the Wheel, in the edict that any magic was inherently evil. But his light made her understand why Tamar might have once called them that.

"You are a remarkable woman," he finally murmured. "And have already proven yourself more fearless than I ever have. Why do you want to help me?"

"Because, I like you, Omar Sabri." She laughed, a little. Just a whisper.

He made an airy sound of surprise, his head ducking toward hers and stopping only a hair span away. Then his body pushed, a fraction closer, crushing the fabric she held between them. Fire or ice or both lit every bit of her skin, and it was all she could do not to meet him. The moment stretched, strained and excruciating. After a heartbeat more of sensibility, she gave in and blew a little stream of air across his cheek in lieu of the kiss she wanted so badly to press there.

"That does not help me," he intoned, "evil girl."

"Or me," she said.

"No?" he murmured. "What would help you?"

"To know you have been practicing silencing your magic. Show me."

The light of his magic extinguished, abruptly, leaving her completely blind in the ensuing dark. Dilay smiled in triumph. She gave the balled-up fabric she held a little shove against his belly.

"Good," she murmured.

"If I succeed at this," he said, his face so close his words whispered over her lips, "will you let me kiss you?"

"I would never let a student kiss me." She thought she did an admirable job of sounding flippant when she was so close to disintegrating into a puddle at his feet.

"Mmm," he said. "What about a prince?" Her body buzzed like she stood in the center of a lightning storm. Or a Sabri tempest. Who knew someone so quiet could raise such a storm in a person?

"Which prince?" Dilay teased. He chuckled softly. He stroked one hand down the door to her left then straightened.

"I should go."

Stay. Her body screamed. But that was foolishness of the highest order. He did not belong in her tiny bedroom, in her tiny house, bordering the poorest parts of the city. The son of a man who would have her hanged for defying his laws. With her near-revolutionary father just on the other side of the door. They did not belong together like this, wanting each other for the most tenuous of connections. She was being a fool, and once again Seda was right.

Dilay held the fabric up between them. Omar took it. He hesitated another moment before he stepped away to wrap it around his head.

She eased her window open. It was so small, she felt terrible watching him wedge his way out of it. She hoped none of the women who sat knitting at their windows to collect gossip could see him in the dark and the drizzle.

"I will come to the University tomorrow," he said when he had collected himself on the other side. "We can try again." He winced and grabbed the back of his neck. "The magic, I mean."

"Tomorrow," Dilay said. He walked backwards a few steps, then turned and disappeared into the dark.

EIGHTEEN

"SHALL I HAVE THE WATER mages draw a bath for you, Efendim?" Ruslan asked as they strode down the hall toward Omar's rooms.

"No, thank you." He was too tired, too shredded mentally, too raw to be around anyone for another moment. Ruslan sensed that, he thought, but would never fail to perform what he considered his duties.

"Food?" Ruslan reached for the doors of the rooms, glancing at Omar as he pushed them open.

"I have kept you enough," Omar declined. Ruslan's brows rose, and he almost smiled.

"Be careful," he said, quietly for an earth mage, "she seems to be rubbing off on you."

Omar grinned, easing past Ruslan into the sitting room that lay between his bedroom and his bathroom. Ruslan closed the doors behind him. Omar started to take a deep breath and stopped halfway through. His father sat on the only full chair in the room, his elbows propped on its arms, his fingers tented in front of his face. All the joy left from his time with Dilay shrank and disappeared. Something heavy pressed down on his shoulders so he thought he might go to his knees.

178 %6 J. D. Evans

"Sultan." Omar bowed, and when he straightened he clasped his hands behind his back.

"Who is rubbing off on you?" His father's voice could boom, filling a room and demanding every bit of attention in it. But at this moment, it was quiet. Measured. And dangerous.

The only appropriate answer was silence. Fear for Dilay sealed his voice for him, turning his insides still and cold. What had he done? Who had told the Sultan? Had likely followed him when he thought he was safe, perhaps now knew Dilay. Bile seared the back of his throat and a wave of nausea made his scalp tingle. He squeezed his hands tighter at his back. He could grasp hard enough to chain himself, to silence all his feelings and protests and ideas, all his wants.

"You think I am an utter fool. That I do not know when my own son is out wandering the city like a vagrant?"

"Of course not, Efendim."

"I indulged this pointless waste of time—this observing at the University. And now you seem to think you are free to do whatever you wish, no matter how it reflects on me and my rule."

"Father—"

"Sultan." He leapt to his feet. Omar ducked his head.

"Do you have any idea what you have done? Every guard and servant in the palace now knows I cannot control my own son." His voice rose, ricocheting back at them from the walls.

"I was careful, Efendim. I disguised—"

The Sultan's face turned purple.

"You are forbidden to leave this palace without a full contingent of guards and attendants. You will not attend the University again, you will not walk the streets again unless it is by my command, and only in your capacity as Vali Ahad. And you will never *disguise* yourself. You are a prince of Tamar, not some common market hawker. If you disobey me again, I will have you confined to your rooms."

It did not matter that Mazhar was allowed all those things with nary a thought from their father. Omar was not a person. Not to his father. Not to anyone. Omar's rising temper cooled and fell, pooling in his belly like tepid, two-day-old tea. Choose who and what he wanted to be, indeed.

"How can you confine me away from the city, the entire land I am supposed to one day rule? From its people? They do not know me, they know my clothes," Omar said in disgust. "They fear my power. That is what you want?"

"They should fear you. A Sultan is feared and respected and from that comes obedience, and from that…love. You are weak-hearted, like your mother. And now, you have found some little diversion to entertain yourself—"

"Don't," Omar snapped. Fury melted the cold that held him frozen.

The Sultan raised an eyebrow, growing calm. Dread filled Omar once more. He only looked like that when he had won.

"The Viziers have presented the candidates for your marriage. You have done nothing more than embarrass yourself and whatever poor girl you have disillusioned."

The air in the room funneled away.

"Your mother has the names, and has been looking for you all evening to discuss them before I make my decision."

Omar bowed, because he could do nothing else, say nothing else. His father left without another word. Omar released his hands from behind his back, and shook them out, trying to banish the pins and needles of numbness. He sat on the floor, on the single step that raised the entry of his room above the sitting area, and tried to summon control.

All he summoned was Dilay. Her whispered voice, and her nearness. He could still feel the cool touch of her breath on his cheek, the ghost of the kiss he had wanted it to be. Wheel and spokes he wanted more than he should. More than he could ever have of anyone, let alone her. What a complete fool he was being. Letting this happen between them. He couldn't have anything of her, even if he had been a normal man with restraint. And now his father might know who she is. What she was.

Omar pushed to his feet and left his room. Ruslan was gone, thankfully, so he walked in lonely silence.

Isn't it lonely? she had asked.

He was lonely. Empty. Worthless.

He stopped in front of his mother's door and knocked. Beste opened it, took a lingering assessment of his clothes, and said not a word as she opened the door wider. Omar moved past her into a room very much like his own sitting room, but with more pillows thrown about. And tassels. He had never understood all the tassels on everything. His mother stood half turned to look at him, as if she had been looking out the glass doors into the garden when he arrived.

"Anne," Omar said.

She smiled sadly. "If you had told me, I could have helped you."

"Helped me what?" he said, though he knew exactly what she meant. It didn't feel quite as freeing to escape the palace as a grown man if he used his mother's help. She batted away his pointless question with a flick of her fingers.

"Do you wish to see these names?" she asked. Omar crossed the room and sank onto a bench, propping his arms on his legs and hanging his head.

"Do I?" He could probably guess a few. The men his father most favored from the Council. One for each of the remaining four Houses on the Wheel. Women he knew in passing at least.

"Zehra Demir is the kindest. I think she would understand… everything…the best," the Sultana said, as she sat on the little stool across from him. "Would you like some tea? Coffee?"

"Arak?" Beste offered in her brash way. Omar couldn't help but smile a little, though he looked at neither of them.

"Zehra is also the most social. I cannot imagine a woman like that being content with being married to someone who…" That infernal burn at the back of his eyes began again. "Who would not—"

"I understand," his mother said. Silence swelled for a moment before she spoke again. "Instructor Akar's lessons…have they," she hesitated, "have they helped you at all?"

He let out a sound that was neither laugh nor breath, a pained sound, and clutched at his head, bending deeper toward his knees, as if it would help crush the rising feeling of despair.

"I know you don't want her to help me, Anne, but I cannot live like this," he said. "I cannot bear it."

He looked up reluctantly when she said nothing, and he caught sight of a tear sliding down her cheek before she stood abruptly and turned her back on him.

"Is that who you were meeting in the city?" she asked.

Omar nodded, even though she was no longer looking at him. He hadn't meant to cause her sorrow. Wheel, he could only disappoint people, couldn't he? His father because he was not the man he was expected to be; his mother because he tried so hard to walk in his father's path; whatever woman he was to marry because he was no kind of husband; Dilay because he had been such a selfish, smitten fool.

"Yes," he said. He had never lied to her. Not outright. Not after what he had seen in her mind. What his power had stolen from her that day was forever etched in his memory. The sadness, the loneliness. Her blazing love for him and Mazhar. The tenuous grip she had on her crumbling self-pride. He could not bear the deeply etched pain of others. The brutal, human truths entombed in each person's mind.

"For lessons?" There was hope in her voice, and despair.

"Yes," he said. "And"—he released a breath—"and I like her."

"I see."

"Anne," Omar said, and his eyes and throat burned like they were on fire, "I like her so much."

Air hissed between her teeth as she looked at Beste. He buried his face in his hands again because he could not bear the pity he knew was about to be bestowed on him.

"Tell me about her," she said, instead.

"I can't." He laughed bitterly. It was locked inside him like a precious secret, feelings he could neither control nor stop, and if he spoke them out loud they would only hurt more. "And now I can't…" The realization punched through him. How would he ever see her again? She wasn't going to be able to help him if he couldn't see her. "Father confined me to the palace."

"There is nothing but pain in this," she said, gently, but firmly. "More than you can understand."

"I know. I did not mean for any of it to become this."

"Then perhaps your father's edict is for the best," the Sultana suggested. Still her voice held that gentle tone, as if he were going to shatter apart.

"Yes, Anne," he said, and forced neutrality into his voice, "tell me the other names." He could mourn and rail by himself. As he always had.

She read them off, none of them a surprise, but with each he went a bit more numb. He did not know any of them well. But he knew of them. Zehra Demir, daughter of the Grand Vizier and a well-known socialite. She was kind, friendly, though he did not know if she had any particular interests beyond people. An earth mage, like her father. It could be hard, for more than the obvious difficulties. Air and earth were in opposition on the Wheel, and often butted heads.

Kadri Gur, cousin to Kudret and Sirhan Yavuz, he had met her once, at a season celebration. He remembered her as funny but judgmental. A fire mage. He could only imagine the judgment she'd level on a husband who would not touch her.

Afet Erem, daughter of the Vizier of Agriculture. He had never met her, did not think he had ever even seen her at court. Air. His head began to throb as the muscles between his shoulder blades drew tighter and tighter.

"And Lalam Kahya," she said. Water. Omar kept his flinch mental. Lalam was beloved at court. Beautiful, smart, and lively. Behram knew her…quite well. The Second House was a sensual House. Known for its love of all things pleasurable. Omar did not think poorly of that, he just knew she would suffer at court for it. Something she did not deserve on top of being saddled with a husband who could give her nothing of what she wanted. He liked Lalam, what little he knew of her.

None of them deserved to be chained to him. To this life.

"You choose." He stood.

"Think about it, then I will if I must," his mother said. She handed him a stack of envelopes, each with calligraphy and wax seals that had been broken when she read them.

A prison door closing on him might have felt less soul-numbing. He nodded, and turned.

"Omar, stay," she said. His chest tightened.

"I cannot." When he looked at her she nodded, hiding her pity with a downturned face. He tried to smile for Beste, who had as good as raised him and Mazhar alongside their mother. But her expression was the same. Sorrow. He left.

He could not leave Dilay like this. With no explanation, no reason for disappearing. Could he send Ruslan with a message? But that would be insulting, wouldn't it? Not only to be discarded like she had never meant anything to him, but to find out through someone else.

A letter. He could say more in a letter, explain why he couldn't give her access to the library, like he had promised. He wouldn't risk the gossip or his father finding out who she was, if he did not already know. And at least a letter was something she would have of him. If she even wanted it. Or maybe the letter was for him, and not her at all.

NINETEEN

ILAY LOOKED DOWN AT HERSELF, kneeling on the stones in front of her home, covered in dirt from repotting the fig tree she had been trying to coax into growing for several seasons. It had produced a single fig in its life span and appeared to believe its job complete. She had employed every trick from every green thumb in the neighborhood, and nothing helped. She turned the pot one way then the other and scattered more dirt in to fill around the edges.

"Dilay?" her mother said. "Will you go to the market for me?" Her mother stood framed in the doorway to the house, her hands wound in her apron as she dried them.

Dilay forced a smile as she looked up from her planting project. "When I finish this. What do you need?" Another task would be good, to distract her from the peaks and valleys of her hurt and confusion. Omar. No matter what she did to free herself from thoughts of him, he crept back in. Memories of his voice or words mixing with the fact of his sudden and continuing absence. He had not shown up to the University. Not when he said he would, or the day after, or any day in the next small turn. Still, like a fool, she kept hoping. And was embarrassed by her hope. By how he had shoved her so easily off course.

"That tree will never grow in that pot. It needs space you cannot give it. A place to stretch its roots." Her mother looked at her with

184

sadness. She suspected her daughter's malaise, Dilay knew. Hiding her emotions from her mother was a near impossibility, but she would never pry. She always waited for Dilay to approach. But this time, she couldn't. When Dilay didn't respond, her mother sighed. "We need more of your father's herbs. A bundle of rushes for baskets. Flour. Oh and honey, if you can get it."

Dilay nodded, absently scooping dirt that had missed the pot from the cobbles.

"You may have to pretend for everyone else, but you don't have to hide from me," her mother said, gently.

"I…" Dilay's words died.

"Is it a man?" Her mother's tone was almost hopeful. Dilay rolled her eyes.

"It is more complicated than that," she said. A man. A prince. Her own foolish naivety. What had she thought was going to happen between the two of them? If anything did happen, what then? And all of it was distracting her from her most important task. The first tribunal hearing was in a few days and she still hadn't found anything to help. If she didn't before then, she would lose her chance.

If she attended, she would be forced to see him again. Would he ignore her? That sent her spiraling back into melancholy. What a stupid girl she had been, thinking what she had thought, wanting what she had. Thinking he had wanted anything from her at all.

Or perhaps his mother had forbidden him from getting any more lessons from her, if she had seen progress. If that were the case, why hadn't he contacted her? Sent a note? Or even a voice cast? Dilay had thought about trying once or twice, but her pride would not allow it. If he did not wish to speak with her, or even explain his sudden absence after all the things he had said, then she would not be the one to grovel or beg. To what end, in any case? For a few more marks? For a kiss? He was a prince, and the more time she spent with him the more she jeopardized her dreams in a variety of ways.

"Dilay Akar," a male voice announced. Dilay looked up to see three palace guards. Her mother made a distressed noise, her hands fisting in her apron. Dilay scrambled to her feet, dusting her clothes off, her heart pumping. She recognized one of the guards, the one with some rank, who had been with Omar at the University the first time she saw him. Her brow creased.

"Yes?" she said. A thread of fear wound through her. Was this about Omar? Or about her? About the school?

"Can I help you?" Her mother was not a physically intimidating woman. But the tone she used just then sent chills down Dilay's back. It garnered the lead guard's attention. He glanced at her then pointed at Dilay.

"You are to come with us."

"What? Where?" Her mother stepped out of the house.

"Not unless you tell me why," Dilay said. The lead guard motioned to his men with a hand, and the two of them stepped forward without a word. Dilay tried to dodge, but each grabbed her by an arm and dragged her away from the house.

"Dilay!" her mother cried, moving as if she would follow.

"Stay. Tell Father," Dilay ordered over her shoulder as the men forced her to march up the hill away from her home. They had grips like iron, so there was no use struggling, and she did not want to give them an excuse to cuff her. They followed their leader to the border of the Air District, where he stopped beside a carriage. The two men shoved her roughly into the box. Dilay landed on her hands and knees on the wooden floor and immediately spun to try and bolt free.

A booted foot stretched across her field of vision, slamming against the frame of the door to block her escape.

"Tsk. After all the trouble I went to to find you."

Dilay looked up, brushing handfuls of her hair out of her face. The Sehzade sat on the bench that backed the driver. Dilay sat back on her heels. "You sent those men to drag me away from my home and toss me about like a criminal?"

"Well"—he stretched his arms across the back of the bench and feigned a wince—"they were only supposed to escort you. But our commander does take his job quite seriously. I apologize if you were damaged. Have a seat."

"What do you want?" Dilay started to get up then tumbled onto the bench across from him when the wagon jolted forward. So much for dignity.

"So rude. Is that what my brother sees in you? He is not accustomed to anyone speaking back to him." He considered her critically, then looked sideways toward his hand as he picked at a loose thread in the bench's upholstery. The mention of Omar made her calm a fraction, but irritation swiftly replaced it.

"I have just been forced into a carriage against my will and left my terrified mother behind. I haven't even begun to show you rude, Efendim."

The Sehzade raised an eyebrow and looked at her from the corners of his eyes. "You may save it for my brother. He is the one who wishes to see you."

"The Vali Ahad sent these men to kidnap me?" She did not believe that for one single moment.

The Sehzade looked regretful and hummed a sound of disagreement. "Not exactly, no. I am merely…" He frowned. "…doing him a favor." Dilay slouched against the back of the bench with an impatient huff. It did not sound like she was prison bound, at the very least. She wondered how long it would be before her father had stormed up to the palace and demanded to see her.

They were awkwardly quiet for what she estimated to be most of the distance to the palace.

"This is best," the Sehzade finally said, quietly. "If they believe you a prisoner. If they believe you are here against your will."

"I am!" Dilay retorted.

"So…you do not wish to see the Vali Ahad?" He turned his gaze on her. His eyes were not like Omar's. Not warm brown. His were hazel. Pale. A twinge of hurt and longing made her glower harder at him.

"I had assumed he did not wish to see me, or he would have. Will he appreciate you forcing me on him?"

"He better." The Sehzade grabbed his entari and tugged it down, then dug a finger under the collar as if it were too tight. "I had to pay Ruslan three turns' worth of my allowance to tell me where you lived." His voice had taken on the whine she had only ever heard from the wealthy, when they were speaking of some monetary inconvenience.

"You could have found me at the University," Dilay said.

"Would you rather I have dragged you from there? I was thinking of your reputation."

"How kind you are," Dilay said snidely. He appeared chagrined, or faked it well.

"You haven't a groveling bone anywhere in your body, have you? How you must vex those old buzzards that call themselves headmasters."

"They like me even less than I like you, I think."

"I'll collect my thanks later." He said it as they pulled to a stop. Dilay did not have time to respond before the carriage door was opened from the outside and the two guards reached in to drag her free once more.

"Stop pulling me about, I can walk," she demanded. They looked to their commander, who narrowed his eyes, then to the Sehzade as he stepped down.

"Ah…yes. I think you can allow her to walk." He winked at her. "They'll see you inside, my dear." Dilay glared at him until she had to crane her neck to do so.

There were no crowds in the courtyard beyond the Morning Gate, thank the turn of the Wheel. Only a few interested parties stared as she passed, and no one she recognized. Until they reached the steps. And as they did, Semih Kadir strode out of the palace, with Behram only a pace behind. Behram started to smile in greeting, then he noticed the guards to either side of her. Semih stopped to take in her little parade, and humiliation burned bright in her cheeks. If she did see Omar today, he was going to regret it.

"Dilay?" Behram asked, confusion marking his face as she was escorted past him and up the steps. Fire sparked in his eyes. Before she could even attempt to answer, the commander grabbed her arm and turned her roughly inside the doors and down a hallway.

"I said to get your hands off me." Dilay wrenched her arm away. "Do it again and I'll start screaming."

He looked at her in surprise, then barked a laugh. "And embarrass yourself in front of the entire palace?"

"I have just been dragged halfway through the city. I am already embarrassed. I will happily return the favor."

The three of them walked in a triangle around her, announcing wordlessly to anyone who saw her that she was a prisoner. She certainly looked like one. She was wearing clothes she reserved for dirty work like gardening and cleaning. They were old and tattered, the hems in poor repair, dirt-specked and stained. Her hair was in a loose braid, now falling apart because of their rough handling of her. And she did not require a mirror to know her face was dirt-streaked. Just lovely.

They stopped in front of two of the largest doors Dilay had ever seen inside a building, nearly as large as those at the palace entrance. These were dark wood, with intricate carvings of the Wheel and its sigils. She had one blink to admire it before the great thug took hold of her again and reached to pull the door open.

"Let go I said!" Dilay kicked him in the shin and tried to jerk away. His grip tightened and he spun her to face him, grabbing her other arm too. Dilay tried to scream, and he shook her. Hard. The sound she had meant to be piercing came out as a keen instead when her teeth snapped together. Her vision swam, and she tried to collect herself from the dizzy whirling in her head. Shapes moved and scattered. Her vision sharpened to normal in the same moment she heard Omar issue a command at a volume that filled the hall.

"Release her this instant."

So that was what he sounded like when he wasn't holding back. She was so addled she almost giggled when his voice boomed at them from her right. The guard did not obey immediately. Omar appeared beside her. His hand clapped down on the back of the man's neck. It must have been a painful grip, because the guard's hands immediately released and he went to his knees. Or had Omar…but there was no sign of his power. No bright light, no dancing swirls, his eyes were clear and dark and furious.

"Omar…" Dilay whispered, pointing to his hand on the man's neck. Omar withdrew it immediately, the fury in his eyes replaced by horror. But the guard only looked up, surprised.

"What is she doing here, and why are you touching her?" Omar ordered, in that same reverberant voice. He gripped the hand he had grabbed the guard with in the other.

"The Sehzade ordered her brought to you," the guard said. Omar motioned him to his feet with a flick of his hand, and swept that same hand over his shorn hair as he grumbled his brother's name.

"Go," he said. They scurried to obey.

"Are you all right?" He faced her.

"You touched him," she puffed. He ducked his head to look at his hands, and Dilay saw past him into the room. She gasped at the narrow view she had of soaring shelves and endless books. His head twitched up, and he turned to follow her line of sight. Then he smiled.

"Welcome to the palace library," he said. Dilay took a step toward the open door, then stopped, and looked at him askance.

"Am I welcome?"

He stared at her with a helpless expression. "Dilay, I…" But why should he feel helpless? She was the one left to twist in the wind. She narrowed her eyes at him, her hurt making her voice sharp.

"Of course you needn't explain yourself, Vali Ahad. I just hoped you might. Especially since your brother had me dragged away from my home in broad daylight like a criminal. My mother is probably in a panic and my father on his way here to demand my release."

"I will kill him," Omar muttered. "One moment," he said to her, and she felt a thread of magic swirl between them like a breeze as he began a voice cast. She could barely make out that he was speaking to Ruslan, ordering that he find her father and pass along that she was safe.

"Thank you," she said grudgingly when he appeared to have finished. He nodded. "It appears that I am unexpected. If you will point me in the proper direction, I can remove myself from the palace."

"Please," he said. "Stay."

"I don't want to," she lied. Not like this. No apology, no explanation, brought against her will to someone who clearly had not asked for her.

His stony aspect crumbled. He looked so tired. Beaten. Her anger, fueled by wounded pride, spun to concern.

"What is happening?" she said, more gently. "You disappeared. I am dragged here by strangers…you were able to touch that guard. Explain. Please."

He nodded toward the library. "Not in the hall."

Dilay obliged and Omar shut the doors behind her. The room was circular, with books stretching up on two stories, a narrow balcony winding around the second level. Ladders were scattered about, and benches tucked against the walls between shelves. X-shaped bookstands were placed around the room, as were several low tables with cushions and one high table. That one was set with coffee. Dilay stared in greedy awe for a moment.

When she turned back to Omar he was looking at his hands as if they were someone else's. He flexed them open then curled them into fists and dropped them at his sides.

"I don't understand," he said, softly.

"Something you wanted more than to punish yourself," Dilay suggested, picking it apart in her mind. He looked at her in bewilderment, then his mien softened, his gaze roaming her face, then her clothes, surely noting her dirty hands and shoes. Dilay hugged her arms around herself and turned her face away from his scrutiny. "I apologize, I wasn't given a chance to change into appropriate attire." The entire ordeal was embarrassing enough, but she did not even have the authority of clean and tidy clothes to bolster her.

"You are beautiful," he said. No. No, he was not going to smooth her feelings with such a simple, meaningless utterance. She tried to sneer at him. But his lost look said tomes more than the words had. His gaze touched in a way most people might have with their hands, a brush here, a stroke there. "I missed you."

Heat rose in her throat, anger, and confusion. "You missed me?" Dilay dismissed the thought with a disdainful look. "That explains a small turn of abrupt silence."

The tenderness vanished from his face and he looked down as he rubbed his fingers over his brow. "My father found out about my trips into the city and had me confined to the palace," he said without looking at her.

"I see," she said. So he had just accepted it. That said a great deal as well.

"I was afraid he knew about you, about everything. The school. I was afraid to draw any more attention to you than I already had."

His professed worries felt more like veiled concern for himself rather than for her. She wanted to believe him, but the hurt of the abandonment made her wary.

"His edict must have also prevented you sending messages or casting your voice. Or any communication at all. What must it be like, to simply decide to discard something, or someone, when it is no longer convenient to you?" Dilay said. "And have no worry for the consequences of it."

Omar flinched. Good. She felt like wounding him. She had been hurt, and now she was humiliated.

"I was fetched like a toy."

"That was not my doing," he said, sharply. "I would never have done that to you."

"Why would you when others can do your dirty work?"

That raised his temper, she could see it in the stiff set of his jaw and his clenched fists. He leveled a cold stare on her. "You are overstepping."

"Yes of course. I have not rolled over and shown my belly because you are displeased. How dare I expect common decency from you." She dropped her hands to her sides. Her father had taught her. If one was going to fight, do it full-on. Do not hide behind yourself, do not appear unsure, or hobble your physical presence. "Thank you, Vali Ahad, for your generous consideration." She mocked a bow.

Storms of anger rolled over his visage. "You have no idea what is happening here." He clasped his hands behind his back.

"No, and I do not want to. You will find no sympathy in me for people who do not fight for what matters to them. Why should I care about someone who does not care about themselves? Why should I waste my time on someone who does not even stand up for the smallest of things he wants? You have no excuses." Tears burned at her eyes and she willed them away with her magic. She would not cry where Omar Sabri could see her. "I thought we were friends."

"I want that," he said, stepping closer, the temper in his countenance guttering out, "please, Dilay. I want that."

She held her hand up, palm out, between them. "Touch me," she ordered. He recoiled.

"No. I cannot control it."

"You just did." Dilay did not raise her voice. Never raise your voice, her mother had warned. It takes your power from you in their eyes. "You controlled it to lessen someone else. Now control it to come to me."

He lifted his hand, fingers outstretched to meet hers, then dropped it to his side.

"No, of course not." She curled her fingers into her palm. "No. You can yoke your power to make yourself a protector. To *save* me. But not to be my friend. To meet me where I wish to meet you, on even ground. How disappointingly typical." It broke her heart, to say it out loud. She had wanted him to be different than that. Different than the people who fought her at every turn, who would never see her as someone equal. "You never wanted help. You wanted permission to fail." She dropped her hand. "Find someone else to give it to you."

She started to turn away.

He stepped after her and reached. Dilay stopped, and he gripped her wrist, over her sleeve. His breath quavered as he slid his grip to her balled fist. Warm fingers just barely closed around hers, like a bear clutching a bird's egg.

"I do not want anyone else." Both stilled, her body as tense as his, both staring at his fingers curved over hers. She could not help that she was a bit afraid, but also elated. She lifted her hand, slowly, between them and he turned his grip to press his thumb up to nestle in her palm. His magic stuttered in flashes over his skin, writhing, and his brow knotted. Light danced and winked out in his eyes.

"I am so angry with you," Dilay said, weakly. Omar almost smiled. The wrinkle in his brow deepened.

"I deserve it. Very few people believe in me"—he pulled, gently, urging her the remaining step that separated them—"believe I could be something more than I am. Expect me to be." His fingers twitched over hers, as though he wanted to stroke but was unsure.

"I believe in you," she said.

"I do not wish to lose that."

"You could have come to me. Standing up to your father cannot be harder than this," Dilay said, gripping the gaping pocket of her work apron in her free hand. The desire to hug him in celebration nearly eclipsed her caution. She did not trust his newfound control enough to touch him any more than they already were. Ghosts of power slipped through the warmth of his eyes again. Little flashes of warning.

"Before you, I would not have agreed. But now I do." His smile was bitter. "You are torture."

"Thank you very much," Dilay sniffed.

"You said I could kiss you," he murmured. What calm she had mustered was obliterated by the catch in his voice.

"No I did not," she said. "And you are not ready for that." Was she?

"I leapt a chasm and am hanging by my fingernails on the far edge. You are going to tell me I cannot climb to the top?" he said, a smile dancing around his mouth but not materializing. The crease in his brow concerned her, the tension that hardened the tendons around his neck.

"I can see your magic already."

"Don't you want to see more?" he teased. Dilay laughed softly, and gently extricated her hand from his. Resignation relaxed his expression then changed to surprise when she pressed her fingertips to his entari, over his collarbone. He reached for her, then swung his arms behind his back and clasped his hands.

"Do not panic." She used her gentlest tone, one reserved for her youngest students. When he released his hands she walked her fingers up, slowly, watching his skin for signs of his magic fluxing harder. When she reached his collar she raised her finger and stroked the side of it softly down his neck. Holding his gaze as she did it.

His eyes closed and exhaled in a rush.

"Omar." She curled her fingers over his collar and used it to pull his head toward hers. "Are you sure?"

"Don't know." He opened his eyes. "Probably not."

She started to release her grip, to give him space, but he pressed a flat hand against her back to hold her.

"You are so small." He looked startled, and Dilay laughed. "Or you feel…small." His face relaxed, and his fingers curled against her back then spread again. The magic glowed stronger in his eyes.

"Are you all right?"

"Yes?" he said, his voice uneven. He touched the tip of his nose to her forehead. She was nervous, her own hands shaking. Because he could hurt her, without even meaning to. Because she was being foolish, allowing this. And because she wanted it so badly. His hand moved in little, stuttered strokes against her back, and his other was balled into a fist at his side.

Dilay traced her fingers over the back of his fist, to coax it open. "Relax," she said. "If you are afraid or tense it will only make things worse."

"It might not be very good for you anyway," he said in a near whisper. It took her a moment to understand, then she laughed a little.

"I meant holding the magic," she said, running the back of her hand over his, then twisting her fingers together with his, "not the kiss." She liked his hands. The way he gripped desperately but gently, fumbling a little, like an overeager puppy Seda had found once that tumbled and jumped and tripped over everything. "I want you to," she murmured. He made a soft sound and lowered his head to touch his lips against her cheek. His beard brushed her skin, neither soft nor coarse. A sensation she liked.

"Soft," he murmured. "Wheel, you're soft."

One of the doors flew open, startling Dilay nearly to shouting. Omar practically lunged away from her, though he still gripped her hand in his. Behram stormed through the door, fire in his eyes and wreathing his arms.

"Where is Dilay?" he demanded. Even as he said the words the sight of the two of them registered on his face, and his anger turned to fear. The fire guttered out. He reached and wrenched their hands apart. "I said never—" He stared at his hand on Omar's wrist.

Behram let go. He paused, then grabbed Omar again. They looked at each other, and both grinned, then Behram gripped Omar's shoulders and laughed as he gave him a little shake. It was possibly the most indecorous thing Dilay had ever seen Behram do as a grown man, and it made tears threaten, despite her racing heart and guilty flush.

"Careful," Omar said, pushing Behram away.

"You did it," Behram said. "How?"

Omar looked at Dilay, reluctant, but still smiling. "She called me a coward."

"I did not," Dilay gasped. Omar sniffed.

"Everything but."

Behram turned to her, looking at her as if it were possible to assess any damage done to her. "Are you all right? I saw those guards dragging you in here, but I was unable to get away."

"I am angry, but unhurt," Dilay said. She brushed at her arms, still able to feel their grip. Omar's good mood disappeared.

"They will be punished," Omar said.

"Do not punish them for the orders they obeyed. Punish your brother," Dilay said in exasperation. Though they had been unnecessarily rough.

"The Sehzade's doing?" Behram said, some anger reigniting in his voice. Then he seemed to cool. "Does he know?" Behram gestured to Omar, his hands.

"No one knows." Omar looked at his hands again. "This is the first time." He flicked his gaze to Dilay, and a little, secret smile started on his mouth that called another rush of heat to her skin she had to banish with magic.

"Not even the Sultana? This will certainly be good news for your betrothed." Behram grinned in a lurid way that made Dilay's thoughts stutter to a halt. All the joy in her drained away, leaving her clammy and cold and sick. She wrenched her gaze from Omar's panicked one. "Did you make a decision on who yet?" Behram asked, still looking at Omar as if he were seeing him for the first time. It took all her willpower to stand where she was with a stiff smile plastered on her face, when all she wanted was to bolt from the room. What a great, simple fool she was.

"No," Omar said. She would not stand there and be humiliated while they talked about a woman Dilay had just unwittingly disgraced.

"I should return home, Vali Ahad. My family was very worried, and as you can see, I was in the middle of chores."

"You do look a bit like a field worker," Behram said, reaching to flick a bit of dirt off her sleeve. "You are the only person I know who can get away with looking like a servant in front of the Vali Ahad."

"She does not look like a servant," Omar said, acidly. Behram snorted.

Dilay clasped her hands in front of her, trying to control the race of her heart and the burn in her throat. No tears. No tears in front of them because she was an idiot.

"I had little choice." It didn't matter, of course. She could have worn her finest caftan and entari, or her University uniform, and it would place her no closer to belonging where she was standing, between a prince and a future Vizier. Oh great Wheel, she'd almost kissed him.

The vile liar. Dilay swiped her fingers over her cheek where the feel of his lips lingered. Omar's skin paled.

"I…" Omar began. His gaze started to slide to Behram then flicked away, turning to the ceiling instead. He clasped his hands behind his back. She wanted to wrench them apart. He owed her so much more than that, but it didn't matter. She knew that from fighting her way into the University. She was due no explanation, no courtesy, no apologies.

"I can take you home," Behram offered.

"I think the Vali Ahad owes me a carriage for my trouble," Dilay said.

"More than that," Omar said, and had the decency to look miserable. But was he miserable because his lie had been revealed, or because he had hurt her?

Dilay kept her frozen smile as she replied, "A carriage will do, thank you." No extra gifts for being a diversion. She would rather burn the place to the ground.

"Let me walk you to the courtyard, at least," Behram said. Dilay ducked her chin because there was no refusing him. Then she looked at Omar, at his face. She met his gaze and shards pricked her all over. There was pain in his eyes, in the set of his mouth. Words he wasn't saying.

"Good bye, Vali Ahad." She bowed. Behram took her hand and led her away, and she forced herself not to look back. They were in a long, dim hallway when Behram finally spoke.

"You think I cannot feel your anger?" he snarled. Of course he could. Fifth House presided over passion. Love, hate, anger. Those emotions resonated against their magic.

"I told you I was angry. I was dragged…"

"Why did he touch you? What did he do to you?"

She knew that tone in Behram's voice. That simmering threat. She had never cared for that part of him, which claimed right to stand as her protector.

"Nothing," Dilay said. Not exactly a lie. "He's done nothing to me." He hadn't turned her in for teaching illegally. He hadn't really been a friend. He hadn't meant anything he said. The promises he had made had been empty. He hadn't even said good bye.

Nothing.

TWENTY

OMAR PRESSED HIS FOREHEAD AGAINST the carved doors once they were shut again, folding his arms above his head and closing his eyes. It was all jumbled inside him, joy and lust, anger and crushing despair. His pulse raced, and his skin felt seared down to his bones. The magic had fought him, fought control he was not accustomed to exacting, like a muscle unused and suddenly strained to the brink.

It had hurt to touch her, and it had been revelatory. Like he had not been alive until he'd felt her skin and her breath and heard the secret, coaxing warmth in her voice. And then it was all gone. That look in her eyes had turned to disgust.

There was a feeling in his hand like hers was still there, her fingers entwined in his, and he closed his fist, afraid for it to fade, because he knew he would never have it again. It would be someone else's hand, someone else's voice and he…did not want that. He wanted her bright mind and her confidence and her unflinching expectations. Something wrenched down on his chest, warning that if he tried to inhale he would fall apart.

He had waited a decade for this. To be fixed. To be whole and capable of touching someone. But he felt more broken, and the only one he wanted to touch would probably never even look him in the eyes again.

The door bucked as someone pushed from the other side. Omar stumbled back. It opened to reveal Behram had returned.

"She is well?" Omar said, though he did not want her name between him and Behram. He wasn't a fool. He could see she mattered to Behram far more than a friend. Behram did not answer immediately, looking at Omar in cold assessment, and Omar felt shamefully laid bare by the look.

"I have never asked you for anything," he said. Omar could tell his friend was angry, but was unnerved by the silence of his magic. Behram had never been one to hide his power.

"No," Omar agreed. Dread sank where despair had been.

"Whatever you are doing with her, end it now. Leave it. You cannot have her anyway." Behram said each word carefully, and barely moved as he did.

"I know that," Omar said. The fire came then. First lighting Behram's eyes, turning the brown to amber, then in little flames around his fingers. Omar did not fear Behram, and never had. Fire could not burn without air, a commodity which Omar held vast control over. That was, he thought, one reason Behram respected him, chose him as a friend. Behram honored power above all else, and in their relationship, the power belonged to Omar.

"Then you should never have allowed anything at all between you."

"This is not your concern," Omar said, his own temper swirling up in a storm of magic all too ready to be released. It did not matter that Behram was right. He had hurt her, and it was because he was selfish. But he would not be lectured by Behram, who seemed to think he owned her, yet had happily dallied with any woman he considered attractive enough.

"Dilay is my concern," Behram said. "She has always been my concern. I know her. You know nothing about her. She is only a novelty to you."

For one instant Omar lost his grip on his emotions and his magic, and it flashed to life in a blaze of light that made Behram's eyes narrow. Behram had no right to speak to him in such a way, to tell him who or what he could care about.

The anger fizzled quickly, buried beneath his logic. He had just lost Dilay. And he had, selfishly, pursued her when he knew Behram cared about her. When he knew things could not go anywhere. He did not also want to lose Behram, who understood things about him that no one else did.

Omar looped chains of control around himself, sinking into the cool rationality of his magic. It helped to ease the sting of Dilay's departure as well, to blunt the anguish. "I do not wish to fight with you. Whatever you're worried about, you needn't be. If she speaks to me after today it will be a Wheel-blessed miracle."

Behram softened, marginally, the little flames dancing over his hands snuffing out. "She will forgive you. She is incapable of holding a grudge."

He thought Behram might not know Dilay as well as he thought, if he believed that. She was a woman of conviction, and while he thought she likely gave Behram more chances than were fair, he was certain there were lines people should not cross with her. Like pursuing her when it would ultimately hurt her.

Besides, he wasn't certain he wished to be forgiven. What was the point? He was to be married to a practical stranger, and being close to Dilay in any way would only hurt. As well as strain his friendship with Behram. He wiped a hand down his face. A sharp throb arced through his skull, warning of more to come. He entertained a short, excruciating fantasy of Dilay's cool, gentle fingers on his head, soothing the murderous headaches that plagued him.

"I think you should tell the Sultana," Behram said, in his approximation of a gentle voice.

"Tell her what?" Omar said, trying to push his thoughts away. Void and stars he wished he had never touched her. Each new moment with her introduced a new and searing anguish.

Behram made an exasperated face. "About your newfound control. Did Dilay truly call you a coward?"

You never wanted help. You wanted permission to fail.

"Yes," Omar said. Because she had believed in him. What had he done? The urge to smash something overwhelmed him so fully that he could only stand there, mute, as he wrestled it away. He clasped his hands behind his back.

Behram chuckled, oblivious to Omar's state. "That is not so surprising. Do you know how I met her? She ran off a group of dockworker thugs when we were children. I still remember her lecturing one of them, his name was Zeki. I don't think I'll ever forget that name."

"Zeki?" Omar said. "The one that plays guard for her school?" She had reformed him, apparently, from bully to guardian of children. Omar started to smile, but stifled it. She had a talent for inspiring men to betterment.

"Her what?" Behram said, dark brows drawing together. A cold spear arrowed through Omar's throat and belly. They stared at each other. He thought Dilay and Behram were close, did he not know about Dilay's night school? If she had kept it from him, it was for good reason.

"I thought I saw him at the University," Omar said. "Or at least, someone named Zeki. But it is a common name." He shrugged. Behram was not an easy man to lie to. It was hard to trick someone who had spent their entire young life being betrayed by the people who were supposed to care the most.

"I see," Behram said. "Unlikely to be the same. He would not have been allowed to attend the University." His tone was too neutral. Trying to rein in his panic, Omar gestured at the hallway.

"I was about to head to the Sultan's wing. Care to come?"

Behram stared past him, into the library, and did not answer.

"Behram," Omar said. Behram looked at him and smiled.

"No. I was only able to escape my father by telling him I had forgotten something here in the palace. I should return." He gave a perfunctory bow and turned away. Then he stopped and glanced back. "I would not wish a touchless existence on my worst enemy." They stared at each other. "I am pleased for you, my friend." The unspoken conditional hung between them like a truce flag offered and unaccepted.

As long as nothing more happens between you and Dilay. Omar acknowledged it all with a tilt of his head. Behram walked away, and Omar stared at his back, his red and brown entari and gold-embroidered tiraz. Was there flame on his hands, again?

Worry niggled him. Had he revealed something to Behram that Dilay did not want revealed? Should he warn her? Would she even trust him now? Surely Behram would not do anything to hurt her. No. Behram cared for her. That was the entire problem, in Behram's mind. He cared for her and did not want Omar to take her away.

Omar stared at his hand, the one Dilay had twined her fingers with. They had felt so small and delicate compared to his. Her skin was cool and silken, her breath warm, her voice and magic like pitch on his desire. Why had he touched her? Broken Wheel it burned beneath his skin. He wanted more. He had felt addiction in the mind of more than one criminal, the gnawing, consuming need for poppy or alcohol. That was what it felt like, to a degree. When they had separated, he'd felt pulled in two, a gaping absence. Omar curled his hand closed and dropped it to his side.

Was he fixed? Or had she been a crutch he needed, the only desire strong enough to silence his magic? He did not want to test it. The consequences of failure were unacceptable. Still, she had told him exactly what he was doing. If he was conscious of trying to punish himself, or as she had said, to fail, could he control it when he needed to? Omar stepped out of the library and closed the door.

He had been so excited to show her the library. To see her face the first time she laid eyes on it. That passionate, covetous desire he had witnessed in her eyes when he had offered her just one book. But the circumstances had stolen that from him. Now all he wanted was that look to be directed at him, and it never would be. He did not deserve her, and as Behram had so painfully pointed out, could never have her.

Omar gripped the entari over his chest as he walked. The thick silver embroidery and dense fabric felt too heavy, too bright. She had been radiant standing in front of him in dirt-stained work clothes and tousled hair. Someone who knew who she was. He was just a puppet in a costume. Nothing.

He stopped in front of his mother's doors and paused to collect himself into some kind of mental order. He knocked.

Beste opened the door and smiled in greeting, though it faded when she saw his face. He could not guess what showed there. The pain of the growing headache? Confusion? Sadness? Beste had known him all his life; he was as transparent to her as he was to his mother.

"Is everything all right, Vali Ahad?"

"Fine." Omar moved past her and into the room. His mother was midway into a sip of coffee when he entered, and Mazhar sat across from her. His brother bore an amused look, and all Omar's futile anger spun up inside him. He strode across the space toward Mazhar, whose mirth disappeared as he lunged to his feet.

"Never do that again." Omar shoved him, and Mazhar fell back into the seat, pale-faced and silent.

"Omar," his mother said sharply. He turned to her. She was half out of her chair, her coffee cup lying on the rug, its contents staining the white and silver fabric. Her panicked gaze slipped between Omar and Mazhar, one hand stretched toward them ineffectually.

"You *touched me*," Mazhar said.

"If you set guards on her again, I will knock your teeth in." Omar rounded on his brother once more.

Mazhar blinked at him, then made a sound of revelation. Omar stared, his anger still a windstorm whipping his wits into a frenzy. "You touched me," he said. "Perhaps you should thank me for interfering." Mazhar settled back in the chair, looking delighted.

Omar nearly lunged at him again, his fingers balling into a fist.

"What is happening?" the Sultana said, interrupting Omar's next attack. Beste worked to pick up the coffee cup and dab at the stain with a rag, but her gaze was on Omar. He faced them both as Beste rose to stand at his mother's side. She gripped the Sultana's elbow.

Omar hadn't meant to do this. To give them hope. "It is working," he said. "I do not know how well, I—"

His mother stepped toward him, her eyes wide, hands outstretched. Fear grabbed him in clawed fingers, ratcheting his pulse. He was going to hurt her. Take from her again. He could feel the magic, whipping like tendrils from his anger and his sorrow, ready to steal. He stepped back, his body tensing. But he remembered Dilay's touch, stroking the back of his hand, coaxing him to her, to relax and trust. And when his mother cupped his face in her hands he held his writhing, snapping magic as she looked into his eyes and hers welled with tears.

"My son," she said. Ache shrank his lungs, a decade of longing and isolation, and he reached for her, wrapping his arms around her and pulling her to him. Beste sobbed, pressing her hands over her mouth. Omar did not remember his mother feeling so slim and fragile. He remembered her as soft and warm. Safe. He closed his eyes because they ached as much as his chest. His mother cried against his shoulder. The familiar smell of her perfume filled him with visceral memory, shrinking him into a boy's body with a skinned knee and tears. And then there were real tears, hot on his cheeks.

It was too much. The magic writhed, trying to twist free. Tangled in his feelings of failure. Dilay had given him this, and he had failed her. He did not deserve this comfort. Omar stepped away and held his hands up to fend them all off, his head ducked as he practiced what Dilay had made him do on the roof. It was just another spell, his power, under his control.

"I am pleased to see this," his father's voice came from the door to the hall. Omar's eyes opened, his grip on the magic slipping away. It sizzled under his skin, hissing and burning. Voices whispered. Memories that were not his, welling up in his panic. "Pleased to see that you are finally taking control of yourself. As a man should."

Omar bowed to his father.

"Leave him be," his mother said. The Sultan did not normally move in silence and appear unannounced. But then, he might not have been. The emotional scene had distracted them all.

"You are ready to take on more of your uncle's duties."

"No," the Sultana said, demanding and pleading. The Sultan ignored her, gazing instead at Omar.

"Do you refuse?"

"No, Sultan."

"Omar, please," the Sultana said. When Omar sliced his gaze away, she turned on the Sultan. "How dare you ask more of him. Wasn't your brother enough?"

"The Wheel demands for the gifts it gives," the Sultan said, then looked at Omar again. "There is a tribunal in the morning. You will attend."

Omar ducked his head. All the feelings were whisked away by his father's appearance. Replaced with cool apathy. He had known the price for more control. It was as silent in the room as it was inside his head when the Sultan departed.

Omar looked to his mother, and her face was pale. She sat abruptly and Beste knelt beside her chair, gripping the Sultana's hand between her own.

"It's all right, Anne. This control will help me manage the rest. The headaches and the bleeding."

"Leave me," she said. Mazhar looked sullenly at Omar, but rose, and they left together. In the hall, Ruslan waited for him.

"A dampening, please, Ruslan," Omar said. He turned to his brother once Ruslan had cast it. This time he did not touch Mazhar, certain the silence in his head and body were a lie and that the magic was coiled and ready.

"I was trying to help you," Mazhar said. "I cannot bear watching you dragging about like a beaten dog."

"I was not."

Ruslan gave a polite cough, which earned him a conspiratorial look from Mazhar. "Yes, you were. And everyone was starting to whisper."

"Commander Isler dragged her about like someone bound for the Cliffs," Omar said. "What were you thinking?"

"You know the man is a fanatic. You should replace him."

"Mazhar—"

"Brother," Mazhar interrupted, and glanced at Ruslan, then back. "I watched your light go out." He shrugged, because he had never been one for displaying emotion he considered sappy. "All these Turns I watched you grow dimmer, and dimmer. Whatever she is to you, I could not care less. But she lit you up, and that is all that matters to me. I would drag her here a hundred times over and never regret it."

"I think she is quite capable of making you regret it," Omar said. Mazhar laughed.

"What happened?" he asked.

Omar pressed his fingers to his temples. "We…" He flushed. "I tried to kiss her."

"Was that part of the lesson plan?" Mazhar guffawed. "Well done."

"Shut up," Omar barked. He had been surrounded all his life by men who had no idea what it was like, what it meant. Mazhar had taken full advantage of his position and his looks from the time he was old enough to care about women. Behram was no different. Even if he'd been able, Omar would never have been like that. "I hurt her."

Mazhar's brows drew together. "Not your magic?"

"No. I mean…I never should have touched her. I didn't tell her about the betrothal." His guilt wound harder when Ruslan made a sound of disapproval, but when Omar looked, he appeared only to be concentrating on his spell.

"Ah," Mazhar sighed. "Yes that was ill advised."

"And Behram," Omar admitted. He did not keep much from his brother, but he had no wish to drag more people into the mire.

"I cannot imagine Semih Kadir allowing Behram to consort with a judge's daughter, even if she is a noble. I don't know what he imagines his claim is there."

"They've been friends even longer than Behram and I," Omar said.

Mazhar nodded, silent. It only lasted a moment. "Did you send her away?"

"She left," Omar said. "Behram mentioned the betrothal."

Mazhar made a sound of exasperation. "Of course he did. Just like he mentioned your trip into the city in front of Father. All very innocent."

"He what?" Chill slowed Omar's pulse and thoughts. Surely Behram knew what the Sultan's reaction to that would be? He would never do something like that. He knew what it was like to be leashed.

Mazhar raised an eyebrow. "They were discussing the guild tribunal schedule, and the mood in the city. Behram said perhaps you could assess it the next time you took a trip into the city."

"It was not purposeful," Omar said. Behram had accidentally let it slip, just as Omar had let slip about Dilay's school. Mazhar and Ruslan exchanged a look. Irritated, Omar made a gesture and Ruslan dropped the dampening spell. Mazhar winced and tugged at his ears, shooting Ruslan a look of disapproval.

"That finesse, Ruslan."

"My apologies, Efendim." Ruslan bowed and Mazhar pursed his lips.

"What now?" Mazhar asked Omar. But he could hardly think straight, too tangled around Dilay and Behram and his own struggles with his power.

"I'll return to the library," Omar said, absently. Mazhar made an impatient sound.

"Not what I meant, but as you wish." He moved as if he might clasp Omar's shoulder, but Omar stepped back. Mazhar dropped his hand and smiled regretfully. Then he left, down the hall toward his own rooms. Omar stood for a moment, unable to muster the desire to go anywhere or do anything.

"Are you simply going to let her go?" Ruslan asked. "What about her help?"

Omar glanced at him, but the steward maintained his usual impassive facade. If he was judging Omar, it was earned. "Why would she want anything to do with me after today? Besides that"—he knew it was obvious to Ruslan he cared about her—"to have her near when I cannot—" Omar winced.

Ruslan looked at him dispassionately. "Her worth to you is only measured in your attraction?" He paused, raising his eyebrows when Omar glanced sharply at him. "What about all that she has done, and is doing for the city? For your people?"

"That is all illegal, and my attention will only turn eyes on her that put her in danger."

"I know what kind of Sultan you wish to be, Efendim. It is the only reason I continue to serve you." Ruslan glanced at the doors to the Queen's rooms.

He knew? That was interesting. Omar didn't even know.

"What does Dilay have to do with that?"

Ruslan stood straighter, his mouth twisting, then relaxing. "Everything, Vali Ahad. You can surround yourself with people like Kadir Pasha, who grasp and connive for power, or with people like Mistress Akar, who sacrifice and fight, and that is how you will define what kind of Sultan you will be."

"I do not have much of a choice in who I surround myself with. The powerful families in Narfour—"

Ruslan scowled. "You always have a choice. She is an invaluable loss to you, Efendim, and not simply because you care about her."

Stunned, Omar stared. Ruslan had never spoken so freely to him. A smile came, unbidden and uncontrolled.

"Be careful," Omar said, "she seems to be rubbing off on you."

Ruslan appeared startled, then smiled. "So, what will you do?"

He might not be able to give her the entire library, now. But there was something much more portable. He tipped his head to indicate Ruslan should follow.

TWENTY-ONE

DILAY READJUSTED THE MARKET BASKET on her arm as she picked through the herbs on the table. The kind, elderly woman manning the booth waited patiently. Her hair was braided and coiled at the back of her head, a plain cloth pinned over the top to protect her from sun and dust, but grey curls escaped from beneath. Perhaps she sensed Dilay's mood, or perhaps she could tell Dilay knew what she was looking for, but she remained silent, instead of naming them all as Dilay touched them. She selected the ones she needed as a stab of regret pierced her belly. She had promised her mother she'd do this days ago, but...

She handed the bundled herbs to the woman, blinking away the sting in her eyes. The woman smiled and patted the air with her hands in denial. When Dilay hesitated, the woman bent forward, beckoning Dilay closer. Dilay turned her head down.

"You teach my granddaughter, Belma. She is much happier since she started. And I can see you are not happy. Take these this time."

"I cannot possibly." Dilay straightened, digging into her pocket for coins, which she held out. The woman cupped Dilay's hand between her own, closing her fingers around the coins.

"You will, today you will. It is all I can give." She smiled and shooed Dilay away. After a moment more of hesitation, Dilay ducked her head and deposited the herbs in her basket. The smile she attempted faltered, and she turned away.

The morning was just beginning to brighten, and as she walked to the southern end of the market, more people were arriving to do their shopping for the day. The morning market was always quieter than the afternoon and evening ones. People were in more peaceful moods in the morning, their shopping more reverent than rushed. Dilay preferred it, when polite smiles and greetings were subdued and the noises and smells of the city hadn't yet mingled together into chaos. The market smelled of fresh, warm bread, spices, coffee, and herbs. Moving through sections was marked by a change in dominant scents. Now she was surrounded by the smells of herbs. Some sweet, some astringent, some were even foul.

On her way down the hill, to the far southern end of the market where the fishmongers were, she passed through the largest section of spice sellers. Always cumin struck her first, sometimes coriander. Ground chilies burned her throat if the powder was being scooped as she passed. Sometimes there was cinnamon, brought from beyond the Odokan plains by traders on the Spice Road. Of course, dozens of purveyors of the best za'atar, that blend of wild oregano and other spices that was absolutely non-negotiable in cooking. Pungent and savory, it always made Dilay crave man'oushe. Fresh from a stone oven, drizzled with olive oil and a good dusting of za'atar.

And that craving brought Omar to mind. Dilay hugged the basket closer to her, letting the rushes cut against her arms. She would be back at the University in just a bit, and that would distract her. That had been all she had been able to do since seeing Omar in the palace, hurry from distraction to distraction. She could not face her anger and hurt without also admitting she had been wholly responsible for allowing herself into an inappropriate situation. She just did not have the emotional strength to deal with any of it at the moment. Not with so many things that needed her attention and focus.

Dilay stopped briefly to purchase a clay pot of honey. Normally she would have brought their own to refill, but theirs was ancient, and had finally cracked the day previous when she had set it down too sharply. The merchant touted the benefits of the honey and how special his particular bees were and the litany of flowers they preferred as Dilay paid and tucked the jar into her basket, nodding and trying to smile. This was not her, this quiet ghost that barely smiled or interacted. She hated that she allowed herself to be so shaken by Omar. She barely knew the man. In fact she knew him even less than she'd realized, when she stood ready to kiss him on more than one occasion. She had arrogantly thought herself above such silly things. Always judging Seda about her flights of fancy and girlish infatuations. The Wheel had certainly turned the mirror on Dilay.

She brooded as her humiliation filled her, crushing. It dominated her thoughts as she strode past booths of jewelry and baubles. The road turned sharply to run parallel to the harbor, leading eventually down to the docks and warehouses. The pier market was along the hill that led down. It abutted the Grand Market, but was not considered the same entity. This was where one found coarser goods. Craftwares and supplies to be turned into other things. Today she sought rushes. But first she had to make it unscathed through the gauntlet of shouting jewelry sellers, charlatans selling visions of the future, and persistent rug and linen salesmen. She directed her gaze to the cobbles at her feet, best to avoid encouraging eye contact.

A familiar cadence of speech caught her attention as she tried to dodge a particularly tenacious silk scarf salesman, who kept trying to rub one against her hands and face. Dilay batted him away when she stopped, turning toward the voice. Across the street from her, Behram was half-ducked into a booth selling Meneian jewelry.

He gestured violently as he bartered with an equally enthusiastic Meneian merchant. As she drew close she could hear that they were speaking Meneian. Dilay had always envied Behram for his talent with languages. Some he learned by necessity, because the Merchant Guild encompassed even those merchants who came temporarily or who were not originally from Tamar. Menei and its many and varied languages, for one. He could speak Common Trade, a remnant of the Old Sultanate that had its roots in both Tamar and the Republic, the land across the Sun Sea. And, supposedly, on a bet, he had also learned to read and write old Corsan, the mother tongue of the Republic. No one else spoke it, at least in Tamar, so no one could verify he had actually learned it. But he had read her poetry in the language once. It was a language of hums, where the syllables bled together into a kind of drone. She thought there were a few too many *m* sounds for it to be beautiful. She had concentrated her studies at the University on magic and its fundamentals, so that she could better teach her charges. There had not been extra room in her schedule for languages. If she ever rose high enough in the University she would do her best to make certain every student could take at least one.

Dilay tucked in beside Behram at the corner of the booth. It was typical of its kind, just a merchant behind a shelf, with a piece of tassled, brightly colored fabric laid over it to attract the eye to his wares. A frame above supported another cloth, woven of reds and purples.

Behram held a big, clunky ring with a polished but uncut garnet in it. "That is hideous," Dilay murmured when Behram looked at her in surprise. His brows knit together, then he turned his attention back to the merchant. The merchant smiled to Dilay, ducked his head, then said something to Behram that was clearly about her, waving a hand to indicate her. Behram looked at Dilay again and said something that seemed to be a denial. The merchant threw his hands up with a loud, "Bah!" They exchanged ring for coins, and Behram turned away smiling like a cat pleased with its kill. He pocketed the ring.

"What could you possibly want with that?" Dilay asked as they moved away from the booth.

"The stone. Garnet is greatly underappreciated."

"That is because it is ugly. Sapphires and diamonds are much more beautiful," she teased. Each House had many things associated with it, things believed, or proven, to have an affinity for the magic within. Garnet, like ruby, was a fire stone, and sapphires and diamonds stones of air. Stones could hold magic, as enchantments. But that was illegal in Tamar. Enchantments were made by trapping intention, and without a mage's focus to guide them, the spells trapped within were often far too broad to be useful, and objects could easily kill whoever they were interacting with.

"You have expensive taste on a pauper's earnings, Dilay," Behram said. "Perhaps if you behave very well, I will gift you one for your birthday."

"No thank you." She laughed. "What would I do with such things? Wear it with my University uniform?" She tugged at the edge of her caftan.

"You deserve such things," Behram said. Dilay looked at him, startled. "I want to give them to you." He stopped, gripping her arm and turning her toward him in the middle of the street. Dilay flushed as people looked and whispered, with knowing looks in their eyes. As though the two of them were lovers. "Why are you wasting your time giving your knowledge away to scrubs and urchins? What do you think the University will think if they find out?"

Dilay stared, her voice disappearing. He knew. How did he know?

"What?" she managed. He made an impatient face.

"I know about your school. The Vali Ahad told me." He clicked his tongue and made a face of disdain as though she were a child he had caught sneaking candy. Omar? He'd betrayed her again? Dilay struggled to wrap her mind around it. None of it felt like him. Why would he tell Behram?

"That nonsense is a waste of your time, Dilay. I can give you everything you have ever wanted, if you marry me, I can make certain none of those old goats at the University ever stand in your way again. I can buy you fine clothes and sapphires. What do you think all I've been doing is for?" His gaze roamed her face in a way that made her panic. "The guild? You told me you thought I could be more than I was. So that is what I'm doing. For you."

Dilay tore away from him, stumbling back, throat tight and breaths too fast.

"I know it is sudden, I had meant to do it differently, but decided I should not hold off any longer."

"No," she choked. "Behram. No!"

He stared at her, as if unable to understand.

"You think that is what I want? Jewelry? A keeper? You think I meant you should become more powerful?" She stepped to him again, gripping his caftan at the tiraz, the embroidery harder against her skin. Sigils of fire. "I wanted you to be a different man than your father is. More than he is."

"I will be. I will head the Merchant Guild, and the only man who outstrips me will be the Sultan." The ferocity of his words was so intense it frightened her.

"Behram," Dilay pleaded. "I meant I wanted you to be kind. To leave your father's brutality and selfishness behind. You are better than this. You know me. You know it isn't *things* I want. I want a better world. You could help me with that, if you had power in the Merchant Guild you could help build schools for all the neglected—"

He tugged away from her with a huff of derision. Her fingers slipped away from his sleeve. "I will not be married to someone slumming around with the worst dregs of society," Behram snapped. Dilay dropped her hands to her sides.

"Behram," she said, softly, her heart breaking, "I can't marry you. I don't." She met his eyes as tears burned hers. "I don't love you that way. You know what I want. I don't want to be shackled to parties and society and pretending all is right with the world because I am comfortable in it."

"Ah"—Behram smiled, but it burned with fury—"unless they are palace parties and society? Unless it is with a prince?"

Warmth and sense vanished, leaving her cold and stiff. "No."

"It is not all about love for you, not truly, is it? You thought you could snare yourself a future Sultan, instead of a Vizier. I have never been enough for you. No matter what I do."

"Stop it! You are not listening to me."

"No, I've heard more than enough." He turned to stalk up the street. Dilay watched him, as people stared at her and whispered. She tried to ignore them, swiping at the tears that escaped her before she reined in her emotion with magic. There would be privacy later. That was when she could cry.

Miserable, she turned in the opposite direction he had gone, and made her way to the basket merchants to purchase rushes. There had been more on her mother's list, but she struggled to remember it.

By the time she circled back to retrieve the last item, flour, to be delivered by wagon at the end of the day, she was struggling under the weight of the rushes and unwieldy basket. The rushes sliced at her hands and wrists as she wrestled them into the house, though none of the cuts were serious or did more than sting for a few moments. She dropped everything in the entryway and made her way to the University for her classes. Perhaps they would be enough to distract her from the upwelling of sorrow that continually bubbled up past her magical attempts to seal it away. She absolutely could not cry in front of her students or the other instructors.

Few things diminished a woman more in the company of men than tears.

TWENTY-TWO

OMAR TUCKED THE THREE BOOKS into a bag he slung over his shoulders. He hadn't even left yet and his body hummed with nervous energy. He wiped his palms on his caftan, but it didn't help the tingling or the damp feeling much at all. A large mirror hung opposite the windows of the tower study to reflect the light, and he caught his reflection as he turned toward the stairs. Wheel and stars he looked haggard. Four tribunal confessions in four days, with a half-dozen meetings between about the upcoming Merchant Guild tribunal and a territory dispute in the valley between two minor Viziers. He had barely slept, and it showed in the dark circles and red rings around his eyes.

Well, he wasn't trying to woo her. He was just going to give her books and ask for her continued help. Perhaps looking much worse for wear would help his cause. Her short lessons had helped him manage his pain better these last two confessions, the aftereffects were much less, but the frequency was making up for it. Voices had whispered in his dreams, memories like ghosts, lives that did not belong to him. He tried not to dwell on those things. Things he had never told anyone about. The things that frightened him.

Omar turned from the mirror. A book with a bright blue cover caught his eye, and he picked it up from the stack, tucking it into the bag as well. A little extra incentive, just in case. He went down the stairs. Ruslan waited at the bottom, and they walked together through the halls toward the palace entrance. Omar hadn't disguised himself today. Neither had he chosen audacious clothing. Instead he walked the middle, with clothes he would wear on a day he did not expect to interact with anyone of import. Comfortable but well made, in shades of grey and blue. He wore no turban or wrap over his hair, and he didn't plan on sneaking out of the palace.

As they walked the main hall toward the entrance, his nervousness grew. He imagined he could feel his father's stare on his back, the heat of his disapproval. Omar had neither asked permission nor told his father, so he half expected to be hauled bodily back into the palace by guards sicced on him by the Sultan. But the only person he saw, besides the usual shifting tides of people in and out of the palace and various Viziers' offices on this eastern side, was his mother.

The Sultana stood at the outlet of the main hall into the entrance foyer. Beste beside her, both of them stiff-backed and sour-faced. Omar's steps faltered. He forced himself to walk on, to meet her, though he did not reach to touch her. He had done so only twice since their first embrace. A squeeze of her hand when she checked on him after the first tribunal. Her fingers on his shoulder when he bid her good night the evening before.

"Sultana Efendim," he said. She ducked her head as Beste bowed to him and Ruslan to her.

"Where are you going?" Her words were clipped, and her eyes disapproving. Beste traced a sigil on her palm in chalk she kept at her waistbelt, and a dampening spell shuttered them in.

"I gather you already know," Omar said dryly, though he could not imagine how she knew. How she always knew. Mothers had a special magic designated only for them on the Wheel and no one ever spoke about it, he was certain of it. Especially First House mothers, who seemed prescient at times.

"Please do not do this." Some of the sharpness in her voice was replaced with concern.

"Do what?"

"Go to her. Take her lessons. The more you study, the more you control this, the more he will ask of you. Look at you." She gestured at him. "I cannot bear to see you in pain, and it will only grow worse."

"It is already better. I've hugged you! I have endured twice what I could have before and I have only just gained this measure of control."

"Can you not see where this leads you?" The grief in her eyes was alarming. Omar frowned.

"You want me to spend my life isolated from everyone? Unable to produce an heir? I can see where standing back and doing nothing leads me. I want control of myself. If I cannot control myself, how can I control my life? My future?"

"I will never condone this," she said.

"Are you going to stop me?" He tensed. She did not have guards with her, but they were only a whispered cast away. "Or make good on your threats to Instructor Akar?" He would do everything in his power to prevent that. She looked at Beste, who gave her an apologetic smile and shook her head. His mother closed her eyes in resignation, and Beste released the spell by smudging her thumb through the chalk on her palm.

"I will return soon, Anne," Omar said. He wanted to do something, touch her, to offer comfort, but he was woefully unpracticed in such things. So he ducked his head to her and left.

"One angry woman stalled," Ruslan said, "though I think the next will be more difficult."

"Thank you for your observation," Omar rumbled. Ruslan barely managed to stifle a smile. Ruslan had already ordered a carriage, one of the smaller, less ostentatious ones, prepared. Six guards waited beside it, including Commander Isler.

"Only three," Omar said, when they arrived. He wanted to avoid drawing any more attention to himself than he had to. Commander Isler exchanged an irritated look with Ruslan, then jabbed a finger at two of his men. The rest crossed the courtyard toward the low, long barracks building on the east side of the grounds.

Omar swung up into the carriage and Ruslan sat across from him. They did not speak as the carriage trundled and bounced through the Morning Gate and into the city. The sound of the city was muted by the carriage, though Omar could still hear the guards' horses trotting alongside. A few turns after leaving the palace road and the carriage rocked to a halt. Ruslan exited first, and Omar followed.

The sight of the courtyard brought the unease back, and the tingles over his skin. What if she refused to give him a chance? There were few students in the courtyard, classes had already begun for the morning. The steep, wide stairs of the entrance seemed to stretch longer than they had in his previous visits. Normally, anyone who was not a student would wait in the small foyer tucked in between two of the wings until someone could escort them where they needed to go. But Omar did not want to draw attention to the reason for his visit. He hoped to find her before the Proctors descended on him.

He glanced up as soon as they passed through the second set of doors between the foyer and the atrium. There were a few students lingering in the wide-open space, and he drew their notice immediately. But Omar looked up, toward the First House Wing. Would she be in class now?

"The library first," Omar said to Ruslan. Isler and his two men followed at a reasonable distance, but Omar wished they were not there at all. Perhaps the worst part of his position was that he was rarely, if ever, truly alone. Even when he couldn't see people they were there, just around a corner or down a hall. A guard, or a steward. A maid sent to wait on him even when all he wanted was a moment of silence. He should be grateful, but over the Turns he'd just grown tired.

The library master sat in the same place he had been during every visit Omar made, on a couch directly to the left of the library doors. He was bent over a book, either reading intently or asleep, and did not look up as Omar strode by. He did issue a soft snore before Omar was out of earshot, and Ruslan made a sound like a stifled laugh.

Dilay was not down any of the aisles of books, or at any of the handfuls of tables. He paused to think.

"The office," Ruslan murmured while shooting a disapproving stare at a man who ogled them too long. Omar nodded. They wound back through the shelves and to the farthest corner of the library. The door to the little office where she had taken him the day he brought her Hanim's book was closed, but not latched.

Omar stood for a moment, trying to sort what he would say, if she was inside. The door swung open and Dilay stepped out, head bent, book hugged to her chest. He tried to speak but only grunt, and she reeled back after nearly walking into him, her head tipping up.

"Oh I'm so sor—"

Her dark eyes widened, then narrowed, and her lips thinned together. She dropped her gaze and turned her head away. His chest constricted. How could he do this to her, ask her for more? He had humiliated her.

"Vali Ahad," she said, grudgingly. Ruslan cleared his throat. Her gaze darted to him, then up to Omar's face. "You came to make me bow?"

"Of course not." He glanced back at Ruslan, who bowed and retreated into the aisle of books, herding Isler and his men along with him. Omar turned back to Dilay. There was a pretty flush on her cheeks and an infuriated look in her eyes and for a moment he could only stare. He could not do this. He could not ask her to be a friend, an adviser, when he could not look at her without losing half his sense.

"Has the Sultan lengthened your leash for the day?" she asked, gesturing to him blocking her exit. The insult burned like coals in his throat.

"I would like to speak with you, if you have a moment." He shifted the bag of books against his back. All the emotion disappeared from her, a magical trick he used himself, often. But he hated that she was using it with him, though he knew he had earned that distrust.

"I do not."

Omar inhaled and closed his eyes, briefly. When he opened them she watched him with raised eyebrow.

"I need you," he blurted. Heat swirled into his face when her eyes widened and her lips parted. "Uh." He tore his gaze from hers. "I mean, you are an invaluable asset to me and I..." he trailed off as her other brow rose, and a mocking smile curved her lips. He was not this stupefied in front of his father's Council of Viziers, why could he not make any sense now?

"I apologize, Vali Ahad Efendim, but my services are not available, in any capacity, to anyone. I am happily employed here at the University." Her smile shrank and soured.

"Dilay," he pleaded.

She folded her hands in front of her and cast her gaze toward the ceiling. "Instructor Akar," she said.

"Could we just"—he pointed into the office—"sit? Please? For a moment? I brought you something."

If she had been a fire mage with flames in her eyes she would not have looked more furious. Inside he felt small and useless.

"No. I do not want your gifts. Your *bribes*," she practically hissed. "I may not be important enough to you to warrant the truth, but I cannot be bought, for anything or any price. And that you even thought this…" She cast a scathing gaze up and down him that left him feeling vastly inferior. "…pathetic appeal would work shows you do not know anything about me at all."

She moved to slip past him, and Omar grabbed the frame of the door on either side to block her, frustrated nearly to shouting.

"I know you," he forced, in a hard whisper. She looked daggers at him, then his arms, her nostrils flared with her exhalation and all he wanted in the world was to hold her and whisper his heart and he could not. His magic writhed, uncontrolled because of his fatigue and his stifled feelings. "I know you are the most fearless person I have ever met. The strongest. I know that I need you, people like you. I want…" He grit his teeth. "I want to be half the person you are. I want the things you want. I do. But I cannot do it like this." He waved a hand to indicate himself, the magic he was certain flashed in his eyes at the very least.

A crack appeared in her demeanor. Omar seized it.

"I did not mean to hurt you." He glanced over his shoulder and lowered his voice. "I did not intend for things to go as they did." A flash of hurt in her hazelnut eyes nearly broke him in two. Could he try? He could try. Just, take her in his arms and back her into the tiny office and hold her. "I have never known anyone like you. How could any man be expected to not be drawn to you like moth to flame, Dilay? You burn so brightly."

He was only trying to show her his heart, but her eyes shimmered with tears and she sucked in a breath. Those were not happy tears. Panic erased his words and his line of thought and he dropped his hands immediately to give her space. Had he frightened her?

"I just want to live my life," she whispered. "I did not ask for anyone to feel anything for me or give me anything. I wanted to help. I wanted to be kind. I did not…" Her voice broke in increments as she purged the words. "Please don't do this."

"Do…" He laced his fingers together to prevent himself reaching for her and gripped his head. "Do what?"

"Tell me these things. Don't tell me how you feel, or what you want, or need. Don't. I tried to help you, and now I have been humiliated, and Behram won't speak to me because he thinks you are the reason I won't marry him." She pressed a hand over her mouth. Then her tear-filled eyes narrowed. "I don't want anything from you. From either of you. Leave me alone."

Omar bore down with his hands against his head, trying to untangle all the things knotted in his chest.

He could not have her. Not like that. So he should not feel jealous, or angry, or panicked that Behram had asked her to marry him. No. He was here because he needed her. The way his father needed the Grand Vizier, or any of his advisers. Just as Ruslan had said. She was invaluable, not because she made his heart ache, but because she was courageous and intelligent and cared about his people. Because she was taking action.

"It seems"—he tried to smile—"that you have had an exhausting small turn."

Fat tears streaked her cheeks as she gave a single, shaky nod. His heart shattered, his inhale arriving like fire in his chest. "It was selfish of me to burden you with this. But I had to try, at least, to apologize to you. You *are* important enough to me to warrant the truth. I am so sorry, Dilay."

"Do you know what they will think of me if I go in front of my classes with eyes swollen from tears?" She wiped at her cheeks, avoiding his gaze.

That she was beautiful. Real, and true to who she was and what she felt. Omar closed his eyes. "What can I do to help?" he asked, his eyes still closed. He ached. From head to toe, with need. To comfort. To make it right. But he could not. He had not controlled himself and their path enough from the start, the very least he could do now was control this selfish need to comfort her in an effort to soothe himself.

"Come inside," she relented. Omar let his hands fall to his sides, relieved, and trudged into the room after her. She walked to the other side of the little table in the middle of the office and dropped to her knees on the floor cushion. Omar closed the door and sat across from her. There was a lamp and a fading mage orb, so the light flickered and changed, making it hard to see and read her face. "Why are you here?"

"Please forgive me," he said. "I should never have allowed anything between us. I hurt you and I did not intend to."

"Did your father give you permission to come?" She swiped the heels of her hands against her cheeks.

"No," he said. Dilay assessed him for a moment, then one corner of her mouth kicked up. Omar tore his gaze from her face, cinching his fingers together in his lap. Void and stars, this was going to be just as excruciating as he imagined it would. Especially with the added memory of their brief touches.

"I am proud of you," she murmured. Omar rolled his eyes up to stare in supplication at the ceiling as heated joy sprang open in his chest. Pathetic. He was utterly pathetic.

"Ah yes. Like a toddling infant, I have let go of my parents' fingers to wander on my own."

She burst into quiet laughter, and all his tension melted away. She traced a circle on the tabletop with a finger, and he thought of her in the palace library, disheveled, with dirt beneath her nails and her hand entwined in his.

"What were you doing? That day Mazhar brought you to the palace? You were covered in dirt."

She blew upward to dislodge a bit of hair that had fallen in her face. He bent forward to lock his arms between his chest and the table edge so he did not reach forward.

"Planting." She gave a little smile. "I am not a talented gardener, unfortunately."

"I am so happy to hear you have a single failing," he said, suppressing mirth when she eyed him sidelong. She smiled back, though it appeared grudging.

"I have many failings," she said, haughtily.

"Liar." He straightened so he could unsling his bag's strap and place it on the table.

"I am terrible at maths," she said. "And languages. I am clumsy and stubborn."

"Stop," he said. "You will only endear yourself to me more." He pushed the bag toward her. It might have been the light, but he imagined he saw another blush on her cheeks and he wiped his hand over his face. Torture. He should have stayed at the palace and…no. "These are neither gifts nor bribes," he said when she leered at the bag in suspicion. "They are an assignment."

She narrowed her eyes playfully, twisting her mouth to prevent a smile. "Oh? I was certain I said my services were unavailable."

"The guild tribunal is very soon. I know you are invested in the outcome. I think we both know, despite my father's preferences, that it would be best if Altimur Pasha were to continue in his role. I cannot interfere. But you can."

She pulled the bag flap open and pulled out one book after the other, stacking the three Hanim books together. Then she took out the larger blue book, curiosity bright in her eyes. Omar pulled the bag back to give her room as she positioned the book in front of her and framed it with her hands. Her thumb stroked the cover, up and down, her gaze downturned as she did. Omar could look at nothing but the slow movement of her thumb, hot spikes shooting up his inner thighs and into his belly. Wheel save him. What had he been thinking, locking himself in this tiny, dark room with her?

"What is this?" she asked.

"The Book of Chara'a," he said.

Her gaze flashed to his. There had not been a Charah since the Sundering. More powerful than Sival, mages of legend, who had broken the world for their Sultan. The ultimate expression of magic, their power came not from words, like Aval, or sigils, like Deval. Pure energy fueled them, like Sival, but not their own. They were the only mages capable of drawing from the power of others. It had been power like that which had raised the Engeli and fenced Tamar, and magic, away from the rest of the world.

"Do you mean to stand a Circle?" she asked in a quiet, awe-filled voice. He had thought of it on occasion, of balancing the Wheel and righting the wrongs of the past. Omar huffed a laugh.

"That would require there to be living Chara'a. The High Council would soil themselves if anyone even suggested such a thing." The High Council of Viziers had replaced the Circle of Chara'a as the advising Council to the Sultan after the Sundering War demolished the Old Sultanate. He doubted they would respond well to the idea of being made obsolete.

"It would be impossible for other reasons, I suppose," Dilay said, reverently flipping the cover of the book open. "One cannot make a circle with only four Houses. I believe that's called a square."

"Your grasp of geometry is sound, yet you said you were bad at maths," Omar teased.

"Can you imagine?" She turned the pages carefully, gasping at the illuminated letters. Dilay touched the brilliant depiction of the Wheel with her fingers, tracing the Sixth and Third spoke with a forlorn look in her eyes. Houses extinct. Mages that would never walk the earth again, destroyed in the war. "I know so little about this. About Chara'a," she whispered, as if speaking at normal volume would damage the book. Omar could not help but feel glee that he had chosen to bring it, that he could watch her like this. Immersed.

He rose to his knees and crawled, unable to resist, around the table to sit beside her. Dilay did not protest or even acknowledge the move, but turned another page.

"You could try, couldn't you?" Dilay said. "Think of all the possibilities."

"It would take someone with a great deal more faith in the Wheel than I have to conjure up two extinct Houses and the most powerful mages of each to stand a Circle," Omar said.

"First, balance Tamar, then the Wheel," she said, teasing, without looking at him. Then she leaned forward over the book. "Look at this." She traced her finger over the Poem of the Wheel, with its painted and gilded dropped letters and illustrated representations of each of the Houses. "*I am balanced for I am broken,*" she recited, though the poem was written in old common. "Do you know it?" She glanced up at him, and he could only stare, enthralled by her joy.

"I know it," he said, swallowing against the lump in his throat. Dilay's lips parted, and he tried not to look at her mouth. Her brows drew together.

"You do not look well," she said, softly chastising.

"I am better now than I have been in days," he said. Because he was with her.

"You've been attending tribunals. How many?" She laid a hand over the page she had been looking at. Her other moved toward his face, but stopped, a question in her eyes.

"Four," he said. Could he? For just a moment, he could hold it, that writhing mass of threat and seething fangs that was his magic. He needed it, her touch, like he needed air. He canted his head a fraction, so her fingertips brushed his cheekbone. She pressed her fingers back, stroked her thumb over his cheek, then cupped it. Abruptly she withdrew her hand, leaving cold in the absence of her warmth.

"Forgive me. I should think more before I speak…and act."

"I would rather you didn't," he tried to tease.

"It can be misleading," she said. "The way I act. The way I care."

Did she mean him? He was not especially practiced in physical interaction, but he had been fairly sure all their intimacy had been mutually desired. Had he forced himself on her? Had she done things she did not want to because he was…who he was? Nausea knotted in his stomach, and he gripped the table edge. Dilay looked at him, and her brows pinched together, then rose.

"Oh, no," she said, shaking her head. "Not you." She folded her hands in her lap.

He was momentarily confused, then thought he understood. "Behram," he said. She flinched as if he'd struck her. "He asked you to marry him." Was that because of Omar? To stake a claim?

Dilay gave a jerky nod. "As much as Behram *asks* anything."

"He cares about you." Omar thought he did an admirable job of sounding neutral, instead of devastated. What would he do if she chose that? If she and Behram attended palace functions together and he had to watch them dance and laugh and…he silenced his thoughts with a gust of magic.

"He does. Yes." Her gaze flicked to his, some question in her eyes he could not interpret, then she looked away. "He wants something I can never be. I don't want to be married. I want this." She gestured vaguely around them. "And my…hobbies. I worked so hard to get here."

"I know."

"He knows about the school. He said you told him," she murmured. The look she gave him rent his skin like claws. She thought he had betrayed her.

"I did not mean to. It slipped. He wouldn't do anything about it? Anything to hurt you?"

"I like to think not, but he was very angry."

There was a knock on the door, then Ruslan poked his head in. "Forgive me, Efendim, you've been"—he clicked his tongue—"summoned."

Ah. His father had discovered his defiance. Omar nodded to Ruslan, who slipped away again. Omar looked at Dilay, who regarded him with worry.

"Will you be punished?"

"Undoubtedly," Omar said. Would he be under guard now? How far could he push this newfound daring in bucking his father's tie lines?

"So." Dilay slid both hands over her hair and stroked them one after the other down her braid. "What do you want from me?"

"Forgiveness for hurting you." He folded his hands together on the tabletop and stared down at them. She shifted to her hip and propped her elbows beside his arms. She set her chin in her hands.

"Who are you going to marry?" she asked. The question felt like a lead weight dropped on him.

"I don't know. There are candidates but…how do you choose a stranger? How do I tell her…" that he could not touch her. Would he even want to? He chanced a look from the corners of his eyes as Dilay pitched forward and buried her head against her folded arms on the table. It was unbearable, how badly he wanted to touch her. Even just her hair, the rope of her braid, frayed, the color of unadulterated coffee.

"She is just as frightened as you," Dilay mumbled into her arms. "Treat her like a person, and I think you will find most women would be understanding."

"You do not know court," Omar said. The wrong woman with knowledge of his lack of control would wreak havoc on his reign, sow dissension amongst his Council.

"No." Dilay propped her head on her wrists, and stared at the door. "But I know you, a little. I know you would keep her at arm's length, with your very sternest face. And likely never even give her a chance to try."

"Is my face that stern?" He mirrored her position, laying his cheek against his folded hands so he could look at her.

"Yes." She smiled. "It is your most frequent manner. You should smile more."

"Should I?"

"I like it," she said. His heart thumped.

"Then I will." He demonstrated, and she giggled. "Forgive me," he said, "and I will smile whenever you wish."

"You must promise to sit on the other side of tables from me," she said. He chuffed.

"Why?" He couldn't muster a smile then. He knew, but he needed the words. To keep in his heart when he wanted and could not have her. Not even truly as a friend.

"You are the only shiny, expensive, gaudy thing I have ever wanted," she said, straight-faced.

"Gaudy?" he said in affront.

"All that blinding silver," she said. "I much preferred you in the tower…" She dropped her gaze to her fingers, her lips pressing together, and her hands balling into fists.

"When I was sweaty?" he murmured. His memory of the way she had looked at him was sharp and clear, causing him much agitation every time it came to mind. Her thick, dark lashes fluttered over her eyes.

"Normal," she said. "Just, simple clothes. And no guards, or stewards. I liked the spectacles too." The look on her face birthed a fiery ache in him.

He ducked his face against his arms. "A table's length may not be adequate. Perhaps a room. Or several."

"We cannot be friends, can we?" she said, like admitting defeat. He didn't think he could manage it, despite his best intentions. It was perhaps the only time the limitations of his erratic power were a boon to him. That touching her had such devastating possible consequences.

"I still need your help," he said.

"You have everything you need. You just need practice. Something to anchor you."

"Please."

"I have to think about it," she said. When he tried to gauge her face it was shuttered, and she straightened. "Should you go? Will your father have the University raided?"

"He might." Omar followed suit, and stretched. He was so tired.

"Omar," Dilay said when he moved to stand. He looked at her. She closed the Book of Chara'a and pushed it toward him. "Whoever you choose, do not choose a First House mage."

There were multiple barbs on that verbal arrow, and he stared at her in silence. She rubbed her hand over the cover of the blue book, keeping her gaze trained away from his.

"Veritors are only ever borne of two air mages," she murmured. "Make it end with you."

"I will try. I may not have a choice."

"You are a prince of Tamar. You always have a choice," she demanded. "You are a more powerful mage than your father. Do you realize that? And a better man. I will not lose another friend to the shadow of his father. I won't." Her voice wavered. Angry. Anguished. "If that is what you are going to do, to choose, then no. I will not help you."

"I have to go," Omar said, trying to hold himself still, to not grab her and pull her to him.

"Of course you do," Dilay taunted.

He smiled, burning on the inside like he was suddenly possessed by the Fifth House. "You will not lose me to my father. Not if you promise to always speak to me like that."

Her eyes widened in surprise. He bore down on his magic, like holding a writhing cobra with a boot to its hood, and pressed his lips to her cheek. He wanted more. Her mouth. Her body. To be with her the way he had never been with anyone, absorb her ferocity and conviction. He wanted that more than he had ever wanted anything. And he could not bear it a moment longer.

She made a tiny noise in the back of her throat and turned her face toward his. It took everything in him to stroke her hair away from her face with both hands and hold them apart instead of meeting her.

"I have to go, because if I do not, I will do something that we both regret, or I will truly go mad."

"I thought if I saw you again I would have more sense," she murmured in a husky, silken voice that stripped another thread of his control. "I swore I would."

"I am selfishly pleased you do not." Want was all he was. A great, hard ache. She might have been formed of magnetic stone the way he could hardly keep himself apart from her.

"That is very selfish, yes," she said. His desire was scraping away his hold on his magic, and he dropped his hands away from her. Dilay watched his face, and a soft smile made her more beautiful. "I like it when you shine for me, Sabri Sultan. Someday, I hope you shine for them all. So they see you like I do."

"What if I only wish to shine for you?"

"You cannot," she said, admonishing. "You bear us all on your shoulders." She studied him a moment more before she swayed forward to nuzzle her nose against his cheek. Then she stood and collected the Hanim books in her arms. She paused, glancing down at him, then left. Omar sat for a few moments, in the silence, and sought calm before he got up to return to the palace and face his father.

Twenty-Three

DILAY SAT ON THE EDGE of the bench she had claimed inside the guild hall foyer. There were many lining the walls, so people could wait in comfort for whichever office they required. As her classes at the University had ended she rushed to the hall. The day before, she had discovered a chapter in one of the other Hanim law books Omar had given her. It might actually be of use, but she had to announce her intent to the tribunal judges or she could not stand before them today. Her father was in Altimur Pasha's office, along with Semih Kadir and the other judges.

People were already beginning to gather for the tribunal, a weak tide pulling them toward the meeting hall in ones and twos past Dilay as she waited. She hooked her arm over her bag. The four law books Omar had lent her lay tucked inside. After torturous candlemarks of the driest reading she had ever suffered through, she'd found Judge Hanim's writings on laws within the guild framework. Laws which had not found their way into newer books, but which would be honored, as most Old Sultanate laws were within Tamar.

The law she hoped to bring before the tribunal dealt with moral delinquency in someone who held a leadership position within the guild. The subject was tucked in among others, a brief but thorough exploration of the qualities that were unacceptable in a leader. *The purview of morality in guild leaderships.* The paragraph began with: "A tendency toward immorality in personal matters points to an equal propensity for amoral behavior in business matters. It is therefore this judge's edict that anyone properly proven to have committed amoral acts in their personal life are subject to removal from leadership positions within the guild structure, and may not be considered for new leadership. Any acts that cause Unbalance, or which break the Wheel, will be considered grounds. Any acts which place personal gain before the well-being of guild members, the Sultan, or the Sultanate, will be considered grounds."

This was a fine line to walk. Mediation, whether personal or professional, was always broken into two sessions. During the first, all grievances had to be voiced. Each was documented. Then, in the second session, proof in the form of witnesses could be brought for each grievance. No witnesses could be brought forth for grievances not voiced in the first session. And grievances without witnesses were dismissed. If the law Dilay had discovered was not brought to bear in this session, it would be too late.

If she proved Semih Kadir unsound, by Old Sultanate Law, then she hoped the judges would favor Altimur Pasha in their judgment.

Guilt prickled her like nettle spines. Behram had confided many things to her over the Turns. His father's many shady alliances. His ill treatment of Behram's mother as well as Behram. The underhanded dealings his father had used to climb his way up the guild ladder, leaving a pile of ruined rivals in his wake. Their silence in the face of his threats and blackmail.

She had considered all day whether she could bear to stand as a witness, if called. And she would be called. If she gave the book to her father and the judges decided to use the old laws to prevent Kadir Pasha from taking power, they would need witnesses to testify about his moral corruption. Behram would never testify against his own father, from whom he hoped to inherit the reins to the guild, as well as half the city. But Dilay could. And her position as instructor at the University would give her enough authority to do so. But it was an unforgivable betrayal of Behram's trust. Especially since they had not spoken since their argument in the market.

She hoped, if she left him out of it, concentrating only on Semih Kadir's illegal business dealings, that Behram might forgive her. She would not drag his pain and humiliation in front of a guild hall full of strangers and colleagues.

Dilay stood, her urgency making her too anxious to sit still. The back half of the guild hall was walled off for the large, rowdy meetings that were held every few small turns. An expansive, decorative arch led inside. There were no doors, signifying all were welcome, though that was not entirely true. Women were a rare sight in the guild hall, though Altimur Pasha's wife had been slowly making inroads there. Before the meeting hall, the foyer took up the other half of the building, and was as grand and ornate as any room in the palace.

Dilay reached into her bag and withdrew the book. She stroked her hand over the cover as she lounged against the wall opposite Altimur Pasha's office. A white feather, one of the many that always found their way into her clothes, marked the page she needed.

The Wheel, and magic, depended on balance between things. Life for death, fire for water, air for earth. There were acts considered to close the circle, or turn the Wheel. Marriage was one. A broken marriage was a broken Wheel, and it was for that reason that outside the nobility and their arranged marriages aimed at breeding high-order mages, marriage was uncommon throughout Tamar. Certainly people had lifelong partnerships, like her parents, but there was no ceremony binding them. No ceremony to irrevocably close the circle, inescapable. So adultery and divorce were two of Judge Hanim's Unbalanced acts. Murder was another, an act which did not give for what it took. Taking without giving, like stealing, or blackmail, was another Unbalanced act. And Semih Kadir had done a great deal of taking over the course of his life. She doubted he had ever committed murder. Certainly abusing a child was an Unbalanced act, but she would not bring Behram into it without his permission.

Dilay bent forward without separating from the wall to look down the foyer and into the meeting hall's wide-open doors. Six low, backless seats sat in a row at the very head of the hall. Four for the judges selected to mediate, one from each of the four remaining Houses, one for Altimur Pasha, and the last for Kadir Pasha. Behind them sat the final chair, raised above the others on a platform. For the Sultan, or in this case, Omar.

The mood in the foyer changed, like a storm had descended, the rhythm of the conversations that kept the hall from ever being silent changed in pitch and tone, and the collective attention of everyone she could see turned to the entrance. Dilay pushed away from the wall, glancing to the front of the hall as Omar entered, Behram and Osman flanking him. What appeared to be half the palace's contingent of guards preceded them, breaking off to take up positions at the door and intervals along the walls as Omar strode forward. Ruslan and his own smaller entourage of lesser attendants followed behind.

The door to Altimur Pasha's office opened, and he exited, Dilay's father and the other three judges with him, then Kadir Pasha. Every man in the group wore tension, in their faces, or the set of their shoulders. Kadir Pasha was the only one who appeared nonplussed. But then, she had never seen the man look anything but fully in control. Something his son had not yet learned, despite being nearly into his fifth Cycle of age.

In contrast, Omar had a look like he had just finished laughing. Behram and Osman looked similarly amused. The distinction between the younger group and the older struck Dilay, nearly causing her to miss her chance to give her father the book. She wanted to shrink against the wall to avoid Omar's notice. It was difficult enough to do what she needed to without becoming flustered because of the way her knotted-up feelings about him addled her.

She slipped between several people separating her and the judges and caught her father's sleeve. He looked at her in surprise. Before she could hand him the book, she was interrupted.

"Gentlemen," Omar said from behind her. She bowed as the others did, her pulse too fast and her palms cold and damp. The men straightened, and Dilay waited one more beat before she did the same. Reluctantly, she raised her gaze to look at Omar. She hoped, and feared, that he would be looking back at her. When she rose and met his gaze, Omar smiled at her with so much pleasure it knocked her thoughts off course again. Before she could settle them, Behram was at her side, and Altimur Pasha led the others into the meeting hall.

Omar lingered a moment, tense and unreadable, then glanced after Altimur Pasha. Finally he smiled at them and angled his head, then strode away. Dilay turned to Behram. His glimmering gaze coasted over her, lingering in places it should not, and discomposing her even more. He smiled as though there was nothing out of the ordinary hanging between them.

"I need to speak with you," she said.

"After? I wanted to buy you something anyway. To make amends." He reached up to pluck at the collar of her entari, his fingers brushing her neck. Dilay pushed his hand away.

"No. No presents. And I need to speak with you now, before the tribunal."

He sighed, glancing around them at the shifting crowd. Then he took her arm in his grip and steered her toward an alcove.

"Behram!" Semih Kadir barked from the doorway of the meeting hall. Behram bared his teeth. He looked at her, and his gaze went to the book she hugged against her chest.

"What have we here?" He plucked it from her grip, his fingers tracing hers as he did, deliberately, she thought. He was an unrepentant flirt, despite his disdain for women in general. He opened the book to the first page, which described the contents. After he had read enough to ascertain what the book was about, he raised an eyebrow. "Do you wish to be a judge, next?"

"You know I do not." She tried to take the book back, but Behram shifted it away, chastising her with a frown. Her stomach clenched, and her throat squeezed. If he saw what she intended to bring up at the meet, she did not trust that he wouldn't burn the books to ashes.

Dilay made another grab for the book, and when he moved it away she stumbled into him. The people around them stopped to stare, whispering to each other. Dilay flushed in embarrassment as she tugged at the sleeve of his upheld arm.

Behram grinned down at her, his free hand settling lightly at her waist. "I am accustomed to women throwing themselves at me," he said as he lowered the book for her to take, "but not you."

"I'll throw something at you." She snatched the book out of his grip and pushed his hand away. He chuckled, tucking her arm into his and turning them toward the doors. The path between them and the hall miraculously cleared, people shuffling aside as Behram led her in. Dilay submitted to his hold because of the convenience—the crowd stayed out of his way—and also for the sick burden of guilt weighing her every step. Having a particular moral code, she had learned, of putting the many before the few, did not ease the ache when the few were hurt by it. And despite the difficulty of caring for Behram, she did. She was also aware that she might be the only person in Tamar who did. Except, perhaps, for Omar.

"I have to go up there." He pointed.

"But—"

He gave her an apologetic smile and lowered his head to kiss her cheek, which he had not done in Turns. It made her feel cold. What was he thinking?

"Forgive me. I will find you after."

Dilay grabbed for him, but he slipped into the crowd. She cursed, which earned her several chastising looks from men passing into the hall. She hitched herself over one of the benches and wove her way through people trying to find seats, to the front of the hall, where the judges were circled together, chatting. Dilay edged between several men, one of whom questioned her parentage at a volume designed for her to hear him.

She cast him a scowl before she turned and grabbed her father's sleeve, again. He looked at her in surprise as she slipped the book into his hand. She touched the feather, meeting his gaze. His brows rose, then his eyes narrowed. The other judges noticed her, turning toward her as one. She could not tell her father anything with all of them, including Altimur and Kadir Pasha staring at her like she was a fish that had just leapt out of a bucket to land at their feet.

Her father would know, if he managed to read the page before things began, what she intended.

"Now," Dilay said, as a steward of the guild rapped a stick against a brass bell to signal time to start. Her father nodded. She turned, and as she did, she caught sight of Omar, standing beside the chair he was meant to sit in, watching. Dilay smiled at him.

"*You're all right?*" his voice whispered. She nodded to him. Why wouldn't she be all right? "*He didn't upset you?*"

Oh. He'd seen Behram and her. Dilay smiled at him again and made her way back through the people to the section of seats for those who intended to bring up grievances. She looked first to her father, who ducked his head at her, acknowledging he understood. Some of her tension bled away, but returned when her gaze passed by Behram. He stared at her, hard, an edge of suspicion in his eyes. Dilay turned her face toward the floor and busied herself with unslinging her bag to set beneath the bench. Magic was forbidden inside the guild hall, so she dared not use it to control her reactions, though she wanted to. That rule did not seem to bother Omar.

The hall grew quieter as everyone found a seat, and Dilay was sandwiched between two older gentlemen she knew by reputation but not personally. She acknowledged both with a forced smile and stiff nod. They made themselves quite comfortable, sitting with knees spread and hands on their legs, with elbows caging her. The smell of day-old sweat filled the gaps between their limbs, making her wrinkle her nose. When Dilay tried to lean forward to see around one, the other gave a grunt of disapproval when she blocked his view. So she sat, fuming, as Altimur Pasha called the meet to order and Omar took his seat behind the judges.

Low murmurs continued even as Altimur Pasha gave the introduction to the meet, and introduced the judges.

"Today you may speak in favor of or against either Kadir Pasha or Altimur Pasha as it pertains to their future as leaders within the guild. In two small turns we will convene again, and witnesses must testify in verification of any grievances brought against either man. If you do not bring a grievance forward today, it will not be considered in the judgment."

Dilay arched backward to see around the man to her left, since the other wouldn't abide her leaning forward. She managed to position herself exactly right to see between the dozen attendees on the benches to the judges, and behind them, Omar. Her father fidgeted with the hems of his sleeves, his gaze whipping back and forth as people began to rise, marking that they had something to say. The other judges acted similarly. One chewed a nail, another shifted position every few moments. The last was as still as a statue.

And Omar. Straight-backed and serious. He looked like a stranger up there. But he wasn't, not anymore. As she watched him, his gaze flicked to hers. She smiled, more to remind him of that than anything else. He returned it, his shoulders moving as if he laughed a bit. And when he looked away, the smile remained.

Her heart fluttered. It had been days since he had sought her out in the library. They had not spoken or seen each other since, and she had missed him. She had worried and fretted.

Could she help him? Should she? He appeared stripped to the bone with weariness. If helping him control his magic meant he was forced to use it more and more…His mother's threats loomed in her thoughts. A mind broken. She had to tell him. She could not keep it from him anymore.

The judges called on people who had stood, who would voice either words for or against one of the two Pashas. This first candlemark went quickly, but the second dragged. As those still standing dwindled, Dilay's unease returned. Her gaze bounced between Behram and Omar. Behram sat with his father and both Osman and Altimur Pasha on the same bench. Behram occasionally slanted his head close to comment to his father, most commonly when someone spoke against him. His father always smiled his approval at whatever Behram had to say. Twice Behram looked at her, catching her eye and glaring when he did.

When three speakers remained, Dilay clutched the strap of her bag, looped over her knees, shifting so she could stand quickly without entangling herself with her seatmates. She concentrated to calm her pulse. When the last man began his speech, she wiped her hands, one after the other, on her thighs.

The last man sat.

The judges conferred. Dilay tensed. "Is there anyone else?" her father called. He turned his head to her. He had seen the passage. Her nerve failed her. Her body would not obey, her muscles tensed and unresponsive. And Behram looked at her. His gaze arrowed onto hers. She did not know what gave her away, but the smile that started on his face fell. His eyes slitted.

"Then I call this tribunal—"

"Wait." Dilay popped up.

"What is the meaning of this?" Semih Kadir asked, standing. "Can just anyone speak now? A woman? She is not even a member of the guild."

Dilay grit her teeth and forced her back straight, looking at Behram and his father, instead of to her own. That would only hurt her cause. Everyone here knew Judge Akar's daughter. The woman who reached too far. They knew her as a troublemaker. The guild did not abide troublemakers.

"Anyone can speak," one of the judges said. "You know that, Kadir Pasha. Many have spoken in favor of you tonight who are not members of the guild. Any can speak tonight, but must provide witnesses at the next." That judge was a friend of her father's. One who had spent many nights in their home, smoking and solving the world's problems.

Dilay kept her gaze on Behram, whose surprise was now fuel for the fire of his anger. Flames flickered in the depths of his eyes. Fire could burn for warmth, and joy, but Behram's never did. Passion and anger fueled his magic, and now she feared it always would. She did not want to be his enemy, in honor of the boy he had been, and because, if she let it, his anger frightened her.

Around her, the crowd chattered. While some were happy to have anyone speak against Kadir Pasha, many were disturbed by her. As for her father, his face remained impassive, but she knew him well

240 J. D. Evans

enough. He did not like her standing up, making a target of herself for Kadir Pasha. He had never liked her friendship with Behram.

"But this is a sham," Behram's father said. "She is the daughter of one of the judges. Your tribunal is meant to be unbiased. If the children of the judges are speaking against or for one person, we cannot expect a fair ruling."

"She will speak," her father's friend said. Semih sat down, fuming. Dilay did not look at Behram, but she could feel his stare, as if its fire were actually burning her skin.

"I speak to question the personal morality of Kadir Pasha, as governed by the Sixth Law of Judge Hanim, Book Three, outlined in his governance of guild mandates," Dilay said.

"What? We are making up laws now?" Kadir Pasha laughed. Dilay's throat was dry, her hands shaking. She tangled her fingers in her entari, then released them, reminding herself to stand straight and confident.

"These are Old Sultanate Laws." Her father held up the book. "Which we are still, as decreed by the Sultan, bound to obey."

Dilay could not help but look at Behram, whose gaze was fixed on the book. She knew he was looking at the feather, knew it to her bones, and the muscles in his face relaxed as understanding came to him. When he slowly turned his head to look at her, fury burned like a firestorm in his gaze. Her heart sank, and her eyes stung. He leaned in to his father, and Semih ducked down so Behram could whisper something.

Semih straightened, smiling. Dilay's hands clenched at her sides.

"Are those University books? How did you come by them? University books are not to leave University grounds," Semih Kadir said. "Yet here you stand. Can we trust the word of a thief, a thief who questions the morality of others?" Semih looked at Dilay. Behram's gaze bored into her, so intently she could not meet it. She grit her teeth. She absolutely could not reveal they were a gift from Omar. That would paint a picture of their relationship that would ruin Dilay's reputation and destroy the credibility of her arguments. Better she was a thief than a lover accepting gifts, which was exactly what they would all assume.

"I did not steal anything," Dilay said at the same time her father said, "How dare you accuse my daughter of being a thief." Her father stood, nearly toppling his seat as he did.

When Omar spoke it silenced everyone and riveted every gaze in the room on him. "Those books do not belong to the University."

Slowly, gazes turned back to Dilay, while hers remained on Omar. She hoped that was not all he intended to say. He shifted, propping a hand on one knee as a smile flitted then disappeared from his mouth.

He did not look at her. "They belong to the palace."

Dilay could not help looking at her father. Surprise then disbelief suffused his face, then was gone, replaced with a mask. A mask she could not manage for herself in the moment. But she knew what lay beneath it. He understood immediately that Omar had given them to her. He would be irate, with this evidence of favor from the Vali Ahad. That was two people who mattered to her betrayed in one moment.

Whispers hissed through the room, and Dilay set her jaw, trying to control her embarrassed flush with focus instead of magic.

"The Queen Sultana was impressed with Instructor Akar's accomplishments and took an interest in her future advancement."

Dilay's muscles relaxed. It was not the entire truth, of course, but neither was it a lie. If she could have beamed at him without looking like a smitten fool, she would have. Instead she addressed the judges.

"Judge Hanim wrote four books on the laws of the Old Sultanate. He served as judge for decades. The book Judge Akar holds has an entire chapter dedicated to the governing of guilds. One of those laws pertains to the moral behavior of guild leaders."

"Citing new laws now? In the middle of a tribunal?" Semih scoffed.

"They are not new laws, Kadir Pasha"—Dilay bowed when he looked at her—"but foundational laws written by the brightest minds of the Old Sultanate."

"The grievance holds," her father's friend said. The other two judges looked at each other, and Dilay waited to see if they disagreed. But each nodded. Her father sat. Dilay collapsed into her seat, jostling the men to either side, both of whom cast her disapproving glowers. She felt lightheaded. Her stomach roiling and tumbling as the judges made their required speeches.

When the steward rang the bell to announce the end of the tribunal, Dilay lunged to her feet and dashed for the exit, trying to avoid the press of crowds. She had to get away. There were tears barely held in check, and she was not sure she wouldn't faint or be sick. Neither could she face Behram.

"*Dilay*," Omar's voice whispered. She couldn't respond. She needed out of the hall and into the fresh air. But the crowd did not move in her favor, and just as she made the door from the hall to the foyer, Behram caught up to her. Because people moved aside for him. Not for her.

He did not look at her, simply appeared beside her, curled his fingers around her upper arm to steer her, and pulled her with him as he strode out of the hall and down the road, ducking into the first alley that would allow them privacy. Dilay did not fight him, she only stumbled along after him, brokenhearted and resigned. Night had fallen over the marks they had been in the tribunal, and the streets were lit by orbs. The smell of the food vendors in the nearby market made Dilay gag.

Behram stopped in the mouth of the alley and spun her to face him. The light from the mage orbs meant to illuminate the street did not quite reach into the alley. Which made the fire in his eyes shine sharper. Angrier. Dilay's tension wound tight around her chest. Behram's grip burned. Wheel and spokes he was as hot as a forge fire. Sweat broke out across her entire body, as if she were standing in the sun in the deep heat of summer.

He could hide his anger on his face, when he wanted to. But he could never hide his fire.

"Tell me," he said, with flames licking at the ends of each word, "that this was not your idea. Tell me your father put you up to it. Or Omar. Anyone." When she did not answer right away he bared his teeth. "*Tell me.*"

"Behram," she said, weakly. His bared teeth became a mocking smile, and he dropped her wrist as if it were a dead rat. She reached for him. He jerked back.

"You are the only woman I have ever unburdened myself to," he said. "The only one I trust."

Dilay swallowed. Tears bit at her eyes. Her nose stung. "I had to."

"You are trying to take everything from me," he accused. "And you have made a mockery of my trust."

"This is about your father. Not you," she said. He gave her a mocking sneer. "I don't want to take anything from you. Even if you do not have control of the guild, you have so much. More than I ever will, more than most of the people in the city. There is so much more you could do and be. Let me free you from him."

"I will be free when I have more power than he does, when I can control him. But you cannot stand that, can you? I must always be poor Behram to you. That broken boy."

"No." Dilay pressed her hands to his chest. The heat of his magic receded a fraction, his lids half closing, but then the fire returned, his mouth twisting in concentration. "Please," she said. "This is not about you and me. It is not about trust and betrayal or power. It is about what is right, and good, and fair for everyone."

Behram sneered. "Little Dilay, always worrying about the greater good instead of herself. Instead of her friends." There was more than anger in his gaze. There was hurt as well. "You will never learn that *everything* is about power."

"It does not have to be." Dilay took a chance, and wrapped her arms around his waist, laying her head against his chest. "Please don't do this, Behram. Please trust me. You always have. I have never done anything to purposefully hurt you."

"Intention," Behram intoned, one hand clasping the back of her neck, the other flattening against her back, "is both the weakest and most powerful tenant of magic. Your intention does not stop the bleed, Dilay."

His hand on her back tightened into a fist in her clothes and fear curled up her spine.

"There is another law from the Old Sultanate you should consider studying." He pulled her hard against him and ducked his head down to her ear. "The law of reciprocity," he murmured, with fire lacing the words, "an eye for an eye." He released her as abruptly as he had grabbed her, and stepped back. "I find a pleasing balance in the concept."

Her throat tightened, he smiled, and the heat, the fire of his magic, winked out, though it burned still in his eyes.

"Good night, Instructor Akar." He walked away.

Dilay collapsed against the alley wall and sank to the ground. Tears spilled down her cheeks as she wrapped her arms around her knees and tucked her head against them.

She'd hurt him. Wheel and void, it hurt. To know that there was no right and wrong here, just a joyless, endless grey.

Twenty-Four

DILAY SAT NEXT TO HER mother, sandwiched in the cushions of their couch, watching her father argue with himself as he walked between the kitchen and the front door. He was eating a pastry, one of three Dilay had bought at the market as a peace offering.

"Is he ever going to forgive me?" It had been three days since the guild tribunal.

"I imagine," her mother said, preoccupied with the cloth she was mending. "He is also very proud of you."

Dilay slouched against the back of the couch, angling her head to look at the ceiling. "How can he be proud and angry?"

"Because," he said without stopping his pacing, proving that he was not as lost to his agitation as she had thought, "you were very brave."

She started to smile.

"And stupid. Utterly stupid." He stopped with his back toward the front door and brandished his pastry at her, flinging bits of pistachio over the carpet. Her mother's fingers stilled with the needle, as she frowned at the scattered crumbs. "What were you thinking, accepting bribes from the palace?"

"They were not bribes." Dilay cupped her hand over her eyes. "An exchange. To help the Vali Ahad, he agreed to allow me access to the palace library. I thought it might have books to help with the dispute, and I was right."

"So now you are on their leash. What will happen when they find out about your school?"

Nothing, Dilay thought, half amused, half bitter. "They have better things to do than follow me about, don't you think, Baba?"

He screwed his face up.

"Please sweep that up, Roshan," Dilay's mother said placidly as she tugged a stitch. He immediately went to the kitchen to retrieve a broom, but launched into his lecture as soon as he returned.

"And now Semih Kadir sees you as a threat. You know he has only tolerated your bizarre friendship with his son all these Turns because—"

"It is not bizarre," Dilay huffed, sitting up. Or at least, it hadn't been. It was becoming so. There was hardly anything of their friendship left. "And what other choice did I have? I only just found the chapter."

"Do not interrupt me." He jabbed the broom at the rug.

Someone knocked on the door. Her father stopped his attack on the crumbs and yanked the door open. Three women stood on the other side, bunched together. The one in front bowed to her father. He stared. They were wearing palace uniforms, finely cut brocade, silver embroidered over entari the color of their magical Houses. Her mother hissed when she pricked her finger on a needle. She grabbed Dilay's wrist as if she meant to yank her to her feet.

"Can I help you?" Dilay's father asked.

"We are servants of the Queen Sultana. She requests the presence of Dilay Akar."

"For what reason?"

"Baba," Dilay protested as she stood. Her mother gripped her hand, making a soft sound of protest.

"You see? How many times have you been forced to go now? This is exactly what I said would happen." He turned and stormed into the room he shared with her mother, slamming the door. The head servant continued smiling cordially, though a line marked her brow. The Sultana had said she would give Dilay time to decide before she summoned her again. Apparently, her time was up. This time, Dilay would not be bullied. She had opinions about them all keeping secrets from Omar, and since she would be there anyway, it was the perfect excuse to tell him the truth of what would happen to him.

"I have to go." Dilay squeezed her mother's hand. "Anne, it is all right." She smiled.

Her mother stood as Dilay stepped away from her, face set with worry. Dilay nodded encouragingly at her over her shoulder. Inside, she was not as cheerful. Would she lose Omar now as well? He could not be expected to forgive her complicity in the lies everyone was telling him.

She smiled at the women, swallowing back the ache in her chest.

THE RIDE TO THE PALACE was much more pleasant than the last. The women chatted with her, asked her what it was like being an instructor, and were friendly as they escorted her to the Sultana's chambers.

Beste answered when they knocked and offered Dilay a reluctant smile. That did not bode well for the Queen's intentions. Dilay clasped her hands in front of her and strode into the room. The Sultana was seated in the same place she had been on Dilay's first visit. Her manner was much less friendly this time. Dilay bowed, then took the seat that was indicated for her, a cushioned stool with no back, in front of a table with ibrik and cups. Beste poured coffee. Dilay picked the cup up but did not drink.

She and the Sultana stared at each other for a moment of loaded silence.

"I would like to thank you," the Sultana finally began. Dilay turned the tiny coffee cup in its saucer, gazing into it. The foam on the top was honey colored, the coffee beneath black. The sharp scent was enough to ratchet her pulse. "I embraced my son for the first time in more than a decade." The Sultana took a sip of her coffee and it clinked as she returned the cup to the saucer, then both to the table.

Dilay nodded. The impending *but* seemed to fill the room, and she felt no need to delay its arrival.

"Have you considered my offer?"

Dilay inhaled slowly through her nose, straightening her spine as she did, and lifting her gaze to meet the Queen Sultana's. She had defied the ancient traditions of a University, broken the laws of a Sultanate, faced a tribunal of guild judges, weathered the firestorm of Behram's anger, and nearly estranged her parents. What was an angry Queen Sultana?

"Your threat?"

The corners of the Sultana's mouth twitched up, and she sipped her coffee, waiting.

"I have a new bargain. You will allow me to help him gain control, and you will stop lying to him about the consequences of his power." A sound buzzed in her ears. Perhaps the fear she was suppressing. The woman was not physically imposing, by any means, but her cold composure and the reach of her power was threat enough.

"My dear, a bargain has two halves. Usually the second begins with *or else*," the Sultana prompted. The mockery was clear, though her tone remained civil.

"*Or else*, when I tell him the consequences of his magic, I will also tell him who forced me to keep the truth from him." Dilay matched the Sultana's lifeless smile.

"Oh? Did I force you? I thought I offered you a very generous alternative."

"I will not allow him to walk blindly into his fate, Efendim. I do not care what you do to me." That was not entirely true, but she did know she could never live with having kept such a thing from him for her own welfare.

"While I am pleased by your show of spine, and what is obviously affection in your misguided attempt at protecting my son, I am not the one hurting him. You are."

Dilay grit her teeth to silence her immediate retort as she set her coffee on the table. When she summoned enough composure to speak, the Sultana interrupted her.

"Stand at the window," the Sultana said, crisply. She indicated the wall of arched glass windows and doors. Dilay stared in confusion. A hand caught her, gently but firmly, by the elbow. Dilay stood at Beste's urging, and Beste led her to stand in front of the window just behind the Sultana. "I thought you might be interested in sharing my view of things."

Dilay watched the empty garden beyond. There were gravel paths cut through, carefully manicured sections of grass and tidy bushes. Some flowering vines, but it was sterile. Perhaps the Sultana enjoyed the bit of greenery as a break from the inside of the palace, but Dilay did not care for it.

Just as she started to turn away to ask what she was supposed to see, movement at the far end caught her attention. The garden seemed to connect different areas of the palace, and as she watched, a cluster of men appeared from the end nearest the palace entrance. They advanced through the garden. She recognized palace guard uniforms. Then Ruslan.

She did not recognize Omar until he dropped to his knees in the gravel.

Ruslan knelt beside him, but no one touched him. No one tried to help him up. And he needed help. His head lolled, and blood dripped from his nose and trickled from the ear she could see. Dilay grabbed for the handle of the door, panicked.

"No," the Sultana ordered. She stood and circled her chair to press her hand to the glass. "This is your fault."

"My fault?" Dilay pressed her hands to the glass, frantic. Why was he bleeding? "What have you been doing to him? How many confessions are you demanding of him?"

"He demonstrated control, he showed more tolerance. So now he will be used up until there is nothing left of him. You sentenced him to this."

"If you had not kept the truth from him, he would not try so hard to please the Sultan," Dilay snapped. "Let me out of here. I can help him."

As she spoke he pitched forward, pressing his hands to the ground, and staggered to his feet. Ruslan handed him a cloth, which he wiped against the blood. Dilay's fingers curled into her palms. Omar walked like he was drunk, and if he collapsed right there, drained from using his power, what would they do? Leave him out in the dirt?

"What you may do is leave the palace. And if I ever hear of him meeting with you again, for any reason, I will destroy you."

Dilay shivered. Beste moved to her side, but Dilay swiveled away when the woman moved to take hold of her arm again. She turned from the glass and stalked to the door, which she yanked open before Beste could reach it. Dilay heard the door close, loudly, behind her, and assumed they had shut it. She made it four steps before she stopped, holding in a sob. She pressed her fingers to her eyes to chase away the tears.

Gentle, female fingers closed on her arms. Dilay jerked in surprise and whirled. Beste held a finger up, over her lips, and took Dilay's hand. She turned her around, and led her in the opposite direction down the hall. Beste walked so quickly Dilay had to trot to keep up. The older woman stopped at a door four removed from the Sultana's and pressed her ear against it.

After a moment she jerked as if startled, grabbing Dilay's hand again and tugging her into a curtained alcove on the opposite wall. The doors opened, and Ruslan exited, with the guards at his heels. Beste peeked around the curtains, made the shush sign to Dilay again, and tiptoed to the door.

Burning with questions, Dilay obeyed Beste's request for quiet. When Ruslan and the guards disappeared around a corner, Beste carefully pressed the door handle down, easing the heavy wooden panel open. Dilay followed her inside. It was set up almost exactly the same as the Sultana's room. A sitting area facing the formal, tidy garden. The patterns and upholstery were different, but did not veer from the white, blue, and silver of nearly all the palace.

Beste turned to her and gripped her shoulders, pulling her close to whisper. "You may go to him. But do not speak unless the Vali Ahad tells you it is safe. The Sultan listens."

"The Sultana—"

"He is mine as much as he is hers, and you have done more than just help his magic. She is afraid she will lose him. But I believe you are helping. I will speak to her on your behalf."

She smiled as she pulled away, sneaking out as quietly as she had snuck in. The door clicked shut, and Dilay glanced around. There were doors to either side. A droplet of blood marred the marble tiles to her right. The door opened suddenly, just a crack, and Beste stuck her arm through, waving it frantically toward the other end of the room. She spoke to someone in the hall. Someone male.

Dilay ran through the sitting room and opened one of two white doors, slipping into the room beyond just as Beste escorted someone in.

"It is too soon, he is only just arrived back, Efendim."

"Just let me see him." That was the Sehzade's voice. Dilay took stock of the room she was in. A washroom. In the dim light filtering in from the sitting room beyond she saw marble and wood, stacks of fluffy towels on a bench by an expansive tub set into the floor. It was bigger than her home's kitchen; the tub alone was the size of her bedroom. What her home must have looked like to Omar. She cringed.

In the room beyond, footsteps scuffed the marble, whispered voices. Dilay opened the door a crack and peeked out. The door on the opposite side of the sitting room was ajar. Beste stood just inside. When Dilay peeked, Beste cast a quick look back and saw her, then immediately looked away.

Dilay retreated a bit more into the shadow of the washroom, waiting. She tugged and picked at the fabric of her caftan.

"Efendim, he needs his rest," Beste insisted. Was he asleep? Could he have been in mage sleep? If his magic was depleted enough, it was possible. But how he had managed to get to the room under his own power was a mystery then. Mage sleep was not something a mage chose, it happened when their magic was exhausted and they began drawing on their own life to cast. She pressed her hands and forehead against the cool marble and closed her eyes.

With a thin, dancing thread of silver magic, she pictured her mother in her mind's eye. Dark-haired and dark-eyed, calm like a summer breeze.

"*Anne*, I am safe. But I will be some time," she whispered into her power. The filament resonated, twisting and swirling until it dissipated. A little jolt of dizziness made her doubly grateful for the cool stone.

"I'll send the physician," Mazhar said, his voice growing louder. Moving toward the door.

"As you wish, Efendim. But wait. Give him a few candlemarks of sleep before someone comes to interrogate him with questions."

Mazhar sighed, the sound accompanied by the door opening. "Yes, Teyze."

Dilay risked a look, just as Mazhar bent to kiss Beste's cheek.

"You will stay with him?"

"I will ensure someone is always with him." She smiled serenely. Mazhar left. The door swung shut. Dilay poked her head out of the bathroom. Beste's smile fell as she stared at the door, then she turned and strode to the washroom where Dilay hid. She dipped her fingers into the pouch at her waist and they came away with rust-colored chalk, which she used to draw a dampening spell.

"I will tell Ruslan he is not to be disturbed, but you must be alert, do you understand? Ruslan cannot keep the Sultan out. Or the Queen Sultana. When you leave, do so through the garden after it is dark. Straight east will lead you to the courtyard."

Dilay nodded, swallowing back her nervousness. What if someone caught her? Beste searched her face.

"You are a kind girl, Mistress Akar. He needs people like you, to remind him that he is also kind. Yes?"

Dilay nodded once, and Beste left her. Dilay stood for a moment after the door had closed to the hall, afraid the moment she stepped out someone else would appear. But she needed to see him. She advanced a step from the washroom into the bright, cheery sitting room. The afternoon light outside was warm, casting all the pale colors of the room as peaceful. She crossed the marble landing that stretched between the rooms, one step above the sunken sitting room in between.

The doors that led to Omar's room were double, two halves of an arch, painted white and carved with the Sabri crest. She touched her fingertips to the wood, pausing for a heartbeat before she gave a tiny push. The door opened smoothly and quietly. The room beyond was a bedroom, unnecessarily enormous. As big as the sitting room at her back, capable of hosting a dozen people with room to spare. Dilay blinked at the bed, bedecked in silver and white and blue, piles of brocade quilts and feather-stuffed pillows. Her entire family would fit on that bed. As a child she would have delighted in jumping on it. Had he?

But there was no cheer in this room, not like there should have been in a room so large and lavish. It was lonely. The feeling fell like a weight on her as soon as she stepped inside the doors. Cold, despite the warmth of the spring day outside. The windows were turned at an angle to the garden that did not let the sun in. Besides that, the curtains were closed. Rather than look at Omar, who was lying on the bed, unmoving, she crossed to the windows and yanked the curtains open, irrationally angry. This room felt like a prison.

She returned to the bedroom doors and closed them, and when she saw the silver, filigreed bolt, she locked it. It would give her an extra moment of warning if she needed it. A mix of determination and self-consciousness turned in her chest as she faced the bed and circled it to the side where Omar lay.

He was on his side, had apparently managed to strip to his caftan and salvar before he laid down. Both were soaked with sweat, and as she sat on the edge of the bed, he shivered. The muscles in his neck and jaw stood out, then relaxed, though a crease remained on his brow. A spreading circle of blood marred a cloth someone had tucked beneath his head, where his nose occasionally dripped onto it. Dilay tried to breathe, but it was noisy, and her brow furrowed.

"Hello," she murmured around the hitch of emotion. "It's just me." She thought he might not like her to see him like this. "If I touch you, are you going to let your magic hurt me?" She doubted it. That lashing out was conscious—self-loathing and the only way he could bear to defy his father. By having no control.

He was not on the edge and not quite to the middle of the bed, which would take him at least two full rollovers to occupy. Dilay toed out of her shoes and laid down, facing him. He was hot, a fever, or some reaction of his magic. She could feel it even with an arm's length between them.

"Do they always do this? Just leave you by yourself in here?" She hated that. Leaving him alone and in pain, with whatever he had witnessed in the minds of others still playing in his head. Dilay folded her left arm under her head and reached to him. She hovered her fingers over his temple, wondering if there was truly a way to ready oneself to have their mind invaded. But maybe, if he did, he would see how she cared for him, and it would help.

She brushed her fingers over his skin, from the corner of his brow to his ear. His face scrunched, and she withdrew her hand. "It's me," she murmured. He relaxed and she tried again, following the slope of his cheekbone with the pad of her finger. Dilay adjusted her head higher up on the pillow she'd claimed.

"My father is angry with me." She rubbed her hand over his short, dark hair. It was soft, though she wished it were longer so she could stroke her fingers through it. Omar's body relaxed. "He thinks I've made myself a puppet of the palace." She skimmed her nails over his head. His hands eased out of fists. "I suppose I am. Just look at me. Not a very respectable way for an instructor to conduct herself. And where shall I begin with your mother, hmm?"

A vein throbbed in his temple, and she massaged the area with her thumb, pressing her fingers back over his head as she had watched her mother do for her father. Omar seemed to take a deeper breath.

"Are you awake? If you're pretending, I will be very cross," she threatened, smiling. But she could tell, by the still heaviness of him, that he was indeed asleep, and was unlikely to wake soon. It might not be a true mage sleep, but he was undoubtedly overtaxed. She used the cloth to wipe another droplet of blood off his nose, blinking away angry tears. How could they let him do this to himself?

"This bed is the most comfortable thing I have ever felt," she said. Leagues away from the hay-stuffed, coarse linen mattress on her own bed. The cost of the bleached linens and pillows alone could likely buy an estate. Dilay hummed a song. The silence made her sad, so she had to fill it. She propped herself on an elbow so she could tuck one hand under his head and continue her gentle massage on both temples. When her hands began to ache she folded her arm under her head once more. She was embarrassed by how much she wanted to explore his skin. Despite his pain, despite that he was not awake to agree to it.

Dilay withdrew her hand and tucked it under her cheek to prevent herself acting on her desire. She watched him. His breathing seemed steadier, though she was no physician, with experience judging such things.

She should go, before someone came and found her. But she hated him being alone.

"I'll stay a bit longer, all right?"

Twenty-Five

His mouth tasted like he'd eaten something rancid. Omar groaned and rolled out of bed. When he stumbled to the door it would not open, and it took him long, confused moments to realize the bolt was turned. He cursed Ruslan as he crossed the sitting room to the washroom. He relieved himself and recoiled from the grizzly swath of dried blood that marred his cheek when he looked in the mirror. That explained the taste in his mouth. He splashed water on his face from the basin, and grumbled about why they still gave him pristine white towels.

It was tempting to lay down on the cold marble floor, to ease the waves of heat that racked him every few steps. But he just wanted sleep, not to wake up stiff and freezing in a dark washroom. He had no idea what time of day it was, except that the rooms were dark, so he had apparently slept the rest of the afternoon away. Not terrible, considering the state he'd been in. Before Dilay made him understand why he couldn't control things, he would have slept through the night. His head ached less too.

The mage orbs in the sitting room needed to be renewed, they were fading to uselessness, and he stubbed his toe on the table in the entry as he went, nearly toppling the decorative vase on top. He righted it, considering removing every single piece of nonessential frippery that someone else had chosen to put in his room.

The orbs in his bedroom were in better shape, so he made it around to the pitcher of water on the stand beside the bed without incident. He poured a glass and downed it. He would just sleep more. The idea of speaking or facing anyone was too much at the moment. He set his glass down and tugged his caftan up and off, dropping it in a heap on the floor. He poured another glass, noticing only then that the curtains to the garden were open.

Odd. Ruslan usually closed them. Earth mages liked things dark. They were like moles. Omar snickered to himself, then winced when his head throbbed. He raised the glass to his lips again. His gaze dropped to the bed.

A cascade of dark hair covered the pillow on the far side. He blinked, taking a careful sip of his water as he squeezed his eyes shut. Was that a memory? His? Someone else's? He opened his eyes. Still there. Carefully, he set the glass back on the table and put one knee on the bed, half afraid this was the beginning of a nightmare. Should he…talk? He braced himself on his hands, and the figure…person… whatever, rolled toward him.

He nearly choked on his fast inhale at the sight of her face. "Dilay?"

Her eyes opened. Her brow knitted, and she jerked her head up to look around as if she was as confused as he was. She looked at him again, and her gaze tracked down, from his face, to the rest of him. Her entire body jolted, and she squealed as she rolled off the far side of the bed and landed with a thump on the floor.

He lunged across the bed and looked down at her. "Are you all right?"

She lay on her back with her hands over her face. "Mmhmm."

He stretched out on his belly, muzzy-headed and still trying to understand what was happening. "Come back."

"No, thank you. You are naked."

"I am not naked," he said. He was, in fact, very close to naked.

"I didn't mean to be here. I fell asleep. Oh Wheel," she groaned.

"At least sit up."

She obeyed, and he scooted back from the edge, sitting in the center of the bed.

"Not that I object to waking up with you"—he heaved a breath—"in my bed. But it is not exactly the circumstances I imagined."

Her face brightened, her eyes widening, and she pressed her face into her hands again. He felt bad for embarrassing her, but she was also charming, and he was still too groggy to be entirely polite. Besides. She had been in his bed. He'd slept next to her. Some of the ache in his neck and head faded, replaced with a thrum of pleasant warmth.

"Your mother"—she looked in several places, none of them were him—"wanted me to see what the tribunals do to you. So I would stop helping you. Beste snuck me in when you returned. And like a simpleton I fell asleep. What if someone saw me?"

"The door was locked. Was that you?" If someone had seen her his waking would have been much less pleasant.

She nodded. He grunted, rubbing his hands over his face. That made sense, now that his mind was clearing. Ruslan couldn't have locked the door from the outside.

"Are you feeling better?" she said.

Her presence had certainly distracted him from the usual array of symptoms. Flashes of memory, more pain. And he had not vomited once. But he hadn't been awake very long. He should make her leave before she bore witness to any more of his weaknesses. Or…

"Come up here," he said.

"I am not coming up there with you while you are naked," she said in exasperation.

"I am not naked," he insisted.

"Half naked." She scrunched her face.

"Fine, I'll put this on." He retrieved his caftan from the floor. Dilay recoiled, he could only assume because it was stained with sweat and blood.

"You don't have a clean one?"

"Somewhere, probably," Omar said, discarding the caftan again.

"Somewhere probably?" She climbed onto the bed and sat, folding her legs in front of her. Omar made an experimental shift closer.

"I don't know where Ruslan keeps my clothes…he just brings them." He moved again, scooting in front of her.

"Great Wheel," she exclaimed, then displayed something between a smile and a grimace. "Do you know how unbearable you are? You don't even know where your own clothes are."

He shrugged, mostly to irritate her. She gave his shoulder a tiny backhanded slap of admonishment. She immediately straightened, clutching her fingers against her chest.

"Forgive me, I… When you were asleep I thought it was safe to touch you."

"That was risky," he said in disapproval.

"No," she said. "I don't believe it was."

She had touched him? He obviously hadn't hurt her, and he was relieved for that.

"I told you, I think you choose to do that."

"To hurt people?" What joviality her presence had caused faded.

"To hurt yourself. To defy your father. By showing him he cannot control you, or your magic."

"So"—Omar pressed his fists to the mattress and levered himself close, so their knees almost touched—"do you think you're safe now that I am awake?"

She cocked her head, and he took a moment in the silence to appreciate the tempting mess of her mahogany, sleep-tangled hair and the fact that it had been made so while she slept next to him. That was an unexpected pleasure.

"Am I safe, now that you're awake? Safe from you? And your father? Beste says he listens."

"Sometimes," Omar said. "I usually know when he is." He was not interested in talking about his father, at the moment. "What exactly do you mean you touched me, while I was sleeping?" Would she do it now that he was awake? Did he trust himself to let her? His magic was as drained as it had ever been.

"Don't be lewd," she reprimanded. He grinned. Dilay lunged sideways to grab a pillow, which she smashed into the side of his face.

He grunted in surprise, then laughed in disbelief. She withdrew the pillow, gave him a little glare, and smacked him again.

"Give me that." He tried to wrestle it from her.

"Get your own. You have enough on this ridiculous bed for thirty people." She hit him again.

"Ridiculous? This is a prince's bed," he taunted.

"A prince who cannot even dress himself." She shoved the pillow over his face, and he obliged by falling under the pressure, landing on his back.

"Are you attacking me? I'm wounded," he protested.

"Poor Vali Ahad." She pressed the pillow up to his forehead and looked down at him. "Poor, poor you."

"Keep it up," he said. Void he wanted her. Laughing and messy and bright and beautiful. "Taunt me again."

"Oh?" she said. "I thought you were wounded."

"You've bested me. Be merciful."

Her expression took on a different edge, less humor and more contemplation. A swirl of hope and desire lit in response, burning in his belly.

"What is mercy?"

He pushed the pillow away, up toward the headboard, and since she was holding it her arms stretched above him, lowering her face closer to his.

"You should touch me again," he said, gripping the fabric of the pillowcase to prevent himself grabbing for her.

"You want me to touch you…while you are naked and in your bed." She raised an eyebrow. His body clenched from head to toe, silencing his voice and fogging his mind. "That is a very bad idea. How are you going to be Sultan with terrible ideas like that?" She clicked her tongue. "I thought we agreed on at least a table length between us."

He relaxed as he chuckled, closing his eyes. "You were the one who snuck into my bedroom."

She shifted beside him, releasing the pillow, and dragging her hands down the sheets to cup his head. He reacted on instinct, grasping her shoulders and opening his eyes.

"Betrothed," she murmured. "Why are you always testing me so?" He liked that look in her eyes. So close to the one she wore for the books he had given her. Desire.

"Not technically." He tried to smile. Not yet. But this would make it hurt more, wouldn't it? Yet he couldn't stop it, couldn't stop the want.

"You would make a fine tribunal judge," Dilay said. "Ruling your nation on technicalities."

"I'm not trying to rule a nation just now," he said, pulling gently on her shoulders while trying to convince himself not to, "just convince you to kiss me." He closed his eyes again. The dim circle of thoughts in the back of his mind, the ones warning him they shouldn't, could not, because of who he was, and who she was, because of Behram, because of everything, went silent when she brushed her mouth against his. It felt little more substantial than when she had blown a breath across his cheek in her home, but the result was to immolate him.

"Please." He opened his eyes to see her looking at him, her mouth hovering over his. Dilay's fingers pressed harder against his head, and he heeded the wordless command, tilting to meet her. She made a sound when they connected, a little *mmf* that destroyed the fine threads of self-control he had left. Her lips were soft like he had never known, giving when he demanded, urging him to a rhythm they could meet together. She taught him with little examples, gently guiding his head and nudging him with her nose when he lost himself. When he thought he had begun to master it, she flicked her tongue across his bottom lip.

His body understood something he did not, raging hotter, aching. He pulled back. Dilay swiped her thumb over his mouth. Her cheeks were flushed, her eyes dark.

"Tell me…" he said, "what to do."

"Just"—she returned to him, her lips moving against his as she whispered, "open your mouth." She kissed him. He obeyed, and when her tongue met his, graphic thoughts of all the other things he wanted, needed, nearly sent his body into convulsions.

"Void," he cursed, in a brief pause. "Dilay." He swallowed, squeezing his eyes shut. "I have lacked imagination all these Turns. That is miraculous."

"You are a fast study." She laughed, and tucked her head into the crook of his neck, mouth on his skin, her fingers stroking his temple and hair on the other side. Lightning sizzled under each touch of her mouth, warmth then cool, too much to feel and not enough, every nerve in his body burning and needful. His magic churned, depleted and impotent, surging in time with his hammering pulse. Dangerous.

"I think you've cured my headache," he said roughly, gasping when she placed a breathy kiss on his ear.

"Oh good," she said, brightly, and sat up. "My work is done."

He snarled playfully at her and grabbed her shoulders, pulling her down on top of him. She laughed in surprise, her hands pressing to his chest. Her cool palms were like ice brands on his burning skin. Could he tell her he wanted to know what her hands felt like everywhere? He couldn't say that. "I'll say when your work is done." It was never going to be done. This want was never going to ease, he could feel it into his bones. "I want to know what you did while I was sleeping."

She adjusted on top of him, her weight so foreign and exquisite he could think of nothing else for a moment, feeling every wrinkle in the fabric between them, every place her body weighed on his. Some places on her were soft and full, making his hands feel empty and electrified. Secret curves and dips he wanted to know, by touch and taste. Her hips shifted over his, settling perfectly aligned with his, her legs and his woven between each other. The pressure of her pelvis on his, new and rapturous torture, made him groan, though he hadn't meant to.

She pressed her toes against the top of his feet, her face heating as she dropped her gaze from his face to his chest. He felt her in his heart, settling inside him like her weight had over his body, the little push of her feet against his a tiny reprimand. Adorable and arousing in an entirely different way. It made him possessive. He wanted that to be his. Little things no one else knew about.

He tangled his fingers in her hair, holding her head as he raised his to kiss her again. Her feet pushed again, and she slid up so he could lay his head back. But her hip pressed against his arousal in the best and worst of ways, and he hissed against her mouth. Her fingers curled against his chest, and he had never been so grateful for a sweaty, bloodstained caftan he couldn't wear, that his skin was naked to the simplest of her touches. And he was just as grateful his magic was barely a flicker, depleted by exhaustion.

"If this was the way I always woke, it would not matter how many tribunals I had to do," he stated when they broke apart. She went still. Edginess took the place of languor. "What is it?"

"Do they always leave you alone?" She tucked her head into the slope of his neck again, resting it on the bed beside his. He did not like her tone, the sadness that had manifested, but was so in love with the feeling of her snuggling into him that he was too confused to understand her question.

"What else would they do? Sit and stare?"

She made a pained sound, pressing a kiss behind his ear. Another place he would not have known was so sensitive to touch. She stroked her hand over his head, her thumb brushing his ear as she did. Yes. He could stand to be petted like that for the rest of his life.

"You shouldn't be alone. When you slept, I talked to you, and…" She stroked his head again and pressed her thumb against his temple, as he had imagined her doing on more than one occasion. For a few moments, she continued, her hands cupping his head, thumbs rubbing circles, her fingers pressing up and down his neck and the back of his head. Desire and an ache for sleep twisted together, his body relaxing in increments, tension trickling away with each press of her fingers.

How long would it be until someone came to check on him? Long enough to give him time to hold her and sleep? He doubted it.

"Omar." Dilay's voice quavered, and she slid off to lay beside him. He turned his head to look at her. "I have to tell you something."

He did not need the pain in her expression to know he wasn't going to like it. But somehow, with her hands on his head and the warmth of her body next to his, it was all right. Whatever it was, he could bear it. He looked at the ceiling and nodded, closing his eyes.

She dipped her head forward to press her brow against his temple. "They are all lying to you," she said, then took a shaky inhale, "and I have been too, ever since your mother told me." Her hand stroked down, over his neck and chest, to rest over his heart. He covered it with his own, gripping her fingers in his. "She told me they hid books from you. Books that tell what happened to the other Veritors. Your uncle did not die of consumption."

His eyes opened, and he stared hard at the pattern on the ceiling, geometric shapes interwoven with the sigils for air, in blues from pale to dark, made grey and black by the dim light of the orbs. He should have felt something, but he was empty. All he felt was her hand, on his heart.

"His power killed him. And it will kill you. In bits, pieces of you…" Her voice broke, her words wheezed. He could hear the tears, but he could not look and see them. It would break him open, drown him in whatever emotion lay just beneath the surface of his numbness. But this revelation…wasn't a revelation at all. He knew.

He had always known, somewhere deep inside him, locked away, he could feel himself dying away with each mind he took, replaced by others. The whispers let in by cracks opened by his power. He closed his eyes and released a slow, hard breath.

So this was what it felt like to be sentenced to death.

Omar snorted a bitter laugh. That was the Wheel's balance. To give him a power that could condemn people, only to condemn him by its use.

Dilay shifted, her head lifted, and he cracked his eyes open enough to see her. There were tears on her cheeks, her eyes red-rimmed.

"Are you laughing?"

He shook his head, releasing her hand so he could wipe her tears away. It was too easy to be able to touch her like this, and not worry. Everything felt exactly as it was supposed to. And that was lies too.

A tiny sliver of time where the fangs of his power had been rendered impotent.

"Why did *you* keep it from me?" He looked in her eyes. More tears glimmered there, and his chest ached under her fingers. His pain was all right, but he could not bear hers.

"I thought I could help. I thought I could change it. But I saw you today and I—" She closed her eyes. "Am I helping? Or am I speeding you to your fate?"

"You have done more for me than anyone."

"Please stop. Please, don't do any more. The tribunals will function without you, without threat of your power. Please."

"When I am Sultan—"

"No," she demanded. "Your father could live decades more, force you through hundreds more minds. Those people do not deserve that and neither do you. What about your family? Your mother and brother. Beste. They love you. You will have a wife, and children, please don't." She sucked in a ragged breath and tears spilled over. "Please don't make them…" She paused. "…make me…I cannot watch you die."

Her emotion mingled in his, choking him and filling his chest until it felt like he couldn't draw air, and he hated every word she had said. Hated the idea of his family's pain, of sentencing them to watching him waste away. And someone else, a stranger, mother to children he fathered, someone he promised a life to. Someone who was not her. Not the woman who had believed in him and fought for him when she barely knew him. Not the woman who scraped and clawed her way to a dream the world would have denied her, only to risk it to teach those deemed unworthy. Not her. And even if it were her, in some imaginary world, how could he betray her like that? Force her to watch him disappear, Turn by Turn, day by day?

A sound built in his throat, until he could not hold it, a cry of pain, or rage, or both. What was he? What was he to the world, to anybody? All these Turns he had been trying to be what his father wanted. When what his father wanted was to use him up like a plow ox, until he dropped dead of the work. The purge of the anger opened a fissure in his mind, and a memory washed over him that was not his. In the space between the moment he was himself and the moment he was overlaid with someone else, his muscles went taut, bowing his back.

Pain lashed his mind, and stuttered, broken remnants of a dinner scene, the sound of glass smashing, a man's shouting and a woman's scream, sorrow that was not his.

"Omar."

Hands touched his face. Cool hands. It wasn't right, it didn't fit.

"Come back."

That voice didn't belong either. It was perfect and matter of fact, a simple order, calm and sure. Not like the people in his memory. Not his memory. What was happening? Those hands on his skin, the image in front of him fragmented, and he could see her face. Dilay.

The other images, false memories, scattered away, and his body relaxed.

"Hello." She stroked his brow. "Are you back?" She had wrapped herself around him, her leg over his, her body half on top of him.

"Thank you." He closed his eyes while he tried to steady his breath and heart. "I am sorry you had to see that." He wanted to pretend he was whole and well for her, but he certainly couldn't after today.

"You don't have to hide anything from me," she said, gently, and brushed her fingers up his neck. "But I can go if you would prefer." It pierced him, like an arrow down his center. She was the only one who cared what he wanted. Had never asked him for anything except to keep living. He rolled to his side and captured her mouth in his, frenzied with the upwelling of care and longing he felt for her. She made that noise again, the little grunt of surprise, his new favorite sound.

"Don't go," he murmured. But he had to let her go. This was unfair to her, to whoever his mother chose for him. "I don't want you to go."

"What will happen if I am here when someone shows up to check on you?"

He kissed her again, too harshly, and when she responded without hesitation, that flame in his belly for her that never went out roared to life. It wasn't enough, laying side by side, rocked apart with each little movement. He wanted closer, wanted the weight and press of her again. Omar reached over her shoulder and grabbed a handful of blanket, and tugged, rolling her beneath him. Again she made no protest, but he released their kiss to look down at her, to make sure he saw no uncertainty or concern.

"You are feeling better," she teased.

"You," he said, adjusting so he could move her hair away from her face with his fingers, "you make me feel alive. And happy."

"Are you certain it isn't the kissing?"

"It is absolutely the kissing," he said. "And also you in my bed, it is also that. Did you know I thought about this?" He ducked his head to kiss her throat. Her skin smelled like flowers, crisp air. Just like her magic. "Not this, exactly, but…"

"I have tried very hard not to think of this," she said against his ear as he continued the revelation of kissing her skin. Her hands touched his back, first fingertips, then palms, then nails. Shimmers of lightning pleasure raced over his skin. The sensation left him breathless.

"Again," he demanded, then tasted her skin with his next kiss. Salty, and… Dilay arched her back with a soft mewl, and her nails skated down his back. It was too much, again, her sounds and nails, and the sensual roll of her body underneath him. Her hips pressed to his, sending jolts between his legs that made him want to press back in return, and he had to freeze exactly as he was to allow the overwhelming sensations to fade.

"We should stop," Dilay said, while also trailing her fingers and nails down his back again, as if it wasn't like striking a spark against lamp oil.

"Your argument is unconvincing," he said. He had never had to fight his body so hard. Fight to keep his senses.

"I didn't actually mean it." She laughed quietly when he scoffed at her.

"So you are staying?" He shifted his weight to one side, to splay his fingers over her belly. Entari and caftan barred him from her skin, but he had gotten very good at imagining, over lonely Turns. Or he thought he had, until she had kissed him and he realized how monochrome his daydreams had been.

"How long?" She pressed the fingers of one hand against his chest, her gaze flickering away from his and back, then away again as she drew them down over his skin.

Forever.

"Until I have memorized you from head to toe?" he suggested instead. She traced his ear, thoughtful. That she did not refuse outright made his skin prickle all over. He had to send her away. This was foolish, testing himself in this manner. He brushed his fingers along her jaw. Even drained as he was, anything more than this was a threat. Even nearly spent magic could flux, and her hands on him, or Wheel be merciful, her naked skin, would probably send him into paroxysms.

She trailed a touch down his ribs, and his hips involuntarily pressed harder to hers. Her lashes lowered, her lips parting, silent pleasure that erased the mote of rationality that remained to him. "Am I allowed to memorize you in turn, Vali Ahad?" Her hand settled where his salvar crossed his hip, her thumb drawing a circle in the dip of his abdomen.

He tried to speak, but only one corner of his mind seemed to be functioning, and it was not that one. All he managed was her name, more plea than anything else, and her fingers tucked into the waist of his salvar, urging him fully on top of her again. His mind blanked as though he had been overtaken by another, except he was still there, with her, and the only thing possessing him was need.

The door opened. Dilay lunged up, burying her face against his chest and holding her arms up, trying to hide.

"Out," Omar ordered, stunned and useless for more than the one word. He did have the presence of mind to wrap an arm around Dilay's shoulders to hold her where she was while he sat up and turned to look behind him at the doors.

Mazhar stood there, one arm folded over his chest, his elbow propped in that hand while he covered his mouth with the other. He was laughing, stifling it with his grip over his mouth. The panic and anger drained out of Omar.

"Go away," he said, irritation the only lingering emotion. Mazhar would not dare give Dilay away. Not with all the illicit trysts Omar had to hold over his head.

"I could go, but I would only be replaced by an onslaught of physicians and servants. I want to know what magic you worked to sneak her in here."

When Dilay heard Mazhar's voice she made a little groan against Omar's chest and peeked over his shoulder. Omar hugged her tighter. Mazhar released his grip on his mouth to wave his fingers at her. His abrupt arrival had shocked the lust right out of Omar, leaving a haze of irrational temper smoldering in its place.

"The same magic you are going to use to sneak her out," Omar said.

"I don't need his help. I can get myself out," Dilay protested, looking up at him. How was he ever going to think of anything but kissing her? There was still a flush to her skin and her lips from their play. She lowered her gaze from his. "Beste told me to go through the garden."

"Father is in the garden with Semih Kadir and his family. Consider yourselves lucky he didn't walk by your window and see this…conversation." Mazhar crossed the room as he spoke to pull the curtains closed. "What were you thinking, leaving these open?" He tsked. Omar hadn't been thinking much of anything. Except about her.

Dilay sat back on her heels, breaking Omar's grip on her. She stared at the curtains, panicked, and she appeared as if she might be sick. "They're out there?" she asked. "Behram?"

"For a time, at least," Mazhar said.

"What if he saw us?" She looked frantically at Omar. Before he could respond, or even understand the ugly knot of feelings that bloomed in his chest, she scrambled off the bed. "I have to go. Forgive me."

"Dilay." Omar clambered after her, but she bent to pull her shoes on and moved away from him.

"I have to. You don't understand. What I did at the tribunal…if he saw us, what it would do to him. This was…" She turned a quick, concerned look at the windows.

A terrible idea. He didn't need her to say it. And when she motioned to Mazhar, who looked to him for assurance, he could only nod. The door closed behind them, softly, but it might as well have slammed shut.

Omar turned his anger on the windows, and threw open the curtains. The garden was dark, too dark to see from inside a lit room. He pushed the doors open and stepped outside. He wanted to shout for Behram, but that was just his temper, and anyone who witnessed would think he had lost his mind.

So he listened. But it was quiet. No voices, no men talking. If they had been there, as Mazhar said, they were gone now.

He had been angry, at Behram, for reasons he could not quite put name to. Or perhaps he was angry at him for wanting the same thing from Dilay that Omar did. To take—to take from her, fill up the holes in himself with all that she was.

Omar walked the gravel path, his anger turned inward, realizing a few steps in that he was still half naked. He stopped, and stared up at the night sky, soothed by the spring chill in the air around him. But not as soothed as he had been with Dilay. In her absence, it all came back to him.

He was dying. They were killing him. And he was letting them. Choosing to let them. That was what Dilay had said to him, those turns ago. Choose to be a good person. Choose to fill himself up with the decisions he felt were right. Choices he made for himself. His own triumphs and joys. Not to steal them from someone else.

TWENTY-SIX

"**L**IKE THIS," DILAY SAID, HOLDING the young boy's hand to show him the order of sigil strokes. The feather he was trying to control bobbed off the ground as a puff of air stirred it. "Good!"

He screwed his mouth up in concentration and tried again, and Dilay did her best to give him the courtesy of concentrating on him instead of all her other concerns. Behind her, Seda guided three young fire mages through breath control, a beginner method of managing the size of the fire they controlled in their palms.

Having to teach all day had been a somewhat effective distraction from the maelstrom in her mind. Omar, and Behram, the guilds—emotions she could not untangle or separate. Men she cared about for the same reasons, and for disparate ones. And she was hurting both of them, knowingly. Behram, by betraying his trust, and Omar, by keeping his fate from him while simultaneously ushering him toward it.

She didn't know what to do. All day she had waited to see Seda, to unburden herself to the only person she could think to. Seda would understand, while Dilay's parents would not. Her friend knew what it was to be unable to push someone from her mind, even if she knew she should. But there had been three new children waiting for her when she arrived at the warehouse school to set up, and now she would have to wait until their class finished.

"Dilay!" Turgay burst through the front door. "The Watch, they're here."

Just as he finished the sentence, someone yanked him backwards out of the doorway. Seda put her arms around the three children she had in front of her and hurried them toward the back door as Dilay bolted to her feet. But it was too late. Eight men, who in the moment looked like frightening monsters in their dark uniforms, moved through the door and surrounded the room, yataghans drawn.

"You are all under arrest, by order of the Sultan, for subversion," the largest of the men said, mechanically.

"Subversion?" Dilay said in disbelief. "These are children."

"They will be held until their parents turn themselves in." The speaker came toward her, hand outstretched.

"Please don't take them," she pleaded.

"Those are our orders. Come quietly or be dragged." His companions were already rounding up the children, all frozen in shock and fear. The youngest of them were crying, and a handful of the older ones did their best to comfort them. Dilay stared, mute, as they were herded out of the building.

"Dilay!" Seda cried out when one of the guards grabbed her roughly by the arms, wrenching them behind her and shoving her forward.

"Let her go," Dilay demanded, lunging forward. The guard in charge, nearest her, grabbed her by the elbow, wrenching her around so hard she thought he'd dislocated her shoulder. "We haven't hurt anyone," she said as he steered her forward, not bothering to lead her on a clear path, so she tripped and stumbled on pillows and discarded supplies. His companions not involved with the children went to work smashing everything in sight. Dilay tried to turn to look, to protest, anything, but the one who held her only twisted her arm until she cried out in pain, shoving her through the door and into the small open space in the alley in front of the school.

Zeki and Turgay were on their knees, hands bound with rope at their backs. Zeki wove in place, and she could see blood from one nostril and a swiftly darkening patch over his left eye. The children had huddled close to the two men, and when Seda's captor released her she quickly dropped to her knees to put her arms around the three youngest, two girls and a boy. Toulin, the void who had spoken with Omar, was one of them, and she was the only one of the three not crying. She stared, resolute, into the darkness. More accustomed, perhaps, to being treated like so much refuse.

"This is madness," Dilay tried again, unable to think past the moment or the simplest of protests, but the man holding her gave her a rough shove and she stumbled forward. Turgay turned to try and break her fall, but could do little with his hands tied. She caught his shoulders as she fell but abraded her knees on the stones of the alley.

"All right?" he asked as she sat back on her heels and he pressed his shoulder to hers to give her balance. Dilay nodded. What had she done? How had they found the school? She must have been too careless. Someone had seen her.

"All of them?" The man in charge directed his question into the shadows of the alley and someone stepped into the light of a mage orb one of the guards commanded.

Behram, dressed in red and gold that looked threatening in the mage light. Dilay tried to say his name, but her voice failed as her heart broke, a hard, aching pain in her chest. He looked at her, and there was nothing, absolutely nothing on his face or his eyes. He had never looked at her so coldly.

"You rotten, burning son of a bitch," Zeki spat at him. Behram smiled, and Dilay's blood froze. He strode to her and held his hand out. Dilay offered hers, unsure, and he pulled her to her feet. When she was up he grabbed her shoulder and yanked her against him.

"If you cannot make good choices, I will make them for you. Do you understand?" he said low, for only her to hear.

"How dare you. Let me go," she said, icy from head to toe, afraid and furious.

"I am not the one breaking the law, Dilay." Fire hissed in his words, even if she could not see it. "You think because you're playing whore to a prince you can do whatever you wish in this city without consequences?"

She slapped him. The sharp lance and shock of impact emptied her of all feeling except the hard sting of her palm. She staggered a step back, and he did nothing as one of the guards grabbed both of her arms and drove her to her bruised knees on the stones. Tears streaked her cheeks, but she had not felt them arrive or fall until they were hot on her skin. She made harsh, high sounds as she tried to calm herself, but those gasps did nothing to make her feel quenched for air.

Behram touched his cheek, staring at her, then dropped his hand to his side. "The Cliffs. All of them."

"Yes, Master Kadir."

THEY WERE MARCHED THROUGH the alley and out onto a main street. Though Zeki and Turgay's hands were tied, Seda and Dilay were left free. When they began their trek up the main road, Dilay removed her entari and gathered as many of the children together as she could, commanding them to hold hands, and threw the entari over their heads to hide their faces. If they were freed, she did not want their faces to be known, to be discriminated against. Seda did the same, for as many as she could.

At the outskirts of the Earth District, they loaded into a wagon and rode a candlemark or more, up the palace road and west, to the Cliffs. The prison was carved into the sandstone below the palace, over the sea, and could only be reached by a treacherous staircase cut from the rock. Dilay had always imagined it was populated by violent criminals and angry-faced guards. Not by children and their teachers. But she should have known better, after all the stories her father had told her.

They were escorted through an entrance cave, where the two men who were on duty in what appeared to be a cavern repurposed into an office took the details of their arrest and crime. It was dark but for the lamps that held orbs. No sun reached them in the tunnels where the cells were. Water dripped somewhere, echoing through the dank cells cut out of rock.

Zeki and Turgay were placed in a cell together, the boys in another, and the girls with Seda and Dilay. As if the boys would not also need the comfort of an adult when they had been torn from their parents.

Dilay had never known anger like the thing that burned in her belly. It felt like the worst hunger she had ever known. It was fire, burning down her limbs, making her mouth taste like lightning and her thoughts spin endlessly in visions of fury and revenge.

Once the tears of the children had subsided, and some of them slept, her anger cooled to a simmer, though she could feel it twisting and changing. Into hatred. It was the closest she had ever come to understanding Behram's obsession with retribution. That it was Behram who had brought the feelings about in her was how she wrestled them more fully under control. She would not become him.

"Will your father come?" Seda whispered when everything was too quiet. Dilay didn't know if he could. She had committed a crime. They all had. Those same guards were supposed to return to the city to hunt down the families of the children. Thinking about it made her feel like vomiting.

Seda leaned in, trying not to disturb the two girls using her lap as a pillow. "What about the Vali Ahad?" she whispered. "Since you're helping him?"

Helping him. Lying to him. Abandoning him without any explanation. What must he have thought when she ran away at the mention of Behram's name? What could he do? He had kept her school a secret because he couldn't do anything if it was found out. She was tired, and hungry. Angry. She could hardly think straight, let alone muster enough control to cast a whisper through stone and distance to the sprawling palace. Even if she managed it, she could not, in good conscience, ask him to show favor to her, to a criminal.

"That is complicated," Dilay murmured. Who knew how much the guards listened to prisoners?

"No. You think everything is complicated. He came to the school. If you think he did that purely from the goodness of his heart, you are not as smart as I thought you were. At least try. You have his ear." Seda glanced at her and away. "At the very least." She brushed a bit of hair away from the face of one of the girls as she stirred.

Dilay wanted to tell Seda everything, but this was not the place, with too many possible ears. And too much emotion. "I am sorry you're here, Seda. This is all my fault."

"I made my own choices. If it is anyone's fault, it is Behram's. I warned you, didn't I? All the care in the world cannot help someone who does not believe they need help."

It was a bitter medicine to swallow, the idea that Seda had seen Behram more clearly than Dilay ever had. But the evidence was too strong. Dilay tried to smile but failed, and laid her head on Seda's shoulder instead.

"I think it will be all right," Seda said. "Even Sabri Sultan cannot possibly think keeping a dozen families in prison will be tolerated by the city?"

Dilay was not as certain. He thought allowing his son to kill himself with dangerous magic was all right. What did he care about common families?

They did not talk for long, silent marks. One of the men snored. Dilay could hear one of the boys sniffling, quietly, trying to hide it but thwarted by the way sound echoed on the rocks. Her heart ached. Her back hurt from sitting on cold, uneven stone, allowing the girls to take turns resting against her.

When light poured into the tunnel, accompanied by the scuff and strike of shoes and boots, she did not know how long it had been. All night? The burn of a few candles? Seda slept against her shoulder, and Toulin in her lap. Two guards, bubbled in the glow of another mage orb, strode down the stone hall and stopped in front of her cell.

"That one?" the man on the left said, pointing at Dilay.

"Which one of you is Dilay Akar?" the other asked.

"You do not even know who we are, but you're willing to keep us jailed? Women and children?" Dilay spat, spewing some of the seething anger in her heart. It felt good for a moment, but the one on the right smiled mockingly.

"I keep the cells closed and the people inside unless they're asked for. And you've been asked for. Get up." He unlocked the door. Seda stirred.

"No," Dilay said, as Toulin wrapped her arms around her neck with a whimper. "I will not go anywhere without the others."

"Bring her," the right-hand guard ordered as he swung the door wide. Seda gasped as the other advanced, and Dilay hurriedly passed

Toulin to her and stood. The guard grabbed her and slung her out of the cell.

"That way." He pointed down the dark tunnel toward the entrance. "Under your own power or with help."

Her legs and feet ached with pins and needles, and she stumbled for the first few strides, until feeling returned. They led her back into the low-ceilinged cavern at the entrance to the Cliffs, where several more guards now loitered, sitting on cushions scattered about carpets. Three were rolling dice. Two sat at the table where the guard present at their arrival had noted their number on a logbook.

Behram stood near the exit, looking bored and disgusted. When she appeared, he glanced to her feet and back up. One eyebrow cocked. All the anger that had been fermenting as she sat in the prison coiled and burst inside her, unlocking her grip on her magic and her wits.

She lunged, but the guard behind her caught both her arms and she stumbled, nearly dropping to her knees yet again. He tugged her back. Dilay tried to rein in her anger, but she did not have enough control to speak, to do anything but stare at Behram, as if that were enough to make him manifest a conscience.

"Ah, ah. Behave," the guard said.

"Release her. I'll take responsibility for her."

"No!" Dilay said. "I am not going anywhere with you, and not when all the others are still back there."

Behram made a sound of impatience. "Don't be foolish. You want to stay in prison to prove a point? No one cares that you're down here, Dilay. Besides me. Now, come with me, I am certain your family would like to see you."

The guard gave her a little push. Dilay set her feet. Behram rolled his eyes and advanced. It was the very last thing she could bear, seeing him come for her, to force her, again. Her magic exploded outward, a rush of air away from her that made Behram and the guards nearest her stagger back and knocked all the papers and pens from the table on the far side of the room.

"You will leash that, or I'll put you back in a cell for assault," the guard at her back said, his hand closing like a manacle on the back of her neck.

Dilay wrenched away from him. Behram tugged at his entari, frowning at her, and jerked his head to the guard. The man shoved her forward again.

"Go on, get her out of here."

"Dilay," Behram ordered. She looked behind her, gritting her teeth. She could not do anything for them from inside a cell, but was abandoning them any better?

She rounded on the guard. "Those children need food, and water. They've been here all night."

He started to sneer at her. He wore a tiraz with two sigils of the Fourth House, and bore a scar over his jaw.

"What is your name?" she asked. He scoffed. She pointed at the thick scar. "That is a recognizable mark. Easy to describe. I will make certain everyone knows exactly which of you denied food and water to children."

His sneer darkened.

"They'll be fed on schedule like every other prisoner. We don't starve people in here," his companion said, shooting an exasperated look at Behram.

"Seda!" Dilay called. "I'm coming back, I promise."

Behram crossed the floor and reached as if to take her arm.

"Do not touch me." She turned away from his reach. He tsked as if she were a spoiled child and led her out through the entrance tunnel and onto the ledge over the ocean. The bright, salty air should have cleared her head, made her feel better. But each step away, leaving the children behind in the caves, rent her heart deeper. They would think she had abandoned them. She *had* abandoned them. She had no plan. Nothing to leverage to free them.

Behram climbed the stairs in front of her and she couldn't even look at his back. He was so familiar to her. She had known him practically all her life. But he suddenly felt like a stranger. Someone dangerous she didn't understand and couldn't trust. The stairs switched back and forth up the cliff face, an exhausting climb that left her panting and sweating at the top.

A carriage waited there, on the flat expanse of field that crowned the cliff. It was painted in the audacious colors most fire mages who could afford finery preferred. To the north the palace sprawled, almost sparkling in the early light. Yet another thing that should have inspired her to a better mood, but it seemed all she could feel was bitter anger.

"I'll walk." Dilay could not imagine sitting cramped into a carriage with Behram without trying to strangle him. She started through the field.

"Absolutely not," Behram scoffed. "It will take you all day."

Dilay turned, using her magic to silence her emotions, because he did not deserve to see how upset she was. Did not deserve truth and vulnerability from her anymore. That had been to make him feel safe, so he could be the same way.

"You do not control or command me, Behram. This is my life, and my choices, and I invited you to be my friend, not my keeper."

"Dilay, you broke the law. Defied the Sultan. I do not know what you thought would happen, but I hope you've learned your lesson?"

"When I met you, you were a broken, lonely little boy. Do you think you are the only one who has ever existed or will ever do so? The only one who deserves someone to treat them with kindness? Or do you truly believe you were due my care because you were born with more than those I teach now?"

"Now is not the time to talk about these things." He dismissed her with a smile and in that instant he looked just like his father. She swallowed a surge of disgust.

"I'm not certain I ever want to see or speak to you again. I will never forgive you for this."

He laughed. "Of course you will. You always forgive me."

She wanted to scream at him. To make him understand what he had done, but the sick feeling in the pit of her stomach was the truth. If he did not already understand, he never would. She had lost him. Even her magic could not stop her tears then. Dilay turned from him and strode away.

"Dilay!" he called, a thread of disbelief in his voice. But she ignored him. He had failed her just as much as she had failed him, and she could not forgive him for it. "I saw you," Behram said, "I saw you in his bed."

She stopped and turned.

"You said"—he dropped his head back, gave a soft, bitter laugh, and lowered it again—"you said you didn't want power, and society."

"I am sorry, for what you saw," Dilay said. And she was. She had never meant to flaunt her relationship with Omar to him. But she also resented that what should have been a precious, tender moment between Omar and her alone was now tainted with Behram's bitterness.

"It doesn't matter." He gestured at the palace. "There are heights even you cannot reach. And Omar is one of them. Did you think he wanted you? That he would not cast you aside the moment he has himself mastered? You truly do not realize you're just a novelty, the first person he has been able to touch in a decade?"

"Behram," Dilay said, her maelstrom of emotion buried beneath a veneer of calm. "I know exactly what I am. I have always known. You are the one who cannot see what you are. What you are becoming."

"I know what I am. And now I burn too brightly for you, don't I? You are afraid." His eyes narrowed, flames outlining the dark of his irises. "But you forget, you gave me my fire. You *are* my fire. The reason I burn. For you."

He was not pleading, not revealing care nor passion. Not the way she wanted or needed. This was anger. Accusation. Possession. He frightened her.

"He will never love you the way I do." He pointed at the palace. "He will hurt you."

"*You* hurt me," Dilay snapped, then reined her flashing temper under the cool logic of her power. He could not hear her. He did not, could not understand. "I am sorry I hurt you too. But what is between me and Omar…it isn't your business. My school isn't your business, and now I, and everything I do, is no longer any of your business."

Again she turned away and walked east through the knee-high, wet grass, toward the city.

TWENTY-SEVEN

"**D**O YOU EVEN KNOW WHO Anne chose?" Mazhar asked as they walked toward the Sultan's receiving room. Omar did not feel like discussing the matter with anyone, let alone Mazhar or any of his friends that strode behind him. He wanted to get it over with, survive through the celebration afterward, and then be left alone to attempt to come to grips with it.

"Zehra Demir," Omar said.

Mazhar hissed. "Well, at least you can be comforted to know that she has had enjoyable relationships before yours." He glanced over his shoulder, where Behram, Osman, and the brothers Yavuz walked. "Yes, Osman?"

"Mazhar," Omar commanded. "Do not speak about her like that."

Omar caught a glimpse of Osman's flushed face when he looked at his brother, and immediately looked away.

"How immoral of you, Osman," Behram said, with an oddly gleeful tone. Omar did his best to ignore them and did not hear Osman's muttered reply. He did not care. He cared that they were speaking about her. It was no one's business but hers, and apparently Osman. He was, in a twisted way, happy for exactly the reason Mazhar said. At least someone had given her what he doubted he would be able to.

Though if his father knew about Osman and Zehra it would be acceptable grounds for a cancellation of the betrothal. Being free with one's lovers was something the lower classes did not mind, but in the nobility, where everyone cared about magical power, it was frowned upon and conducted more illicitly. Omar did not want Zehra shamed, no matter that the information had given him a short-lived glimmer of hope for ending the entire thing. He brushed the thought of annulment away.

But he didn't know what he was going to do with Zehra. Ever since the night Dilay had been in his room, he had been completely unable to hold the magic. At least he was now able to identify when it was going to lash out. He had avoided hurting anyone. He wanted to tell Dilay that. It felt like a triumph, despite the backslide of control. Not exactly the cure he had hoped for, but better than before. Something to manage himself.

If he thought about his power, controlling it, moving forward in his life, he didn't have to think about Dilay. About what she had told him. That his power was a two-headed serpent, poisoning him every time it struck someone else. He didn't have to think about how she had so naturally understood how to bring him back to himself, and that she would probably never put hands on him again. He might never see her again. He turned his thoughts away, trying to think of anything but her or Zehra. But how could he not think of either of them, when he was walking toward a betrothal to one?

The doors to the receiving hall were thrown open, and a small crowd lingered in the hall. They parted for Omar and his companions, murmuring. Tension gripped his neck. The receiving hall was half the size of his father's Council Hall, furnished more comfortably, meant for conversations. Usually, betrothal ceremonies were held in the courtyard near the Morning Gate, so citizens of Narfour could attend. Omar had not been told why they were holding the ceremony inside. It wasn't weather—the morning had promised a beautiful day.

He turned to ask Mazhar, but their mother approached, and both of them bowed. Mazhar kissed her hands, and Omar made an attempt at a smile. She returned it, sadly, and returned to sit beside their father.

The families of the women who had been offered as candidates sat on the left side of the room, with a wall of open-air windows at their back. The windows were covered with lattice frames, which were open to the cool morning air. He wished it could have been outside. Perhaps he would have been able to think out there.

The room was filled to the brim with nobles, most seated, many still standing and chatting. When he and Mazhar entered and his friends broke away toward their families, the chatter faded. Omar approached his father, with Mazhar to his left, and they bowed.

Eymen stood to his father's right and smiled amicably at Omar. He already looked very pleased, but how could he not? Surely the Sultan had already informed Eymen of his daughter's choosing. Omar sat on a bench to his father's left, Mazhar next to him. He cast a single look at the four women on the bench on the opposite side of the hall. He knew what they all looked like, had seen them before, had spoken to them. None of them looked back, most stared at the floor. Trying, just as he was, not to look miserable.

Zehra sat nearest the front of the room. Since she was the Grand Vizier's daughter, she held the highest rank among the four. Her black hair was knotted in elaborate braids arranged around her head and decorated with strings of pearls. She wore the traditional colors of the Fourth House, golds and yellows, cut with white in honor of the occasion. As Omar looked at her, he saw her look across the room at Osman.

At least they would be equal in that—both thinking of another. He closed his eyes briefly against thoughts of Dilay.

Eymen called the ceremony to begin, and the few continuing whispers died out. Each father stood with his daughter, detailing their assets and why she would be an auspicious match for Omar. The women tried to smile but looked half frozen, and he could not blame them. He knew how marrying a stranger played out, at least for his mother and father. There were also happy marriages among the nobility, but those were equally split between luck, and people whose parents had chosen partners who already cared for each other.

The Queen Sultana stood when everyone was finished, poised and smiling, radiating joy Omar knew she did not feel. She was an accomplished actress, his mother. He would need many more lessons from her to navigate the rest of his marriage. Just as she had learned how to do.

"The Sultan is pleased to announce the betrothal of the Vali Ahad to Mistress Demir. May the Wheel spin for the balance between the First and Fourth Houses and bring joy and prosperity to Tamar and her people."

Omar stood. This was the moment he had dreaded for the two days since he had last seen Dilay. Betrothal required touch. And he did not know how to tell Zehra, or avoid it, without causing an uproar. He had hoped, until Dilay's abrupt and panicked departure had broken what control he'd gained, that he had enough to make it through these few moments.

Zehra stood, smiling stiffly, and strode toward the platform where the Sultan sat as the room applauded politely. Two servant girls placed four cushions on the floor. Zehra knelt on one, with her left side oriented toward the Sultan. Omar joined her, kneeling opposite. His mother retrieved a ribbon and a length of rope from a tray that Beste held and knelt on the third. The Grand Vizier knelt on the fourth, to Omar's left.

A mother always betrothed her sons, and a father his daughters. For balance. The Queen gave Omar a look he could not read.

"*Do not touch me,*" Omar cast his voice in an imperceptible whisper to Zehra, who twitched as if startled, her hazel gaze locking against his. "*I will explain later.*" She had been crying, he could see now, so close and looking right at her. Her eyes were red-rimmed and swollen, which showed despite the kohl outlining her lashes. Her cheeks were splotchy beneath the dusting of powder she wore.

Omar held his hands out between them, palms up. Zehra hesitated, and her gaze darted to her right, he thought hopefully, then back. She was supposed to put her hands in his, but she complied with his command and hovered them just above. His mother gave a tiny nod of approval, and Omar simply hoped no one else would notice.

"The Wheel severs us and brings us together, circles broken and remade. In betrothal we are a circle unbreakable, one for another," the

Queen recited, dropping the ribbon over Zehra's left wrist, "and the other for one. Be betrothed and be bound, in glorious celebration of the Wheel." She handed the jute rope to Eymen, who dropped it over Zehra's right wrist.

"Silk, for the soft, and the gentle. For the strength to hold each other up." His mother knotted the ribbon loosely. Zehra stared at it, and Omar fixed his gaze over her head, concentrating only on his smallest movements, to jerk away if he needed to.

"And hemp, for hardship," Eymen said. "For that which can be frayed by time and negligence unless it is cared for." He knotted it. Zehra offered a tremulous smile as she raised her head. He could not match it, only stare at her. The smile faded, and her gaze dropped. Omar felt like a monster. He would smile for her. Just as Dilay had told him to. He had to give her a chance. His heart seized, and his throat worked as his mother and the Grand Vizier stood. She pronounced the betrothal official, and everyone except Zehra and Omar stood, cheering and clapping.

Omar carefully extracted his hands from the loosely hanging binds, and Zehra followed suit. He untied the hemp to retie it in a larger circle, which he dropped over her head to hang around her neck. She did the same with the silk ribbon, and though her proximity made him uneasy, she did not touch him. When his mother and Eymen had moved into the crowd to speak with others, Omar looked down at his hands, curled into fists on his knees, and forced them open.

"I am sorry," he said, underneath the uproar, and knew he sounded too gruff.

Zehra gave a single, airy laugh. "I know you did not choose me, Vali Ahad. So you needn't apologize. Shall we go pretend to be happy?"

She was trying to be lighthearted, but it struck like a blow. The first acknowledgment of a lifetime of pretending. He stood, but Zehra waited, looking up at him expectantly. He stared.

"Oh." Her brow creased, and she got to her feet without the help she had clearly expected.

"I promise to explain, after all of this. But for now—"

"It is fine, Vali Ahad, obviously, you do not have to touch me if you do not wish to." She smiled, but it was sharp, and judgmental. Dilay had given him the same, and had eventually forgiven him, he reminded himself. Zehra might too. But he could not say to her what he had said to Dilay...*I did not say I didn't want to touch you.*

They walked side by side out into the hall, where others were lingering in conversation before entering the ballroom. All bowed and offered congratulations and well wishes. Omar caught Zehra looking flushed and pleased when he did look at her. In one morning she had gone from noble to Princess Sultana. There were some benefits for her, beyond the hardships. He had to remember that.

She enjoyed the attention they received on their way down the hall, growing more and more animated, greeting friends and elders with enthusiasm. Meanwhile Omar withdrew more and more inside his *too stern* face, as Dilay had called it, and people offered much more subdued, and distanced congratulations to him. He clasped his hands behind his back and his shoulders tensed.

They passed through a section of hall clear of others, and Omar's shoulders relaxed but his grip on his hands did not. Zehra heaved a sigh.

"It is unfortunate the ceremony could not be held in the courtyard, don't you agree? It would have been a nice distraction for the people from all that mess in the Earth District."

Omar puzzled over her words for a moment, but could not understand.

"What mess?"

Zehra made a dismissive wave with her hand. "I know very little. Father mentioned it when we were riding to the palace this morning."

When he looked at her, she cast her gaze sideways and up at him, reaching to fidget with the pearls in her hair. She flushed. Omar cringed inwardly. How could she have no more information than that? Her father's estate was on the edge of the Fire District, she could probably see the Earth District from her windows. But he shouldn't fault her more than himself, this was the first he had heard of anything happening in the Earth District.

The ballroom was rarely used for actual balls, outside the celebrations hosted at each turn of the seasons, the Wheel spinning from one House to the next. For the betrothal, long, low-set tables had been placed throughout, in lines down the center of the circular room. Cushions served as seats, and tray upon tray of beautifully arranged food decorated the tabletops. Omar wondered what Dilay would have to say about all the excess. But thinking about her chastising him only made him think of her in his bed, hitting him with a pillow, and his amusement swiftly disappeared.

"May I?" Zehra asked, when they had walked through the doors and the cheering had died down. She pointed to the far side of the room, where a group of young women had gathered, including the other three women who had been potential candidates. Were they all friends? Of course they were. Would she mention his odd request to not be touched? Omar ducked his head. She started away from him, then turned and bowed before angling away again.

Omar watched her for a moment, the way the others anticipated her arrival with whispers and smiles. She really was quite lovely, and deserved someone who would look at her and not long for another. He rubbed his fingers over his brow. He needed to find Eymen or his father and ask about the Earth District. It was too much to ask of Zehra to know details of events like that. She would not have been raised to, and today she had other things on her mind. But she would learn to pay attention. He hoped.

She was enveloped into the group of women as Omar cast about for his father. Mazhar and his mother stood talking with a group of people near the windows. Omar did not see his father anywhere, and that was strange. The Sultan was not one to fade into the background. He looked for Eymen. The Grand Vizier was conspicuously absent as well. Omar looked for any of the highest-ranked men in his father's Council and found them all absent.

He skirted the edge of the room to avoid the crowd, though well-wishers slowed his progress, as he had to stop and talk for at least a moment with each. Finally Mazhar saved him, breaking away from his own conversation to stride to Omar's side.

"How are you?" he asked, looking concerned. And also exhibiting the beginnings of drunkenness.

"Where is the Sultan?"

"Ah," Mazhar said, then cocked his head. "I thought you had heard."

"Heard what? And when would I have heard it? I have been trapped in my rooms all morning putting this on." He snatched at the betrothal outfit, all shining silver embroidery and thick, stitched brocade. The turban weighed heavy on his head, making him hot despite the cool spring weather. He felt like one of his father's ceremonial horses, decked out in bells and tassels.

"He called an emergency meeting of the Council to deal with a"—Mazhar squinted, searching for words—"small uprising in the Earth District."

"An uprising?"

"More riots than uprising." Mazhar tilted his hand from side to side.

"Why am I just now hearing about this?" Omar asked. Mazhar shrugged, wide-eyed.

"It is your betrothal day. I assume Father did not wish to distract from it any more than he had to."

"There are riots in the Earth District and all the nobility is up here, eating and drinking and celebrating?" Omar said. Mazhar twisted his mouth in thought then shrugged a shoulder. "That doesn't bother you?"

"Of course it bothers me. But it doesn't surprise me. Does it surprise you? Besides, what am I going to do, clap my hands and send everyone home?" He gave Omar a pointed look.

"No. Not you," Omar said, fuming.

Music began, musicians on a platform at the north end of the room keeping it low to facilitate conversation. The light, bouncing melody made Omar's fingers twitch in dissonance, and he felt an urgent need to be away from the charade in front of him. He turned toward the doors.

"Where are you going?" Mazhar asked, dryly. Omar tossed a withering glance over his shoulder and strode away.

"Vali Ahad," his mother called. Omar stopped and pivoted stiffly toward her as she approached. The smile she wore was no different than the elaborate necklace of diamonds and sapphires that adorned her neck. An ornament. She continued smiling as she came to his side, displaying it for everyone watching.

"You cannot leave," she commanded.

"Are you aware of what is happening in the city?"

She ducked her head to someone who greeted her in passing. "Of course I am," she said.

"You did not think to inform me?"

"Smile," she said, softly, "people are beginning to notice." People were staring at them, looking more curious than jovial. Omar forced a tense smile.

"Anne, what is going on?"

Her eyes narrowed and her smile faltered. She set her wineglass on the tray of a servant who drifted by.

"I would have informed you after the celebration. This is where you need to be, what you need to be doing. This is how you win influence and navigate the circles of Viziers. The City Watch has it in hand. Your concern is here."

"Has what in hand?"

Her brow furrowed and her gaze darted to his then away. A sinking, heavy feeling filled his belly at the regretful look in her eyes that she quickly hid. "Last night the City Watch raided a warehouse in the Earth District."

"What warehouse?" There were hundreds of warehouses in the Earth District. Hundreds. But in that moment, only one mattered to him.

Her gaze slid to his again. "It was being used as a school, for voids and lowborn mages. They took the children and the adults who were present. They are in the Cliffs."

The room shrank around him, so he could neither see straight nor make his thoughts calm. He could not immediately determine whether the swirl of emotion building inside him was despair, or rage. It seemed to begin in his chest, spiraling like a hurricane, spreading outward through his torso and into his limbs, like ice.

"Omar," his mother admonished, "this is not the time to cross your father. Dispense with your duties here, first."

"That is exactly what I intend to do." He strode for the doors. He had just stepped out of the ballroom when two hands closed on his left arm. A lancet of pain shot through the limb and exploded in his head, his vision going instantly white, then filling with mixed-up, frantic images overlaid with foreign emotions that eclipsed his own—Zehra. He managed to rip his arm away and stagger back. He heard her gasped apologies, and he tried to focus on her voice as he had Dilay's, but he tumbled deeper into her stolen memory.

Betrayal. His heart ached. It was the city, somewhere in the city, a crowded street. An alley ahead of him…Osman Altimur was in it, had a woman backed up to a wall, and she looked pleased about it. As did Osman. They were laughing, and that made Omar furious, and hurt. She wasn't even pretty, just an earthborn whore or scullery.

He braced to shout Osman's name, but he was suddenly out of the memory and in his body. Zehra stared at him, tears in her eyes, and Mazhar was whispering to her, his arm twined through hers, trying to tug her away.

"I don't understand," she said. She appeared unharmed, and Omar hoped she had not realized his mental invasion.

"Come, dance with me, all right?" Mazhar said, shooting a look at Omar.

"Go with him," Omar said, an ache blossoming in the front of his skull. "I will return shortly."

She frowned but obeyed. Omar reached up to touch his nose, to make certain it wasn't bleeding. He cast a look over his shoulder at his mother, still standing where he had parted from her in the middle of the ballroom. Beste had joined her and whispered in her ear. His mother appeared…resolute.

Omar turned and headed down the hall toward the Council Hall. Each step stirred that storm of emotion, worry for Dilay, for the children who had been imprisoned. And anger. Inside, his magic whipped, tendrils of air magic like coils. He had to fight to keep it off his skin and out of his eyes, and wrestling it gave him somewhere to focus his energy, instead of on the desire to rush immediately to the Cliffs.

The voices of the High Council filled the hall long before he reached the doors. They were raised in argument, though not yelling yet. Omar turned the last corner before the hall just in time to see a contingent of City Watch and wardens from the Cliffs escort a group of prisoners through the door. Omar recognized Dilay's friend, Seda, Zeki, Turgay, and two of the older boys. Dilay was not with them, which only increased Omar's alarm. Was she still down there? Were they questioning her? His skin prickled, and he sped his stride, reaching the doors a few moments after they had swung shut behind the group.

He shoved them open and strode into the hall.

The Sultan jumped to his feet, nearly toppling his ornate bench. "Explain yourself."

Omar did not stop until he stood even with the City Watch Captain, who bore a stricken look, glancing between Omar and the Sultan. Seda looked at Omar as well, glanced away, then looked back with wide eyes.

"I am informed there are children in the Cliffs," Omar said. He did not bow, could not bring himself to. He had never believed his father would condone such a thing. No matter what led to it.

"They are being held until their families have been apprehended, Efendim, then they will be released," the Grand Vizier said, accompanying it with a tense, censuring smile.

"Released to what?" Omar demanded.

"We will discuss this later." The Sultan sat, the movement also a dismissal of Omar.

"Sultan," Omar said, "release them all, or I will discuss it now, in front of your Council, and guards, and anyone who cares to listen."

His father's face went still and cold, fury to match Omar's. They stared at each other.

"You are overstepping," the Sultan finally ground out, "and will leave this room immediately."

There had been a time he would have gone, escaped to his study and his books and his self-pity. But not today. Not when brave, bright Dilay was in prison for what she believed in.

"You will make orphans of those children, for what? To prove what point? They are the children of dock workers and drudges with only a flicker of magic."

"These are *my* laws, and *my* subjects. And you are my son and will obey me."

Beside him, the Grand Vizier gripped his staff of office, casting worried looks toward the blustering Viziers.

"No," Omar said. "Not in this. Release them, or I will." He was burning from the inside out, terrified of his father's reaction and ready to strike him. His words and his actions barely registered as decisions, they simply happened, nearly outside his control, his magic a tempest beneath his skin, his thoughts and words more instinctual than planned.

The captain's eyes bugged. Half the Viziers leapt to their feet and began shouting and chattering.

The Sultan turned his head to the side, as if that was all it took to end things, all it took to deny Omar. "You will do no such thing."

You are a more powerful mage than your father, do you realize that?

Omar released his tenuous grip on his raging magic, saw the flicker and dance of light as it raced over his skin. The chatter of the Viziers died down, and the Sultan's attention switched to him again, shocked.

"This Council will be mine someday. I will remember that not one of them spoke against you, against the imprisonment of children. Against an act of tyranny against your own people. I will not forget."

Omar turned to the City Watch Captain, who flinched back, eyes like a terrified horse's, wild and white-edged.

"Release them," Omar said.

The man fumbled for the keys on his belt, staring at the floor as he unlocked Seda's manacles, then Zeki and Turgay. Omar stood, magic fluxing and whipping across his skin. Once the boys were unlocked, he pointed to the doors.

"Escort them to the Morning Gate. Then return to the Cliffs and release every person who was arrested at that warehouse. I will be there shortly to see I am obeyed."

The captain cast one last look at the Sultan before turning to comply. Dilay's friend rubbed her wrists as she gave Omar a head-to-toe perusal. "She isn't there. Someone took her," she said, quietly, before she turned and trotted to catch up with the others. Omar turned to follow them.

"If you leave this room—"

For once, he was glad for a power that made him untouchable. He did not turn to look at his father, only released his final hold on his magic, so that he could see his own light out of the periphery of his vision.

"Who is going to stop me?"

TWENTY-EIGHT

DILAY HISSED AS SHE HELD the poultice against her bruised and scraped knees. Zel, the woman who lived next door to them, tsked. A longtime herbalist, she had rushed over the moment Dilay made it home. She was not the only neighbor in the house, several had congregated when news of Dilay's arrest had spread, to support her parents. Her mother's two sisters were also there. Her father's cousin, and his wife. Dilay thought the entire extended family might have arrived, if they did not live in the valley. For all she knew, they might be headed across the mountains at that very moment.

Everyone had stayed when the protests began, because the entire affair was one wrong encounter from becoming violent.

Dilay's mother and her aunts were in the kitchen, preparing food, and their husbands were sitting scattered on the couch and seats through the living room. No one was speaking, everyone was listening to the commotion outside. Two of the men smoked, the pipes filling the room with sweet, eye-watering smoke. Dilay flinched every time she heard breaking glass or a rise in volume of the protesters. They had moved up through the Earth and Air Districts and into the Grand Market, where damage would be the most costly.

"Baba—"

"No," he snapped. Dilay fumed, and he stood and paced to one of the front windows, standing to the side in case anyone realized theirs had yet to receive a brick. She started to rock in place with her pent-up agitation, and Zel slapped her thigh in reprimand.

"We're just going to sit here? And watch?"

"I think you've participated quite enough," her father said without looking at her. "This is all because of you."

"It is because of the children," Dilay corrected. He cast her a look of rebuke.

Dilay exhaled impatiently. Zel peeled the poultice away. She made a thoughtful sound and wiped roughly at Dilay's knees.

"Ow!" she gasped.

"You would rather the gravel stay in, hmm?" Zel said, continuing her rough ministrations. Dilay bit her lip to stifle her grunts of pain.

A commotion in the kitchen, the sound of worried women's voices greeting someone familiar preceded the appearance of Seda from the back. Dilay tried to stand, but Zel held her in place with a hand on her shoulder and a chastening look.

"Did they release everyone?" Dilay asked as Seda rushed around the couch to drop onto the seat beside Dilay and pull her into a hug. Dilay hugged her back, relieved as Zel tsked at them.

Seda pulled back, sweeping her mussed and dirty hair behind her ears. "No, it was just a few of us—"

"What on the Wheel—" her father cursed as he stared out the window. Her mother stepped out of the kitchen with a large, flat dish of tabbouleh.

Someone pounded on the door.

Everyone looked, and Dilay's two aunts poked their heads out of the kitchen behind her mother. Dilay's father hesitated, looking at Dilay in accusation, then stepped to the door and opened it a crack.

"Is she here?" Dilay's muscles went slack at the familiar voice, but she didn't believe it until her father pushed the door open wide and she saw Omar framed by it. Seda put a hand over her mouth, glancing at Dilay. Behind him Dilay saw Ruslan, and guards, too many to count initially. Was he there to arrest her? No, that made no sense. They wouldn't send him to do it. But then, she could not have imagined Behram turning his overinflated sense of vengeance on her either. Who knew what ways she had misjudged Omar?

Omar took a step into the house like he meant to rush at her and everyone jumped to their feet. Glass shattered when her mother dropped the dish of food on the tiles. Seda gripped Dilay's hand urgently, rising to her feet. There was a confused melee of bows and standing, and Omar crossed to her like he was blind to all of it. He looked at her exposed, bloodied knees and she saw a flash of anger. Dilay jerked to her feet, and Zel tugged her caftan down over her bared legs.

"I have looked everywhere for you," Omar said. His eyes were frantic, white magic zipping through them, appearing and disappearing on his neck and cheeks. Except for his voice the room was silent, tension tight like instrument strings.

"Why?" Dilay said. She was too wounded for this. For whatever he was about to inflict on her. She could not bear anything else. Before he answered, her gaze caught on his throat. At the pale ribbon that hung around it like a necklace. Only then did she notice the rest, realize he was wearing enough white and silver to blind her, that his turban was tucked beneath Ruslan's arm, who stood stoic in the doorway as her father eyed him with malice.

Dilay lifted her gaze to his.

"Dilay." Seda tugged gently on Dilay's hand, but Dilay ignored it.

"I was going to ask if you're all right," he said, his gaze straying as if he would look at the multitude of people gaping at them like sardines. "But…"

"But that would be a foolish question," Dilay said. He nodded, unflinching at the sharpness in her voice.

"You should control your magic," Dilay murmured, because she could see fear on the faces around her.

"I will be able to in a moment," he replied.

"Why are you here?" Dilay didn't know what else to say. What was there to say? They were worlds apart. She had spent the night and morning in prison, the afternoon fighting her way home through protesters, and he had been cozied up in the palace with wine and mezze.

His gaze darted when her mother crouched to begin cleaning up, and her aunts crept from the kitchen to assist.

"I need your help," he said, which caused a stir, and the swirl of magic in his skin was replaced by a rise of color in his neck. Omar glanced to Seda, whose fingers tightened on Dilay's hand.

"Vali Ahad, please," Dilay's father said. "She has done enough, been through enough."

Omar's brow wrinkled as he searched her face. "I know. I'm sorry, Dilay," he said. His use of her name elicited a gasp from her mother's eldest sister. Dilay glared at him in censure. He brushed a hand over his hair, looking worn. Dilay wished she did not have to talk to him with half her family and neighbors staring at her. Zel fiddled with her basket of healing supplies, but her gaze was directed at them, unflinching. Seda stood stiff and awkward against Dilay's side, her lips pinched together. "I want you to come with me to address the rioters."

"Why should I?" Dilay asked. "You have no idea what I've been through—" Did he care? Or did he simply think parading her about and riding in like a hero would be enough?

"But—" Seda murmured. Omar gave his head a shake, and she pouted.

"I know you spent the night in the Cliffs. I was unaware until this morning."

"Come with me," she said, and turned toward the kitchen as she extracted her hand from Seda's. She would rather have more privacy between her and all the perked ears, but she couldn't very well shut the both of them in her bedroom with everyone watching.

Dilay led him into the kitchen, and out the back door. The chatter began immediately and escalated to arguments quickly. They only had a few moments before someone came to interrupt. She turned her back to the embankment behind her to face him and folded her arms over her chest. He stopped a few steps out of the door, allowing her space.

"Do you even know why I was in the Cliffs?" Dilay asked. Omar took a moment to answer, his eyes fixed on her arms, bared by the short-sleeved under-caftan she had stripped down to. Dilay followed his line of sight to the rising bruises, darkening in the shape of fingers.

"The City Watch raided your school." He clasped his hands behind his back and a furrow appeared on his brow. The magic on his skin flickered and faded, but the muscles in his neck tightened.

"They arrested all of us," Dilay said.

"I know."

"You know? Yet you came looking for me instead of helping them."

"Dilay, I—"

"Behram sent them. Did you know that as well?" The emotion came back, the choking stranglehold of hurt. "To teach me a lesson because he saw us."

Omar's face went slack, and his gaze cut sideways and up, toward the palace.

"Fix this yourself. Or better yet, tell him to fix it. I have fought and scraped and played the games I had to play, so that I could help. So I could make things better. And I see what that means to the people it threatens. I will not help you. Not one single time more."

He exhaled, and his shoulders relaxed, his hands falling to his sides. The magic in his skin and eyes swirled away completely.

"I want to hold you," he said, without looking at her.

"Why?" Dilay asked. To soothe himself, she suspected, rather than to comfort her.

"Would you like the truth, or a pretty answer?" Omar said wryly, still staring toward the palace.

"Guess," Dilay snipped. One corner of his mouth tilted.

"So I do not forget why I left the palace this morning, and instead return there to strangle Behram in full view of everyone at court."

"I wanted the pretty answer." Dilay turned her head to the side so he couldn't see her irritation.

"Because you are so loved by my city that they will riot for you. And I would like to join them. Holding you seems a better course of action."

"You read too much poetry." Dilay dropped her arms to her sides. "They are not rioting for me. You imprisoned their children. Took them hostage."

"I know," he said. "And they are rioting for you, their champion. I have spoken with a number of them."

She glanced at him. "Have you? With your magic like that?"

He nodded. She snorted. "I could hardly help it," he said. "No one knew where you were. I abandoned everyone at my betrothal. I put my guards at risk in a riot. Today has not been a good day."

Her eyes slitted. "My heart bleeds for you."

"You are angry with me, I understand," he said, tiredly.

"I don't want you here. I don't want your help. I don't want to feel anything for you. My feelings have done nothing but hurt me." As she said it she heard a shuffle in the kitchen and rolled her eyes toward the sky. Brilliant. The last of her self-respect. "Can you hear all right in there?" she called. Another shuffle, urgent whispers.

Omar pressed his thumbs to his temples. "I will make this right, I will. But it will take time. I cannot move mountains in a day, especially after leaving the ceremony this morning. It would be best if the city did not burn down between now and then. Come with me to the Grand Market, we can speak with the riot leaders together."

"Is this sudden heroism salve for your guilt? Because of us?"

Omar flinched. "I cannot change what I did or who I was yesterday, Dilay. I did not understand what a coward I was until I met you. Until I was staring at a room full of laughing people eating food and drinking while you were in prison for helping people who had nothing. I didn't understand. And I cannot change the truth of that, but I can change tomorrow."

"I will not care about you a moment longer. I have nothing left to give." She wanted to believe him, but she was shredded inside, and the only thing she felt was anger.

"All right," he said, a cool mask falling into place.

"No"—she pointed at him, at the magic he was using to hide himself—"you show me the truth."

"You just lied to me," he said.

"You do not deserve my truths. You do not deserve my hurt. Any of it."

"I am not Behram."

"No. You are Omar Sabri the Sixth, Vali Ahad of Tamar. You are the most powerful air mage in Narfour. And I am just me. Powerless. Barely a noble. And nothing I have achieved or done has made any change at all. That was made very clear to me last night. Just exactly how meaningless and powerless I am."

"I am the Vali Ahad," he said. "The most powerful air mage in Tamar. And I cannot stop the riots in this city without you." When she looked at him he smiled tentatively. "Who is meaningless?"

They stared at each other, and he did not cover his emotions with his magic. She could see how badly he wanted to reach out to her. And her desire for it ached inside her, but that ribbon around his neck was yet more proof of her insignificance.

"No," Dilay said. Her father was right. She had done enough. Given until there was nothing left of her. She walked past him and into the kitchen, through the gauntlet of her mother and neighbors and family and into the living area. Her father and his friends leapt to their feet, but she ignored them as she crossed the room to her bedroom. Dilay slammed the door closed and sat on her bed, trying to settle. She bent forward, pressing her face into her hands and holding back another flood of tears.

A quiet knock sounded just before her door opened and Seda slipped inside.

"Did he leave?"

"Yes." Seda sat beside her on the bed. "Why are you in here?"

Dilay turned a teary-eyed look on her friend. Seda smiled apologetically, tucking her hand into her sleeve and blotting at the tear that escaped onto Dilay's cheek.

"Air mages have such tender hearts," Seda said. "Because they don't practice with them often." Her tone was gently teasing. Dilay swiped at her eyes and looked away.

"I give and give and all they want is more."

"No," Seda said. "Not they. Just Behram. It was the Vali Ahad that released us. In front of the Council, and the Sultan. He threatened them with his magic. Dilay, he was so frightening." She set her hands in her lap, curling her fingers together. "He went to the prison to make certain the others were released. Didn't you pay attention? He left his betrothal to come find you. He defied his father, and disrespected all those nobles, just to help you, and us. And now he is trying to make the rest of it right and you won't help him in return."

Dilay's eyes fluttered closed. The pressure in her chest was incomprehensible. Was she pleased? Grateful? Or enraged.

"I know you are too smart to think that all these things you have done, all this defiance, was going to be easy? You did not think you would sit quietly at the University and nudge an entire nation to change? This is your real chance, Dilay. He is." Seda brushed a bit of Dilay's hair behind her ear. "You've invested all that time and forgiveness in Behram, but you cannot muster the same for the Vali Ahad? Someone who actually deserves it." She smiled brightly when Dilay looked at her from the corners of her eyes. "You never can see these things. Which is why you will always need me."

She could see them better than Seda believed. Now, after having layers of denial and delusion ripped away so brutally. Behram had never once tried to change, to move toward her. Omar had done nothing but try to meet her, to be better. Even when he failed. He listened, and learned. He tried again. As he was now, alone, in a city full of angry people. What if someone attacked him, and his magic lashed out? What if…

Dilay lunged off the bed and tugged down a fresh set of clothes. "You're right."

"I know," Seda said with a martyred sigh as Dilay stripped out of her caftan and pulled the clean one on. Seda held up her entari and helped her shrug into it.

"He said he was going to the market," Dilay said as she buttoned her entari.

"That's where the leaders are. Or leader. I don't know who or how many, I avoided the riots on my way here."

When she and Seda emerged from her room, Dilay's mother was waiting. She observed Dilay's change of outfit with a resolute nod. She moved in as the family and neighbors whispered behind her, taking a moment to straighten the clasps of Dilay's entari and then brush at the fabric with her fingers.

"Dilay." Her father stepped forward from the bench on the far side of the room. Dilay's mother cast him a look that silenced him, and he sat back down. Dilay did not say another word, just strode to the front and pulled open the door, Seda only a step behind.

They had to take a winding route through the neighborhood to get to a road that would funnel them to the market. The protestors had blocked off alleys and side roads with piles of crates and other detritus. The streets in her neighborhood were eerily quiet, deserted. But she could hear the shouting from the protests in the market. Or riots. Some combination of the two. The closer they got, the louder the cries became. Some were even comprehensible. Outcries against the nobility, against the Sabris, vile things that made Dilay glance at Seda. Her friend had a tense smile set on her mouth, her eyes narrowed.

They reached the edge of the protestors, mostly families from the Earth District, dockworkers, laborers, and tradesmen. Their wives. Older children. The road was strewn with debris, broken crates, the remnants of windows. Dilay saw one door torn off its hinges and laying in the road. She did not see or smell any fires, and she was grateful for that. The moment fires started there would be no stopping disaster. The palace would deploy its entire guard force, the city would be shut down. It could lead to things she couldn't bear to think about. Civil unrest. People dying.

"Dilay!" Turgay and Zeki shouldered their way through the crowd. The four of them crashed into a tangled embrace. He had done this, freed them. Omar. When she could do nothing, he had stood up for her, had faced his father and whatever rumors his defiance would cause. After the greeting, Zeki and Turgay took up positions to either side of Dilay and Seda, holding back the crowd as it surged and shifted like the ocean.

As they turned onto the main road, and the cries of the crowd became so loud, the mood more volatile, Dilay heard someone cry her name, again, and stopped. She peered between Zeki and Seda and saw Belma's mother waving. Dilay broke away from her friends and edged her way toward the woman.

"Is she home?" Dilay asked. The woman nodded, and hugged Dilay.

"Thank you," she said.

"I didn't…it was my fault."

"Thank you for what you risk to teach her." She smiled tearfully, swiping at her cheeks with her fingers. Then she turned, and called into the crowd. "She's here!"

Dilay took a surprised step back as the group, who had been chanting, turned inward, and familiar faces appeared out of the melee to come forward and offer gratitude, some hugs, some simple kisses to her cheeks. Seda joined her, and then Zeki and Turgay.

"You should thank the Vali Ahad. He was the one who spoke up against my arrest. All the arrests," Dilay announced. She did not know how they would take it. Despite their friendly greetings she could tell they were angry, edgy. "I am looking for him, have you seen him?"

Belma's mother pointed, toward the top of the market, where fire from torches and mage orbs glowed brightly, and the shouts of the crowd were the loudest. "You best hurry, Mistress. The ones up there aren't likely to welcome him."

"That's right," a male voice crowed. "He comes down here to silence us, he deserves whatever accidents befall him."

Seda called over the voices that cried out in favor of something violent happening to Omar for his trouble. "He freed us. He freed your children."

"He might be the only one at the palace who is sympathetic at all. Can you imagine what they might do if something happens to him?" Dilay said. "Come with me now, and help. It might be our only chance to negotiate with anyone from the palace."

"You think he'll listen to us? Care what we have to say? He is only here to shut us up."

"He will listen," Dilay said. "Won't you try? Anything is better than this—the city on the brink of burning."

"What do you have to lose by trying?" Seda asked. Dilay squeezed her friend's hand in gratitude.

There came a few grumbled rebuttals, but no one outright said no. Dilay glanced at Seda, who nodded her encouragement, and they walked farther. Similar encounters happened throughout the district as they walked. A young couple, the husband an ironworker whom her father had saved from a prison sentence. A student who had aged out of her school two Turns prior. The man down the street from her parents' home who baked bread for the neighborhood whose grand-children Dilay taught in exchange. All joined their group.

By the last encounter before the market, she estimated more than a hundred people followed them up the hill and toward the Grand Market.

A WALL OF ANGRY PROTESTORS, ARMED with torches and makeshift weapons made of boards, bricks, stones, or anything else they could find, prevented any further progress by Omar and his guards. Omar could see his destination from where they were. In the center of the market a platform made of crates and wood planks served as stage for a man who paced, giving an impassioned speech about basic human decency and the right to survival for all.

"We can find another route," Omar suggested to Commander Isler, who had a look that suggested to Omar he was itching for a reason to escalate things. That would do far more harm than good.

"If you allow them to dictate your movements, Vali Ahad, then you have conceded to them," Isler said, gesturing his men from their current circle around Omar to a line like an army about to charge. Omar shifted, hands gripping his reins so hard they cut into his palms. Isler was his father's man through and through, a bully all too happy to apply violence when understanding was a better tool. Mazhar was right. He was a fanatic.

"By order of the Sultan, you will move aside, or you will be punished." Isler drew his yataghan, and his guards did the same. Before Omar could voice his protest, the crowd responded to the drawn weapons with louder taunts, and by pushing forward, forcing Isler and his men to move their horses back.

"Commander Isler!" Omar ordered, a moment too late. The commander spurred his mount forward, knocking people back, and two young men fell to the ground, saved from the horse's hooves by quick-witted companions who yanked them out of the way. Isler reined the horse back, his men closing around him.

For a moment everyone was still, the abrupt silence more threatening than the shouted taunts a moment before. Ruslan maneuvered his horse nearly against Omar's, his face tense, his fingers tucked into the chalk bag at his waist, for fast spellcasting.

"Move back!" Isler barked. A rock sailed out of the crowd and struck his shoulder.

Fire ignited in Isler's hands, crawling up his arms.

Voices railed against the show of magic and temper. Shouting anger at proof that nothing came from the palace but violence and subjugation.

"That is enough, Commander," Omar said, loudly enough to be heard over the cries.

"These people are just rabble. You are the Vali Ahad, you do not mean to let them—"

"I am the Valid Ahad," Omar said, "and I gave you an order."

Answering fire sprouted among the crowd, flames igniting in hands and on clothes.

"Ah! The palace has acknowledged us," the man on the makeshift platform announced. "With the Vali Ahad, no less. Are you daring, or foolish to show your face here?"

"Narfour is my city too." Omar dismounted. He felt pulled as taut as a drawn bow. There was no mistaking the sense that a single wrong move would ignite the tempers of everyone around him, and possibly the city. Wherever he looked, every face, he saw hostility. A woman turned away when his gaze fell on her, hiding her face against her companion's shoulder, clearly afraid of him. They thought he was there to hurt them.

As the muscles in his back and neck tightened, he thought of Dilay, and forced himself to relax, to hold his writhing magic, excited by the threat.

"Your city?" the speaker mocked, to laughter from the crowd. "You do not know Narfour, and it does not know you. What do we have to speak about? You have only come out of your pretty palace because we interrupted your festivities." He turned to the crowd. "Didn't we?"

Cries went up again, a wave of sound through the gathered people, who grew more restless.

"Vali Ahad—" Ruslan cautioned.

"Efendim," Isler said, in a tone like an order. Omar handed his reins to Ruslan, casting Isler a castigating look. "This is pointless. Every one of these people should be in prison." He did not bother to lower his voice, the accusation easily heard over the tense quiet.

"Sabri tyrant!" someone howled in response, and a clamorous bellow erupted in agreement. Torches were thrust into the air. Isler motioned with his left hand, the one empty of a weapon, and conjured a fire ball.

A bolt of fear froze Omar for a heartbeat. As Isler drew his hand back to throw the fire, and dozens within the crowd did the same, the fear evaporated behind a surge of instinct. Omar released his hold on his magic, wrapped magical hands around the air surrounding Isler and yanked it away. His fireball snuffed out. Omar extended the reach of the magical command. He could steal the air from a man's lungs, if circumstances were dire, but instead he whisked the air around the market square and extinguished every mage fire, every torch, every flicker he saw.

Darkness settled, along with stunned silence.

Omar was the only light left, his magic radiating from him like the light of a rising sun, illuminating the circle around him.

"Enough," Omar used that same magic to amplify his voice, loud enough to reach every corner of the market. "Please. Violence is not the answer here. I am here to speak for the palace."

"But who will speak for you, Vali Ahad? You took our children, for the unspeakable crime of *learning*, and we are done being treated like animals," the speaker answered into the dark market.

Omar clenched his hands at his sides. The silence that followed was answer enough, weighing everything down, a hopeless void.

"I will speak for him."

Omar knew Dilay's voice, the signature of the magic she used to amplify it enough to be heard. A mage orb shimmered into existence, illuminating her in the darkness, standing amidst a circle of faces he recognized. Seda stood beside her, lowering her hand from conjuring the orb. Omar's body relaxed, air filling his lungs and clearing his head.

"And me," Seda said.

"All of us," Turgay said from Dilay's other side, and Zeki, next to him, nodded in agreement as Turgay swept a hand to indicate a cluster of people around them.

"Yusef, ask any of these who imprisoned them, and who released them," Dilay addressed the speaker. "Ask your daughter. Ask Toulin what she knows of the Vali Ahad. And then let him speak, or it can only be assumed you are more interested in your temporary power than you are a solution to injustice."

Yusef faltered, looking at Omar as he contemplated. Torches flickered back to life, and a few more orbs floated up to light the market once more.

"Let me through," Dilay commanded. The crowd between her and Omar shifted, opening a path for her to cross the street. She smiled at him across the gap. He clasped his hands behind his back, so he did not grin like a simpleton as he strode toward her. Ruslan dropped out of his saddle, and a few of the quicker guards did the same to hurry behind him.

When he reached her, he clasped his hands harder, and smiled.

"*Hello*," he cast. She cocked her head, and a wisp of cool magic swirled up the back of his neck. The greeting made the rest of his tension bleed away, and he released his grip on his hands.

"Very well, Vali Ahad, come tell us what you have to say." Yusef stepped off the platform and gestured to it as if it were a dais, exaggerating a bow. Omar held a hand out in front of him in invitation.

"You first," Omar said to her. "So they can see I will defer to you."

"Will you?" Dilay asked as she stepped in front of him, trying to tease away her tension and her emotions.

"Yes, Instructor Akar."

She couldn't look back at him, though she wanted to. He wasn't teasing, even his cast voice held promises she did not want to hear. Promises he could not keep. She swallowed the lump of hurt, and pressed a hand over her frantic heart as she walked forward.

The crowd parted for them, or for Zeki and Turgay forging ahead of her. A few of those up front were familiar to her, faces she saw in the market; the elder woman who sold her herbs grasped her hand on her way by; a city messenger whose void son had taken classes from her until he had taken work on the docks. Dilay squeezed hands that were offered and returned smiles until she stood at the platform across from Yusef.

"Did the Vali Ahad free you too, Dilay?" Yusef asked. Dilay had only met him once. Yusef was Toulin's father. His daughter was a void, but he was clearly a fire mage, for both the charisma he obviously possessed, and the scorch-marked platform upon which he stood. If she remembered correctly, he was a smith for the guild.

"He asked me for my help," she said. Yusef's thick brows drew together. Omar moved to her side and stepped onto the platform. Dilay looked up at him, and he held his hand out. She raised an eyebrow in question, because magic still sizzled in the brown of his eyes and glowed over his skin. He had darkened the entire market, dozens upon dozens of fire mages. That anyone had ever thought a lack of control was his issue seemed laughable now. He gave the smallest nod, and she took his hand. He tugged her onto the platform beside him.

A restless hush descended on the crowd. Dilay looked out over their heads, to the market beyond, where vendors had done their best to barricade their stalls. Some stood in front of them with makeshift weapons, some cowered within. Some had left the stalls to join the throng that stretched down the market road toward the pier. Hundreds.

"You are angry." Omar's words to the crowd did not even need a push of magic to carry. Dilay repressed a smile and a glance at him. There was symbolism there, between the voice and the man. The mildness he affected, the quiet manner and reserved conduct. But that wasn't him, and she thought that perhaps he was emerging from that imperfect mold cast over him to be the man she was certain he could be. A Sultan who saw his people. "I understand."

There was laughter in response, some shouted insults. Omar waited for the quiet to return. "I like to think"—he looked at Dilay—"that Dilay Akar is my friend."

She gave a single nod, because she could not speak. It was not friendship dark in Omar's eyes, but adoration. Dilay looked at the crowd instead. Seda, Turgay, and Zeki stood in the front, along with a few of the others who had followed from the lower districts. A wall like the ineffectual palace guards should have been, but who instead milled by Commander Isler.

"What happened last night was my fault," Omar announced. She glanced at him in surprise. A rumble went through the crowd, accompanied by an uptick in the agitation that was already palpable in the air. Dilay did not know if Omar possessed the speaking skills to calm a crowd, or rally them behind him. But this was a trial by fire. If he failed, she could see in some faces enough anger to fuel violence to kill, despite his earlier demonstration of power. "I have been to Instructor Akar's night school. I have seen what she, and the others"—he gestured to Seda and the two men in the front row—"are trying to do."

"And what is that, Vali Ahad? What could you possibly know about our children and what they are denied?" Yusef said, and was echoed through the crowd. Omar waited again, started to clasp his hands behind his back, and Dilay tugged gently on his sleeve. He relaxed.

"I know what it is to have magic that controls you more than it is controlled, and I would not wish it on anyone. I also do not believe in talent wasted, and I have seen Instructor Akar's talent for drawing out the best in her students." He gave a slight smile, but he did not look at her. Something fluttered in her stomach. Pride, or the same adoration she had seen in his eyes before. "I should have done something, the first time I went to the school and saw what she was doing. But"—he relaxed his shoulders—"I was afraid. And so I inadvertently caused this. All of this. The arrest of Instructor Akar and her students, the fear you feel, the entirety of the injustice is on my shoulders."

People shouted agreement, and not in a friendly way. When they quieted to a discontented rumble, Omar continued.

"So I will do what I should have done the moment I knew about Instructor Akar's efforts. I will enlist her assistance in developing a plan for more schools like hers, for each district. Schools that anyone can attend."

Dilay believed him, her entire body filled with sparkling, incandescent excitement. But the crowd did not. They responded with a mix of stony silence and scornful chatter.

"We have been lied to enough, Vali Ahad," Yusef said. "You cannot simply appear down here for the first time and begin promising things and expect us to believe you." He gave a sharp laugh. "We are not the fools your breed think we are. The Sultan will never agree to anything like that."

"I believe him," Dilay announced, using a push of magic to carry her voice to the far edges of the crowd. "What will this anger solve? What will violence do but cause more hardship? Look at this market." She pointed. "What will you do, strip them of their livelihood to prove your point?"

"We have been reduced to this," Yusef said, addressing the crowd and not her. "If they will not listen to us peacefully, then they will listen when we burn their city."

"I am listening," Omar declared. That booming voice demanded silence, and achieved it. "It took me too long, and for that I am sorry.

But I am not my father. And all I am asking of you today is a chance to prove that to you, before anyone else is harmed."

"It is my school," Dilay said. "And my choice to help. And I choose this path."

"And me!" Seda called. She stepped up to stand at the base of the makeshift platform and face the crowd. Turgay and Zeki joined her. A moment passed that felt like a collective breath held.

A few others broke from the crowds. Parents of those Dilay taught. Friends from her neighborhood. They joined Seda in facing the protestors, silent in support. A trickle of them continued, and Dilay's body was light with relief.

"Go home," Dilay said. "Everyone. Go home to your families. You have the attention of the palace, and a promise. Let it rest at that, today."

There were rumblings, a few flashes of fire amidst the crowd, mages that would prefer to maintain their anger. Hope flickered when Dilay saw one such fire extinguished by a man standing next to someone, who then gave a quick, angry admonishment.

"For today," Yusef said, giving Omar a tense, angry frown, "you have won. But if you do not keep your word…"

"I understand," he said. Yusef raised his arm. The signal worked on most, as a large slice of the crowd began to turn and scatter, a disorganized dissolution. Enough remained and began to cluster that Omar stepped off the platform as Yusef turned away.

"Yusef," he said. "If we cannot disperse them with words, then I will have to bring the City Watch in, and I do not wish to."

Dilay could see that most of those who remained were men, drunk on alcohol, the promise of violence, or both. Yusef stood beside Omar, surveying the milling group, many of whom still held clubs made of broken bits of wood or other detritus they'd found along the way. But they were dispersed as the crowd absorbed them, many forcibly steering them away. Dilay stepped down.

She laced her fingers with Seda's, looking toward Omar. He and Yusef had their heads bent together, talking. It did not look friendly, but neither did it seem antagonistic. Dilay turned toward

Commander Isler, who stood with arms folded over his chest and a sour glower. Perhaps he had wanted a more…energetic outcome. He had certainly tried for it.

"Have you been home yet?" Dilay asked Seda.

"No. We spent all our time returning the children. Come on, you can walk me back."

"Wait," Omar said, turning away from Yusef with a hasty farewell. "May I?" He gestured in the direction of her home.

Seda pressed her lips together to repress a knowing smile Dilay was all too familiar with. "If you wish it, Vali Ahad."

"What did you say to Yusef?" Dilay asked as they fell in step together.

"We spoke about Toulin."

Dilay beamed up at him. There were so many things she wanted to say, but this was not the place. A small section of his guards, along with Ruslan, followed them through the streets. Seda gave Dilay a farewell hug when she turned down her street.

"I will check on you in the morning," Seda called as she broke into a jog toward her home. Dilay waved.

When they reached her house, it was quiet. Perhaps the neighbors and family had returned home. Or perhaps they were all huddled, listening. The night was darker for the lack of mage orbs in the lamps. Everyone had been too busy participating in or avoiding the protests to light the lamps. Omar's men waited at a reasonably discreet distance up the hill.

"Will you be all right?" Dilay asked. She did not know what waited for him back at the palace. He shrugged.

"I doubt I am in any real danger. No imprisonments or hangings. So, I will bear it." He stared at her so hard heat crept up her neck.

"I…never told you congratulations," she said, succeeding in making the moment even more awkward as she pointed to the betrothal ribbon around his neck. He clutched at it as though he meant to rip it away but dropped his arm and shifted his gaze away from her instead. "Who?"

"Zehra Demir," he said, with all the emotion of crushed stone.

"I am glad," Dilay said, her throat closing. "That it is not an air mage. That you will not have to see a child—"

"Stop." He rubbed a hand over his face. "Please stop."

"All right." They stood in silence for a long, painful time, until she could bear it no more. "I should go."

Omar nodded.

"I am so proud of you," she said, because she wanted him to know, to feel some of her bursting triumph. When she started to bow he stopped her, his hand cupping her face and urging her up.

"Don't," he said on a shaky breath. His thumb swept over her cheekbone. "Thank you." He stepped close and pressed his lips to her brow. She closed her eyes, unable to breathe or speak. "For being my strength."

She grabbed handfuls of his entari, her chest a single, crushing ache.

"I"—he drew back, his fingers tightening then relaxing against her cheek—"will love you until the day I die. Even if I do not remember myself, I will remember you. Always."

He dropped his hand, turned, and strode away. She wanted to scream for him to stop, but she could not. He did not look back, not once, and Dilay was shattered and reformed by the single, shredded breath she was able to draw.

TWENTY-NINE

OMAR KNELT ON THE COLD tiles of the Council Hall in nothing but his salvar, his hands pressed to his knees so he did not fall forward under the strike of the cane. He had lost count, but Eymen had said there would be fifty when he announced the punishment to the Council. It was all a crescendo of pain now, each new lash sending it soaring, erasing thought and self. Enough time between each so they did not blend together. The only thought that lingered was that when he was Sultan, he would abolish this punishment, and perhaps even bury a stack of canes with his father, as a last, final jest.

His skin had broken. He could see droplets of blood land on the pristine tiles when the guard flicked the cane. He tried to count them between, to still the animal in his brain that wished to lash out. The instinct to turn around and put hands on the man assigned to lash him, and erase his mind. Violence beget violence—he had come to deeply understand that concept over the last two days.

The next lash came, and for a moment he was nothing but pain, it resonated through his limbs and teeth, blackening his vision and his sense. And in that dark and silent place of nothing but pain, he and his magic came to an agreement. That he did not need protecting anymore. He could face an angry city and subdue them. He could defy his father and survive. Despite the pain.

"Fifty, Sultan Efendim," the Grand Vizier announced. Omar breathed. His magic coiled and curled inside him, quiet, and controlled. His skin was clammy, his muscles shaking involuntarily. He still couldn't see quite straight when he bowed to touch his head to the marble. For a moment he thought he would pass out.

"Well taken, my son," the Sultan said, calmly. Omar had no delusions that his father would be emotionally affected by the sight of him being struck. He was newly settled with that revelation. Because he did not need his father's approval, if he approved of himself. Omar sat up. "I trust you will also handle your duties today with the same composure?"

"Yes, Sultan," Omar said in a voice he did not recognize. The Council members who were present stirred. It was clear many of them disapproved of the Sultan's choice of punishment for his wayward son. But none of them saw fit to voice that dissent.

Ruslan hurried to kneel in front of Omar, bearing a tray with a glass of water. It wobbled as he held it out, his usual stony manner strained. Omar drank, and set the cup back.

"The physician," Omar's mother ordered, in a thin voice. Ruslan nodded to her.

"You may go, son. To prepare for the guild tribunal," the Sultan said.

"There is a matter I wish to address first, Sultan," Omar said, "if I may." Perhaps it was a poor idea to address the Council half naked and bleeding, nearly delirious from the throbbing pain. But Omar had been dealing, and functioning, with pain all his life.

"You have earned my ear for the moment," his father said. Omar did not stand; he wasn't certain he could without toppling over again.

"I wish to annul my engagement to Zehra Demir," he said. He wanted to smile, because bringing it up felt akin to spitting blood at his father in defiance. This new dynamic between them suited Omar well.

"You cannot possibly," the Grand Vizier said, glancing frantically between Omar and the Sultan.

"Have you not caused enough disgrace in this court already, Vali Ahad?" his father demanded. "How dare you insult the Grand Vizier, and I, with such a suggestion."

"It is not meant to insult, Grand Vizier, I apologize. I am honored to be betrothed to your daughter, as any man would be. But Sultanim"—he returned his attention to his father—"I am concerned that this will mean I am the last Veritor in the Sabri line."

The Sultan looked immediately to the Sultana, who stared at Omar with angry disapproval. So. That had been her plan in choosing Zehra. As well it was, or he would not have been able to think of an excuse to annul things without shaming Zehra, which he did not wish to do. But, this solution was Dilay's, not his. Though she probably did not realize she had given him the idea when she mentioned it in parting. He could not think of her. Of his foolish confession to her. She didn't need the burden of his feelings on top of everything that had already happened to her.

"Sultan Efendim, I understand that this is a concern, but please consider the ramifications for my daughter." Eymen turned to bow as he spoke. The Sultan tugged at his beard, his gaze trailing up to the patterned ceiling.

Though his back was numb, or hurt so badly Omar could no longer distinguish the pain, he could feel blood oozing over the undamaged skin lower down. Sitting through the Merchant Guild tribunal would be agony. But if he could achieve this single triumph, he could also endure that.

Because he had understood, standing in front of a crowd ready to trample him into the pavers with Dilay at his side, brave and beautiful and torn asunder, that there would never be anyone else for him. He would not pretend. He would spend his lifetime alone if that was his only choice. She was a Queen in his heart, and was all he would ever see.

"My son makes a valuable point, Grand Vizier," the Sultan finally said. Omar almost collapsed forward to his hands, relief making them unsteady. "But I will not shame your daughter. There are a multitude of fine young men who would be proud to call her wife. In fact"—the Sultan stood—"Semih."

Omar's relief turned to dismay as Semih Kadir stood, smiling serenely. Omar grit his teeth.

"Your son would be a fine match for Mistress Demir. Would that please you, Grand Vizier?"

Omar tried frantically to come up with something to stop the Grand Vizier from accepting. If Behram married Zehra, it would put his father in line for Grand Vizier. If he also controlled the Merchant Guild…It was too late to redact his request for annulment. What had he done? His gaze whipped to Mazhar, who sat pale and silent on the bench nearest their father. They met gazes, and Mazhar discreetly spread his hands at Omar's silent plea.

"Yes, Efendim." Eymen bowed again. Omar gripped his knees to prevent himself clutching at his own hair or beard. Fool. Trying to manipulate the Council without thinking of all the possible outcomes. Of course his father would choose Semih, who also valued the division in classes, adherence to tradition.

"Then consider it done. My wife and I will reassess potential First House matches for the Vali Ahad once the dispute within the Merchant Guild has been dealt with. Those with eligible daughters may present them to the Grand Vizier."

As Eymen turned to look at Omar, he raised an eyebrow, because he knew what setting Semih Kadir in line to replace him meant. Omar dropped his gaze to the floor. He was going to have to get a great deal better at this, if he was going to survive his reign as Sultan.

And Behram. What would he do now? He had avoided seeking him out, even after returning to the palace. He needed far more time before he could face Behram as a rational, thinking person.

The other side of that coin of betrayal was his own. He knew how Behram felt about Dilay, and had not honored it by controlling himself. He had betrayed Behram, and now, forced Behram into the same situation he had just relieved himself of. Marriage to a stranger when he cared for someone else.

Omar braced himself with grit teeth and pushed to his feet. He bowed.

"Thank you, Sultan Efendim."

HE WANTED TO STAND. Sitting made his entire body ache, distracted him with the fiery pain of his wounds as the shock and numbing salve wore off. But he could not, or risk distracting everyone from the proceedings. So he sat, tense and miserable on the narrow bench as he tried to concentrate on what was being said by witnesses of the tribunal.

Things were balanced, so far. Character witnesses for both men attested to their interest in bringing the guild forward into the modern age, for the glory of the Sultan, of course. Each grievance was met with counter witnesses.

It was during this impasse that Dilay stepped into the witness box. Even at a distance Omar could see how upset she was. Despite what Behram had done to her, Omar knew she would never intentionally hurt anyone. But standing as witness against Behram's father… Omar glanced to the benches where Altimur Pasha and Kadir Pasha sat. Behram was beside his father, arms folded over his chest, gaze fixed unwavering on Dilay. A surge of his lingering anger zipped through Omar. Behram blinked, his head turning, his gaze locking with Omar's. They stared at each other. After a moment, one corner of Behram's mouth curved up, and he looked away.

Dilay spoke, her voice level and pitched confidently, though Omar could feel the bit of magic she used to keep it that way. Her gaze was fixed on her father, he thought.

"As outlined by Judge Hanim's law of morality, I believe Kadir Pasha is unfit to serve as a guild leader." She paused, her gaze flinching to Behram and away again, fixing on her father. The honeyed color of her skin turned ashen, and she swallowed. "He has bullied and blackmailed his way to his position."

Behram shifted in his seat, his jaw tightening as his father shifted to look at him. Dilay and Behram's mutual discomfort seemed to seep into Omar's body. Those gathered murmured to each other as Dilay outlined instance after instance of people bribed to give Semih Kadir advantages within the city, blackmailed or sabotaged those who could not be bribed, or simply threatened them into compliance. Each example stirred those who supported Semih into louder murmurs and restless shifting, and made Omar's apprehension about Semih Kadir having access to the position of Grand Vizier even more pronounced.

When she was done, she took a breath, and for the first time that day looked at Omar. It did not last long enough, just a flick to and away of her gaze. He had worried that his confession might have pushed her away. Now he understood it might seem childish to her, with so many other concerns weighing on her mind.

"Do you have witnesses for these accusations, Instructor Akar?" one of the judges asked dispassionately. Dilay did not look at the benches where the Pashas sat. Her hands curled into her entari then relaxed.

"I am witness to these events, as they were told to me by Behram Kadir."

"Master Kadir, do you corroborate these accusations?"

"Is it the habit of this court to take the word of criminals against generous, contributing members of society?" Semih asked, blandly, a look on his face like everything was beneath him.

Omar heard Dilay's sharp inhale, but anything else was buried beneath the uproar that ensued. People, a few faces Omar recognized from the protests, stood, shouting, and others rose to meet them, throwing verbal accusations across the aisle at each other. Behram and his father wore matching smiles of contentedness, as if they were happier in the chaos than in the order of a moment before.

Dilay's father stood, and cast his voice toward the high ceiling so it thundered in an order to be seated and silent. When everyone had complied, Semih stood and bowed toward the judges and Omar.

"This would be a simple matter to clear up, yes?" He looked at Omar. Omar managed to repress the shock of repulsion that went through him. Dilay gripped the rail of the witness box she stood in, her skin losing some of its warmth.

"My magic is not a trivial matter, Kadir Pasha. Are you suggesting that I use it to identify whether you are lying?"

Surprise registered momentarily in Semih's eyes, then fire, then nothing.

"It is not my word we are questioning, is it? Is the court not aware that Instructor Akar was arrested for illegal instruction? That she fomented riots in the city?" Semih said, calmly, as though it were surprising and amusing that he had to inform anyone. Beside him, Behram shifted, his face uncharacteristically unreadable.

"And you are unaware that she was pardoned, and that the Sultan has agreed to legalize her school, and others, throughout the city?" Omar said. "Your arguments about her character are unfounded, Kadir Pasha."

Behram appeared momentarily stunned, his mouth pressing in a thin line. His father glanced down at him for confirmation but Behram did not respond, and Semih recovered with a tense smile.

"Efendim, that may be the case, but she chose to practice illegally. To defy the Sultan. I have done nothing but support the Sultan, as you know. Clearly you can see why it is concerning that a dissenter be allowed to bring charges of errant morality against me?"

"I will submit to it." Dilay's voice shook and cracked. "I will submit to a confession."

Semih had not planned on that, a look of surprise spasmed across his face.

"No!" her father barked. Omar's stomach cramped, and he grit his teeth, leveling a glare on Behram he wished held the power of immolation in it. Semih held a hand up toward Dilay in invitation to Omar. Omar tried to think past the panic. Dilay looked at him, sorrowful. Apologetic. Because she worried more for him than she did herself. He balled his hands into fists then relaxed them. He stood, stiffly, and waited while the flash of dizziness and stiffness faded.

The distance between him and the witness box was a matter of twenty strides, but each one was excruciating, for the physical pain, the pull on his wounds, the blood he could feel seeping through his bandages, and for his fear. *I am in a poor state to do this, Behram. You are putting her at risk you do not understand.* Omar cast his voice in a whisper. *"Are you so loyal to your father that you are willing to risk her sanity?"*

Behram's eyes narrowed as Omar reached the witness box. Dilay opened the wooden gate and stepped down to stand in front of Omar. She smiled at him, tremulous. He did not want this, to know the secrets inside her.

The absolute silence of the hall made Omar sick. He could feel every gaze on him. He did not need to read their minds to know what was in them at that moment. Monster.

He lifted his hands and tried to imagine he was going to touch her face as he had only a few times before. In caring.

"You are bleeding, Vali Ahad," one of the judges said, in alarm.

"Yes," Omar said, without turning. Dilay's gaze met his, searching.

"Why are you bleeding?" Behram hissed from his seat. Omar turned his head to look at him.

"That was the price to free the people you put in prison," he said, then looked at Dilay again. "Forgive me," he murmured. A tear tracked down her cheek, her lips pressing together as she nodded once.

As Omar reached to her, Behram bolted from his seat and ducked into the space between Omar's hands. Omar had already committed to the action, and his hands settled on Behram's head.

"Behram," Semih barked in denial. Behram gripped handfuls of the front of Omar's entari, twisting so the fabric tightened against his back and his wounds, and curled his lip.

"Do it, and be damned for what you see," Behram snarled quietly. Omar hesitated, and Behram gave a little jerk of his hands in Omar's clothes. Omar released his magic.

A burst of light and pain razored through him, shredding him open at the same time it drilled into Behram's mind.

Minds manifested in many ways. Behram's burned. It was chaos. An inferno of rage and apathy that quickly consumed Omar's own reality. Distantly, he heard Behram grunt in discomfort. Then he was lost. Blow after blow, physical and emotional. Emptiness that was never filled with pleasure or pain. Burning desire to be better, more, to see that people who betrayed were punished. That they hurt like he did, that they were empty like he was. Hate raged, fiery creatures consuming every good thought he stumbled upon.

He was burned away, his grip on himself and his magic lost in the tumult inside Behram. He could not sort memories, fragments of things he observed twisted together with the punishment of observing them.

Permeating it all, loneliness crushed him. Every small joy was strangled by it, made a lie by a life of abandonment. Nothing. He was nothing. It did not matter what he achieved, what he became. No one saw him. No one cared.

But her. Dilay. A girl of wind and joy, everything he was not, everything he wanted to be, to know. But her pristine image was fractured, crumbling apart, rays of black fire shining through her. Betrayer.

It was that image that gave Omar a thread of himself back, enough to clutch and pull his mind from Behram's.

The moment he was back in his own his eyes popped open, his gaze meeting Behram's. Blood seeped from one of Behram's nostrils, and fire flickered in his eyes. The last dying flames that clung to embers. Omar dropped his hands to Behram's shoulders, barely able to breathe, even back in his own skin. All he could think of was to pull Behram into an embrace, but the look on his face warned against a display like that. Behram had a feral look in his eyes that told Omar he had been stripped too raw to be safe. The room came to him in pieces, first smells, then sounds. Behram wiped his bleeding nose against his crimson sleeve, elbowing Omar's arms away at the same time.

"What did you see, Vali Ahad?" he asked. Omar stared at him, still lost in the tumult. Wheel and stars, it would take him a lifetime to pick apart everything he had felt inside Behram. But their mirrored feelings for Dilay...

Guilt rose up like bile, gnawing, tearing him apart. He had contributed to this. To Behram's loneliness. What kind of friend was he? And more to come, as he had just that morning sentenced Behram to more pain. The guilt bowed under Omar's anger for a moment. But what he had done to Dilay was not love.

"Are you both all right?" Dilay asked, gently. He could not look at her. Not with Behram there, not with his friend's emotions still tangled in his own. He managed to nod and stepped back.

"Your back." She pointed. He dismissed it with a shake of his head. Magic was stressful on the body, and one that was not whole was taxed more than one that was. He would not be surprised to look in a mirror and see his back covered in blood.

"I cannot verify anything," he announced. Some minds he could pick apart, follow threads and memories with ease. But Behram's was a tangled lifetime of fear and anger. If someone spent their entire life being made into an animal, reacting to pain after pain, there were no tidy pathways to find truth. Truth became warped.

Dilay closed her eyes in defeat. Omar looked at Behram. "I am sorry."

Behram seemed to falter, then returned to the bench beside his father.

"Vali Ahad, are you able to continue? Shall we recess?" Dilay's father asked, one hand raised as if to hold Omar up.

"Continue," Omar said, then took careful steps to return to his seat at the back of the hall. Ruslan moved to his side, his teeth clenched, face tamed to stone.

"Efendim," he began, but Omar raised a hand and Ruslan grunted in resignation. Omar was, perversely, happy for the pain that throbbed and burned on his back. His aching head. The bloody nose that Ruslan handed him a cloth to deal with. Penance. For what he had taken from his friend. For the invasion. For his own betrayals. That was a caning he deserved.

"As these accusations cannot be verified," Semih said in leading. The judges huddled to whisper to each other. Dilay returned to the witness box and clasped her hands in front of her entari. And he had failed her again as well. Omar controlled a grimace of regret with a little push of magic.

"I am sorry, Instructor Akar, but without another witness to verify, we cannot accept this as evidence," one of the four judges said.

Dilay managed to school her face as she bowed in acceptance. Omar propped an elbow on his knee and pressed his forehead into his palm as people shuffled and whispered.

"Kadir Pasha, do you have any final grievances to bring?"

"In the interest of balance, also referenced in Hanim's law of morality, we would like a chance to rebutt," Semih Kadir said.

"The charges could not be verified," the same judge said with an edge of impatience.

"That is not the point," Semih replied.

"They are allowed a chance," Dilay's father said, pressing his fingers against his temples. "You may step down, Instructor Akar."

Dilay obeyed, returning to her seat. Omar could not see her there, tucked in amongst the crowd.

"Proceed, Kadir Pasha," the other judge said. Behram stood and stepped into the box, causing another flurry of speculation to go through the onlookers. Omar dreaded what Behram had to say, what more he might do to Dilay.

"I was witness to a very disturbing conversation, in which it was revealed that Osman Altimur had an affair, outside the sanctity of a closed circle marriage, with Zehra Demir. And, that affair has continued despite her recent betrothal to the Vali Ahad." Behram looked at Omar with a feigned frown of apology. "I am sorry you had to find out this way, Efendim."

Omar kept his head propped in his hand, but curved it over his mouth to hide his grimace. Semih had clearly not informed Behram of that morning's decision.

A few scandalized gasps were overshadowed by the sudden increase in volume of whispered conversations and Omar straightened, gripping his knees against the new twinge of pain. This was exactly what he had not wanted to happen to Zehra.

"And, although I regretfully cannot corroborate this with a witness, I have it on very good authority that this is not uncommon for Master Altimur, that he is far too free with his affections. Is that moral? Who knows how many bastards he has fathered?"

Osman bolted to his feet, gold magic breaking open over his skin like fissures.

"You cannot bring items to the tribunal with no evidence, with no prior notice." Osman's magic rumbled behind his voice, and the building shifted on its foundation.

"Accusations were brought against my father with no evidence, so, as he said, these in balance." Behram gave a dismissive shrug. "And if you wish for evidence, you need only demand another confession."

"Those are not the traditions of a tribunal, Master Kadir," Dilay's father said. "Grievances and evidence are the traditions. We have never needed a Veritor to confirm before, and I do not intend to make that the new convention."

"It is only fair, Judge Akar, that the same methods be used for both sides of this dispute," Semih Kadir said.

"That is enough." Omar stood. "The court has more than enough evidence to consider in this matter, and I will not risk another mind for petty tit for tat. I am, with agreement of the judges, closing this tribunal to more evidence."

Dilay's father stood and turned to bow to him, and the others did the same. "Yes, Vali Ahad Efendim, we have enough evidence to consider a decision."

"Gentlemen, thank you for your service to the Sultan," Omar said. They parted as he stepped off the dais and between them and their seats. The aisle that led to the main portion of the guild building and the exit beyond appeared to stretch for leagues. And his bloodied back would be visible to everyone as he moved.

The two guards who had stationed themselves at the back of the room moved forward as he did, and Ruslan walked close enough that he could offer assistance if Omar faltered. Everyone stood as he walked, bowed as he passed, and whispered behind him. But then he heard shuffling, and glanced behind to find Behram had dropped in at his back. Omar turned his attention forward, and Behram followed, silent.

Once outside, Omar's guards formed their customary ring around him, and Behram continued in silence until they reached the carriage.

Omar stopped there and turned to face him, nodding to Ruslan, who cast a dampening then stepped outside its ring.

"Speak," Omar said. He was not ready to confront Behram, about anything. But he owed it to him to be there if he was ready to do so.

"I would have given anything to you. Anything you desired," Behram said. The fire was gone, his voice was uncharacteristically cold, and even. "You took her from me. The only thing I wanted. The only thing I ever asked you for. And gave me your castoffs."

Omar closed his eyes. So he did know about Zehra. And had disgraced her publicly anyway. The pain of regret speared him, for what he had condemned her to. For selfishness. How many people was he going to hurt because of Dilay?

"I did not take her. And she was not something to be passed between us like a tea set. She is a person, who feels, and bleeds, and loves as she chooses. I cannot change who she is, or what she wants, and I would never want to. That is the difference between us."

"I love her. I have always loved her. *She* is my fire."

"You love her?" Omar said scornfully, then willed away his rising temper. "You put her in prison. For doing something she loves and believes in. You hurt countless people to enact your revenge. You fueled riots in *my* city. That is not love."

"But what you feel is? You have not even known her a season. I thought we understood each other, you and I. Her betrayal was enough, but yours…" He looked away.

"I did not mean to hurt you," Omar said, foolishly, he knew. Behram gave a derisive laugh.

"Have her, if you think you know better. She will betray you, just as she betrayed me." Behram looked toward the guild hall, where people were beginning to exit. The judges wouldn't make a ruling for at least a few days, there was no reason to linger now. "You speak about her beliefs as if they are some honorable thing, but the moment you do not serve them, she will turn from you. Wait," Behram said, heat coming into his voice, "and when you come crawling to me with a broken heart, you will see that there is no difference between us at all."

He turned and strode toward his father, who emerged from the hall. Omar shredded Ruslan's dampening spell with a flick of his fingers, fuming. He lingered for a moment, agitated beyond the ability to speak to anyone. Ruslan remained silent, waiting.

Dilay exited, walking beside her father, and Omar watched her. People flocked to speak to her. Just as they had at the protests. They listened to her. She was one of them. She could walk the line between highborn and lowborn because that was exactly where she existed. If he was going to change Narfour's, and the entirety of Tamar's perception of the Sultanate, he needed that. He needed her. That felt akin to standing at the bottom of the Kalspire and deciding he was going to climb it with nothing but his hands and his will.

But if he did not try, he would know, for every remaining day of his life, that a poor judge's daughter was braver, and had managed to climb far higher than a pampered prince, with far less.

Omar smiled grimly as he turned and climbed into his carriage.

THIRTY

DILAY KNEW SHE LOOKED RIDICULOUS—trudging through the courtyard of the palace carrying a tree. People stared. They remarked on her carefully braided hair and the fact that she was wearing her instructor's uniform while carrying a potted plant to the palace. She continued on, resolute. The guards at the palace entrance were so dumbstruck by her cargo that she made it all the way through the doors before one of them called out for her to stop.

She had practiced a little speech for just such an event, about being invited to discuss the ongoing negotiations to reopen her school. But it was unnecessary. As the guard hurried to catch up to her, Ruslan appeared from a side hall and saw her. He stopped to stare in consternation, until the guard came up beside her and took her arm to pull her back outside.

"I can handle this," Ruslan said, striding into the foyer. There were a handful of people standing in the sprawling entry, and they stopped their conversation to take in the spectacle. The guard bowed to Ruslan and stepped away, and Dilay smiled gratefully at him, propping the pot on her hip and tucking her hair behind her ear.

He moved to take the pot from her, and she turned it out of his reach. "I can manage, thank you."

"The Vali Ahad is in the tower. You intend to carry it halfway across the palace and up the stairs?"

Dilay blew out a breath of impatience and thrust the tree at him. "Fine. But the next time you are in the city, you will come to my parents' home and have tea with us."

"Of course, Instructor." The tone was formal, but she could tell he was amused. The message that had been delivered to her the day before had been too vague to be useful. She was not even certain Omar had written it. Just that she was to arrive at the palace for discussions about legalizing her school and others. So, she had dressed in the best clothes and spent extra time arranging her hair into braids wound around her head. Just in case Omar intended for her to meet with any of the Council. She had not seen him, outside the tribunal and its awful events, since he had left her after speaking at the protests.

"How are you, Ruslan? Well, I hope," she said, to take her mind away from Omar and all the things between them. Was he healing? What had he seen in Behram's mind? She had seen them speaking together after, and had been worried and relieved. At least Behram was speaking to Omar. He was not completely alone.

"I am, Instructor, thank you."

"You may call me Dilay," she said. He threw her a horrified look. Dilay laughed, which made him relax, marginally.

"May I ask why you are carrying a tree?"

"A gift," Dilay said. And a farewell. Something that represented birth, and death. Something she had nurtured and neglected, and had hopes for that she would never see realized. Gifts for those about to get married were meant to have a history, something to pass along to two people who did not have one yet.

He did not reply, and they walked in silence down the long halls, passing a few more people, though it was not a busy time of day at the palace. When they arrived at the familiar little hall at the base of the tower stairs, Ruslan invited her to precede him with a duck of his head.

Dilay climbed the stairs, and halfway up could hear the low pitch of male voices. She hesitated, wondering who was with him, but didn't want to stop Ruslan's momentum. The fig was not yet large enough to be very heavy, but it was awkward.

At the top of the stairs she could see through the open stone arch into the study. The Sehzade was sprawled on his back on the long bench beneath the windows, which were thrown open to the spring morning. Omar sat near his feet, much as he had been the first time she had visited the tower, with a book propped in the stand before him and his spectacles on. They looked at her simultaneously as Ruslan came to her side and set the tree down. Dilay bowed. Omar's brows drew down as he looked at it.

"A new hobby, Instructor Akar?" the Sehzade asked, his head turned sideways against the bench as he eyed the tree.

She had not expected to explain herself in front of others, but perhaps it was better. Being alone with Omar had proven time and again that she had no self-control.

"A gift," she said. "A betrothal gift. I thought the gardens outside the Sultana's rooms looked bereft, and a fig is a lovely way to start a marriage." Dilay was proud of her smile. The Sehzade snorted as he sat up, his gaze trained on Ruslan and a mocking smile barely hidden.

"Well done, old man," he said caustically to Omar as he stood. "Nice to see you again, Instructor Akar."

"This is much preferable to the last time," Dilay said, irritated by whatever had passed between him and Omar. He smiled at her and gave Ruslan's shoulder a pat as he headed for the stairs.

"You brought me a tree and had someone else carry it for you?" Omar asked, a smile tugging at his mouth. Dilay laughed softly.

"It was quite heavy."

"Do you require anything, Vali Ahad?" Ruslan asked. Omar looked at Dilay in question, and she shook her head. Ruslan bowed and departed down the stairs.

Dilay clasped her hands together in front of her, painting a smile on her face that she hoped did not look as uncomfortable as it felt. Omar leveled a nettled stare on the tree. As if he were offended by it.

"I thought you and Zehra might like to plant it together," she offered, weakly. "Where the Sultana can see it?" He pulled the spectacles off his face and rubbed the bridge of his nose, then replaced them. "May I?" She gestured at the bench beside him. He nodded.

She sat, with enough distance that they did not touch, and folded her hands in her lap. "You wanted to speak about my school? The sooner we can at least reinstate mine, the better off you will be in the eyes of the city. If you still mean to?" She could not help the niggling fear that his promises would be forgotten in the wake of everything else.

"Of course I do," he said, tersely.

"Are you cross with me? Or are you hurting?" She leaned forward and moved her head so she could meet his gaze. He looked at her sidelong.

"You have not spoken to Behram."

"No." Dilay turned, tucking one leg beneath her and sinking sideways against the back of the bench so she could look out the window. "I don't know if I ever will again." She wanted to say it out loud. She wanted to tell someone how much it hurt, and Omar might be the only one who understood.

He collapsed back, dropping his head against the wall.

"I wanted so much for him," Dilay said. "He is so brilliant. And I thought there was still kindness in him."

"He is brilliant. He helped me study my languages. He was always better at them." Omar's eyes were closed. That did not dim the allure of the spectacles. Dilay looked away from him, trying to guide her thoughts away. "And maths. And almost every subject."

"Not magic." Dilay smiled. "He is gifted, but I can see you have more potential." Anyone who could leverage such powerful magic to subdue a crowd the size of that which gathered at the protests, without hurting anyone, was a gifted mage indeed.

"Now I do," Omar said. "Because of you." He did not look at her. She wanted him to. And she didn't. Did he still feel it, what he had told her the night of the protests? That he loved her? What did it matter? Her gaze cut to the little fig tree, then back to the window. Gulls circled outside, white flickers against a steel ocean. Did it matter that she felt the same? That she had wanted to shout it at his back? To run after him and tell him. It had kept her awake that night.

"Your control is better?" she said instead.

"I believe my power and I have come to an agreement," he said.

"Oh?" She rested her chin on her arm, staring at him. That was all that was allowed to her anymore, she reminded herself. No touching. She followed the straight line of his nose and the curve of his mouth. Looking was hard. It made her want to reach out, to follow with her fingers where her gaze went. Over the coarse brown hair of his beard. Was that a grey hair? She bit her lip. Sometimes she could look at men and know they would only grow handsomer as they aged, when grey streaked their hair and the softness dissolved from their features. He was one.

"Somewhere around the thirtieth strike of that cane I realized it was the worst my father could do to me, and while I would not wish to repeat it, it was no worse than what my power had been doing to me for Turns…And I succeeded."

"I hate that he hurt you," Dilay murmured. She wanted to touch him, or hug him, to connect. Perhaps it was no longer his power that kept them apart now, but the distance felt as great. She thought for a moment of laying with him in his bed, his bared torso and desire in his eyes. She closed hers because it hurt to think of it, and threatened to bring her to images of him like that with someone else. It was so much worse now that she had a face to stick in her torturous imaginations.

Would Zehra be kind to him? She hoped so. She knew little of her, but that she seemed like a gentle person.

"It was a lesson well learned," Omar said.

"What lesson?"

"That decisions I make for myself, triumphs I earn by my own efforts, are armor against others who wish to control me."

She smiled. Then looked out the window again. What was the difference? Why could Omar find himself in the midst of it all, while Behram could not? Was it her fault? Deep within she knew it was neither her fault nor her responsibility, but she could not let go. She could not let Behram go, could not convince herself he was completely lost to her. But…

"You're thinking about him," Omar said.

"I can't help it."

"Me either," he said. "I am so angry with him, but I cannot help but feel this gnawing guilt." He turned his head toward her, opening his eyes. "He loves you. I saw you in his mind." He pulled the spectacles off and gripped them in his hand. "But"—he took an unsteady inhale—"there is so much else there. Poison. Fire. More rage than I think even you could wade through. In his mind, the world sees him as nothing."

"I could not survive Behram's mind. How did you?"

Finally, he smiled. It was tiny, just a lift of one corner. "You. Just as you pulled me out when you held me the night you were in my room. You were just as beautiful in Behram's mind as you are in mine."

"I betrayed his trust." She could not respond to Omar's compliment, it only broke her heart, for all three of them.

"Yes. We both have. And he betrayed ours. I want to make amends, to make my part of it up to him, but I do not yet know how."

She could not speak of it anymore. "What are you reading?"

He sat up abruptly and closed the book, a thick tome that appeared to be in good repair. The spine was buried in the bookstand so she could not read it.

"History," he said.

"Of what?"

"Tell me about that tree," he said. Dilay sniffed in irritation, and he smiled without looking at her.

"I have been attempting to grow it in a pot for three Turns. It is doing well with what it has, but I feel it would do much better with space, more soil to spread out in. And since I have not had a chance to give you a gift, and I was so sad to look out your mother's window, I thought you could give it room to grow. I…also liked the idea of you having something to look at that I gave you." She tried to smile again, but it failed when her throat tightened and her teeth clenched together. "Maybe that's selfish."

Omar reached to her, snaking an arm around her waist and pulling her to him. She made a sound of surprise, and he lifted and dragged her so she sat on the small bit of bench between his spread legs. He held her there with one arm around her waist, his chest pressed to her back, his head hooked over her shoulder. He pulled the book open with his free hand, flipping quickly through the pages until he finally stopped. He nudged the back of her head with his nose.

Dilay shifted forward and twisted to look at him, and he jerked his chin toward the book. With a tsk of frustration, she turned back.

"How am I supposed to read like this?" She feigned annoyance. She did not want to do what she should, which was pull out of his embrace. Couldn't she have one more moment? One more memory of his warmth to keep her. She touched the page and bent forward. Omar opened the wires of the spectacles and placed them on her nose. She laughed as the words blurred into illegibility. "You need these?"

"Just for books," he said. She turned to look at him, mimicking the stern set of his mouth. He made a little sound. "You are very charming, Dilay."

"That is not how I would describe you in these." She took them off and carefully placed them on his face. Flutters danced in her stomach.

"No? Embarrassing? Old? Tutorish?" He regarded her in an approximation of a tutor's disappointed leer.

"That is not a word," she admonished playfully.

"Come up with a better one."

Wheel she wanted to kiss him. What a weak, spineless mess she was. "Tantalizing," she whispered.

His arm around her waist tightened, his gaze dropping to her mouth, which made everything so much worse. Dilay spun around to stare at the book. It took her a moment to anchor herself to the text. A history of the Sabri family tree, it seemed.

Omar placed a hand on her shoulder and ran it down her arm, making her shiver, then cupped his hand over hers. He straightened her index finger and touched it to the middle of the right-hand page. His play made her joyful and bitter. She read. Then read it again.

"I don't understand."

"Tarkin Sabri, who ruled after Ediz Rahal's murder of Omar Sabri the Third, took a wife from the valley to reaffirm to the scattered remnants of Tamar that they were united." His cheek touched the back of her head as he spoke softly against her ear. "She was common born. Tamar was attempting to recover from the Sundering War, and he

believed taking a wife from the commoners would give them something to believe in, when they no longer had faith in their rulers."

A flicker of fragile excitement made her swallow hard, afraid to
look at him.

"I do not want to spend my Turns looking at your stupid tree," he
murmured. Her brow furrowed and she snapped her head around to
look over her shoulder at him. "I would much rather look at you."

"Betrothed," she forced out.

He shook his head, slowly. "I cannot produce tiny Veritors to torture the people with if I do not marry an air mage. My father was very
concerned when I brought it up. He annulled my betrothal."

"Omar…" She felt like she was tumbling through the air, not certain where or how she would land.

"I need your help." He cupped her waist with gentle hands. "To
convince the Council that now is the time to show Narfour I will not
be my father. That I have their interests at heart."

"How?"

He touched his nose to her chin. "Be with me. Like you did at the
protests. At my side."

"As an adviser? Like a Vizier?" She could barely make her voice
work.

"No," he said, laughter bright in his eyes. "Not like a Vizier. Like
a Queen."

She huffed, searching his face. "I am not a Queen. I am not…"
This was what Behram had done to her. Panic swirled in her belly.
"Please don't do this to me."

"What am I doing?" he said worriedly.

"Behram did this."

"No, Behram had you arrested," he said, lingering anger coloring his
voice. "I love you. I want you to be exactly what you are. Exactly what
I admire, what I have admired from the moment I met you. Do not
be anything else. Please. Except mine. Be that as well." He stroked her
waist, once, twice, and again, his hands restless, his gaze more so.

"Even if I agreed, you cannot believe your father will ever let you
marry me."

"For you, I would endure a hundred more lashes with that cane. And it is the Council I need to convince. Not my father. They can occasionally be outmaneuvered."

"I don't believe you at all," she said, eyeing him. "And if you think I'll just stand by while you get beaten with a cane you are mad."

He looked at her with adoration just before he caught her mouth in his, tugging her body hard to his. The angle was awkward, but she did not care. She thought of his kisses entirely too often to deny even one.

"I know, and you cannot imagine how that knowledge makes me feel," he said.

"You cannot simply spring that on me. I have to think," Dilay said. How could she think?

"All right," he said. She wanted to tell him how she felt, how her heart ached any time she thought of him with anyone, thought of never seeing him again. But this…

She turned a little more, and tucked her head into the slope of his neck. It was perfect, to lean into his embrace, feel him clasp his hands together against her back. He rubbed his chin against the top of her head, his beard snagging in her hair.

"I worked very hard on those braids," she protested, but did not move. He made a throaty sound, cupping her head with one hand, and his fingers traced the knot of them. Then he dug his fingers in and claimed a pin, which he pulled free. Before she could protest, he found another, and she let him continue, her pulse a hard thump in every limb. She closed her eyes, tucking her head into the curve of his throat as he continued his work with both hands. The braids tumbled against her shoulders, and he combed them with gentle fingers. She shuddered in pleasure at the touch, his fingers against her head, the warm grip of his hand on the back of her neck.

"You didn't like them?" she had to say something, his intense silence was stifling.

"I have wanted to touch your hair from the moment I met you." He buried his nose in it, taking the strands in his hands with another sound that made her body weaken.

"Oh." She slipped her mouth against the side of his neck, not a kiss, more like a warning. His hands urged her closer, and she did kiss his skin. Little pecks, tasting the salt of him, inhaling the inexplicable way he always smelled so clean. Like fresh air and soap. Somehow, addled as she was, she did not care that the open arch to the stairs loomed at her back, threatening. Anyone could walk in on them. Doing this.

"I miss you so much when we are apart," he said.

She slid her hands up to his face and tilted it toward hers to kiss him. He responded ravenously, his hands returning to her hair to hold her to him. He gave a short, sharp moan that made her ache. She pressed harder against him, her whole body to his. He scooped an arm under her hips and lifted her up, using his other hand to shove her entari and caftan out of the way so she could kneel over his legs.

"Me too," she said, breathlessly, aroused and embarrassed to be straddling him. She looked at him, heat rushing into her face, and his eyes were wide and dark as he looked back.

"Dilay." His voice dropped in pitch, a husky timbre that made her languid. Her hands pressed against his stomach of their own accord as she touched her brow to his. She tugged apart the clasps on the lower half of his entari, finding the caftan beneath and bunching it out of the way. In the deepest dark of her thoughts, she knew she wasn't acting sensibly, but she did not care.

Omar turned his face into the slope of her neck, whispering encouragement as her fingers found skin, and the top of his salvar. Light flickered awake on his skin when she curled her fingers underneath the waist of the salvar. His head lifted.

Dilay brushed the fingers of her free hand over a pool of light that pulsed against his throat, meeting his gaze. Light spun in his eyes as well, and a furrow creased his brow. She smoothed it with her thumb and started to withdraw her hand from his waistband. Omar caught her by the wrist, his other hand cupping the back of her neck, as he pressed her body to his and her hand into his salvar.

"Omar," Dilay cajoled in a near whisper. If his limit was already tested, grabbing at his most intimate places was not going to help. Despite her rational thoughts, her fingers twitched against the heat of his abdomen.

"My magic is all right"—he brushed his lips over hers—"but I will not be all right if I am denied what I want one single time more."

"Oh?" she hummed, curling her fingers until their tips brushed the hot, silken skin of his erection. She gripped him. "What do you want?"

His breath rushed and caught, his muscles going taut beneath her. He swore.

"Efendim, I am sorry to disturb you," Ruslan called from well down the twist of stairs. Wise man that he was. Dilay's head snapped up, and she yanked her hand away. Omar grabbed for it and missed as she scrambled off his lap and onto the bench.

"If the palace isn't burning down I will kill him." Omar hunched forward, jamming his spectacles on and crossing his arms over his knees to hide his undone clothes. Dilay fumbled her hair into a quick braid, to at least appear somewhat in order. Ruslan arrived at the top of the stairs, oozing reticence, and looked entirely too relieved to see them sitting, awkward and stiff.

"Yes?" Omar asked in a remarkably cool tone of voice. Dilay wasn't certain she could speak at all. Ruslan held out an envelope as he approached, like a truce flag. She recognized the seal on the back, the mark of the tribunal court.

"A decision has been made in the Merchant Guild dispute. A messenger just delivered this."

Omar straightened and took it, and Ruslan's gaze flashed to his bunched-up entari then away. Dilay fidgeted with the cuffs of her sleeves.

"Thank you." Omar started to rip it open before Ruslan had even bowed. He unfolded the paper within and read it, then rubbed his hand over his face and muttered a curse.

"Who?" Dilay asked, though she suspected his reaction was enough of an answer.

"Semih Kadir."

THIRTY-ONE

ILAY WAITED IN AN ALCOVE across from the Council Hall, where Omar had gone to inform his father of the decisions of the tribunal. Her own father was likely entrenched at a teahouse somewhere, venting his fury to anyone who would listen. People passed her little hiding spot, but only a few noticed her, and only briefly. While she waited she repinned her braids, though not as tidily as she would have done with a mirror and a comb. It would have to do. She doubted she would go in front of the Council now, with this new development. The leadership of the Merchant Guild was a much more pressing issue to the Council than an errant teacher and her wild ideas about public schools.

She stared at the doors, wishing she could hear more than the rise and fall of muffled voices. What would it be like to be able to be present at these meetings? Where the decisions that affected the lives of everyone in Tamar were made? That was so out of reach even she could never have dreamed of such a thing. But…if she agreed to Omar's proposal, would she be allowed in? Could she maneuver the Council? Influence them? Dilay huffed. She had not even swayed the tribunal with laws and truth, how could she hope to move the Council in a direction they did not wish to go?

Omar made it sound easy. Could he teach her? Dilay leaned against the back wall of the alcove, staring at the Council doors and trying to imagine herself inside. Dressed in heavy silk and brocade, with jewels, quiet and proper and subdued like the Queen Sultana. She tried to imagine fighting Viziers the way she had fought the Headmaster and Proctors at the University. That was nearly impossible.

Guards inside the hall opened the doors and stood outside as the men inside got to their feet.

Dilay's alcove was offset from the doors, so she did not see Omar until he was near the hall, walking beside Mazhar just behind their father. The Queen Sultana was not there at all. Did that mean sultanas were not allowed in? She folded her arms over her chest. No. She could not imagine that. Being a ruler barred from participating in ruling.

Omar's gaze darted over the hall. Did she see disappointment? Was he looking for her? Warmth filled her, both for the hope that he looked for her the moment he could, and for the heat that lingered from their…discussion in the tower.

"*I am here,*" she whispered into her power. He looked again, and she stepped forward into the frame of the alcove. His posture relaxed, and he smiled. Dilay tried to ignore the way it made her own body do the same. She could imagine that. A man who was excited to see her even if they had been separated no more than a candlemark. Mazhar followed Omar's line of sight and saw her too, and some of the warmth fizzled away when he said something to Omar that made his face tense.

When most of the Viziers had moved on, down the hall toward the main palace, Omar crossed the hall to her. He had a look on his face she liked, as though he were considering backing her into the shadow of the alcove for more kisses. But there were people still in the hall, and of course they knew exactly where he was and who he was talking to.

"What happened?" Dilay asked, instead of reaching to pull on him as she wanted to do.

He indicated the hall with a jerk of his head and Dilay stepped out to walk beside him, though she left a respectable distance between them. Hopefully enough of one that no one suspected she had been in his lap not so long ago. Dilay banished the heat in her face with a wisp of magic.

Three Viziers stood chatting together by the doors to the Council Hall, but their conversation stopped when she and Omar passed. Dilay reached up to brush a strand of hair behind her ear and dropped her chin to stare at the floor. She probably looked strange next to him.

"They see what you want them to see," Omar said, without looking at her or them. "You have done far more with far less than anyone in this palace, remember?" He smiled without looking at her and Dilay nodded. Of course.

"What should they see, when they look at me?" Dilay asked as they turned down a hall that she believed would return them to the Sultan's wing, where all the private rooms were.

"If it were up to me, they would see a Queen," Omar said, when it appeared the hall they were in was empty. Dilay cast him a little smile, which he returned. "But you know who you are, Dilay. The trick is to never allow them to forget it."

"So wise for someone who would not even leave the palace for fear of his father not so long ago."

"I apparently only needed the right incentive," he replied. They exchanged a glance that warmed Dilay like a summer breeze.

They walked in silence the rest of the way, though she didn't know where they were going. After another turn they arrived in the hall where his rooms were, which is where he stopped. Dilay looked up at him uncertainly.

"I thought"—he pushed the doors open and motioned her inside with a tilt of his head—"you might like to plant a tree." He whispered the last in her ear as he shut the doors behind her. Dilay turned to face him with her brows raised. It was not exactly what she wanted, but it seemed a silly thing to say out loud.

"Do you know how to plant a tree?"

"No idea," he said jovially as he unbuttoned his ornate silver entari and tossed it over a chair. "Although I imagine one has to engineer a pit."

"A pit?" Dilay laughed, following his example and shedding her own entari. Omar stepped into the sitting area and crossed to the glass doors, which were already open, revealing that the little fig tree had made a magical appearance on the stone veranda beyond. He ducked his head out to examine the sky as he rolled the sleeves of his caftan up to his elbows.

"If we hurry, we can beat the rain," he announced.

She stopped to lay his entari flat over the bench, so it did not wrinkle, and did the same with hers. He observed her, smiling guiltily when she raised an eyebrow at him.

"What do we need?" he asked when she came up beside him.

"A shovel would be helpful. Unless you care to dig with your hands."

"I have something better." He walked out into the garden and she followed. As he stepped out of his shoes, she picked up the fig tree and handed it to him. "Where should we put it?"

"Somewhere the Queen can see it from her rooms. And where you can." Dilay reached down to tug her slippers off. He wandered into the garden and she followed, watching as he glanced between the doors she suspected were his mother's and the grand-looking room at the very end of the garden that was surely the Sultan's.

After a few turns and repositions he stopped and set the pot on the ground.

"Here," he announced, looking pleased. Dilay bit her lip to stifle her laugh and nodded.

"And the shovel?"

He gestured, and Dilay looked toward the far end of the garden, seeing Ruslan as he walked toward them. He did not appear to be carrying a shovel. She turned a scathing look on Omar.

"You did not call him here to use his magic for you."

"Of course I did," Omar said, as though it were the only solution that made sense. Dilay cast Ruslan an apologetic glance when he arrived.

"Would you rather wait while he attempted to figure out a shovel?" Ruslan murmured to her when they stood shoulder to shoulder. Dilay sputtered a laugh, and Omar cast them a suspicious glance. Thunder rumbled, close enough that urgency crept into Dilay's thoughts.

"Here." Dilay put her hand on the grass next to the pot, checking the spot against views from the many rooms that surrounded the long, narrow garden. Ruslan ducked his head and knelt and Dilay moved out of the way. He scratched a sigil in the earth, pressing his palms to the spot she had selected. She took another step back when she felt his magic roll over the ground, itchy at the sensation. The ground heaved apart, and he manipulated it with motions of his hands, scooping dirt out to widen and deepen the hole.

"That should be fine, Ruslan, thank you," Dilay said as he sat back on his heels.

"I will bring coffee to your room, Efendim." He stood and bowed to Omar.

"Should we ask for a dampening so you can tell me about the Council?" Dilay asked.

Omar closed his eyes briefly, and she felt a brush of his magic, then he shook his head. He sat on the opposite side of the hole from her, folding his legs in front of him. Dilay winced for the grass and dirt stains that would likely ruin his expensive salvar. She tugged the pot toward her and showed Omar how to remove the fig from it.

Omar pulled the pot away, leaving Dilay holding the little tree. "My father is pleased with the decision. Altimur Pasha had begun to fall out of favor with him. Despite the opinions of the city, the palace viewed him as too sympathetic to the common man. More troubling, for me at least, is that I have also inadvertently handed Kadir Pasha the path to Grand Vizier."

"What?"

Omar set the pot on the ground. "When I asked for annulment, my father suggested Behram to take my place, so that Zehra would not be shamed, nor her father."

"Oh," Dilay said. Behram would be livid. Had he known at the tribunal? When he had paraded her history in front of everyone? Anger burned away her concern for him. Was he intent on making himself unredeemable in her esteem?

"I did not mean to do that to either of them, and now Semih will be next in line for Grand Vizier with almost no one powerful enough to contest him. And, Osman has disappeared." That surprised Dilay, and she could see regret on Omar's face. They had looked happy when she'd seen them all at the tribunal. Laughing together. Friends. "Some think Altimur Pasha sent him away to let rumors spawned by the tribunal debacle die down. Some think he ran."

"What do you think?"

"It isn't like Osman to run. But I cannot know for certain. Behram said things that would be difficult for Osman to live down." Omar pursed his lips in thought. "The Council is divided on their feelings. Very little was accomplished besides quibbling. They will not convene today about your schools, I'm afraid."

Dilay picked at the roots of the fig, teasing them apart. "I did not think they would, once Ruslan brought the tribunal notice."

"It will happen, I promise. How is Yusef?"

"Edgy." Dilay set the fig in the hole. "Hold here." She indicated the trunk. Omar obeyed, and she carefully corrected him to make certain the tree was straight. She scooped dirt into the hole around it, and Omar held the tree with one hand to help. "I will speak with him tomorrow and tell him what happened. I believe he'll understand." She pressed the dirt to compress it around the tree and sat back to admire it, brushing hair out of her face with her fingers.

Omar made a little sound like a laugh, and reached forward to brush at her cheek. She flinched away in surprise.

"You have dirt there," he said.

"And you are remarkably clean for someone who's been *planting* a tree." She reached over and dragged her dirt-stained fingers across his face. He grabbed her wrist and hauled her toward him, and Dilay scuffed dirt onto his pristine white salvar as she laughed. She braced her hand against his thigh as he tried to tug her closer, flicking more dirt in her face. Dilay wiped her hands on his caftan and he made a startled sound of protest, grabbing both her hands and pulling her to him. The look on his face, pure, unfettered joy, made her bright with her own. And love. She loved him. It was not a new realization, it had been warm inside her for some time, it was simply that she settled into it in that moment. Realized it would not go away, or be forgotten, no matter how complicated things would be for them.

"This is not how you plant a tree, Vali Ahad," she chided, kneeling in front of him. He pressed her hands together so he held both her wrists in one hand and brushed at the dirt on her face, more gently this time.

"I think it is the perfect way to plant a tree. I would not wish to do it any other way, or with anyone else."

No. There was no one else. Just him, the quiet, stern man with laughter and potential buried within him.

"This was supposed to be a betrothal present." She let her gaze rove his face and stroked her hand up his exposed arm.

"It still could be," he coaxed with a smile that made her melt. Little muscles in his arm played under her fingers as he curved a hand around her neck. His gaze flicked to the side, and tension replaced his ease as he released her and stood. A few fat rain droplets began to fall around them as Dilay turned and rose beside him. The Queen Sultana approached, Beste at her side.

Dilay bowed. The Queen eyed the tree as though she did not understand it, then turned to Dilay.

"I was wrong to compare you to a termite," the Queen said. Dilay blinked, and Omar scowled. "You are a thorn I cannot be rid of."

"Anne." Omar took a step forward. The Queen turned her head a fraction in denial of him, her gaze set on Dilay's.

Dilay did not know how to respond, or even how to feel at the Sultana's proclamation.

"I do not enjoy watching the two of you cavorting like otters out here in the dirt"—she paused when Omar made a strangled noise—"but it pleases me to see him smile."

Beside her, Beste ducked her head to hide her own smile, her gaze catching briefly on Dilay's as she looked down. Had Omar told his mother he was going to ask to marry Dilay? She looked up at him, but he appeared both embarrassed and irritated.

"Efendim," Dilay began, but the Sultana flicked a hand.

"You have defied me at every turn, Instructor Akar." She folded her hands in front of her caftan. Dilay pressed her lips together to silence her protests. "I can appreciate a woman who does not buckle. You will need that spine if you are going to survive here."

Beste touched fingers to the Sultana's elbow and the latter huffed impatiently.

"I will do what I can to help you."

The spattered drops of rain fell harder, and the Queen glanced skyward, then at them. "Do not stand out here in the rain like a couple of gaping sandgrouse," she said, then turned back for her rooms. Beste walked beside her, her fingers clutched in the Sultana's sleeve.

Dilay stared at her back, trying to pick apart whether she was angry or baffled. "Will she ever cease to compare me to animals?"

"Only if she ceases to like you," Omar said, with a subdued smile. He glanced up into the darkening sky, then down at the tree. "We should go in." He took her hand, twining his fingers with hers, and urged her toward his rooms. The doors stood open, and when they reached the stone patio outside them Dilay stopped, tugging Omar to a halt beside her.

"Stand in the rain with me, Vali Ahad."

He looked skeptically into the swirling grey above them as the rain fell harder. The spring shower was cold, bracing, and smelled, always, a bit like ocean brine. Omar closed his eyes. It was not a deluge, as it had been the night they were trapped in her room. But they were soon soaked, and water trickled in rivulets down his upturned face.

"To what end?" he asked, but there was a ghost of a smile on his face. The water made his caftan and salvar cling, and Dilay's gaze strayed repeatedly to him. To muscles and expanses she wanted to know by touch, the way she knew his voice as she knew her own.

"You said you never had. Storms are the cusp between the First and Second House, a confluence of air and water, primal. Everyone should stand in the rain, at least once. Especially someone who means to rule over all the Houses."

"But," he said, his eyes opening as he dropped his chin to look at her. To her chagrin, he caught her gaze fixed far too low to be appropriate. As heat rose in her face, he turned her body into his. "I cannot send you home to your family wet and shivering, what will they think of me?"

It was cold, especially as her clothes began to cling and water slipped down the back of her neck. But his eyes were warm, as were his hands, that heat seeping, barely, through the fabric of her sleeves where he held her arms. She did not mind the chill.

He stepped close, his bigger body eclipsing hers. "I'll have Ruslan bring you something dry to wear." He brushed damp hair off her face with his fingers. Dilay nodded mutely. Wet clothes felt very much like no clothes, suddenly, with parts of his body pressing against her she might not otherwise have been able to discern through layers of cloth. The hard ridge of pressure against her belly, for instance. They stared at each other. Surely he was thinking the same thing she was? That it was only that morning she had been in much more intimate contact, and was now craving the same.

When he ducked to kiss her, it occurred to her in the heartbeat before his mouth touched hers that they were likely being watched. Curious servants and a disapproving mother. But the thought was lost swiftly to the new sensation of soft lips and icy rain, his fingers slippery along her neck, their clothes twisting and sticking together. Chilly streamers of wet in contrast to the heat of his body.

He pet his hands down her back. Without the thicker, stiffer fabric of her entari, she could actually feel the friction of his touch, not just the pressure, and her body responded by bowing closer.

He moved, keeping her pressed to him with an arm around her shoulders, and maneuvered her through the doors and into the sitting room. Ruslan had kept his promise, and a tray with a coffee ibrik and small cups sat on the table. Dilay noted them, interested in the idea of a warm drink, but was distracted when Omar stepped away from her.

He closed the doors and pulled the curtains across them, and Dilay brushed self-consciously at her wet, sagging braids, then crossed her arms over her chest. Thankfully her caftan was not white, and transparent when wet, like his. Though she greatly appreciated the view his afforded her.

"You are even more handsome when you are wet," she said when he moved back to her. "While I look like a bedraggled—"

He cupped her cheek, sealing her lips with his thumb. "I like it when you're mussed," he said, "I like how real you are." His gaze fixed on his thumb over her lips, and he stroked across her mouth, so little sharp bolts of sensation popped throughout her body. All she could think about was touching him. She didn't care about dry clothes, or returning home as she should. "I'll call Ruslan." He dropped his thumb away from her mouth.

Dilay caught the fabric of his caftan as he turned.

She stepped close. "Do you want me to go?"

"No." He hooked his hands over her elbows and pulled her hard to his body. "I asked you to stay. I asked you to stay forever. And you still have not answered me. I thought you might like space to think."

"I…" She lowered her hands, working them beneath the caftan and up, to his skin. It was cold, damp, and prickled the instant she touched him, beginning a larger tremor. Magic whispered over his skin, pale light like the promise of morning sun. "…have had enough of distance between us."

"Yes," he said. The magic brightened.

"I want to see." She traced a trail of light along his stomach. Flux, in a normal mage, was no more dangerous than dilated eyes or flushed cheeks. But in Omar…he seemed more settled into his control than he ever had, but she would have to pay careful attention to him.

He held his arms aloft. Dilay shot him a mocking smile. "Do you not know how to remove your own caftan, Sabri Sultan?" He answered with a little, knowing smile, and she took handfuls of the fabric and pushed it up until she couldn't reach any higher. Omar grabbed the caftan at the back of the neck and tugged it up and over. She didn't wait for him to peel it from his arms, but touched her fingers to his waist, gliding them up over his ribs. He stopped with his arms still locked in the caftan, and dropped his head to her shoulder, his arms falling between them. Dilay paused to pull the caftan off then resumed her touches, and his visible magic flared in response, whipping in little hurricanes of light over his skin. She chased them with her fingertips, reminded of the light orb chasing game many children played.

"You have had me like this twice now," Omar said. "It hardly seems fair."

"You were not wet, the last time." She brushed a kiss to his shoulder, circling her hands to his back. He flinched, stepping forward and away from her touch with a hiss. Dilay yanked her hands back, remembering only then that he had wounds. She took his arm and made him turn enough she could look. Black and purple streaked his body, yellowing at the edges. In some places he had been struck so hard the skin had broken.

"Omar." She ran her fingers gently over a few of the unmarked places. "These should be bandaged."

"I was told to let them breathe." He turned to place a kiss on her neck, and when she unconsciously bent her head to the side he continued, from the neckline of her own caftan up to her ear. "It's all right." He turned her to face him once more, his soft kisses upending her thoughts.

"Thank you," she said. Those wounds were for her, and the others. He'd stood up for her, for something that mattered to her, and to him.

"Together, yes?" he said. "All these things, these changes, and battles. We can fight them together."

Dilay nodded, afraid if she spoke her voice would betray too much emotion. He looked down at her for a moment, too serious. He cupped her face in both hands. "I thought I would always be alone, but…"

"I won't let you be alone." Then she kissed him, because the confession made her shy. "I love you," she admitted when they parted.

"So"—he touched his forehead to hers—"marry me." He grabbed fistfuls of her caftan and tugged her to him, then held her there as he stroked her back again. His fingers stretched low, toward her backside, like he meant to grab her there and lock their hips together. But instead he tugged her caftan up over her hips.

"I am still thinking." She drew back but he pulled her to him again, nipping at her lips with his in reprimand. "I would have to give up everything."

He pulled it higher, revealing the thin, pale chemise beneath it. Dilay helped him pull the caftan over her head. He tossed it away.

"I did not intend for you to give up anything."

"How can I teach and be your Sultana?"

"My Sultana," he repeated, hands settling on her hips. He explored her face with his gaze, stroking his hands down her waist, to her hips again, then finally did cinch hers to his. His eyes lit, literally, with his magic. "I have never heard more beautiful words."

"Not even when I said I love you?"

"Do they not mean the same thing?" He smiled, but his gaze had fixed down as he plucked at her wet, clinging chemise. "I knew you loved me when you marched in to save me at the riot," he bent down to say against her ear as he pulled the chemise up and off.

Dilay pinched the sensitive skin of his belly and made a scandalized noise. He chuckled, touching his lips against her shoulder as he stroked her arms. She shivered at the warmth, craving that same everywhere on her chilled skin.

"I did not march." She ran the backs of her fingers over his stomach and up his chest. She had never wanted to touch someone so much, never wanted time to memorize every bit of them. "And you did not need saving."

Omar studied the band of cloth around her chest. "I might now," he said.

Dilay giggled, and he wrapped his arms around her, guiding her toward the couch that dominated the sitting area.

The door to the hall clicked, someone outside turning the latch. Dilay gasped, and he tossed her, with what care he could, onto the couch. She cried out in surprise, ducking down below the back of the couch to stay out of view of the door. Omar flicked the fingers of one hand at the door. Magic flared and died on his skin and the door slammed shut from the gust of wind. Someone shouted in surprise from the other side.

Omar vaulted over the couch and to the doors to turn the deadbolt.

"Who was that?" She sat up as he stepped over the back of the couch and settled beside her.

"Don't care," he said, pulling her firmly into his lap, in the same straddled position she had been in the tower. This time, however, they had on far less, and presumably, would not be enduring any interruptions. Any *more* interruptions.

"You are more athletic than I might have given you credit for, considering how much you read," Dilay teased. He clicked his tongue.

"You'll have to start giving me more credit, considering how often you've misjudged me. Besides"—he cupped her waist, the playful look on his face fading as he stared down at her exposed skin—"the right incentive can inspire a great many things." He rubbed his thumbs up her stomach, causing her to gasp. She curved her fingers over his shoulders as he snugged her hips to his with a low, rumbled sound.

"How…" He studied the band of cloth around her chest. Dilay twisted so he could see the laces at the back. "Do you lace that yourself?" He plucked at it in consternation.

"Of course I do." Dilay laughed. "Some of us do not have servants devoted to the task of dressing us. And *I* know where all my clothes are."

"Of course you do." Omar lay, gingerly, against the back of the couch, a hand sliding up her back to urge her to lay against him. "Your bedroom is a closet."

She gave his chest a gentle slap, then kissed the spot in apology. He tipped his head back, closing his eyes as his fingers tangled in the knot that held the laces of the breast wrap tight. While he tugged and felt his way through them, Dilay took her time tracing sigils on his chest, chasing the flutters of light beneath it.

When the laces finally gave and he issued a small sound of triumph, she stopped, twisting her arms behind her back to tug the band loose, then up over her head. He dropped his hands to her waist with a whisper of admiration. He tried, and failed, to not stare at her exposed breasts, and Dilay stifled a smile.

She dropped the fabric band over the back of the couch and laid against him again, pressing her bared breasts to his chilly skin. The shock of it, cold and warmth, the coarser friction of his chest hair on her breasts and nipples, the surprised groan that escaped him, all encouraged the thrum between her legs. That desire made her bolder, and she angled her hips, pressing the juncture of her thighs against his arousal.

He grabbed her hips with a sharp inhale, holding her to him as his legs flexed beneath her. Dilay nuzzled his ear, kissing, then nipping his earlobe, closing her eyes as she inhaled the calming scent of rain and the cool taste of his magic on her tongue.

"We're getting this lovely couch all wet," Dilay said in his ear. Omar turned his head, capturing her mouth in his. This kiss wasn't like the others, it was frantic. He fumbled at her waist, alternating between trying to yank the knot of her salvar free and simply shoving at them to try and get them off. Dilay assisted, her nails useful tools at loosening the wet fabric of the knot. She rose over him on her knees. Omar slid the salvar off her. Dilay kicked her legs free one at a time, then worked the waistband of his salvar loose as well. Omar's gaze followed her movements, locked on her bared torso, his neck flushed and his eyes nothing but light.

"You can touch me," she murmured. "I want you to." She did, her body ached for touch, everywhere, but especially those places most sensitive. Her breasts, and thighs, and between them.

For a moment he appeared overwhelmed, then he arched beneath her to push the salvar off his hips. When he sat he urged her toward him, sitting up straight to press his face against her lower belly. His coarse beard tickled and scuffed her skin, that sensation scored with soft brushes of his lips, and she thought, his tongue, but she was so lost in the cacophony that she could not parse them. She dug her fingers against his hair, wishing again that it was long enough to grab. Instead she stroked the short strands, holding him to her as he stretched up, continuing the blissful torture over her ribs and breastbone.

"How are you so soft?" He touched the tip of his nose and lips to the inner curve of her breast, and Dilay shivered, her nipples tightening and her fingers digging against his head. "How am I to think of anything but touching you ever again?" He punctuated the reverent question with a kiss, running his hands up her waist to bend her forward so he could reach to continue a series of soft, slow kisses over the circumference of her breast.

Dilay had to grip his shoulders to prevent herself melting off the couch. She nearly collapsed back to his lap when he turned his attention to her nipple, eliciting a gasp from her and an answering sound from him. His mouth had always felt wonderful, whether on hers, or her neck, any of her skin. But his lips, and tongue, on her breasts, sent her spinning into a breathless stupor. She had a brief moment of sanity when he took a break to switch from one breast to the other, his warm hands stroking firmly down her waist to her hips.

"I rarely think of anything else," she said in a quavering voice, which crumbled apart when he pulled her to him. Her bare thighs pressed to his, their skin warming together where it touched. He looked down between them, dropping his hands to her thighs. He opened his legs a bit wider, so her backside sank between them, and pulled her hips flush to his.

"So"—he squeezed—"touch me."

"Is that a command?" She set her hands on his hips, her thumbs sliding up and down the lowest span of his stomach.

"A plea," he replied. Dilay swept her hands up, over his ribs, and chest, to his shoulders, his body bowing into the stroke. She continued it down his arms and he dug his fingers into the curve of her backside, holding her as he rocked their hips together. A plaintive sound escaped her when the hot, smooth length of his arousal pressed against her core, bringing relief and more desire in one.

The magic returned to his skin, flickers of sunlight, racing down his arms, to his fingers, and all the places on his body she wanted to touch, sweeping over his chest and down his stomach then disappearing beneath the place her legs crossed his.

She moved her fingers between them, circling his shaft and he grunted, fumbling for and grabbing her wrists, holding her hands still.

"Wait." He dropped his head against the back of the couch, and Dilay reluctantly released her hold on him. She concentrated on not squirming her hips to his, not pushing him further, though all she wanted was to pet him, to fill up the empty well of longing that had accompanied her since they met. "There are so many things I was not creative enough to imagine," he said, running his hands up her arms. "That your touch would make me forget my own name, for instance."

"Omar," Dilay whispered. "My Omar."

She squealed in surprise when he cinched his arms around her and had her on her back on the plush carpet before she even understood what happened.

"Yes," he said. He rose over her on all fours, and pressed his fingertips to her belly and up, the softest of touches. It bordered on tickling her, but instead of making her squirm in discomfort, she made a little sound of pleading as her skin prickled again.

She dragged her nails down his stomach as he dropped his head to kiss her shoulder, reaching again to wrap her fingers around him. His ragged pant made her shiver, and he looked at her, the muscles in his neck and arms tightening. Light flickered in and out of his pupils.

"Are you all right?"

"Trust me to tell you," he said. She couldn't imagine he wouldn't lose his grip on it at some point, but she did trust him. The aroused part of her kept whispering she didn't even care if he did lose control. But she did, and so did he. Neither of them wanted that between them. Even in love there was room for privacy. A person's hidden mind was theirs, the good, and the bad.

Dilay ran her nails lightly down his back. The magic danced and he visibly trembled before he stretched out on top of her. She murmured approval, for the warmth, and the pleasure of his weight and skin on hers, the shift of his stomach against hers, the hot, hard demand of his erection pressed first against the valley of her hip and belly. A little shift of her hips angled him between her legs.

She offered a kiss with a soft brush of her mouth, and he took it, trying to dig his fingers into her hair and stymied by the damp braids.

He grumbled in irritation, and she tilted her head to give him better reach. He rose on his knees, pulling her up to sitting and they both worked to undo her hair.

"Don't lose the pins," Dilay said when he tossed them carelessly aside.

"I will buy you new ones." He combed his fingers through her hair as he kissed her neck, urging her gently down again.

"I do not want new ones, I want those," she said. Omar shifted to peer down at her with raised brows.

"Shall I stop and crawl about the carpet to look for your rusty pins?"

"They are *not* rusty," Dilay feigned indignation. "And I would be very amused to watch the Vali Ahad scurrying about—"

He tightened his fingers into her ribs and she shrieked a laugh, trying to wriggle out from beneath him.

"Disrespectful girl," he complained, shifting down to plant a line of quick, soft kisses along her midsection. Dilay sucked in a few gulps of air as she recovered from the shock of his tickling. She bent her legs up to either side of him, squeezing against his ribs as he kissed his way back up. He nipped her lower lip, then drew a circle over her right breast with his palm, making her moan, drew a line on the underside with the pad of his thumb, then circled her nipple with it as well. Dilay pressed toward him with a throaty sound and he covered her breast with his hand. He repeated it with her left. Then he did the same with whisper-soft kisses, trailing his bearded chin over her skin until she gasped his name.

She was panting when he moved up to hover his face above hers. Magic shone erratically over his body, and she cupped his face. "Are you all right?"

Omar chuckled. He rocked down and collapsed between her thighs as he buried his face into the curve of her low belly and laughed. And she couldn't help but giggle. Omar nudged his nose and mouth against her skin, then kissed her navel, rubbing slow circles with his thumbs as he worked his way back up to her head, planting a wet, sucking kiss on each nipple. She nearly lunged up to push him on his back, but he covered her, his weight pressing her into the carpet. Dilay twined her legs around his hips, and he edged up another fraction so his erection rested against her core.

She did not want to rush him, but her entire body was a useless throb of want, so she felt half drunk on desire.

"I am surviving," he answered, kissing the place where her collarbones met. "And you?"

"No. You're torturing me." She tightened her legs, rolling her hips up, wishing for much more than little teases of sensation.

"Good torture, or bad?" His face reflected real concern. Dilay took his hand in hers, and avoided his eyes as she guided his hand between her legs.

"Both," she said, a little shyly.

Omar rolled to his side, pulling her with him and urging her to hook a leg over his hip. He ducked his head to hers, drawing a line along her jaw with his lips. "Show me," he ordered. She laid her hand over his, directing his touches, whispering encouragement when he tried without her guidance. He moved too slowly, but each tentative circle of his fingers made her push against him, made her breathing more stilted.

She curled her fingers around him to return the favor, keeping her touch light, stroking him from tip to base. He pressed his mouth to her shoulder, and she felt his teeth scrape, a long, harsh moan vibrating against her skin. His fingers faltered in their touch, leaving damp trails along her thigh as he moved his hand to wrap around hers where she held him.

"Dilay"—his hand squeezed hers tighter—"I want…" His words choked off when she stroked again, pulling carefully to settle him between her thighs.

"You want," she prompted huskily, tightening her leg around his hips.

"You"—he kissed her chin, his hand gripping her hip—"inside you."

She whispered his name as permission, reaching down to help. He slid in, a smooth, exquisite invasion that made her gasp. Omar rolled her onto her back once more, his hips settling into the cradle of hers, his head buried in the slope of her neck and shoulder.

His breath came in unsteady rhythm. His body taut along hers. He dropped unsteadily to his elbows, withdrawing then returning, and gasped an invocation. Magic glowed steadily on his skin, from beneath his lashes. Her own sparkled over her skin, light like starfall, and he slitted his eyes to watch it, holding excruciatingly still.

She pet him, his chest and arms, focusing hard not to move her hips or press against him, to feel that sweet friction her body yearned for.

"You're so beautiful," he said, his voice raw. He dropped his head to hers. "I will not admit how many times I imagined you like this."

"Shall I guess?" Dilay teased. He made an experimental shift, then another lift and return. She whimpered.

"Too many." He stared at her, a wide-eyed look of wonder on his face that would endear him to her for all her life.

"I have imagined you too." She slung her legs over his hips again, low to avoid his back, and rested her hands on his neck. When he began again, watching her face as he did, she helped guide him to an angle and rhythm that made her weak and thoughtless. There was nothing but her body and his, how they came together, the sound of his rough breathing mingling with hers, the taste of magic and heat in the air between them. She had not realized how much time she spent buried in her own mind, until this, until she could exist in no other way but with every physical fiber and sense.

Her magic slipped out of her mental control when Omar made a subtle shift in his position, lighting sparks and sun behind her eyes. Every muscle in her body seized, her fingers digging into his shoulders as she cried out and crashed through her own magic. More light flashed above her closed eyes and she opened them to see Omar, lit like a beacon. His eyes met hers for a moment, his own body quaking, then he clamped his eyes closed and shoved up and off her with a strangled curse. Her first instinct was to reach for him, but he yanked away. His magic whipped, light rocketing off him as he shook and gasped on all fours. Then he dropped to his belly, his face buried in his arms.

"Are...are you all right?" The light was fading swiftly to a more subdued glow, and his back rose and fell unsteadily.

For a long moment he did not respond. Finally, he propped himself on his elbows and scrubbed his fingers over his face before he turned to look at her from the corners of his eyes. Red crept up his neck, and his mouth was tight.

"I thought I had control of the magic," he said, quietly, turning his gaze away again. "Forgive me if I ruined everything."

"Do you have control now?" she asked. He nodded, and Dilay lay down and squirmed her way under his arm, so her face was beneath his. He tried not to smile, but failed, adjusting a bit so he could kiss her.

"You didn't ruin anything," she said, heat rising up her neck. "Did you not feel me, what you did to me?"

He shifted again, hooking a leg over hers, and propped his head in one hand so he could stroke her arm. "I was preoccupied with what you did to me," he said. He searched her face. "What I did to you was good?"

She could not tell if he was blushing, but there was diffidence in his expression. She traced a muscle in his arm. "Hmm..." she mused. "It was so long ago I can hardly remember. Shall we try again?"

He hummed agreement, ducking his head to her shoulder, and his beard tickled her as he kissed her skin. "Perhaps somewhere other than the floor?"

"You do have an unnecessarily large bed." Dilay traced the dips between his ribs, and he shuddered. He sat up, urging her to her feet as he stood.

"You should stay in it"—he turned her around so her back was to him and wrapped his arms around her, steering her toward the bedroom—"with me."

"My city classes resume tonight."

He huffed impatience. "You will move those to the day. I won't give you up every night."

"Oh, will I?" She spun to face him as they made it into the bed-room and he kicked the door shut behind him. She circled her arms around his neck. "Who said I would stay with you every night?"

"You are going to marry me, where else would you stay?"

"I did not say that."

He hoisted her onto the bed. "You have to do what I say, I'm going to be the Sultan," Omar mumbled into her neck as he climbed over her. Dilay laughed, pinching at his ribs as he kissed her. "Or I will leave a trail of books between your classroom and here to lure you back every night."

"Or"—she stroked his hair—"you could agree to a few simple requests."

"Mmm," he said in suspicion. He shifted, and traced the line of her collarbones as he watched her expectantly.

"If I marry you, would you want me to leave the University? I cannot," she said.

"No." He stroked her cheek. "Of course not."

"And the school you promised me?" she said, hopefully.

"Schools," he corrected. There was brightness in his eyes. Teasing and joy. Dilay returned his smile, settling more comfortably beneath him and rubbing her calf along his.

"I won't be paraded around the palace in choking clothes and sit silent and ornamental while you chatter at your Council."

"No," he said. "The palace has plenty of beautiful things to look at, and while you are very beautiful"—he kissed her nose—"that is not why I want you to marry me."

"Or abandoned in my own suite like an unfavored pet?"

His lashes lowered as he murmured denial, and he reached down to guide her leg around his hips.

"You will open the University to all mages who can afford it and pass the exams," she said, with more demand, more assured for the desire she saw warming in his eyes. "All of them, not just nobility."

He proffered a smile. "I will do my best," he said. "Though you will have to learn to argue with the Council beside me."

She scoffed. "If I must do your work as well, then I also want a scholarship for gifted children from the lower classes and poor districts to attend the University." She raised her eyebrows.

He started to reply, but she added, "And I still want access to the palace library, as you promised."

"Are you finished?" he asked. "Anything else? Your own wing of the palace?"

"Spectacles like yours for the children in my class who need them."

He made a thoughtful sound. "As you wish."

"I will marry you," she said, catching his face between her hands and kissing him. He returned it, first with force, then tenderness, tangling his fingers in her hair. "There is no one else in all of Tamar I would rather stand beside," she added when he released her.

"Nor I," he replied. Then his brow wrinkled. "Do you need to go? To prepare for your class?"

"Night is a very long time from now," Dilay said. "Unless I am keeping you?"

"Keep me," he said, touching his lips to her brow. "Keep me forever."

THIRTY-TWO

B REATHE IN. SHE FORCED THE rhythm as she strode forward when the doors opened before her. Then she had to force it out again at the sight of all the Viziers, lining both sides of the aisle leading to the dais. The Sultan sat there, and on a stool beside him the Queen Sultana. Benches at the base of the dais and perpendicular to it served as seats to the most highly ranked in the court. Omar sat to the Sultan's left, then Mazhar. On the bench across the aisle, Eymen Demir, the Grand Vizier, then all the Viziers in descending rank toward the doors.

The tap of Dilay's shoes on the marble seemed remarkably loud. The men did not even whisper as she walked toward the dais. If they had whispered it might have been easier, she was used to whispers. A woman who did not belong.

Omar caught her gaze and winked, and she suppressed a smile. But she did belong. With him. It had come to her in little pieces, every time they were together. That was what mattered. Not the other people in the room, not the fact that her father had refused to speak to her for all of half a day, not that it was new fodder for the people who thought she had not earned the spaces she occupied. Just Omar, and how she had woken up to him in the middle of the night, staring at her with magic on his skin and worship in his eyes.

Dilay stopped between Omar and the Grand Vizier and bowed to the Sultan and his wife.

"Instructor Akar," the Sultan said, "you seem intent on bringing yourself to the attention of my court."

She considered whether it was best to remain bowed forward, so he could not see her face, or to straighten, so he could. Omar had warned her that he could be mercurial. She straightened her back and folded her hands in front of her. Beste had lent her clothes fit for an audience with a Sultan, and arranged her hair in a coil at the back of her neck like the ladies of the Sultan's court wore. She had expected to feel constricted and out of place in such formal attire, stiff, heavy brocade in pale blue, and slippery silk salvar to match. Even the slippers were ornate, with lengthened toes and embroidery. She'd almost tripped and fallen on her face in the hall. A fitting introduction as a potential future Sultana.

But, the clothes felt good. Like armor she had donned, or a disguise. There was, after all, safety in fitting in, one less thing for them to hold against her.

"I am honored to be allowed before you, Sultan Efendim," Dilay said.

"The Vali Ahad seems to think you would make an acceptable Princess Sultana," he said. Dilay studied the sapphire pin on his turban. It was the largest stone she had ever seen. Enough to cover the purchase price of half the Earth District.

"He has mentioned that, yes, Efendim." Her mother and aunts had helped Beste dress her that morning, and Beste had nodded along as her mother imparted the only wisdom she had offered. There is a time to win a battle with force, and there is a time to win a battle with subterfuge. Today was a day for subtlety and deference.

"And do you have an opinion?"

"No, Sultan Efendim. I know only that I love your son, and I love my homeland and this city, and I will serve as best I am able in any capacity."

Someone made a pleased grunt of approval, which felt like a victory.

"You already serve my city, as an instructor at the University. An odd choice for a woman. Though I am told good things about your skill. How had you intended to raise a family?"

Dilay clasped her hands in front of her. "I had assumed I would not, Efendim." That garnered her many mumbles of shocked disapproval from the men who surrounded her. She felt penned in, like a horse on an auction block. She wished suddenly that her mother and father were there, so she could look at them. Instinct told her that looking too often at Omar would make her appear weak.

"Why not?"

"I did not believe I could devote myself to a family and to my students." She knew where he was heading, but saw no way to stop things.

"Do you intend to give up your position if you are chosen as a bride for the Vali Ahad?"

"Not if I can fulfill my duties as Sultana while maintaining my position at the University."

"Preposterous," someone guffawed behind and to her left. Dilay curled her fingers into her palms and forced a neutral smile.

"Master Bugra was a full-time tutor for both princes for many Turns while maintaining a position as a Master Instructor at the University. His duties at the palace had him here night and day."

"He was not participating in decisions of state," someone else said, purposefully loud enough to carry to the Sultan's ears.

"Will I be?" Dilay asked coolly. Even if the Sultana did participate in decisions like that, Dilay doubted the Sultan, or any of the Council, would admit to it. The Sultan's mouth twitched down, and he held a hand up to indicate silence to his Council.

"Speaking of Master Bugra, he has informed me you were very driven to become an instructor. Yet you have changed your plans when offered the possibility of being elevated from daughter of a laundress to a princess?"

Wind swept through her, anger. She struggled to control it with her magic, her gaze drifting from the Sultan's turban, to his wife. The Queen Sultana smiled serenely, her head moving in the tiniest of nods. An unexpected ally. Discreetly, the Sultana traced a circle on her palm. The oldest symbol for the Wheel. Balance in all things, great to small and back again, power balanced with weakness, love with pain, and life with death. Yes.

"I am the daughter of a laundress, yes. A woman who serves the nobility in the chores they cannot conceive of doing themselves. It is a simple thing, and yet, I would guess, no one in this room knows how to do it. Or realizes that scores of common women make their livelihoods at such menial jobs. The ugly, unpleasant jobs that hold a city up and power a society. The water singers who wash the clothes account for a quarter of the Second House mages in your city, Efendim."

His mouth pinched in anger.

"I am also the daughter of a judge"—Dilay forced her chin higher, her shoulders back, and let her hands fall to her sides—"who has seen time upon time what happens when the poor are left to molder where they are, with no chances to improve their lots. Who has watched innocents suffer under laws meant to keep everyone, wealthy and poor alike, exactly where they are."

The hall filled with voices, angry whispers, huffs of condescending amusement. The men to her left and right shifted in irritation, as if they would like to get up and leave the room. Dilay took a moment to calm her racing heart and scattering thoughts.

"I would rather be the daughter of people who see suffering and work to improve it, than I would a princess hidden away in a palace, celebrating while my people threatened to burn my city down."

That made him angry. The Sultan slapped his hands to his knees as though he might stand.

"Tamar is not in balance, Sultan Efendim. You and your Council can choose to let that remain, until the laundresses and the dockworkers and the street sweeps and servants decide they have had enough and rise up to plunge this city into chaos. Or, you can take steps to balance it."

"And you believe you are that balance?"

"I have spent my entire life teaching people balance, Efendim. And I have spent that same time walking the line between common and noble. I can blend in among both groups. Can anyone here say the same?"

"Think how they would praise you, Sultan," the Queen Sultana said mildly. "The first Sultan in generations to do such a thing." Her eyebrow raised and she gave Dilay a pointed look as she turned her face toward the Sultan. Dilay swept away the heat in her cheeks with her magic. Clearly her subterfuge needed work. "How much more deeply they will bow to the Vali Ahad because he will have such ties to his people."

Dilay chanced a fleeting look at Omar. He sat calmly, his face turned down, perhaps to hide his emotions from his father. Dilay tried to picture them both, sitting where the Sultan and Queen Sultana sat. It was difficult to do so. How could the other woman bear it?

"Grand Vizier," said the Sultan. Eymen stood and bowed. "What says the Council?"

"I do not know Instructor Akar, Efendim, but I know her father. He has always been considered a fair man, who bows to the law in all things. He is respected." Eymen looked to the other men. "Does anyone wish to speak?"

"I know Instructor Akar." A portly man stood, scratched at his cheek as though embarrassed. "She taught my son at the University and he learned more there than he learned in all his Turns of primary school."

"That does not qualify a lowborn noble to be elevated to rule," the Sultan said in boredom.

"No, of course not, Efendim. But it does demonstrate an understanding of people, and of balance."

The Sultan waved the man back to his seat. More stood. A few spoke for her, but many complained about the precedent it set. Standing while they spoke about her was humiliating, and made her grow more and more agitated, ready to spin around and storm out. She had not realized it would be more trial than discussion.

"Does anyone else care to speak?" Eymen asked when there had been a short gap of silence after the last man sat. Omar stood. Eymen bowed abruptly, and the Sultan turned a narrowed-eyed look on him.

Omar stepped to Dilay's side and bowed to his father. "I will speak," he said.

Eymen glanced apprehensively from the Sultan to Omar and back again. The Queen radiated a mixture of amusement and exasperation, and the Sultan's face flushed red.

"And as I am the Vali Ahad, that will be the final word. It will be Dilay Akar, or it will be no one."

While they had whispered dissent when she spoke, they erupted with it after Omar's declaration. He slid her a look, a tiny smile, and she felt the burden of judgment sift away.

"That is not yours to decide," the Sultan said.

"I know what kind of Sultan I wish to be, Efendim. And it requires someone to serve as bridge between me and my people. As Tarkin Sabri saw the need for a signal to his people that the Sultanate was united with them after the Sundering War, so do I, now. She is that signal." Omar spoke calmly, almost as though he was disinterested.

The Sultan's teeth clenched and he looked at his wife, who gave a single nod. The Sultan shifted, shifting one way then the other, tugging at his beard, then directing a lour at Eymen. "Grand Vizier."

Eymen bowed again.

"You may submit a date to me for my son's second betrothal." He pinned a narrowed gaze on Omar. "This will be the last, yes?"

"Yes, Efendim"—Omar bowed, and looked at Dilay as he straightened—"the last."

Dilay smiled at him. Mazhar grunted *finally* from his seat on the bench.

Eymen announced the session complete, and Omar took Dilay's hand to lead her to the side as the Sultan and Queen Sultana rose and moved for the hall. The Sultana stopped in front of Dilay and gave her an imperious look.

"We will practice your skill at addressing the Council."

"Yes, Sultana." Dilay ducked her head. Omar squeezed her hand. The Sultana walked away, and Mazhar stood, joining Dilay and Omar as they fell in behind the Sultan. Omar adjusted Dilay's arm so it was twined through his. More proper than holding hands, though she hoped they still would, sometimes.

"They hate you already. This will make sessions much more interesting," Mazhar said. "Well done."

"Mazhar," Omar warned.

"He isn't wrong," Dilay said. They turned in the opposite direction from the Sultan and his wife, down the hall and, Dilay thought, in the direction of the Sultan's wing. It would take her a lifetime to memorize all the halls. "I lectured when I should have been more subtle."

"Subtle takes practice," Omar said. "Perhaps I can take on the role of instructor, for once." He didn't look at her, but his lips curved up.

"I will see you both at dinner, I trust?" Mazhar stopped at the junction with the hall that led back to the palace entrance.

"Where are you going?" Omar asked.

"Well, you have a fancy new betrothed to teach you all the back alleys and debauchery the city has to offer you. I, on the other hand, have to learn myself." He took Dilay's free hand and kissed it. "I will see you again, big sister." He winked, then offered a quick wave and trotted down the hall.

Dilay looked up at Omar. "He gets away with a lot more than you did, doesn't he?"

"You have no idea. I think half the city will mourn when Anne turns her attention to betrothing him." Omar peered behind them, then relaxed his arm, slipping his hand down to lace his fingers between hers. Dilay ducked her head against his shoulder. "There is no one he loves?"

"Not that I know of. Mazhar doesn't talk about love." He stopped to open his doors. Ruslan was inside, setting up an array of food, as well as a tray of coffee, and tea.

"How do you do that?" Dilay asked. "Always have things ready?"

"Magic, Mistress," Ruslan replied with a subdued smile just before he bowed to them. Dilay fidgeted. It would take time to grow accustomed to being bowed to. Only her students did it, as youth to an elder. Having people her own age do it outside the Earth District was…confusing.

"Thank you," Omar said to Ruslan, who looked surprised. The smile returned and he ducked his head before leaving.

"These things suit you." Omar waited until the doors shut behind Ruslan to touch the embroidery on Dilay's borrowed entari.

"They are not as unbearable as I thought they would be," Dilay admitted.

"And everything else?"

"Give me time. I am not accustomed to navigating these things. But as long as we are together, I am not frightened of them." She took a shelled almond from the tray of food. Did they not even have to shell their own nuts?

She looked out the glass doors and calmed at the sight of the little fig tree. Its unexpected new function was to serve as grounding and reminder to her, of where she came from. There were battles to fight now. New ones she did not know how to navigate. Council meetings, politics more insidious than any she had dealt with. Plans for a city, a nation, on a scale she could only previously have dreamed of. Dilay looked at the little almond in her fingers and smiled wryly. Perhaps it was not so bad to not have to worry about the small things, when one had so many big things to deal with.

"I think you will both flourish nicely here." Omar stood behind her, resting his hands on her shoulders. Dilay touched her fingers to his, worries beginning to creep in around the joy of what felt like a battle won.

"Have you spoken to Behram?"

He squeezed her shoulders. "No."

"This will hurt him, you and I."

"I know. And despite everything, that is not what I want."

"I failed him," Dilay said.

"I think he failed you," Omar said, gently, "but if you want to forgive him and try again I will do whatever you ask. I think you mattered to him more than anything else, and I cannot help the guilt I feel for this…for us. Maybe together, we can help him."

"I don't know yet," Dilay said, "if I want to."

Omar nodded, rubbing his thumb up the slope of her neck. "My mother asked me if we intended to continue our lessons, to control my power." He replaced his touch with his lips, and Dilay turned into him. Her skin prickled.

"You know why. She wants to know the same thing I do. Do you intend to continue carelessly using your power?"

"No, love," Omar said. "But trust me when I tell you the only way to win my father over to that idea is profound subtlety, and time. I cannot change that. Trust me, and we will work toward it together."

"And what if our children have your power?"

"I will be the last to use my powers this way—that, I can unequivocally promise you." He looked at her hair, then her clothes, a slow smile lighting his face. "About those advanced lessons?"

"I suppose I can spare a moment." Dilay feigned a put-upon sigh.

"This will take at least two moments." Omar tugged her toward the bedroom and she followed, laughing.

EPILOGUE

ILAY AND OMAR EMERGED FROM the Sultan's wing and into the foyer of the palace entrance. Her parents waited for them there, her father holding a squirming bundle and speaking in laughing tones to Dilay's mother. Beste stood with them, also smiling, the smile broadening when she saw Omar and Dilay.

Beste extracted the baby from Judge Akar's arms, making him frown in disappointment, and handed her to Dilay.

"I expect more time with her this afternoon. You have hardly let me hold her at all," Dilay's father protested.

Dilay smiled coyly at him. "Whose fault is that? I have to bribe you to come to the palace at all." Dilay's mother leaned in to kiss her cheek, then the baby's. Her father huffed, turning his head away but bowing to Omar before he did.

"She has such an easy temperament," Dilay's mother said, and Beste nodded agreement. "Unlike her mother."

Dilay clicked her tongue, then turned a smile on the baby as she held her up. "Are you ready, my little light?" she asked. The baby stared up at her with wide, dark eyes. "Yes you are, my brave girl." Omar had the same giddy adoration cut with exhaustion on his face that he had worn since their daughter's birth. "Are we ready?" Dilay asked him.

The palace doors were thrown wide, allowing in the bright morning sun and the chill of late winter. The sound of the gathered masses outside was something like buzzing bees, uncomfortable for its imagined threat. It was nearly the end of the first season since the princess' birth, the traditional time to present a baby to the public. Dilay was not certain she was ready to share her most precious accomplishment with the world.

"I will never be ready," Omar said, looking toward the doors, where two guards watched them standing there, steeling themselves. He put an arm around her shoulders. "But I am here with my strength." He kissed Dilay's temple. "And my heart." He tapped his daughter on the nose and she smiled at him. "All is well."

"Each new thing is frightening," Dilay's mother said with a smile, "but they will almost always weather it better than you do."

Dilay gave her mother, then her father, a one-armed hug before Beste escorted them away to stand outside with the Sultan and Queen Sultana on the steps.

Dilay glanced up at Omar, and he winked. They waited another moment for a trio of guards to precede them, then followed out onto the broad landing of the stairs.

The cold air braced Dilay, filling her lungs and thoughts with clarity. The brightness of the sun made her blink and the baby fidget and fuss. She went still and wide-eyed when a cheer went up through the courtyard and down the palace road, from throngs of people who had traveled up from the city to mass at the Morning Gate. Only nobles were in the courtyard, everyone else was barred by a wall of guards at the gate. The Sultan and Queen Sultana stood to the left of the doors, and Dilay's parents to the right. They smiled encouragement. Seda was with them, and Mazhar. Seda clapped her hands together once and smiled bright like flame. Of course she had seen the baby multiple times, but today was special. Time for Omar's child to take her place as princess.

Omar touched a hand to the small of Dilay's back as they descended the stairs, where the Viziers of the Council waited to bestow their well wishes. Once they had done so, the princess would be announced to all those gathered. Eymen Demir waited at the bottom of the stairs and was the first to greet them with a bow. He smiled with real joy, and set a tiny pouch tied with a yellow ribbon in a large basket near his feet.

"Sand from the valley, for balance," he said. He bowed again before he moved aside to allow the next. Each Vizier followed suit, approaching one at a time and offering a simple gift, one for harmony or balance. Stones or small toys representing the Houses, clothes in the colors of the First House, as everyone assumed the princess must be. It became a bit of a blur, each man offering a gift, bowing, smiling, saying congratulations. Until the end of the line. Behram was there. His father had died, unexpectedly, only a small turn after the birth of the princess. It was customary for a family to isolate for that first season, so Dilay had only been able to send a letter of condolence to Behram. Seeing him now, taking his father's place as Vizier, made her immeasurably sad. Omar pressed his hand to her back again when she faltered. It had quickly become his silent signal that he was with her. If she needed him.

Behram approached and bowed, then set a small book in the basket. A glimpse at the cover showed it to be a collection of fables. An unorthodox gift.

"If she is like her mother," Behram said as he moved in to touch one cheek then the other to Dilay's, "she will appreciate it."

"I am certain she will love it, Behram, thank you," Dilay said. He did not meet her gaze, but turned to Omar and offered his hand.

"I was very sorry to hear about your father, my friend." Omar grasped Behram's forearm.

"That is the Wheel, is it not? What goes around comes around."

Dilay was distracted from his barbed words when a little boy peeked out from behind Behram. She had seen Behram and Zehra's son only a few times, at court functions. Cemil, named in honor of Behram's father. He was three Turns now, nearing four, she thought. A beautiful boy with dark curly hair and eyes like golden jasper. She regarded him more carefully. He smiled shyly and pointed.

"Beebee," he whispered. Dilay smiled and crouched.

"Would you like to meet her?"

372 ❧ J. D. Evans

He nodded and came closer, glancing repeatedly at Behram as he did. Dilay's heart shuddered and shattered.

She knew that look. That desperate, uncertain look. She had spent her childhood with a boy who wore the same. Cemil offered a tentative reach and squealed in glee when the baby grabbed his finger. "She likes you." Dilay smiled, and touched Cemil's cheek. "You will be great friends." He beamed, giving his hand a little shake, and was rewarded with a smile and a coo.

Behram put a hand on Cemil's small shoulder and he immediately let go, his smile dimming as he retreated to his father's side. Dilay stood, clutching her daughter more tightly. "He is welcome here, Behram. If he would like to play."

"Perhaps." He smiled. "If we have time." He turned to Omar again. "I will do my best to live up to my father's place on the Council, Efendim. Know that I am with you as I always was, that I have, and always will, serve Tamar."

Omar smiled, and nodded, and Behram bowed to them again. His gaze touched Dilay's only briefly before it rested on the baby, and one corner of his mouth ticked up, then the expression was erased as he turned away. Air was ice in her lungs.

"Omar," she said, watching Behram's back.

"The boy," Omar acknowledged. She turned her gaze to his.

"What can we do?" she whispered.

"Keep Behram close. Give Cemil the best chance we can."

Dilay nodded, looking once more at Cemil's little back, so small next to Behram. She refused to lose another one to that violent cycle of Kadir fire.

The Grand Vizier stepped forward and spoke, the power of his Fourth House magic making the earth rumble. Omar gently extracted his daughter from Dilay's arms and held her up.

"The Vali Ahad and Princess Sultana present their daughter, Princess Sultana Naime Sabri ilr Narfour. May she bless all of Tamar with the wisdom and balance her predecessors have." He slammed his staff of office against the stones, and the crack resonated, it seemed, all the way to the Kalspire. The watching crowd roared, and all Dilay wanted to do was run back inside to escape the ocean of sound. Surely it would upset Naime.

But the baby was calm when Omar lowered her into the cradle of his arm, her favorite place to nestle. She looked out over the courtyard as if she were a Queen already, receiving only what was due to her. Dilay thought she might need that composure, in the years to come. There were rumors that the Republic in the north was beginning to expand its borders. That their rulers abhorred magic and its wielders. Rumors that would force Omar to look beyond Tamar's borders.

As Omar lowered Naime back to Dilay's arms and her little face brightened with a smile, Dilay forgot her worry for a moment, wondering in delight just exactly what kind of woman her daughter would be.

THE END

If you enjoyed this book, you can continue on in the series, follow me on social media, and sign up for my newsletter (for fun FREEBIES!) here:

Acknowledgments

IF YOU FOLLOW ME anywhere on social media, you are probably aware that I, like everyone else, have had a very bouncy year. During the writing of this book a pandemic hit, we moved, I got pregnant, and a general haze settled over my ability to create.

If it were not for the people I'm about to mention, I don't think this book would have happened.

First: My editor. I mention her in every book, but I cannot express enough how much of an impact she has on both me and my writing. She has worn many hats since we started on *Reign & Ruin*, but this time around it was the World's Most Patient Cheerleader. I pushed this book finish an ungodly number of times and she did not toss me out on my bum despite also dealing with 2020 and all the joy it had to offer. Really, this book is in your hands both because she encouraged me to write a prequel / gift for my fans and because she rode the roller coaster with me. Michelle, thank you so very much.

Second: My sister. As always, my alpha, beta, brainstorm partner, the only one who knows the ending and the one who Literally saved my writing by asking me to do writing sprints with her one morning. Now we do it every weekday, even though she lives in Montana and I live in North Carolina. We grab coffee, meet at 9am EST, and do sprints for an hour before we have to go our separate ways. Sis. Thank you. You know Tamar wouldn't exist without you. And neither would my maps.

Third: My beta readers. Jess, Kate, and for the first time, Anka. You get what I'm trying to do and your comments and time are so incredibly valuable. This one was rough, but you helped me believe in it and make it the best it could be.

And, as always, Tanya for her absolutely stunning art. This time around Terry Roy not only formatted the inside but also laid out the outside, so double thanks for her awesome work.

Most importantly, I want to thank you, Dear Reader, especially if you're reading the acknowledgments, for taking up valuable space in your TBR with my books and imagination. Really, all of this is so I can share the weird ideas in my head with someone, and when you read and love my books then I truly believe we've created a world together. Thank you.

About the Author

J. D. EVANS WRITES fantasy and science fiction romance. After earning her degree in linguistics, J. D. served a decade as an army officer. She once spent her hours putting together briefings for helicopter pilots and generals. Now she writes stories, tends to two unreasonable tiny humans, knits, sews badly, gardens, and cultivates Pinterest Fails. After a stint in Beirut, J. D. fell in love with the Levant, which inspired the setting for her debut series, *Mages of the Wheel*.

Originally hailing from Montana, J. D. now resides in North Carolina with her husband, two attempts at mini-clones gone awry, and too many stories in her head.

Made in United States
North Haven, CT
01 December 2024

61202573R00233